BLUE
MERCY

BLUE MERCY

ILLONA HAUS

POCKET STAR BOOKS

New York   London   Toronto   Sydney

An *Original* Publication of POCKET BOOKS

 A Pocket Star Book published by
POCKET BOOKS, a division of Simon & Schuster, Inc.
1230 Avenue of the Americas, New York, NY 10020

ISBN: 0-7394-5347-5

POCKET STAR BOOKS and colophon are registered
trademarks of Simon & Schuster, Inc.

Designed by Melissa Isriprashad

Jacket design by Jae Song

Manufactured in the United States of America

For Sparky
(Det. Sgt. [retired] Steve "Sparky" Lehmann,
BPD Homicide),
without whom this book
and my work would be impossible.

And for Chris Brett-Perring,
inspiration and supporter extraordinaire.

Acknowledgments

In the course of researching and writing this work, I have relied on the expertise, wisdom, and experience of many. These are the major players to whom I am indebted:

Vickie L. Wash, Chief, Circuit Court Operations, State's Attorney's Office for Baltimore City;

Mary G. Ripple, MD, Deputy Chief Medical Examiner, State of Maryland;

Det. Joseph Dugan, BPD Homicide;

Det. Mike Hammel, BPD Homicide;

Det. Robert F. Cherry Jr., BPD Homicide;

Det. Lynette Nevins, BPD Homicide;

Bruce Tannahill, Tannahill Funeral Home, Owen Sound.

Any mistakes are my own.

Also, much thanks goes to my readers—Terri Rowe, Jerry "Chopomatic" Hatchett, Patricia Lewin, Jo Gillan, Jackie Gibbons, as well as Pam Myette and Manina Jones—for their time and eye for detail.

Huge thanks to Annelise Robbey and Meg Ruley, who saw the potential, cradled it, and let it be what it was, for their trust and their encouragement. And last, but not least, to Amy Pierpont for her guidance and infinite patience.

BLUE
MERCY

1

SHE KNEW THIS PLACE.

Wet asphalt glistened under sodium-vapor lights. Soaked trash clogged storm drains and gutters swelled. For ten minutes they'd waited in the unmarked car, watching the corner row house as the blue flicker of a television pulsed behind a sheet tacked over the first-floor window.

They didn't need backup, she told Spencer. Her case. Her call.

As she crossed the dead-end street, the rain against her skin was a relief from the hot July night. A dog barked, high-pitched and frenetic. She imagined its eyes, bulging from behind one of the darkened windows next door. Spence offered a wordless nod, then jogged around the east side of the house. As the silence swelled, she gave him time to go up the alley, get to the back door and into position.

She followed the walkway to the porch. Took the three steps. Brushed back the edge of her jacket and unbuttoned the safety strap of her holster. Exhaled. Steadied herself, and lifted her fist to the door.

"Hey, Bernard! Baltimore police."

She waited. Nothing.

"Come on, Bernard. Open up! Police."

The night took another silent breath.

Then it erupted. And he was there—Bernard Eales. All six-foot-four of him, flinging open the front door. He filled the opening. Barging onto the dark porch. Massive. Smelling of booze.

In his eyes, she saw something flare. Wild and primal. Meaty lips parted in a malignant smile, revealing overlapped teeth.

She drew her Glock, the nine clearing leather fast even as the rubber grip slipped once in her wet hand. "Just back up, Bernard."

But her voice faltered.

And Eales grinned. In a million dreams she would never forget that evil smile. Or the lightning-speed jab that cracked her wrist.

She swore at him. His next strike smashed the words back into her mouth, instantly filling it with hot blood. She swung hard, her closed fist connecting with the soft cavity of his temple.

His startled cry came out in a belch of fetid breath.

And then the beating started. One blow after the next. In the cramped and shadowed porch, there was no telling what was fist and what was Eales's heavy, leather boot. She lost count after a half dozen, after her throat gagged against the blood, and her lungs clutched for air.

The world around her lurched out of focus. She thrashed at him, desperate to find a weakness. Another punch took her square in the stomach and she buckled, a burst of air and blood rushing out of her as she tumbled off the porch.

Disoriented, she searched the dark lawn for Spence.

But Eales wasn't finished. Lumbering down the steps, he came after her. She braced herself. Dredging a final burst of energy, she rolled and hooked her leg around his.

Eales teetered. For a second she envisioned two-hundred-plus pounds of Baltimore billy-boy dropping on her. But he caught himself. One beefy hand skidded across the sidewalk inches from her face. He cursed, righted himself, and this time she heard the deep crack of bone when his boot tore into her side.

Against her cheek, the cement was cold. Her own

blood warmed it as she felt her body go weak. And here, on this filthy piece of pavement, in a grime-slicked puddle, she was ready to give up. Close her eyes. Surrender.

Not again.

This time when she reached for the holster at her hip, the Glock was there. She drew it. Fast and fluid.

Eales never knew what hit him. There was the white-orange flash at the nine's muzzle. The satisfying kick of the weapon in her hands. The plume of burned gunpowder. And the hollow-point spiraled from the barrel, twisting through the air in slow motion and driving into solid flesh. In the pallid light, a mist of blood sprayed from the exit wound.

The second shot followed the path of the first. A dark stain bloomed across Eales's chest even before his knees caved beneath him. *This time* when Spencer charged around the corner of the house, Eales was at her feet.

It wasn't the nightmare gunshot that woke Kay Delaney lately, but instead a quiet gasp. From sweat-soaked sheets, she stared at the dark ceiling. The light from the streetlamp below her third-story bedroom fractured through the rain-smeared window and danced overhead.

She drew in several long breaths, trying to calm the drumming of her heart. If only that night had gone down the way it did in her dreams now. If only it were Eales who'd bled out on his front lawn fourteen months ago instead of Spence.

Pushing back the sheet, she dragged herself to the bed's edge, looked at the clock. One a.m. A low pain throbbed at her temples. Kay found the bottle of aspirin in her nightstand drawer and shook out three. A mouthful of warm beer from the bottle she'd brought to bed earlier helped wash them down.

When she tossed the container back into the drawer,

the pills clattered, the plastic striking the metal slide of the Glock.

The 9mm in the shallow drawer lay in shadow. It was more her knowledge of its presence that delineated the square contours of the heavy, Austrian-tooled sidearm. It wasn't loaded. But then, she didn't keep it by her bed for protection. For that she had the .38, tucked in its leather holster, hanging from her bedpost. She'd bought the Chief's Special months ago, a heavy snub-nosed revolver with a Pachmayr grip and a smooth, clean trigger pull. And she'd kept it by her bed ever since. A by-product of the fear Eales had implanted.

Kay hated the fear that lived in her now. Resented that Eales had taken up permanent residence in her head.

She shoved the drawer shut. No, the 9mm was there for only one reason. To remind her.

Spencer charging around the side of the house, the look of disbelief on his face when he took the bullet, the way he seemed suspended for a moment in the thick night air before crumpling to the wet grass less than thirty feet away, his mouth gaping like a fish drowning on air, its rhythm keeping tempo with his slowing heart, and then his eyes. He'd stared at her well beyond his last breath.

The Glock in her nightstand kept the images alive. *Her* Glock. The one Eales had smashed from her hand the second he came out the door. The one he'd used to gun down Spencer.

She imagined the fine layer of dust dulling the nine's once-buffed surface. She hadn't touched it since the day Ballistics had finished their testing, and the technician had casually slid the gun across the counter. She could still remember the strange weight of it in her hand. She'd never holstered the gun again, reverting to the off-duty, subcompact nine that she had qualified to carry. And the departmental-issue stayed in the drawer.

Kay moved to the window, its bottom pane propped open with her Koga, the protection stick's handle firmly wedged against the low frame. The night air sucked at the curtain, heaving the sheer material out, then in again, caressing her naked, sweat-slicked skin.

Below, Hamburg Street dead-ended at Federal Hill, empty except for parked cars. Over the neighbor's roof, she could make out the top of the hill, and past it the lights of the city across the Inner Harbor. The bass of an overamped car stereo pulsed through the damp streets. Then the wail of a distant siren.

Kay shivered, but didn't move from the window. She embraced the bite of reality the chill offered and wondered what her shrink, Constance O'Donnell, would think of this latest slant on the same old dream.

When the phone rang seconds later, it made Kay jump.

"Delaney here."

"Kay? It's Sarge. Sorry to wake you." Sergeant Ed Gunderson cleared the smoker's phlegm from his throat. "But we got a situation. I think you'll wanna be in on this one."

Static crackled over the line.

"Are you there, Kay?"

"Yeah." She lowered herself to the bed again. "What've you got?"

"A murder down here in Canton. Twelve hundred block of Luther. Body's burned up pretty bad. Found it in an abandoned warehouse. We don't have a positive on the body yet, but . . ." More static, only this time it sounded like Sarge fumbling with the cell phone. "Thing is, we could get some heat on this. From the media. And the brass. A real red ball."

6 • Illona Haus

Kay took another sip of warm beer, enough to wet her throat. "What is it?"

There was a burst of interference, then voices in the background. And finally Sarge whispered, "I think it's your girl, Kay. Your witness. Valerie Regester."

2

THE RAIN HAD COOLED the September night air, but had little effect on the charred remains of the former Dutton Mannequin warehouse in Canton. Heat radiated from the concrete floor where ashes and soot swirled in greasy pools of water.

Detective Danny Finnerty sidestepped a scorched mannequin, its head a mass of boiled fiberglass, its blackened arms reaching out. Wearing rubber boots, he sloshed through the debris and sludge, passing the torched delivery-bay door. Outside, another fire truck backed away from the curb, its beeper piercing the silence of the gutted building. A radio car's siren blurted once, then there was only the drumming of water from the rafters overhead.

Finn ignored the residual sting of smoke in his eyes and trained his gaze back to the body. Arson detectives had almost missed her, initially mistaking her for one of the destroyed mannequins.

With Arson scouring the rest of the warehouse, it was Ed Gunderson who kept watch over the body. The toll of thirty years on the job was visible in the big man's posture; under the rumpled tan trench coat his shoulders sagged inward as though he carried the weight of his entire squad on them. And his receding hairline seemed directly proportional to the receding clearance rate of cases within the unit.

In one gloved hand, Gunderson held a purse. He looked decidedly uncomfortable, like a dutiful husband gripping his wife's handbag at the mall. Gesturing to one of the Mobile Crime Lab technicians, he unloaded the scorched purse before turning to Niles Fischer, the medical examiner's investigator.

In the glare of the portable halogens, Fischer's pristine white coveralls and matching hair glared in stark contrast to the burned wreckage around them. He squatted next to the remains, gnarled, latex-encased hands planted firmly on each knee until he lifted his wrist to check his watch.

Finn navigated a path toward them, keeping his breathing shallow. A three-year stint with Arson years ago had taught him a trick or two.

"Give her another ten minutes," Gunderson instructed Fischer. "She's on her way. In the meantime, nothing gets moved." The sergeant's voice had an edginess that Finn doubted was entirely due to the late-night hit of caffeine they'd picked up on the way over.

Fischer stood, sidestepped the body, and started for the exit. "I'll be out in the van having a smoke."

When Gunderson turned his gaze, Finn saw more starkly the exhaustion in the man's pocked face. Well past his eligible retirement, Ed Gunderson was an anchor in the unit. Homicide was the man's life. What he knew best. And the way Gunderson saw it, Finn guessed, leaving would be tantamount to picking out his own headstone and calling it quits.

"Thanks for coming along, Finn," Gunderson told him. "I know you were on your way home. If you gotta go—"

"No. I'll stay." Fact was, he hadn't been on his way home when the call had come in to Homicide almost an hour ago. At the end of night shift he'd had his jacket on and one foot out the squadroom door. But it was O'Reilly's bar he'd been headed to. Last place an alcoholic should frequent. Still, when the desire for a drink was strong, sometimes a familiar setting helped the most, even if he only ever ordered a soda.

"So did you get anything from Arson?" Gunderson asked.

"They'll be a while still. Fire was definitely deliberate though. Perp tossed the gasoline can on his way out. Most of the damage is back here. Luckily there weren't as many flammables in the rest of the place, otherwise it might have taken out the whole building."

"And she's the reason." Gunderson nodded to the body.

Finn followed the sergeant's gaze. It didn't matter how many fire deaths he'd seen while working Arson—the sight of blistered and seared skin, of fabric melted into flesh, was never an easy image to stomach. Harder still was the eerie yet familiar posture of a victim's burned body: the intense heat of the blaze causing tendons and muscles to contract, drawing the limbs of the victim into what the texts referred to as a pugilistic attitude. To Finn, the position had always resembled a boxer caught in a defensive stance, as if the victim might have been alive in the fire, fighting the flames. But it was almost never the case. The heat and smoke usually killed them first.

"So Kay's coming?" he asked Gunderson.

Gunderson nodded, his gaze never leaving the body in the shallow pool of grimy water.

"Does she know it's her witness?"

"Yeah."

"And this was on the Eales case, right?" Finn asked.

"Hm-hmm."

Bernard Eales. Finn hadn't heard the name spoken aloud in months. Not many dared around the offices. Mostly out of respect for Kay, Finn liked to think. But also because of what Eales represented: every cop's worst nightmare.

And it wasn't just Joe Spencer's death, or Kay's close brush herself, that had made the incident a year ago so horrifying. It was that even with six seasoned detectives working the murders of three prostitutes over the span of several months, no one had recognized the potential of Eales as a suspect. Finn, though, had always wondered if Kay *had*.

The media had been all over the story. Like hounds on fresh blood they'd covered the manhunt as every cop—uniformed or otherwise—took to the streets. Finn suspected it was actually the pressure of the media coverage and the citywide alert that had forced Eales to call in and surrender three days later. They'd picked him up at a junkie friend's house several doors down from his own, still holding Kay's 9mm.

The story had gone national after that for a brief time. But Kay had borne the brunt of the local coverage. For weeks. And Finn could do little but sit at the sidelines and watch.

It had been a fleeting moment of redemption when—only a week out of the hospital and still recovering—Kay had convinced Valerie Regester to come forward, positively identifying Eales as the man she'd seen dump one of the women's bodies down a slope in Leakin Park.

"So you're giving Kay the investigation?" Finn wondered if Gunderson was aware of the personal interest Kay had vested in Regester since the girl had agreed to testify, if he knew about Kay convincing her to get off the streets.

"I'm not sure," Gunderson answered.

"You think she's ready for the street?"

"She's been out there."

Finn hadn't heard. He'd stopped keeping tabs a few months ago.

"Sent her out on a couple slam dunks. Easy cases. This one though . . ." Gunderson looked past the glare of the crime-scene lights. "I think I'll let Kay decide if she's ready. She deserves a real case. How would you feel about working it with her?"

"Me?"

"I can clear it with your sergeant. This case needs experience, Finn. And Kay needs a partner. Someone to ground her."

Someone like Joe Spencer, Finn imagined Gunderson wanted to add.

Finn had seen how much Kay invested in each case, never giving up, leaving no stone unturned, and often taking directions others wouldn't even have considered. Spencer had been a good fit for her. An old-school, by-the-book cop who maintained perspective on the case while Kay chased her intuition.

"She won't stand to have her hand held," Finn said.

"I know." Gunderson nodded to the bay doors. "She's here."

She was lit from behind by the strobe of cruisers outside as she stepped over the scattered debris. Still, there was no mistaking her. Or the tension that stiffened her stance when one of the uniforms pointed her toward him and Gunderson.

Finn watched her pick her way around oily puddles toward the circle of lights. She'd cut her hair, and Finn realized then that he couldn't remember when he'd seen her last. Weeks or months?

The cut was short. The kind that gave an air of confidence that might turn most men off but looked damn sexy to Finn. The suit, however, bordered on masculine. He'd seen her wear it before, only now it looked different. The material drew tight at her shoulders, while the rest hung loose off her thin frame. And when she finally met Finn's gaze, the year of wanting her hit him like a ton of bricks.

"Sorry I dragged you out, Kay." Gunderson offered her a hand as she straddled the blackened beam, then he gestured to Finn. "I asked Finn to tag along. With his Arson stint, I figured he could give us some insight."

Kay nodded. Her cool gray eyes caught his, and her fleeting smile seemed little more than professional courtesy. What had he expected?

"So it's Valley?" she asked.

"We found her purse just through the door there. It fared better than she did. ID in the purse is all Regester's. Thirty-two dollars and change still in the wallet. No car ownership or insurance cards. Not even a Maryland driver's license."

"Any vehicle outside?"

"Not in the immediate vicinity."

"So her killer drove her here."

"Unless she walked." Gunderson nodded to where the halogens flooded Regester's body behind him. "You ready to see her?"

"Yeah."

Sarge stepped aside then, allowing Kay to take in Valerie Regester's twisted remains.

"Christ," she whispered, her voice suddenly shaky. "Are you sure that's her?"

3

THE SMELL ALMOST KNOCKED HER OVER. The stench of burned meat. Cooked organs and singed hair.

Kay worked her fingers into a pair of gloves as she moved past Sarge. She brought her hand to her nose, welcoming the usually objectionable odor of latex.

Water rippled in the wake of Kay's duty shoes, washing against the soaked and blackened remnants of the victim's clothing. Squatting, Kay swallowed hard, her breath clutching against the acrid stench. In her mind, Valley's rare smile flashed.

"She was half under this beam." Gunderson gave the alligatored surface a tap with his shoe, letting loose a burst of charcoal shards. "Finn figures the killer counted on it helping with the burning. Old, dried wood fires up better than a fresh body."

Kay shifted, allowing full illumination from the crime-scene lamps. Along the victim's throat she could just make out the braided pattern of a chain. She reached for it, plucking the necklace out of the blistered flesh and sliding her fingers along its length behind the neck. Searching. Then finding what she'd prayed she wouldn't.

From the heat-tarnished chain dangled a medallion. St. Michael. Patron saint of police officers. A medal of protection.

Kay felt sick. She let the pendant drop. "Can we roll her?"

When Gunderson's cell went off, the sergeant retreated to take the call.

"I'll help," Finn offered.

The bitterness of beer and bile rose to the top of her throat. Through the thin latex gloves Kay felt the residual warmth of the remains. Warmth from the flames, not life.

There was a low, sucking sound when they rolled her, as though an air pocket had been created between her back and the concrete. Black water swirled in to fill the place where Valley had lain. With his hand still on one charred shoulder, Finn propped her.

"Amazing," he said, "how resilient the human body is, huh?"

In the glare of the lamps Valley's hands were white, untouched by the flames that had consumed the exposed areas of her body. A yellow cord bound her wrists, and some of her clothing had also been protected: remnants of a pink leather skirt and a pale blouse. She wore no rings, no other jewelry, but her nails were long, sculpted, and polished by a salon, with glittering decals on each.

"The hands look good," Finn said. "You'll get prints to compare to her past prostitution record."

Kay sat back on her heels. "It's her."

"How do you know?"

"The nails. Valley always had them done. She liked them long. Said they protected her on the street."

Hell of a lot of good they did tied behind her back, Kay thought.

"And there's this." Kay caught the St. Michael's medallion between her fingers again, angled it for Finn to see.

"That hers?"

"I gave it to her."

A beat of silence, then: "I'm sorry about this, Kay."

Finn's discomfort radiated off him like the heat from Valley's body. Kay had forgotten the awkwardness that came over him when confronted by genuine emotion.

Behind them, Gunderson jammed his cell into his coat pocket. "I gotta get back," he said. "You two good here?"

Kay stood as Finn released the body. "What do you mean, 'us two'?"

"I'm giving you this one, Kay. But like I said, this here's a red ball, so you're working with Finn."

Kay caught the look that passed between the two men and knew arguing was pointless. The decision had been made before she'd ever set foot on the scene.

"Take it or leave it, Kay."

Six years working under Ed Gunderson had taught Kay

just how far she could push the man. She got further than most of her peers when it came to Sarge, but Spencer's death had taken the wind out of their relationship. Even though Sarge had fought for her when people needed someone to blame, when the brass needed to make an example of her, Kay would never forget the disappointment she'd seen in his eyes when he'd stood at her hospital bedside.

"I lost one good cop, Delaney," he'd said when she'd tried to hand in her shield. "Don't make it two."

Kay had always wondered if there was more behind his hanging on to her. As though, in the midst of the calloused cynicism that came with working murders, she was Ed Gunderson's last link to humanity.

She nodded.

"All right then," he said, snapping the collar of his trench coat. "I'll see you downtown later."

Watching him navigate the debris, Kay knew she should be grateful. A month ago he wouldn't have let her anywhere near the case.

She caught Finn studying her. "So, you're the arson expert," she said. "Tell me about this fire." She bit down on the sarcasm too late and looked past the circle of light to the far reaches of the wrecked interior.

"Well, she was probably dead before the fire was lit."

"And you can tell that how?"

"This scene's got all the signs of someone trying to destroy evidence. And you can smell it."

She took in a breath and immediately regretted it. "What exactly am I supposed to be smelling?"

"Gasoline. There's traces of it just under everything else. He used it as an accelerant." Finn circled to her, closing the comfortable distance between them, and pointed out the blacker areas around the body. "Our boy splashed gas here. And here across the beam. But mostly over the body. The fire characteristically spread up from there. You can follow the path. From anywhere in the building I can show you how the fire originated from this one spot. See the *V* patterns?" He motioned to the wall next to Valley's body.

"These show you the fire's point of origin. And here, where the burning is deepest, you can almost make out the trail of gas he laid. Arson'll talk to the owner, find out if there was fuel on the premises. If not, we can assume our boy came prepared."

"A professional job?"

"Not likely. This guy didn't try to conceal the fact that he was setting a fire. Now that doesn't mean he didn't know what he was doing. See, either this guy was incredibly stupid, thinking he could destroy a body with fire, or he's got a different motive for the arson."

Finn seemed to scan the darker recesses of the burned shell. "I'm betting he torched this place to destroy evidence. An arson scene is an entirely different ball game than anything you've investigated. Often you're looking at minimal or no trace evidence. You've got temps of a thousand degrees ripping through here. Flames and smoke, falling debris. And then you've got your fire crews trampling every last square inch of the place. Doesn't leave much chance for solid evidence. I'm guessing our guy knew that."

"But why not make it really tough on us then?" she asked. "Why did the son of a bitch just leave her purse like that?"

"Because it's not *her* identity he's trying to conceal with the fire, Kay. It's his own."

4

KAY SCANNED THE DESTRUCTION AGAIN. Finn was right. It *was* unlike any other scene she'd worked. It was foreign. Nothing here spoke to her. Nothing cried out with answers.

Her gaze stopped on Finn. It was the first time in months she'd really seen him. He looked rumpled. It wasn't just the creased and smudged suit that his dry cleaner on Broadway would curse him for bringing in. His eyes looked tired and he needed a shave. Between his Latin complexion and his sleek, black hair pulled into the usual ponytail, he looked more like a hit man for a Colombian drug cartel than a forty-year-old, black-Irish murder cop from Baltimore.

She regretted shutting Finn out, Kay realized then. Regretted not letting him be there for her. Of everyone, Finn understood what it was like to lose someone, *and* to feel responsible for that death.

Kay averted her gaze when he caught her stare.

"Any thoughts on whether this could be related to Eales?" he asked her. "With his trial starting in the next couple weeks . . ."

Kay shook her head. "I just don't see it. Eales doesn't have the money or the brains to arrange something like this."

Kay looked to the body. *Valley*. Almost a year ago the girl had finally agreed to meet with Kay. Out on Calvert Street, just down from the glitz and squalor of The Block, the young hooker had shivered in a halo of breath vapor as she accepted Kay's own scarf and gloves. How many times had Kay told the girl she was doing the right thing by testifying? Assured her she'd be safe?

"Then maybe it's random," Finn said. "She could have been hooking again and got picked up by the wrong john."

Kay didn't want to believe it.

"When was the last time you talked to her?" he asked.

"Couple months, I guess. I got her a job in the State's Attorney's Office. Filing. Answering phones."

"Well, hooking certainly pays better than a city wage."

Kay hoped he wasn't right.

"What about family?" he asked.

"There isn't any. Mom bailed, and father died when Valley was six."

"Adoptive parents?"

"No. She was in and out of foster homes." Kay shook her head. "Damn it, Finn, this girl pulled her life together."

"Detective Delaney, at long last." Niles Fischer sloshed toward them, his assistant carrying a litter. They stopped within the circle of light, and Fischer cracked her a dry smile.

"How are you doing, Niles?"

"Complaining never got me nowhere. Seen everything you need to see?"

"Pretty much. Can you tell me anything about her?"

The ME's investigator shrugged. "Not much. Victim was probably deceased before the fire started. Not sure how though."

"What is that, you figure?" Kay pointed to the four-inch gash along the top right side of Valley's skull. The thin layer of flesh beneath glared pink against the seared skin. "Is that a laceration from a blow?"

"Could be. More likely a heat rupture though. With temperatures this intense, the soft tissue splits. Especially tissue close to bone." Fischer arranged the heavy plastic sheet around the body. "They'll x-ray her, look for corresponding fractures. But there's no telling for sure till you let us get this girl downtown."

"All right, then, she's all yours. But bag her hands." *I hope you took a piece of the bastard with you, Valley.* Kay turned to Finn. "Gunderson said they found her purse?"

"Yeah, over here."

He led her through the flame-licked doorway and into the main area of the warehouse. Finn trained his police-issue Maglite across the concrete floor, stopping when its beam caught a slightly charred Coca-Cola can and what might have been foil gum wrappers. It was amazing to Kay how some areas of the building appeared almost untouched by the devastation.

"Right here." Finn pointed. "We already bagged the purse. Looked like it had been gone through. Could get lucky and get a print."

"Yeah, and you could win the Big Game jackpot tomorrow too." Behind them, from the back room, the sound of the zipper on Valley's body bag ripped the silence. Kay hated the sound.

"Face it, Kay. What we got here is a stone-fucking whodunit."

5

WITH THE FIRE DEPARTMENT'S pumpers gone, Luther Street was clogging with press vehicles and TV-satellite trucks. Kay tried to ignore the small crush of media. Several officers monitored the border of crime-scene ribbon that snapped in the breeze. Inside the taped-off corral, more uniforms scanned the ground, systematically working a grid up the side alley and the back.

"Anything?" Kay asked the closest patrol.

He shook his head, kept his eyes to the ground. She saw the end of his cigarette flare as he sucked on it.

"Hey, Slick." She waved him over, snatched the fizzling butt from his lips, and flicked it past the yellow tape. "Don't smoke on my crime scene, okay?"

"Yes, ma'am. Detective."

In his exhale, Kay savored the traces of nicotine that hung in the damp air. It had been a year since she'd last lit up. She had Bernard Eales to thank for that. He'd put her in the hospital for a week, and during that time it had required too much effort to drag herself to the elevator, ride the car down, and limp to the main doors for a smoke. Later on, it seemed senseless to start up again.

Besides, when you'd faced death that closely, when you'd smelled its breath, there was no way the experience didn't change you. It was natural, her shrink had told her, to want to alter things about your life after something like that. And Kay had. Smoking wasn't the only habit she'd given up since the beatdown.

She looked at Finn, his shoulders hunched against the steady drizzle. The harsh blue strobe of a radio car's light-bar washed his face in erratic pulses. Kay wondered how he'd been in the past few months. Seeing the outline of his body beneath the damp jacket and the creased slacks made it hard to forget what they'd shared before that nightmare on Eales's porch, before Kay had pushed everyone away. Especially Finn.

In many ways, she missed him. But it was better like this. She didn't want anyone counting on her again. Ever. It was good that he'd given up leaving messages on her answering machine.

"We're not going to find any eyewitnesses," Finn said. "There's nothing down here." He nodded to the dark windows of the neighboring warehouses, broken panes, and boarded-up frames.

He was right. Luther was a narrow, potholed side street T-ing north off Boston, the main drag that swept out of Fells Point and along the eastern shore. An industrial wasteland.

Finn followed as Kay ducked under the police ribbon and crossed the street. Directly opposite lay a fenced-in lot. Twelve feet of rusted chain-link circled a graveyard of parked trailers and flatbeds, junkers and random piles of sheet metal. Kay felt an involuntary shudder as her eyes searched the murky maze of skids. Her heart skipped when metal clanged and she spotted movement back in the farther reaches. A stray dog, most likely. Nothing more.

The dark made her uneasy now. Made her think thoughts no cop on the street could afford to think. Used to be she was the first one through the door in any situation. Now she didn't know if she could do it. Didn't know if she'd freeze up. And she hated not knowing, hated not trusting herself. Mostly she hated Bernard Eales for stealing her courage.

She turned to study the Dutton warehouse. The three-story, crumbling structure looked hollow. Flames had licked up the east wall through the first-floor windows, blackening the brick.

"So why did he choose this place?" she thought aloud. "Was it convenient or significant?"

"It was empty. And it was isolated."

"Yeah, and so are half the warehouses down here. Why this one?" She pointed to the alley alongside the Dutton building. "You can't see the side entrance from the street. He had to have known it was there. That it was open."

"Lucky guess?"

"No. The building means something. He was familiar with it."

"Come on, Kay, we're getting soaked. We'll come back in the daylight. Rattle some doors. By then Arson will have something for us. We may as well get started on the paperwork."

Kay started to follow him, then stopped. "No. I want to go to Valley's apartment first."

"Now?"

"Yeah. You said her purse had been gone through. This guy has her address. It wouldn't be the first time a perp made a house call after the fact. Besides, we have to check the place anyway."

"Fine. But we gotta get through that." He nodded to the media personnel, each jockeying for a better position along the yellow tape. One broke from the pack. "Here comes Jane," Finn warned.

Jane Gallagher, WBAL's crime reporter, zeroed in, her cameraman scrambling to keep up.

"Detective Delaney, can you tell us if there's been a positive identification on the body?"

"No comment." The red operating light on the camera glowed, and Kay clamped down on a dozen other words she'd rather use.

"Has it been ruled a homicide?"

The microphone bobbled in Kay's face. "No comment."

"What about the fire? Has it been classified an arson?"

There was a time Kay had been civil to Gallagher. Actually liked her. She'd used the reporter herself a couple times on cases. But that had ended fourteen months ago. Paramedics had barely scraped Kay's battered body off Eales's walkway when the reporter had pounced. The next morning, and for several days after, the image of Kay's bloodied and swollen face had flashed across Channel 11's monitors.

But it had been Gallagher's ongoing commentary on the incident that had been the most defamatory: citing bad judgment, a disregard for policy, and a lack of departmental defensive training as the cause of the brutal attack on the two detectives. Kay never knew why Gallagher had such an obsession for the case, but Kay suspected Jane's feelings for Spencer had gone beyond professional, despite his wedding ring. And that Gallagher, like many others, blamed Kay for his death.

"Detective Delaney, are you working the case? Is this your first investigation since—"

Before Gallagher could execute any defensive move, Kay had the mike in one hand. With the other she snatched the lens of the shoulder-mounted camera. The reporter's thin lips stretched into a smile, and Kay despised the amusement she saw in the woman's face.

"Don't go there, Jane. Don't go anywhere *near* there. You are the *last* person who's getting anything on this, you hear?"

"Wait, is that a departmental position or a personal one?"

"You need to ask?"

"I'm just doing my job, Detective."

"Yeah? Then let me do mine or you're going to find this mike so far up your rectum you're going to need a fucking nuclear enema to get it out." Kay gave the microphone a final shove before turning.

Behind her, Gallagher mumbled something indiscernible, then Kay heard Finn's voice: ". . . not like you don't deserve it, Janey. Besides, you know the drill. Talk to the spokesperson. Like everyone else."

Kay couldn't make out the words after that, but when Finn caught up with her, his silence said it all. He'd just run damage control for her, and he didn't like it.

6

VALERIE REGESTER'S APARTMENT was up in Hampden, a predominantly white, working-class enclave in the Northern District. Here there were fewer steel grates over store windows and doors, and the trash sat neatly at the curbs waiting for morning pickup. The four-story walk-up smelled of cooked onions and cat piss, and the humidity from the day still hung in the tight stairwell. It was even hotter on the top-floor landing outside the girl's apartment.

Kay remembered Valley's excitement the day she'd first brought the girl to see the rental. The promise in Valley's eyes was one of those images, those life snapshots, that would stay with Kay forever. But as she envisioned it now, Kay saw her burned remains. And she saw Bernard Eales. *Could* he have arranged the girl's murder?

Kay watched as Finn snapped on a fresh latex glove and tried the knob of Valley's door.

"Locked," he said. "Doesn't look like our boy was here. Does she have a roommate?"

"No."

"You wanna wake the super?"

But Kay didn't have to answer. From the opposite door on the landing there was the slide of a chain, then a dead bolt being thrown back. When the door opened a crack, Kay badged the tenant.

"It's Valerie, isn't it?" Valley's neighbor looked to be in

her early twenties. She clutched a silk kimono around her and twisted a lock of blond hair around one finger. Behind her, through the open door, Kay saw the snow-filled television screen of a station gone off the air.

"I'm Detective Delaney. This is Detective Finnerty."

"Kathleen Koch." Her hand was slim and cool in Kay's. "You're that cop. Valerie's friend, aren't you? I recognize you from the picture in the paper."

"Yeah," Kay said. The same picture everyone else in Baltimore City and twenty-three counties from Worcester to Garrett had seen. "Ms. Koch, do you know if anyone's been here tonight?"

"No. I would have heard. I've been keeping an ear out, waiting for Valerie to come home from class."

"Class?"

"Yeah. She's taking a drawing class at Notre Dame. It's done at ten and she should have been home hours ago. She's got work tomorrow."

"Does she get a ride with someone? Take Mass Transit?"

"Sometimes she catches the Light Rail. Tonight she had my car."

"Would she have driven anyone home?"

"No."

"Does Valerie have a boyfriend?" Kay asked.

"No. Not Valerie. She's had it with guys. That's why she's at Notre Dame," Koch said, referring to the all-women's campus.

"You don't have a key to her apartment, do you, Kathy?" Finn asked.

"Sure." Koch groped the wall just inside the door and produced a key chain.

"Can you tell us what Valley was wearing tonight?" Kay asked.

"Oh, God, what's happened to her?" The first waver of

panic gripped the girl's voice and her knuckles whitened around the spare key. "Tell me she's all right."

Kay shook her head. Looked to Finn. In her partnership with Spencer she'd always been the one consoling, the one carefully choosing words for the victim's survivors. Spence used to tell her she was good at it. But Kay had figured out early on that it was just his way of avoiding the wailing mothers, the weeping spouses, and the hysterical family and friends.

"She borrowed my leather miniskirt." Koch handed Kay the key, her hand suddenly shaking. "It's pink. And a white top, I think. What's happened to her?"

Kay unlocked the door and stepped into the foyer of Valley's apartment. Tonight, she couldn't be the one delivering the news. After what she'd seen back at the warehouse, there was no comfort left in her.

Behind her she heard Finn's muted tones, then Kathleen Koch's sobs. The place smelled of scented candles or some kind of flowery air-freshener. A cheap box fan in one window slapped the heavy night air through the small apartment. The carpeting was worn, but Valley had had it cleaned. She'd painted as well. Kay remembered the nicotine-yellowed walls.

Nowhere in the apartment were there signs of a struggle or foul play. Nothing to indicate Valley had been abducted from her home. Still, Kay pulled a pair of gloves from her jacket pocket.

In the bedroom, the wall switch worked a small lamp on the nightstand. A faded kerchief with a Florentine pattern was draped over the shade, muting the light. The bed was made, pillows carefully arranged. Another fan was propped in the bedroom window, its breeze rustling the leaves of a hanging spider plant and the brittle pages of newsprint tacked to the wall—pages from Valley's sketchbook. Life-drawings, nudes, portraits in broad, bold strokes of charcoal. Kay recognized several of Kathleen Koch.

A paint-chipped dresser with lopsided drawers had been angled into the corner, the top cluttered with costume jewelry, knockoff imitation scents in quaint perfume bottles, and nail polish from Wal-Mart. Tucked in the corner of the clouded mirror was a photo-booth snap of her and Koch. Both laughing.

There were no other photos. No family shots. No childhood memories caught on celluloid. Kay remembered the sound of the zipper on Valley's body bag. *Who would bury the girl?*

Kay tamped down the threat of emotion. The time to grieve was later, *after* Valley's killer had been caught. Right now she couldn't afford to dwell on the girl's loss.

Crossing to the bed, Kay pulled open the nightstand drawer: a dog-eared *Chicken Soup* book and a half-used pack of matches from Donna's in Mount Vernon. She'd taken Valley there for lunch months ago, had jotted her new cell number inside the matchbook. A bottle of NyQuil and two prescription bottles rattled in the drawer when Kay pulled it open farther. She picked them up, turning each into the light: Xanax and doxycycline.

Taking one last look around the bedroom, Kay knew Valley hadn't been hooking again. She shouldn't have been so quick to lose faith in the girl. This was the apartment of someone starting over, someone living on a city wage, leaving a lifetime on the streets behind her. She'd turned her life around, and watching her do it had been one of the few glimpses of humanity Kay had found since that night on Eales's porch. It had given her hope.

In the living room, Kathleen Koch had gotten ahold of herself. Finn looked huge sitting on the couch next to her, cradling a tissue box while she wiped her eyes.

"Do you know why Valley was taking Xanax?" Kay asked her.

Koch looked up with swollen eyes. "She was having panic attacks. Mild ones."

"About the upcoming trial?"

Koch nodded. Blew her nose. "She was having nightmares too."

That explained the NyQuil.

"And do you know what the doxycycline was for?"

"I don't know what that is."

A shared glance with Finn told Kay he'd gotten everything he was going to from the girl. Kay motioned to the door, and Finn guided Koch to the foyer and out onto the stairwell.

"You've got my number if you think of anything or need to talk," Finn told her, returning Valley's key.

The girl sniffed again. "Thank you, Detective."

"One more thing, Kathleen." Kay stopped her before she could close her apartment door. "You said Valley used your car tonight?"

"Yeah. It's a Nova. Gray." She gave them the tag number.

"Valley had her license then?"

"Of course. We went to the MVA just last week to get the photo renewed. It was her birthday."

Kay mentally kicked herself. She shouldn't have forgotten.

"And she carried it with her, right? The license?"

"Always."

"Thanks, Kathleen. Now lock up, okay?"

They heard the dead bolt slide home, then the chain, as they headed down the stairs. Wordlessly they left the building and crossed the street to the unmarked. The sound of Finn's hard-soled brogues against the asphalt echoed through the wet dark of morning.

"Maybe we'll get lucky on the wallet after all," Kay said over the Lumina's buzzer as she opened the passenger door.

"You're thinking the killer took Regester's driver's license? But why, when he didn't take the money?"

"Because the money's just money." She met Finn's gaze over the roof of the car. "Her license has her picture on it."

"Yeah. And?"

"And, it's his souvenir."

7

THEY FOUND KATHLEEN KOCH'S Chevy behind Fourier Hall at Notre Dame College. Dawn had started to lighten the sky over the Chesapeake some fifteen miles east as Kay and Finn scanned the manicured campus and the empty lot, working their way to the run-down Nova.

From a distance nothing was visibly suspicious about the little car: no awkward tilt from a flat tire, no smashed window, and certainly no note on the dash begging the campus parking division not to tow.

The lot's lamps still burned, their yellow glow shimmering off beaded rain across the Nova's windshield.

"Both doors are locked," Kay noted as she approached the passenger side. "Her stuff's inside though." On the passenger seat lay a sketch pad and a small wooden box bearing the name of an art supplies store. A red rain jacket had been tossed in the backseat.

"Maybe it wouldn't start," Finn suggested. "Could be she went for the Light Rail and he grabbed her there. Maybe even grabbed her up in Hampden after she'd gotten off."

"No. Ten o'clock at night, I think she would have called her friend. Gone back inside to use the phone."

"Building might have been locked up already."

Kay circled the car. The paint had oxidized years ago in the blistering Baltimore sun. The bumper's chrome was peeling and the Maryland plates had started to rust. When she came around to the driver's-side door, Kay knew the feeling in her gut was valid. Glass ground beneath the heavy soles of her shoes.

Finn heard it as well. "What the hell's that?"

At her feet, thick shards peppered the wet asphalt, glittering like jewels. Several more glinted along the Nova's roof.

Kay looked up. "The son of a bitch took out the light."

Twenty feet above them the glass-bowl diffuser had been shattered. It had been a good shot. Or maybe it had taken several.

"He targeted her. Knew what car she was driving, where she'd parked," Kay said.

But why was her sketchbook already in the car? Unless Finn was right. Unless she'd gotten in and the car wouldn't start.

"Can you get under the hood without access to the inside?" Kay asked.

Finn had already snapped on a pair of gloves and was prodding through the top of the grill. There was a faint pop and the hood came up.

"External latch," he said, propping the hood, then pointing. "There. Spark-plug cables were pulled."

The rubber ends dangled uselessly next to the distributor cap.

"Son of a bitch." Kay stepped back from the oil-stained engine.

"If this girl is as street-smart as you say, Kay, how'd he get her into his car?"

"She wouldn't have caught a ride with a stranger. He took her by force. Or . . ." Kay scanned the deserted grounds again, grasping for a scenario that felt right. "Or she knew the scumbag. We better get Mobile out here to dust the car," she said, even though she doubted they'd find much. If Valley's killer had put such orchestration into her abduction, he'd hardly leave prints.

They waited twenty minutes for a Mobile Crime Lab unit, sitting together on the hood of the Lumina, first exchanging awkward small talk, then sharing silence. They watched the white Crime Lab van circle a couple times before locating the lot behind Fourier Hall. Leaving the tech to dust the Nova, they headed downtown. Kay let Finn drive, enjoying the rare luxury of being chauffeured through the streets that usually passed her in a blur.

Baltimore wasn't her city. From its glittering tourist-infested Inner Harbor to the crumbling projects where heroin and cocaine perpetuated the decay, from boarded-up row houses to the gluttony of Guilford and Roland Park with their private schools and stately shingled homes, all of it felt foreign to Kay.

There had been no rhyme or reason to her coming here thirteen years ago. Out of college, needing a job and knowing there was no future for her back home in Jonesport, Maine, she'd followed a friend to Maryland on a whim, with two hundred bucks in her wallet and a suitcase in the trunk of her Honda. And when the Department advertised for recruits, the money and benefits looked better than any other prospects at the time.

Thirteen years . . . Another eight and she could retire from the force. If she actually *made* it to retirement. Eight years could seem like a life sentence when the passing of weeks and months was counted by the number of murders up on the board, by the endless list of victims, and the plea bargains for lesser sentences granted by the state simply to keep the system from clogging. Even at the best of times, murder was a thankless business.

Still, she made a difference. It wasn't a view shared by many in her squad, but it was the one thing Kay clung to over the years: the notion that what she did helped people, even if in the end it was only a handful. As a murder cop, *she* was entrusted with the pursuit of the worst possible crime—the taking of a human life. *She* spoke for the dead. And for the survivors.

Even so, after her twenty were up, she'd retire. She'd made a vow to herself: no drop program, no tempting departmental bribes to stay on board just a few more years with the promise of a tidy bonus at the end. She wouldn't let the stress eat what little soul was left. When her day came, she'd be gone. Maybe she'd go back home to Maine. Back to the fishing-village atmosphere, untouched by the plague of violence she saw drugs exert on the city. Away from the crack holes and seedy side streets, from the hot spots where crime seemed to incubate and spread like some terminal disease.

Studying Finn's profile now, Kay remembered a time when the city hadn't seemed so bleak.

"So, have you had lunch with Jimmy Carter lately?" he asked, perhaps sensing her eyes on him.

"No. You?"

Finn shook his head. Smiled.

Together they'd worked with the Habitat for Humanity organization within Baltimore, helping to restore vacant row houses for low-income families. They'd seen several projects through completion in the Northeast District and

even took part in a lunch with the former president as part
of the groundbreaking ceremonies.

Kay missed the camaraderie of the crew, missed the hard
labor and the sense of accomplishment, and she missed
sharing something outside the job with Finn.

"You gonna be okay with this?" Finn focused on the
traffic congesting along Greenmount. "You and me working together?"

"Sure. You?"

He shrugged. "I don't have a problem. As long as you do
the typing."

It wouldn't have been the first time Finn had solicited
her writing skills. Before Spencer's death, they'd often
found themselves in the Homicide offices together. One or
the other working overtime, their hours deliberately overlapping in spite of their alternating shifts. These days,
though, Kay did her best to be out of the offices before
Finn's squad came in, avoiding him when she could.
Obviously Finn had been doing the same.

"Tell you what," she said. "I'll do the typing if you don't
babysit me through this entire investigation."

"Deal." And in his voice she sensed she'd been right
about why Sarge had put Finn on the case. Finn was Sarge's
safety net, his way of ensuring that she didn't screw up, that
she didn't get someone else killed.

He accelerated through the amber light at Biddle.
"Listen, I don't know what you're feeling about this girl,
Kay, but if you want to sit out the autopsy this morning—"

"I'll be there. Thanks for the concern though," she
added.

As they crossed Eager Street, Kay felt the familiar tight-
ening of her spine. It had started two blocks away, but now,
with Maryland's State Pen to her right, the tension twisted
in her empty gut.

The rough-hewn granite of the Transition Center loomed beyond the twenty-foot Cyclone fence topped with accordion coils of shining razor ribbon. Kay wondered if other cops looked at the Pen as they passed it. If they thought about the men they'd put there.

As the Lumina shot past the cluster of buildings, there was only one man Kay thought of.

8

DAY 403.

Bernard Eales felt his feet first. Arches pressed against the cold iron bar at the end of his low cot. The bunk was too small. With no room to roll over, he generally woke in the same position he lay down in when lights went out each night in A Block, the starched sheet still pulled to his chin.

From the farther reaches of the cellblock he heard the echoes of catcalls, distant slammings, even muffled cries. Nothing in particular defined mornings in his corner of the State Pen. No sun. No alarm clocks. But Bernard always recognized morning in his gray double cell: his bladder was bursting and his mouth was stale.

With effort, he hauled himself up. Shambling barefoot across the cement pad to the stainless-steel urinal, he loosened the drawstring of his prison trousers and groped for his cock.

From the top bunk, Darnell Brown whimpered. One month in and the crack-selling street tough still cried for his mama. Especially in his dreams.

Bernard checked his watch, then remembered he'd traded it for smokes last week. He'd ask Patricia for a new one. Nothing pricey. And some more Marlboros. He hated bartering. Always got the shit end of the stick.

Not that it mattered much when he had Patsy, he thought, his urine at last striking the steel bowl. She took care of him. Two visits a week. More, if they'd let her. And always with a little something. All he had to do was smile, nod while she talked about her cats, and pucker a few blown kisses from behind the visitation-booth Plexiglas before she left.

Patsy and her fucking cats . . . If he ever got out, the first thing he'd do would be to get rid of the fucking cats. He kicked the flush with his heel. Darnell stopped whimpering.

Bernard turned within the twelve-by-fourteen cell to the narrow window. Like all the cell windows in the Pen, it was welded shut, its frame painted a bright orange. They did that so the guards could see if you fucked with it.

Next to it hung a calendar, stuck up with shreds of masking tape. Patsy had given it to him, from the garage her old man took the Beemer to. Photos of classic cars. Nothing that turned him on though. Nothing as sweet as his '59 StratoChief. He wondered where the Strat was now. Still in police impound probably. The gleaming black paint job dulling in the glaring sun. The white walls drying out and flat. The battery dead. Sons of bitches.

On the calendar, Darnell had been crossing off the days with bold red *X*'s. Bernard let him. It was Thursday. In his left-handed chicken-scratch Bernard had made a notation to remind him of today's meeting with Grogan. With the trial starting in two weeks, the defense attorney was itching to talk strategy, jury selection, and witnesses.

All a waste of time. Even if Grogan *did* manage to convince a jury he'd shot the cop in self-defense, that he hadn't known they were police at his door that night, and he'd been protecting his home against presumed intruders, even *then* that ball-busting, blond state's attorney bitch was going to have his nuts on a platter for the hookers' murders.

Bernard returned to his bottom bunk, flopped down onto the sweat-dampened sheet. He kicked at the top mattress when Darnell started whimpering again. Then he closed his eyes, rooted a booger out of one nostril, and flicked it across the cell while he imagined himself behind the wheel of his shiny black StratoChief.

9

AFTER A HALF HOUR in the cutting room of Maryland's Office of the Chief Medical Examiner at 111 Penn Street, Finn still hadn't desensitized to the reek of Valerie Regester's remains. Neither the chemical air fresheners nor a constant flow of purified air through the morgue's ventilation system could compete. Kay, on the other hand, had surrendered. The paper face mask hung from her neck, and two smears of Mentholatum sat under her nostrils.

Regester's body had been wheeled out earlier, photographed, weighed, and finally prepped in the autopsy room's sterile expanse of ceramic tile and stainless steel. What remained of her clothes had been peeled from her charred skin and laid out on an adjoining slab. They'd watched Eddie Jones work on her, removing and weighing organs, his gloved hands slick with body fluids as he droned observations to his assistant. Louis Armstrong played on a boom box in the corner, and from behind his mask the ME hummed along with "What a Wonderful World."

"So, finally out from behind the desk then, huh, Kay?"

Jonesy asked as he slid Regester's liver into the scale.

Finn glanced across the table in time to see Kay nod.

"Yeah. My coffee-making wasn't winning me any points. I think they figured I'm less of a hazard out on the streets."

The corners of the ME's eyes creased, revealing the smile hidden behind his mask.

Eddie Jones was a little younger than Finn, closer to Kay's thirty-three. At six-three and with a full head of sun-bleached hair, he was the easiest ME on staff to spot if he was on the floor. He looked like a bird, Finn had always thought, with close-set eyes and a sharp Roman nose. An albino vulture, poised over the city's carrion and waste.

From the moment they'd walked into the morgue, Finn had sensed a rare easiness and familiarity between Kay and the ME. Although he'd never worked a case with Kay before, Finn had witnessed Kay enough on the job to know her briskness. Civil but professional, Kay's social graces sometimes took a backseat to whatever case she was working. He'd seen some of the guys on the unit take that frostiness the wrong way. And even *he* had wondered about her until Joe Spencer had introduced them two years ago.

Kay had been working a new case caught on the four-to-twelve shift when Finn had come onto the midnight. Standing on the eighth-floor terrace of headquarters at 3 a.m., the lights of the city reflecting off the humidity that lifted from steamy streets, Kay had been having a smoke with Joe Spencer. He'd made quick introductions, then left, while Finn and Kay stayed, sharing a half dozen Camels and light conversation as they watched the sun rise.

They'd shared smokes a few more times after that, running into each other by accident, then on purpose. Until one night they ended up at some waterfront bar. Finn couldn't remember which one. They'd gotten drunk, then capped it off back at Finn's boat, and Kay had stayed the night.

In the morning they'd agreed they'd made a mistake, but he was in her bed the very next night. And for countless nights after that. For almost a year.

From the start Finn had known his feelings and his illusions of the relationship went deeper than Kay's. Still, he'd always hoped she'd come around. Even after Bernard Eales, after she'd refused to take Finn's calls and her avoidance of him became painfully clear, he'd waited for Kay. Until several months ago, sitting at O'Reilly's, staring at a double shot of bourbon, on the verge of taking that first drink after twenty-one months of being dry, Finn had finally given up on Kay.

He missed her. But it was getting easier.

"All right, boys and girls." Jonesy leaned back from the table at last. "Here's what you've got so far. Obviously we're talking major charring. Deep burning that was assisted by flammables being poured onto the clothing. She was definitely dead before the fire started. There's no evidence of smoke inhalation, and no traces of carbon monoxide in her blood."

"Can you tell if she was raped?"

"No visible indications of forcible sexual activity. But you do have what appears to be evidence of strangulation. Petechial hemorrhaging in the mucous membrane lining the inner surface of the eyelids. And it looks like she bit her tongue. Both signs of asphyxiation. And then"—he pointed to the back of the neck, high up, where a narrow section of the skin had been protected from the flames— "it looks like you've got some bruising back here. Fingertip impressions."

"He strangled her?" Kay asked.

Jonesy nodded, then circled both his hands around an

imaginary throat. "From the front. I'm looking at a fractured hyoid bone, hemorrhaging in the voice box, larynx
and the neck muscles, as well as damage to the thyroid and
cricoid cartilages."

"Manual strangulation's usually about power," Kay
pointed out. "Anger. Hatred. And if it was a frontal assault,
then maybe it was about watching her die. Unless she was
already unconscious. What about drag marks?"

"Nothing suggests she was dragged. No abrasions or
contusions to the back. Nothing on the shoe she was still
wearing."

"So he carried her into the warehouse?"

"That's a big guy to be able to lift her out of a car and
carry her through all the junk that was in that place," Finn
said.

"Then maybe he forced her to walk in herself." Kay's
eyes never left Regester's remains. "What about the hands?
You get anything from her nails?"

Jonesy shook his head and drew the mask from his face.
"Nothing visible, but we took clippings. We'll see."

Over the blackened body on the slab, Finn watched Kay
while Jonesy droned on. She didn't look well. Her complexion was sallow, and he wondered if she wanted to
throw up, but she remained intent.

He admired that intensity. Until he'd actually met her,
he'd only heard about her being a hound dog. Not just a
detective in a suit, sporting a gun, but a real nose-to-the-
ground, dog-with-a-bone murder cop. During the year
they'd been lovers, he'd seen the effects an investigation
could have on her. And he'd worried about the obsession
that consumed her with each new case.

"What about doxycycline?" she asked Jonesy. "She had
a prescription for it. What would she take that for?"

The ME shrugged. "It's usually prescribed for chlamydia."

"So she was sexually active then?"

"Not necessarily. She could have picked it up long ago and was only recently diagnosed." Jonesy stepped back from the table and seemed to admire his morning's work. "Oh, and another little tidbit. Your boy's got a knife."

"A knife?"

The ME nodded, and behind the silver-rimmed glasses his eyes lit up. Word around the OCME was that if you wanted a gunshot expert, you talked to Tam Nguyen, but if you needed the final word on a stabbing, Jonesy was the top blade man. The man even collected knives.

"Looks like a single-edged knife. Probably something like a lock-back. Straight blade and damned sharp. But not big. The kind that fits in the palm of your hand. It's got a narrow hilt, which suggests a thin handle. And I'm estimating a three-inch blade, based on one of the stab wounds that wasn't as direct as the others. The tip of the blade slipped, skidded up the sternum. Left an impression of the hilt on the tissue."

"A stab wound to the sternum?" Kay had gone even paler.

"Yeah. Actually, several." Lifting back the thin flap of muscle and charred skin that had covered Regester's sternum, Jonesy pointed out a half dozen shallow notches along the white bone.

"Can you tell how they were sustained?" Finn asked.

"Not really. I can say the blade's cutting edge was down, and the thrust was upward. Assuming, though, that she was standing."

"So what then? He was taunting her? Or was it part of the abduction?"

Jonesy shrugged. "Wish I could help you on that one, but with the burning I can't even say for certain if the cuts were made pre- or postmortem."

When Kay finally spoke, her voice was thin. "I need shots of these. Close-ups, showing the placement of them."

"Not a problem." Jonesy gestured to his assistant. "I'll have them sent up along with the autopsy report."

"I need them sooner." Kay didn't wait for an answer. Stripping off the paper gown she wore over her suit, she started for the doors. "And I need this kept quiet. Thanks, Jonesy."

Catching up with her, Finn pulled the mask from his face and asked, "What're you thinking?"

Kay's mouth was a tight line as her gaze went back to Regester's remains, the legs still bent, the blackened knees rising above the stainless-steel slab. In that moment Kay looked lost.

"What is it about those stab wounds?" he prompted her.

But she didn't answer. A muscle flexed along her jaw as she swung open the morgue's heavy door and tossed the paper gown into the biohazard bin. "I've got to get to the office," she said.

"You've seen them before, haven't you? The stab wounds."

There was a distant look in her eyes when she nodded. "I have to pull some files."

"Which ones?"

"Bernard Eales."

10

WITH THE REEK OF THE MORGUE still on them, Finn convinced Kay to grab some take-out breakfast with him down in Fells Point and found a bench across Thames Street. Down by the water, surrounded by the tourist traps and souvenir shops, preppie bars and the Broadway Market, Finn could almost forget what they'd been witness to this morning. And with Kay next to him, unwrapping her usual fried egg on rye, he could almost dismiss the fourteen months of silence that separated them.

"So how have you been?" He had to at least try.

"Fine."

"Sarge says you're working cases again?"

"Just dunkers." Resentment bristled in her voice as she stared at her sandwich. "I get every slam dunk that comes in. Sarge'll send me out with one of the guys, and if there's a lineup of eyewitnesses and a murder weapon waiting for us when we get on-scene, all of a sudden it's my case. Domestics. Street fights. Stickups."

He wanted to say something about it taking time, about how some cops—after a beating like that—would *never* have come back to the job. He wanted to tell her that it wasn't just her who'd suffered; it was everyone on the unit. Trust had to be reestablished. Rebuilt. But Kay knew that, was living it.

"Well, you look good," he said instead. "I like the hair-cut."

From the corner of his eye he caught her quick side glance. Saw the skepticism. "What? I can't give a compliment without you thinking it's a come-on?"

Kay's silence verified he'd guessed right.

"You know, just cuz I say something nice doesn't mean I'm aiming to get you in bed."

"So you're telling me you don't want to get me in bed?" she asked, and Finn liked how the amusement softened her features.

"Well, I didn't say that."

More silence, and Kay looked away. "Thanks," she said. "For the compliment."

He followed her gaze out over the bay. The sun's light scattered in the wake of an early-morning water taxi shuttling tourists from the Inner Harbor to Fells Point.

"So, what am I missing on the Eales case?" he asked. "I never heard about these chest wounds."

"We kept it quiet," Kay said. "The cuts were supposed to be our hold-back, because it was so bizarre."

"And they were on all three of the previous victims?"

Kay nodded. "That's how we finally linked my Harris case to the others."

Finn remembered the photos she'd shown him of the Annie Harris crime scene. Easily the worst decomposition case he'd seen. Based on the tox screen, Kay and Spencer had initially figured Harris was an OD, having gone into the vacant row house to shoot up. Kay had talked about the case, telling Finn how she and Spence had come onto Eales's name on the street, people saying he was an acquaintance of Harris's and that they'd get high together once in a while. That's why she and Spence had gone to see the son of a bitch, to talk to him as a witness, find out if he might shed light on Harris's last days.

"With the decomp we didn't see the chest wounds, but when the ME found the nicks to her sternum, we knew there was a connection to Jimmy Holewinski's dead prostitute dumped in Leakin Park, and Varcoe's Jane Doe a month after his."

Tourists spilled out of the water taxi across the way at Henderson's Wharf and began to fan out along the pedestrian walks.

"But Harris was Eales's first victim?" Finn asked.

"Because of the decomp, the ME put her time of death prior to the other two. So, yeah, she was the first. At least, the first that we know of."

Kay went silent after that, ignoring her breakfast, drinking her coffee and staring at the water. Finn knew her mind was on Eales's South Baltimore porch.

He waited. The water taxi backed away from the pier, its engine revving, before it shuttled back across the harbor.

"So the stab wounds were the same as the ones on Regester?" he asked her.

"I think so. On all the victims, the wounds were shallow, nonfatal. They made no sense to any of us."

"So you're saying, besides the burning, she's like Eales's victims?"

"No. There is another difference. Eales's victims actually looked like suicides at first."

"Because of the heroin?"

"Not just that. Their wrists had been slashed," Kay said. "They'd all been bled to death."

"And what did Eales have to say about that?"

"Nothing. According to the interview transcripts he doesn't remember a thing."

Finn balled up the wax paper from his sandwich. "Well, there is the one other obvious difference between Valerie and those other victims," he said. "Valerie sure as hell wasn't picked up by Bernard Eales."

11

VICKI DiGRAZZIO, the assistant state's attorney, was waiting for them at Headquarters. In her red pumps, she paced the floor outside the elevators, a death grip on her leather briefcase.

"Sarge just called over with the news," she said, tossing loose blond curls over one shoulder, a movement Kay knew fueled more than a few male fantasies within the

Homicide squads. She doubted Finn was immune. "I still can't believe it."

They took the elevator up to the sixth floor. In the blurred reflection of the stainless-steel doors, Kay recognized Vicki's distress. Even though Vicki DiGrazzio was a workhorse, regularly juggling a dozen of the state's tougher prosecutorial challenges for the Homicide Division, Kay imagined the ASA managed to sleep most nights, that she wasn't haunted by the same ghosts Kay was. As a prosecutor, she was one step further removed from the victims than Kay.

With Valley, however, it was different. It was Vicki who'd helped Kay secure the job for the girl. Typing. Filing. Answering phones over lunch. And even though Valley's charm was reserved for few, Vicki had liked the girl.

Kay and Finn filled her in on the initial autopsy results, saving the news of the signature nicks on the sternum for more private quarters. When the elevator car jostled to a stop and the doors shuddered open, Kay could already hear the phones bleating from Homicide.

Down the corridor to the Homicide offices, with its vomit-green walls and yellowed tile flooring, the air was thick with the odor of stale coffee, old lunches, and men's cologne.

Over the past months, though, a new smell had invaded the sixth floor: moldy air conditioners. With extensive renovations under way on the seventh and eighth floors, portable AC units had been installed to alleviate the interruption of the ventilation system. In the side office, one monstrous unit butted up to the bank of west windows, a plank of plywood replacing one pane and supporting an outtake vent. Tape and wire suspended flexible ducts from the ceiling, all leading to or from the rumbling unit, giving it the appearance of some oversize life-support system. But if there was any oxygen in hundred-degree humidity, it could hardly be considered life-sustaining.

They led Vicki through the tight maze of putty-colored government-issue desks. Electric fans oscillated from the tops of file cabinets, rustling papers and stirring the thick heat as if it were soup. Kay's desk sat at the far wall, edged into the corner she protected vehemently from the encroaching squalor of the male-dominated unit. Here she found privacy behind the rattling AC unit and maintained her clear view of City Hall two blocks over.

Kay pulled her chair around for Vicki. "Couple more months of this," she said, clearing a corner of her desk, "and they say we'll finally be upstairs in the new offices."

Finn interrupted, "Listen, while you catch Vicki up, I'm going to pull those Eales files."

"Eales?" Vicki asked, but Finn was already on his way out. "What does he mean the Eales files? What's going on?"

"There's something else," Kay said, knowing the AC unit would shield their conversation. "Something that showed up at the autopsy. Valley's killer used a knife."

"You said she was strangled."

"She was. The knife wounds were nonfatal. Just like with Eales's victims."

Vicki's face tightened. "Wait a second. How the hell is that possible? We kept that back. It wasn't even in the reports."

"Someone's gotten it. Somehow. Whether it was a leak departmentally or came from Eales himself." Kay perched on the cleared corner of her desk. "Either way, Vick, Valley's murder looks like a copycat, or—"

"No, Kay." Vicki raised both hands as though to fend off the possibility. "No. We got the right goddamned guy. All the evidence is there. It's the most airtight case I'll ever prosecute."

"Not anymore."

Vicki was silent for a long moment. Clearly processing. "Son of a bitch," she said finally. "You realize if Eales's lawyer gets ahold of this, he's got his entire defense? You *know* how James Grogan works. This is all he needs to establish doubt in a jury's mind that the prostitutes' killer is still out there."

She stared past Kay and out the window, but Kay doubted Vicki focused on anything. She was seeing months of work slipping away from them. She was seeing justice in the case of the women's murders going unserved. And Kay knew Vicki DiGrazzio didn't take that well.

"This is a copycat, Kay. That information got leaked, and I want to know how. What else have you got?"

"We still need to see what Arson came up with, and if the Crime Lab got any prints off the car Valley was driving last night."

"A witness or two would be helpful."

"We'll go up to the campus again. And back to the warehouse neighborhood."

"There's no way Eales didn't murder those women."

"Something will surface." But Kay could tell Vicki's confidence wasn't bolstered.

"And what about you and Finn? You okay?"

"Sure." Kay wondered if Vicki sensed the lie. Besides her shrink, Vicki was the only person Kay had confided in about her past relationship with Finn.

"Well, if you want to talk . . ." Vicki stood, straightened her fire-engine-red dress, and righted the shoulder strap of her briefcase.

"Thanks."

"Call me when you've got something," Vickie said before starting back across the crowded office, and Kay wondered if the ASA was even aware of the stares that tracked her exit.

Kay wheeled her chair behind her desk. Draping her jacket over its back, she fished out her untouched break-fast from one pocket and tossed it in the trash. Nausea coiled in her stomach. It was the heat. And it was the memory of Valley's autopsy. Seeing the girl being cut, hearing the whine of the Stryker saw as it touched against the bared skull, seeing her organs removed one at a time . . .

"Hey, Delaney. Line four. ME's office."

Kay pushed aside several reports to uncover the phone. "Hi, Jonesy. What've you got?"

"Maybe nothing. Found a couple marks on your vic." Eddie Jones watched too many cop shows and read too many novels. She hated when he resorted to fiction cop-talk. "Can't be hundred percent certain. I'm waiting for Becky to look at 'em for me," he said, referring to the other assistant ME on staff. "She's dealt with these before."

"What are they?"

"Couple small, circular contusions. Back of the neck. Two and a quarter inches apart. To me they look like the kinda marks left by the prods of a stun gun. If I'm wrong, I'll give you a call back."

"Thanks, Jonesy." Kay hung up. Next to the phone, on the top of her stacked paper trays, the plain manila enve-lope had already arrived from upstairs. One complete set of crime-scene photos.

Kay opened the envelope and slid out the stack of pho-tos. They were in the order they'd been taken. Long shots of the warehouse, the side alley, the charred openings of the windows. She could picture the scene before the destruc-tion of the fire. And she could picture the back parking lot of Notre Dame.

He'd waited in the dark, after busting the light. Then nailed her with a stun gun.

Kay saw Valley on the autopsy table. Saw the rope.

You tied her because you weren't sure how long she'd be out. Was she in the backseat? Or did you prop her in the front next to you, your hand on her knee the whole time?

Once you had her in the warehouse, you held her throat in your hands. Did she struggle? Did it make you feel powerful?

Kay exhaled, trying to let go of the anger that flexed along her jaw. She flipped through more photos: the red gasoline can, soot and debris, a mannequin's arm.

You burned her because you'd left evidence of yourself. What? Hair? Fiber?

Jonesy said there was no evidence of sexual assault.

But killing her turned you on, didn't it? It had to have given you a rush. Did you masturbate on her, you son of a bitch? You'd left your DNA all over her, so you had to burn her. Did you watch while she burned? Did you enjoy the flames? The crackle of heat as the fire hissed against human flesh?

But what about the knife? What about the goddamned knife?

Kay flipped through the last of the photos, stopping when she found one of Finn. It wasn't uncommon for a detective to request his picture be taken on a crime scene. Usually for posterity. But Kay didn't imagine Finn had asked for this photo. He'd obviously gotten into the camera's frame, or maybe the lab tech had a crush on him.

In the picture Finn towered over Valley's body, the edges of his jacket brushed aside, his hands on his hips. The flare of the camera's flash was harsh, and Finn was obviously tired. Still, he looked good. He'd never stopped looking good to her, she realized.

For the first time, Kay wondered if he was seeing anyone.

12

"EARLIER THIS MORNING Baltimore Fire personnel responded to a two-alarm blaze here in Canton, at this vacant warehouse north of Boston Street, last operated as Dutton Mannequin. Fire officials are not revealing what sparked the fire, but at this time arson has not been ruled out."

The news camera panned the front of the warehouse and the sea of emergency vehicles lighting up the night. It was beautiful. Like something out of a movie.

But the tint on the TV mounted in the corner of the diner was on the fritz. The Channel 11 reporter's pinched face looked green.

He swilled back the last dregs of coffee from the stained mug, before pushing it across the Formica-topped table, next to the chipped plate. He hadn't finished the eggs and bacon, the grease already congealing and opaque across the strips of fatty pork. A fly landed on a triangle of toast. He watched it suck at the cold butter before his eyes went back to the TV.

"Homicide detectives responded to the scene just after one a.m. Police spokesperson Sergeant Richard Contel confirmed later this morning that the fire claimed the life of a young woman. Further details have not been released . . ."

The footage from last night showed two men in white coveralls as they picked their way out of the wreckage, balancing a litter between them. The black body bag glistened in the rain.

Valerie Regester. It hadn't taken much to find the girl. Even less to actually snatch her. Everything like clockwork.

It was a job, he'd tried to remind himself last night, sitting behind the wheel of his Buick as she crossed the college lot. *Taking care of loose ends.* He hadn't expected the thrill he'd felt as she'd tried to turn over the engine. And when she'd gotten out of the shitbox car of hers, and he'd stepped from his, he'd felt alive for the first time in months. And when she'd turned to look at him, he'd loved how her eyes had narrowed with suspicion. But his smile had eased her concern. It always did.

Then the drive through the city—nerve-jangling, but exhilarating. Her thin, mewling sounds from the backseat had bubbled up old desires. And the need reemerged, like a cockroach clawing from its spent shell, mutating into a stronger, indestructible state. The final metamorphosis.

But it wasn't until he'd finally had her throat in his hands, until he'd felt her life pulse—potent and desperate—against his palms, that he'd been struck by the unexpected jolt of arousal. He thought the fucking Zoloft had killed all that. He would've liked to have spent more time with her. Regretted that he hadn't made arrangements.

Still, there'd been enough time to go back to the car for his knife. And now, as he cleaned his hands with a paper napkin, he was warmed by the memory of that pleasure, the rage of blood in his ears, the thundering of his heart as he'd emptied himself onto her.

On the TV, the camera followed two detectives, the bulge of their suit jackets barely concealing the nine-millimeters clipped to their belts. The camera zoomed in. And his heart fluttered.

She looked different from the grainy, black-and-white photo from the *Sun,* taken after Bernard had finished with her. The photo he'd cut out and saved, of her face all battered and bloodied beyond recognition. But it was her.

Detective Kay Delaney.

13

PAST THE WINDSHIELD and through the haze of afternoon heat, the steep sides of the State Pen's old fort-style turrets loomed over the Madison Street entrance, the granite darkened by more than a century of grime. It was the second-oldest penitentiary in the country, and an unmistakable landmark on the eastern bank of the Jones Falls. An 1800s fortress that could never be confused for anything but a prison.

And Eales was in there. Somewhere beyond the stone walls, chain-link, and razor wire.

She'd toyed with the notion all day, and an hour ago—standing under the pounding water of her shower at home—Kay had at last made the decision: she needed to talk to the one person who had the most to gain from Valley's death. Now though, with the lobby doors less than fifty yards from the nose of the Lumina, her courage was sapped, and the questions she'd so carefully rehearsed scattered.

Exhaustion played a role. It had been a long afternoon with Finn. A walk through the burned Canton warehouse offered nothing. Then, up at the college, Valley's drawing instructor, distraught and shaken, had been a dead end, unable to supply them with anything more than the number for campus security. A couple hours ago, frustrated, Finn had gone home to shower and sleep, taking with him the Eales case files he'd pulled. Kay had her own copies at home, and in their pages she'd found the reference to Dutton Mannequin.

Deeply embedded in transcripts and office reports, Eales had listed Dutton as one of more than two dozen places of employment in his past. He'd been twenty-six, and the job had lasted ten months.

She'd reached Vicki on her cell, somewhere between the State's Attorney's Office and the courthouse, their conversation broken as the cell picked up static in the downtown core. *Just keep the interview focused on links to the new murder,* Vicki had warned her. *No reference to Spence and the upcoming trial.* And as protocol would dictate, Vicki advised her to bring Finn, even though she agreed Kay would likely get more from Eales on her own.

So here she was. The passenger seat of the police car empty.

The smell of old cigarette smoke lingered, the stained velour seats saturated with it from years of her and Spence sharing their habit. She'd cleaned the ashtray months ago and wiped down the interior. A faded air-freshener dangling from one of the vent knobs had lost the battle.

Kay's craving rose. She felt the half-empty pack of Camels in her suit pocket. Her emergency stash. It had taken work to dig it out of the clutter on the top shelf of her closet, but that had been the point. And now they would be Eales's. The cost of information.

Kay closed her eyes, imagined tapping one of the unfiltered cigarettes from the pack right now, lighting it up and savoring the smooth smoke as it filled her lungs and calmed her nerves. She resisted and at last reached for the door handle.

The glass-enclosed lobby of the Reception and Diagnostic Center was cool. Sterile. At the front desk, Kay was handed a visitor's pass and reported to Administration. There, she accessed the prison records and Eales's visitation logs.

She wasn't sure exactly what she was looking for. A name. Someone who came to see Eales regularly. Or recently. Someone who might have done him the favor of killing Valley. But aside from his defense attorney, Eales's only recorded visitor was a woman—Patricia Hagen.

A clerk of Grogan's? An intern? Or maybe Eales had some fanatical girlfriend. An inside-outside relationship, Kay guessed as she took stock of the frequency of the visits. *What kind of woman spent that much time with a sour, ill-tempered South Baltimore billy-boy awaiting trial for multiple murders?* It took all kinds.

From Admin, Kay was escorted through the barren, blue-gray maze of the Metropolitan Transition Center and led to a twelve-by-sixteen-foot iron cage.

"You're in here." The guard motioned her into a holding cell, two sides flanked by barred hallways, the other two, solid cinder-block. And in the center, a table and two steel-cased chairs.

Tension tightened in Kay's gut at the realization of what she was about to do. She certainly hadn't expected to sit face-to-face with Eales with nothing but three feet of stale prison air between them. Back home, when she'd convinced herself to come here, she'd imagined a visitation booth, with its reinforced, Plexiglas partition and handsets.

From somewhere deep in the bowels of the MTC, gates slammed and a yelled chorus started up, then died just as abruptly. Five hundred and forty hot cells, most of them double-bunked, made up Blocks A and B of the west wing alone. A thousand violent men crammed into an oven. And one of them was Bernard Eales.

"Listen"—she turned to the guard—"I didn't request a holding cell."

"Front desk said this was a police interview. Figured you'd want some privacy."

"It's not necessary."

"Look, you got this cell, okay? It's all set up. 'Sides, they're bringing Eales in now."

She heard the chains first. Then another steely slam.

And finally, in the convex mirror mounted high in the corner of the corridor, she watched the image of two uniformed guards leading a large white mass in a tangerine-orange jumpsuit.

Eales.

14

HE WAS HUGE.

In full irons, Eales lurched between the guards. The unmistakable jailhouse shuffle. As he cleared the wall and lumbered past the bars of the holding cell, he focused dead ahead, as though refusing to acknowledge Kay's presence.

Only his size was imposing, Kay tried to convince herself. Eales was white-trash redneck, not some embodiment of evil.

Nice try, Delaney. He pulled the trigger of your duty nine and gunned down your partner.

Kay drew in a solid breath. Felt it tremble as it left her body. Until Bernard Eales, Kay had never known true hate.

The guards stopped him in the doorway. Only then did Eales look at her. Expressionless. He'd gained weight. A lot of it. And he'd gone soft and pasty. *An ugly son of a bitch.*

The heavy brows cast his eyes in shadow, but Kay knew them from her nightmares, raw blue and lifeless. The corners of his mouth curved severely down, the thin lips bracketed by a slovenly trimmed beard. He'd shaved his head. The stubbled regrowth revealed the receding hairline along his glistening pate. A one-inch scar, red and ragged, marked his right cheekbone. It didn't look very old. Kay wondered if he'd gotten it in prison, or if maybe she'd put it there herself fourteen months ago. She hoped the latter.

"You want the cuffs on or off?" one of the guards asked her.

Eales's slow eyes sized her up. She thought she saw a glint of recognition before the challenge shadowed it. He was daring her.

Well, fuck him. "Leave 'em on. This won't take long."

She turned her back to him, trying to contain a shudder of loathing and uncontrolled fear. How many interviews had she conducted in her career? Hundreds? Thousands?

That's all this was. Just another interview.

Eales shuffled behind her, coming to the table. She could sense his closeness as she lay the cigarettes and a book of matches on the table. Sense the presence of the man who had beaten her to within an inch of her life. She almost wished Finn were here. But it was better this way.

Kay pulled out the chair farthest from the door, the legs grating across polished concrete. "Have a seat, Bernard."

While driving here she'd already made the decision to address him by his first name. Keep it cool. Professional, yet casual.

"You remember me, Bernard?"

"Sure." Eales's mass poured over the edges of the seat, dwarfing the chair. His irons clattered against the table and the chair's legs. Elbows planted, he balled one hand into the other, rested his chin against his thumbs, and slumped forward onto the table.

She circled back, but didn't pull out the other chair.

Fresh abrasions marked three of his knuckles, she noted, and there was dirt under his nails. Other than the scar on his cheek and the bloodied knuckles, it didn't appear Eales was having a tough time behind bars. She'd have thought a dumb-ass like him would have been the brunt of more attacks and ridicule. Then again, maybe he was too big for anyone to consider fucking with.

From her briefcase, Kay took out a Miranda waiver and slid it across the table. "You know the drill, don't you, Bernard?"

He took the pen she offered, clasped it between thick fingers, and initialed each warning as she read them out.

"You understand, Bernard, you don't have to speak with me today, right?" she asked him when they got to the end of the list.

He made a gesture somewhere between a nod and a shrug.

"Is that a yes?"

"Yeah."

"You also understand that you can, and in fact are advised to, have your lawyer present?"

Again, a nodding shrug.

"And your presence here this afternoon is completely voluntary, is that correct?"

This time the shrug came with a grunt she thought sounded like a reflection of humor. He dropped the pen and opened his hands to draw attention to the cuffs cutting into his meaty wrists. "Voluntary. Right."

"All right then." Her hands were fists inside the pockets of her suit jacket. A line of perspiration trailed down her back, and she wondered if Eales could smell her stewing in her own sweat.

"So how ya doing, Detective?" It came out *dee-tective*.

Kay circled the table slowly, keeping her gaze on Eales's head. That ugly, shaven scalp with all its cranial ridges and irregular depressions. She shuddered at the evil she knew lurked beneath that misshapen skull.

"Valerie Regester's dead," she said when she reached the front of the table again.

"Don't know who yer talkin' 'bout." His voice was low, the words slurred in a lazy Baltimore drawl.

When Kay leaned across the table, she could smell the musk of body odor coming off him and the sour breath that leaked through his crooked teeth.

"Don't play me for some dumb shit, Bernard. Valerie Regester was the witness who was set to testify against you."

"Oh, right. The bitch that says it was me she seen dump some broad's body in Leakin."

"Yeah, that's her."

"So she's dead, huh?" He eyed the pack of Camels.

"You don't seem surprised."

"Nothin' much surprises me no more, Detective."

"I know Grogan was in to see you earlier. You're saying he didn't tell you the prosecution's witness had been murdered?"

Something twisted at the corner of his down-turned mouth. Kay imagined he'd just amused himself with a thought.

"Naw," he said. "The guy ain't got much of a stomach for that kinda stuff. Weird, him being a criminal attorney and all, huh? So how was she killed exactly?"

"You don't know?"

"How the hell am I supposed to?"

"She was strangled. Then someone set her body on fire. Not exactly your style, is it?"

"What? You think *I* got something to do with it? How's that supposed to work? I bust outta here, kill that lying skank, then break myself back in? Let me tell you, sweetheart, the food ain't that good in here."

He lowered his folded hands on the table, the right half-obscuring a two-foot tattooed snake that coiled down his forearm, wrapped around his cuffed wrist, and came to a head along the back of his left hand. The tattoo was old, the ink green with age, and the reptile's scales had stretched to accommodate Eales's expanding fat.

"Maybe you got someone to do you a favor, hmm, Bernard?"

He didn't answer, and Patricia Hagen's name almost slipped from her lips.

"Funny thing is," she said, bracing her hands on the back of the empty chair and leaning toward him, "she was burned in a warehouse down in Canton. Twelve hundred block of Luther. Ring any bells?"

He shook his head.

"It should. You worked there. Dutton Mannequin."

"Now ain't that a coincidence?"

"Exactly what I thought. So what do you know about Regester's murder?"

"Nothin'. This is the first I'm hearing about it."

Kay's bullshit radar was usually foolproof, but she couldn't get a firm read on Eales. She guessed it was their history that impaired her judgment today.

Yanking out the empty chair, she sat. From her briefcase she snatched the two five-by-sevens she'd selected from the crime-scene photos and slapped them faceup on the table.

She searched Eales's face for a reaction.

"Oo-ee, someone sure went all firebug on that girl, huh? Musta really hated her."

"Someone like you maybe?"

"Hey, I don't even know the girl."

"Knew her enough to call her a bitch."

"Yeah, a *lying* bitch. And a skank. And I'd say it to her lying face, 'cept she's dead."

"What did she lie about, Bernard? Seeing you in the park?"

"No. I was there. Already told police that. She lied about what she seen me dumpin'. Wasn't no body. It's all in the files." His eyes held hers for several heartbeats, narrowed into two slits. Then a slow smile parted his lips. "But you probably ain't read the files, huh? They pulled you offa the case, didn't they? Git the shit kicked outta you and you're probably on desk duty, huh? Doin' a lot of filing lately, Detective? Answering phones? Making coffee? Guess it's better 'n being fired."

"What did you dump that night in the park, Bernard?"

He looked disappointed she wouldn't take the bait. "Shee-it. I was dumpin' my trash is all." He reached for the smokes at last—uninvited—the chains clattering across the metal table. Tapping one of the Camels out, he jammed it between his dry lips, then worked the matches in spite of the cuffs.

Kay held her breath as he exhaled a cloud of smoke. Bad enough she had to breathe his air, she wasn't about to share his smoke. "So you wouldn't find it necessary to have Regester dealt with?" she asked.

"Even if I did, how the hell am I supposed to?" He lowered his head to the cigarette again, the cuffs cutting into his wrists as he took a long drag. "I'm just a low-life thug, ain't that right?"

Kay gave him credit for having no delusions. He exhaled another cloud of smoke and stared at her through it. His gaze slithered down, past her neck and the low V of her blouse, settling on her chest. Kay felt dirty. Felt as though those big, ugly hands of Eales's had just made the journey instead of his groping eyes.

"You look different, Detective. Kinda butch. You change your hair?"

Kay held his stare when it slid back up.

"Y'ain't a dyke, are you? Not that it matters, I guess. At least we'd have pussy in common, huh? I just kinda thought you were an item with that cop I shot, you know? The way you was crying when he hit the ground and all."

Kay swallowed the rage.

"So you sleepin' nights, Detective?"

"I sleep fine, Bernard." She felt her jaw clench again. Only once. But he must have noticed.

"You're not afraid of me, are you?" His lips crawled into a smirk when she didn't answer. "You are. Detective Delaney, sittin' there in her fancy suit, 'fraid of li'l' ol' Bernie."

She took a breath. "Yeah, Bernard. That's right. I'm so fucking afraid of you I'm pissing myself right here in my fancy suit, while you . . . you sorry, sad fuck, sucking on a year-old Camel, you're never going to see the outside of this place again except for a few short drives to the court-house where they're going to convict your murdering ass."

Bernard sat, unflinching.

She leaned in closer. "But we'll see who's really afraid when you're getting strapped down to that table and they stick a cold needle into your arm, huh, Bernie? We'll see who's pissing in their shorts when that countdown starts."

Silence settled on the cell. She could hear his breath whistle through his once-broken nose, then watched his pupils dilate.

"Who's Patricia Hagen?" she asked.

He took another long drag.

"I know she visits you, Bernard. You wanna tell me who she is? Or do I have to look her up?"

Watching his lips clutch the butt of the Camel made Kay never want to light up again.

"You got yourself a girlfriend, Bernie?"

She watched his eyes as the smoke cleared.

"Take me only a few minutes to find out," she said. "I can get her address. Maybe give her a visit, hmm?"

"Yeah, she's my girlfriend. So what?" There was a defensiveness in his voice suddenly.

"What's she see in you, do you figure? Because I sure as hell don't see it. When I look at you, all I see is total vacuity."

She met his stare, unwilling to back down as the silence swelled between them.

"What?" he said at last. "You think I'm some stupid shit never owned a dictionary? Don't treat me like I'm stupid. There's more to me than you think, Detective."

Undaunted, Kay drew herself to the edge of her chair, leaned across the table again. Close enough she could see the pores of Eales's oily skin. "Does Patricia know why you're in here, Bernard?"

"Course she does."

"Does she know everything? Does she know you like your women *dead*? That you hack up their wrists and play with them once they've stopped breathing? What else did you do, Bernard, hmm? Did you have sex with them? Maybe you couldn't get it up while they were alive. Is that why you murdered them?"

Nothing.

"And what would your girlfriend do if she found out? I wonder. What would she think if I showed her the pictures of your little hobby? You think she'd still visit?"

"Fuck off." He shoved away from the table then, dropping the dwindling butt to the floor and crushing it under one laceless sneaker.

Behind her, Kay heard the guard shift at the cell's gate. "So what about your brother, Bernard?"

"What about him?"

"His name's not on your visitation records. He doesn't come see you?"

"He lives in Pittsburgh."

"And he can't drive four hours to visit his big brother?"

"He's got his own life."

"No, that's not it. You probably make him sick, don't you? Probably can't stand the thought of you. Your own brother doesn't even want to see you."

He grabbed up the pack of smokes, tucked them in the cuff of his jumpsuit. "We done here?"

She'd lost him. She'd let her anger take over, and Eales had clammed up. "Sure, Bernard. We're done."

The room came alive with the rattle of chains as Eales stood. Kay pushed back her own chair and followed him.

At the cell door, Eales turned unexpectedly, causing Kay to come up short. But not short enough.

He was too close. "I'm glad that lying bitch is dead," he whispered between clenched teeth.

"I don't see why," she said, refusing to back down. "I'm more of a threat to you than she ever was." In the narrow space that separated them she could feel the heat coming off his huge body. "They've already got a cell reserved for you over there in Supermax. You're headed to death row, Bernard, because you killed my partner. And I'm the strongest witness in that case. *I'm* the one who's going to guarantee you make it to that cell."

15

IT WASN'T HER USUAL CROWD at Rocky's Iron Pit on Pratt Street. Not the late-night muscle addicts who were too absorbed by their own routines to take note of hers. Who never looked twice when she threw a few more pounds on the leg press and shook as she barely made the twelfth rep, then did it all over again.

Trying to ignore the stares reflected in the floor-to-ceiling mirrors past the Nautilus circuit, Kay wished she'd waited until her usual time. But after leaving the State Pen, with the residue of Eales still crawling along her skin, she'd needed the release. Needed to sweat out the disgust that raged through her body.

Her muscles burned and her arms quivered as she lowered the weights back onto the stack. Still, she couldn't abolish the image of Eales. And Valley, her burned remains on the flooded warehouse floor. And finally, Spence.

Sitting, she took the setscrew down yet another notch, adding more weight, and felt the stares as she settled into the last set.

She closed her eyes. Tried to picture Spence. But it was harder now. She hated that Eales's face was easier to conjure up than Spence's. Hated that the one image her mind always came back to was of Spence as the life seeped out of him on that filthy corner of Baltimore City. She tried to remember his quick smiles and his easygoing laughter, his tireless patience as he'd taught her the ropes. But the memories were fading.

When the weights came down this time, they stayed. There was nothing left in her. Mopping her pooled sweat off the vinyl bench with her towel, Kay left the grinding pulse of electronic dance music. In the locker room, she didn't shower, but instead pulled on cool-down pants over her shorts and threw on a fresh T-shirt before heading out.

She thought of Finn. Unlike her, he'd worked a full day shift and then overtime yesterday before he'd ever stepped foot in the warehouse in Canton. He'd looked wasted when he'd left the office this afternoon. As she drove south to Light Street, Kay wondered if he was going over the case files he'd carted home or if he was finally getting some sleep. Ten minutes and she could be at the marina, walking the plank to his boat. At the lights on Pratt, Kay toyed with the idea.

It wouldn't be just for the case though, she realized. This morning, on the bench by the water, she'd wanted to touch him. To answer the simple need for a connection. But she hadn't because she knew she had nothing left to offer him.

So now, Kay drove home.

The converted three-story row house was grander than most in the gentrified neighborhood of Federal Hill, boasting a rare back-alley garden as well as an elaborate roof garden. With Kay's apartment on the top floor, she'd taken over the planters and terraces on the roof when she'd moved in six years ago, an eager and confident rookie to Homicide. She'd found solace on her roof, puttering in the dirt, staking and deadheading, enjoying the company of Mr. Drummond's homing pigeons on the neighboring rooftop.

But Kay had let the garden go. Last fall she hadn't had the energy to plant bulbs, and this past spring, she hadn't had the heart.

Inside her top-floor apartment the AC hummed in one of the tall windows overlooking the Hill. The air felt cool, but lifeless. Sidestepping a stack of bundled newspapers, Kay dumped her bag and flipped on the stereo.

The solo violin in Tchaikovsky's Symphony no. 2 filled the apartment. Kay closed her eyes, willing the music to transport her. But it wasn't the same. She'd bought the CD at the last concert she'd been to with Vicki at the Joseph Meyerhoff Symphony Hall, foolishly imagining she could re-create the oblivion she'd come to find at each performance she attended. But the small speakers of the mini-stereo didn't compare to the acoustics from the orchestra seats of the Meyerhoff.

Kay cranked the stereo anyway and headed for the bathroom. She needed to wash the memory of Eales off her skin.

In the steam of the shower, the stink of nicotine lifted from her hair. Kay envisioned Eales's lips around the butt of the stale Camel. She suppressed a shudder and started scrubbing.

She tried to focus on the music, but the hatred boiled up again, bile-sour. Kay scrubbed harder, the water scalding her rawing skin.

Only eighteen hours ago she'd picked her way through the emergency-response vehicles and personnel outside the Dutton warehouse and stood over Valley's body. Eighteen hours, and they still had no concrete lead. *The first twenty-four hours of an investigation are the most critical.* How many times had Spence said that? But until the results from Arson came in, until she figured out who Patricia Hagen was and how Eales fit into the scenario, there was no direction. And exhaustion was winning the battle.

Turning off the water, Kay wrapped herself in a robe and padded barefoot to the kitchen. Harris, the grizzled tabby who shared her living space, stared at her from the last clear corner of the counter. With one eyelid marred by an old split, he observed her with his typical crooked gaze. Judging, Kay always imagined, as though he knew she was responsible for his owner's death.

He'd been Spencer's cat for only a few short weeks, until his wife begged Kay to take the animal after Spencer's funeral. Grace had claimed allergies, but Kay knew better. The cat had warmed to no one but Spence.

The old stray, with his tattered ears and alley-mauled face, had made his appearance at the Annie Harris crime scene. He'd wrapped himself around Spencer's ankles the moment they'd stepped inside the vacant row house, clearly seeing Spence as his retirement ticket.

It had been hot that afternoon, fourteen months ago, the July sun relentless as it beat against the pitted asphalt of Edmonson Avenue. But it had been even hotter inside the crumbling house. A hundred degrees at least.

The smell from the second floor had hit Kay like a wall even before she'd stepped through the busted-down front door. In the car, before arriving on scene, Spence had tossed a coin to determine who would lead the case. It was the last time Kay had chosen tails.

The first sign of maggots was on the ground floor. Hundreds had wormed through the floorboards overhead and the light fixture before dropping to the littered ground. Upstairs, the air was electric with the buzzing of flies, and if not for Spencer prying off the plywood from one window, Kay was certain she'd have been sick along with the uniform who'd discovered the remains.

What was left of Annie Harris's nude body rose from a pool of decomposition fluids and writhing maggots. Through the varying levels of insect activity and the rate of decomp, the ME's office had made the rough determination that Harris's body had been laid out for at least eight weeks. Identification wasn't determined until the FBI labs came back with prints, carefully lifted from the hands they'd sent to Quantico. And the knife wounds to the chest had been indiscernible until the ME had slopped through the entire mess.

Now, as Kay gave the cat a wide berth and took a Corona from the fridge, she tried to block the mental images of that afternoon.

At the stereo she cranked the volume and tried again to surrender to the music. The movement crescendoed to its climax. In the symphony hall the music would be inescapable; it would crash over her, move through her, until there was nothing but the music. But here in her apartment, with the reality of her life surrounding her, the music was flat. Kay flipped off the CD midstrain and abandoned the stereo.

The second bedroom served as her home office. There, Kay turned on the computer and took several long draws of her beer as she waited for the modem to dial in. She needed sleep, but knew she wouldn't find it. Not until she'd answered the question that had burned in her thoughts since she'd reviewed Eales's visitation records: Who was Patricia Hagen?

16

FINN FELT LIKE AN INTRUDER. He hadn't used the key in over a year. Still, he'd kept it. Wishful thinking. Or maybe just a keepsake. Either way, Kay hadn't asked for it back.

He slid the key home, felt the dead bolt turn, and considered going back down to the car for his cell. But he knew Kay was in. He'd seen her police car at the curb on Hamburg and her 4Runner farther down the block. On the airless landing he'd already knocked for several minutes. And with each minute she didn't answer, the worry in the pit of his gut grew.

An hour ago he'd gone to the State Pen. After catching some sleep on the boat, then spending several hours reviewing the Eales case files and making some phone calls, Finn had concluded that if anyone needed to be interviewed about Valerie Regester's death, it was Bernard Eales.

Unfortunately Kay had come to the same conclusion.

At the Administration offices Finn had seen Kay's signature on the visitors' log, and he'd felt the first stab of anger. He'd canceled his interview with Eales, and the anger grew as he'd left the Pen and driven south to Kay's apartment. Only as he neared her Federal Hill address had Finn understood the real root of his anger. It wasn't so much that Kay had gone alone, but rather that he hadn't been able to shield her from Eales. Just as she had for the past year, Kay had refused to lean on him or turn to him.

At the lights on Pratt Street he'd considered going home, calling her instead. But Kay could hide a lot when she was just a voice over the phone, and after she'd interviewed Eales, Finn needed to be sure she was all right. Needed to see her to believe it.

Stepping inside her apartment now, it took a moment for his eyes to adjust to the dark. Past stacks of newspapers in the foyer and a pair of mud-caked runners, Finn moved to the living room. The coffee table was littered with several empty beer bottles, a pizza box, and a gun-cleaning kit.

He heard the television on in the bedroom, made his way down the hall, past a full laundry hamper and dry cleaning hanging from the bathroom doorknob. He called Kay's name, but she didn't respond.

He found her on the bed, the cold pulse of the television washing over her as she lay in a tangle of sheets and case files. He wasn't sure if he called her name again as he crossed the room to finally stand over her bed. Her robe had fallen partly open, and even though he thought to avert his gaze, he couldn't.

Next to her, the Harris crime-scene photos came to life in the flicker of the TV. Finn remembered the day Kay had caught the case. Remembered a time before Eales. If he thought about it, Harris's murder had been the beginning of the end for him and Kay.

He couldn't be sure what woke her just then. He hadn't even seen her eyes open, but in a heartbeat, Kay rolled, reached to the side of the bed, and came back with a .38 Special.

"Jesus, Kay!" He stared down the barrel of the gun, solid in her hands.

"What the *fuck* are you doing here?" she asked, lowering the revolver.

"I've been knocking for ten minutes." He nodded to where the CNN newscaster highlighted the latest unrest in the Middle East.

Kay searched for the remote and muted the TV. When she slid the Chief's Special back into its holster on the bed-post and stood, Finn saw she was shaking.

"I could have shot you." She used anger as a disguise as she brushed past him.

"I hadn't considered you armed and dangerous. Since when do you take a five-shooter to bed with you anyway?" But Finn knew the answer.

She started down the hall, turning on lights as she went. "What time is it?"

"Almost ten."

In the kitchen she took a glass off the counter and filled it under the tap. Finn spotted the empty bottle of Silent Sam.

"So you saw Eales today," he said.

When she turned, he saw a defensiveness in Kay's eyes. "I was going to fill you in, in the morning."

"That's not the point, Kay."

"Look, I cleared it with Vicki. Eales signed the waiver. Besides, Vick agreed I'd likely get more out of Eales if I went alone."

"And did you? Get anything out of him?"

She held his gaze for a moment, and Finn tried to keep his eyes from wandering to the low V of her robe. "No," she answered.

"I should have been with you," he said, imagining Kay alone in the interview room with the son of a bitch.

"Come on, Finn. With how much you hate Eales, your anger would have compromised the interview, and you know it."

She was right, but he wasn't about to concede it.

And then Kay was onto him. "Wait"—she set her glass on the counter a little too hard—"it isn't procedure you're pissed about, is it?"

"Never mind." He took a step back, needing to distance himself from Kay, and from the truth. "Who's this Patricia Hagen?" he asked, starting into the living room. "Her name's all over Eales's visitation record."

"Eales's girlfriend." Kay followed, then led him to her office. "I logged on to the Department's system from here. I can't find anything on her. No criminal record, no traffic or parking tickets, not even a Maryland driver's license."

She flipped on the green banker's lamp at her desk, and Finn surveyed the extent of Kay's yearlong obsession. Dozens of crime-scene photos had been tacked to the wall: Annie Harris, Roma Chisney, and the Jane Doe from Leakin Park. Over a year later, the dead girl still didn't have a name.

There were shots of the exterior of Eales's row house, and the patch of lawn where Joe Spencer had bled out from the gunshot wound to his chest. A wide swath of blood spread across the sparse grass and mud. And finally the aftermath of the assault on Kay, her own blood staining Eales's walkway.

A light layer of dust covered the photos and Kay's desk, and Finn hoped it meant Kay's obsession was waning. But his memory of that night had never waned. Every detail rang as vivid as if it were just last week he'd paced the tiled corridor outside the surgery suite at Johns Hopkins Shock-Trauma Unit, praying Kay would come out. Only once before in his life had he felt so terrified, so helpless. Five summers ago, he'd paced a similar hallway, only then it was his son's life he'd been praying for. And Toby hadn't come out.

He would've done anything to have traded positions with his son, to have turned the wheel right instead of left so the car had taken the impact of the transport truck on the driver's side rather than the passenger's. For the rest of his life, Finn would replay the accident that had claimed his son's life, in the same way he'd replay those days fourteen months ago when he'd almost lost Kay.

"I figure we should pay Patricia Hagen a visit tomor-row," Kay said. "In the meantime"—she pushed aside case folders and spread four photos across the cleared top—"I keep coming back to these."

"The knife wounds?"

"They're definitely similar," she said, then pointed out each photo in order: "Annie Harris, seven cuts. Roma Chisney, ten. The Jane Doe, more than a dozen and a half. And Valley, five. And with each one the cuts are deeper, Finn. He's actually driving the knife into the sternum."

"But there's no pattern, Kay."

"Patterned or random, they mean something."

"Could be nothing more than a by-product of the abduction, a means of subduing them."

"No. With Valley being burned and Harris too decom-posed, the ME's office wouldn't say for certain if the cuts were made pre- or postmortem. But with these other two, the cuts were *both* before *and* after death. What's he doing to them after they're dead?"

"Whoa. What do you mean *them,* Kay? Someone killed Regester. Singular, not plural. Eales killed those other women."

Kay gathered the photos and started to put them away. "They're the same, Finn."

"Come on, we got the right guy. You saw the reports. I *know* you went over them a million times. How can you doubt the evidence?"

Kay shook her head, examining the photos again. There was a naked confusion in her face. As if she wanted an explanation, needed it, but knew it was out of reach.

"I know you didn't see the evidence, that you didn't see Eales's house. But *I* did, Kay. I was in that hellhole. We got traces of the women's blood from everywhere. Living room, hallway, bathroom. Even in his bed for Christ's sake. They found hair samples that matched the Jane Doe and the Chisney girl, and they found Harris's underwear in his goddamned dresser—with her blood on them.

"Bernard killed those women, Kay. I know it. And so does every other cop who set foot in that house."

"Then how do you explain these?" She held up the photo of Regester's chest.

"I don't know. We've got a copycat. Christ, Kay, except for those knife wounds, the MO doesn't even fit."

Kay shook her head and tossed the photo onto the desk with the others, her gaze lingering on them. "I just want to understand, Finn. I want to know why he cuts them."

"Why? I can tell you why. Because Eales got off on it. Because he liked to victimize women and it made him feel powerful. Because everyone at school laughed at him when he had his first public hard-on in gym class. Or maybe because his junkie mother locked him in the closet with a rubber band around his dick when he was a kid. Who the hell knows? And why does it matter? We got him."

Finn left her office, moving through the cluttered hallway to the living room. Kay followed.

"We got Eales," he said again. "And there's boxes of shit from his house down in Evidence Control that prove it. As for Regester, fine, I'm willing to work with the possibility that it's related to Eales. Maybe she was killed because of her testimony. Or maybe she was more connected to Eales than she let on. But it's a fresh murder, Kay."

"So where do *you* suggest we go from here then?"

Seeing her standing in the middle of her apartment, hands on her hips and her thin robe revealing just a little too much, the memories twisted in his mind, unbidden. How many times had he wished those memories away, wished there'd never been that spark, that fire between them, leaving so many ashes for him to sift through?

"I want to talk to this Patsy Hagen broad. And anyone else Eales is connected to," he said, drawing his gaze from her at last. "Including the knucklehead's brother."

"William Coombs? He can't tell you anything."

"He's the son of a bitch's brother. And *someone's* paying Eales's legal fees." James Grogan was one of Baltimore's top defense attorneys. The man hadn't lost a case in years. That kind of slime cost big bucks. "Unless Grogan's taking Eales pro bono, someone's forking over the greenbacks."

"Well, even if it is Coombs, he and Eales haven't spoken in years."

"And you know this how?"

"Because I talked to him a year ago. On the phone. So did Varcoe and Jimmy Holewinski. Even back then Coombs hadn't seen his brother in years. He didn't even know about his brother's arrest until he read it in the papers. *And* he's never visited Eales in prison. He doesn't know anything, Finn."

"Well, then, he can tell us that himself tomorrow morning. I've set up a meeting with him."

17

THE DINER JUST SOUTH of the Maryland line on the old York Road catered to a smorgasbord of truckers and locals, with the occasional traveler blown off course from the I-83. The diner being less than a couple miles east of the former North Central Railroad, someone had decided on a train motif as the decor. An electric engine and cars rattled along a track suspended one foot below the ceiling and running the circumference of the dining area, while the walls boasted an array of clocks in a locomotive theme.

In his pressed suit and crisp tie, William Coombs looked patently out of place seated in a corner booth at a heavily lacquered maple table. He had waved them over the second they stepped through the door, and Kay decided then that she and Finn looked far too much like cops.

The arrangements Finn had made with Eales's half brother accommodated the car salesman's schedule, forcing him to take only a minor detour off his route to Philly on business. Still, he seemed mildly put out by the meeting, but Kay guessed it had nothing to do with the early hour or the detour.

When he'd pushed aside his breakfast and stood to greet them, Coombs's expression was taut. In his narrow shoulders Kay sensed tension, and a muscle along his jaw twitched as he sat down with them.

She searched for recognition, but found none in Coombs's unsettled expression. If he *did* recognize her from the papers or by her name from over a year ago when they'd spoken briefly on the phone, he didn't let on.

He was a small man, fine-boned and lean, the polar opposite of Eales and clear proof of their different fathers. His face was pleasant, with a neatly trimmed beard, chiseled features, and a cleft chin. His perfect teeth capped the winning smile that Kay didn't doubt sold a steady stream of high-end cars. The only feature he shared with Eales was the eyes. They were the same blue, but on Coombs they worked.

"I'm really sorry, the name doesn't ring a bell," he told them, flashing that endearing smile to the waitress as she collected his plate.

"Valerie Regester was a witness in your brother's case."

Coombs nodded, fastidiously dabbing at the corners of his mouth with a napkin while the electric train took another pass above their table. "The girl the papers mentioned?" he asked. "The one who says she saw him in the park?"

Finn nodded.

"I remember now. And you say she was murdered?"

"Two nights ago."

"You're not thinking my brother had something to do with her death, are you?"

"It's just one possibility we're exploring," Finn said. "If there *is* a connection, we're trying to figure out who might have done it for him."

"Well, Detective Finnerty, I'm not sure how I can help. I honestly don't know Bernard's circle. I haven't seen him in years."

"When was the last time?"

Coombs's gaze fell to the coffee cup he cradled in his

hands as though his mind was tracing back over the years. "I guess it would have been six . . . no, more like seven or eight years ago. Around the time I bought him the house on Gettings Street."

"Pretty generous of you for a brother you never see," Finn suggested.

"I owe Bernard a lot. Our mother died when I was eight. It was Bernard who raised me. But before you get the wrong idea, Detective, my debt to Bernard ended with that house. Even then he was already into the drugs and drinking. I wanted to help out but I wasn't willing to support his habit, so I bought him the house and cut the ties. You understand, I'm married. I have a baby daughter."

"Congratulations," Finn said with sincerity.

"Do you have any children, Detective?"

Finn nodded. "I have a daughter. Fifteen."

Coombs smiled. "Then you'll understand why it is I have to exclude my brother from my life. I have to think about my own family now."

"So you two never spoke? Never called?"

"Sure, Bernard called. When he needed money. But the calls ended a few years ago. I think my wife finally said something to him." Coombs waited as their waitress refilled their coffee. "Like I said to the detectives who called last year, when it comes to Bernard and his friends and acquaintances, I really can't help."

"Do you know a Patricia Hagen?"

"Actually, yes, I do."

"Any idea how she knows your brother?"

"Her father employed Bernard years ago. The Parkview Funeral Home down on Fort Avenue. Why, are Patricia and my brother involved?"

Finn nodded. "You sound surprised."

Coombs shook his head and this time let his gaze wander past the grimy window to where a rusted-out pickup with Pennsylvania plates pulled out of the crowded lot. "At this point, Detective, not a lot surprises me about my brother."

Kay stirred sugar into her black coffee. Working on nothing more than the diner's burned brew, four Excedrin, and a breath mint, she had let Finn do most of the talking this morning. Besides, it was his interview. She'd known already last night they weren't going to get much from Coombs. Last year when he'd been nothing more than a voice over the phone, even with all the hatred she harbored for Eales, Kay had felt a semblance of sympathy for Coombs. But now, sitting across from the man, she felt sorry for him.

Still, Kay had questions of her own. Questions there'd been no need to ask Coombs a year ago when his brother's case was a slam dunk.

"Do you have any idea why Bernard might have killed those women last year?" she asked carefully.

Coombs let out a breath, and she thought she saw a sadness behind his eyes then. "I don't know what went on with Bernard the past few years. I only know what little I read in the papers. And I know he was into drugs and alcohol. I guess I'd like to blame that, the drugs. I mean, it's hard for me to believe my own brother could . . . do those things."

"I think it'd be hard for anyone to believe of a sibling," she offered.

"Bernard always did have a temper though." When Coombs looked at Kay then, she sensed a genuine compassion behind his soft eyes. "But I think you already know about that. You're the detective he beat, aren't you?"

Kay nodded.

Coombs's gaze went unbroken. "I'm sorry for what he did to you."

"Thank you."

Next to her, Finn cleared his throat. "So, Mr. Coombs, you've had absolutely no contact with your brother?"

"No. Like I said, I had to sever the ties. For the sake of my family."

"And your brother's defense? Who's paying for that?"

A flicker of confusion seemed to touch his narrow features then. "I'm sorry. I . . . I'd assumed it was the state, that Bernard had been assigned a public defender."

"Not exactly. He's being represented by James Grogan."

"Should I know that name?"

"He's one of the top criminal attorneys in the city," Finn explained. "And he doesn't come cheap."

Coombs shrugged. "I didn't know that. Honestly, I haven't been following the situation. I hope you understand."

He drank his coffee and looked up as the electric train trundled past, his eyes following its route around the room.

"It's been a difficult year," he said. "My wife, she already couldn't stand Bernard, and then . . . with the media attention . . . You'd think having a different surname would give us at least a modicum of privacy. But it didn't seem to matter. Within days of Bernard's arrest those vultures were circling. The attention's died off a bit now. We've been able to get on with our lives. But you're always waiting, you know? Waiting for the press to swoop in."

When he looked back at them, Kay saw a premature tiredness in his young eyes.

"I guess, with this murder you're investigating, I might hear from them again, hmm? The media?" Coombs asked.

"It's quite possible," Finn said. "If you run into problems, you can call us. There might be something we can do."

"I appreciate that, Detective. But I'm getting pretty skilled at handling it. Do you know, I even found my name on some asshole's website because of all this? I finally had to threaten the guy with a lawsuit so he'd take my name off."

"What website's that?" Kay asked.

"Some guy, Arsenault I think. Yeah, Scott Arsenault. He had a website up and running, about my brother. The murders. God knows what else. I didn't look at the whole site. Stopped when I found my name."

"Do you know if the site's still up?"

Coombs shook his head. "I have no idea. It's not the kind of thing I keep tabs on, you know?"

18

BERNARDEALES.COM was a load of Ethernet horse-shit.

They'd driven back to Baltimore and Headquarters in the same awkward silence that had settled between them earlier on their way up to meet with Coombs. In Kay's silence, Finn guessed she was imagining the content of the website Coombs had mentioned, questioning why someone would go to the trouble, and wondering who Scott Arsenault was.

Within minutes of stepping off the elevator on the sixth floor, Kay had logged on to the last available computer in the unit while Finn pulled up a chair next to her. And as she scrolled through the pages, one by one, Finn felt his hostility unraveling.

The entire site was dedicated to "saving" Eales. A red banner at the top of the main page announced the wrongful arrest of Eales, and the opening notes detailed claims of police brutality, evidence tampering, and a gross miscarriage of justice.

Act now before this innocent man is convicted! A photo showed Eales standing next to a large, black vintage car behind his Gettings Street house, a polishing rag in one hand, a can of Michelob in the other.

Kay scrolled past the smarmy grin and started clicking links to articles about the prostitutes' murders and Eales's arrest, press clippings and evidentiary summaries, court documents, even articles from law publications. At the bottom of the main page, a link offered to take visitors to the Eales message board.

"The prick's got himself his own fan club," Finn said, feeling tension settle in his jaw.

"And look at this"—Kay pointed to the flashing red link beneath it—"visitors can even contribute to a defense fund." She kept scrolling. "Tell me this isn't for real."

"Sure as hell is. And you're lucky visitor number twelve thousand and two," he said, indicating the counter at the bottom of the screen.

Kay clicked the cursor on a link titled *Get the REAL Story*. Together they skimmed an elaborated narration of the events that had transpired on Eales's porch fourteen months ago. All lies.

Finn's mood darkened as he read about police not announcing themselves at Eales's front door and Arsenault's citation of every American citizen's right to bear arms in defense of self and home. Sitting so close to Kay, Finn could feel her tension as well and had the overwhelming desire to take the mouse from her hand and close the entire site so as not to subject her to the propaganda. But he knew there was no prying her from the terminal.

He read on: the exaggeration of Eales's arrest and interview, claiming he'd been "relentlessly interrogated by police" for more than ten hours, when Finn *knew* it had been six, maintaining Eales had been denied restroom breaks, food, and water, when Finn had seen Eales hauled off to the men's room at least four times during that long, hot day in July while Kay still lay in the hospital. The memories were crystalline. Finn could even remember the look Eales had given him each time they'd led him out of the interview room, could remember the hatred that had swelled through him as he thought of what the man had done to Kay.

"Jesus," Kay said, several lines ahead of him, "my name's in here. More than once."

She backed up to the main page again, this time clicking the link *Press Coverage.* More than a dozen links to the *Sun* and video bytes from the local channels ran down the page. Another click of the mouse and Jane Gallagher's voice sputtered over the speakers through the media player. The video stream was choppy and the audio broken, short bursts that didn't sync with the WBAL reporter's image. Kay hit stop the second her own bloodied face filled the screen.

Then, Finn at last commandeered the mouse. Kay's hand lingered under his for a moment before she relinquished it.

"It's all bullshit," he said, tempted to close it down, but knowing they needed to investigate the entire site.

While Kay watched, Finn went through several more pages, bringing them to one titled *The Evidence* just as Ed Gunderson joined them.

The sergeant stood behind their chairs, scanning the contents with them: the summary of the evidence, the victims' slashed wrists, the heroin in their systems, and how each had been bled, then washed before being dumped down a slope in Leakin Park. The address of the row house where Annie Harris's body had been left was documented, along with highlights of the ME's findings. All of it lay before them . . . before the world.

"What the hell is all this?" Gunderson asked.

Kay explained, a new waver in her voice, while Finn scrolled.

"Well, where's all this information come from?"

"Most of it looks like it's been picked up from the media," Kay said. "I don't think there's anything here that isn't public."

"Wrong," Finn said, his hand freezing on the mouse as the text appeared on the black background. . . . *several shallow knife wounds to the chest of each victim* . . .

"How in the hell did he get that?" Kay stared at the reference and finally pushed away from the desk. "If that detail is on the site," she said, pacing, "anyone could have read it."

"Which means your suspect list just got a hell of a lot longer." Gunderson's words were clipped.

"Twelve thousand and two hits on his site. That's a long list."

"Who put this damned site together?" Gunderson asked.

"Some wannabe serial-killer junkie named Scott Arsenault."

"So is this a departmental leak or is this mope some friend of Eales's?"

Kay shook her head, her jaw twitching, her lips tight.

"Well, you're gonna find this little asswipe," Gunderson said, "and you're going to find out how the hell he knows about those cuts to the victims' chest."

19

SCOTT ARSENAULT lived on President Street in an upscale high-rise a world away from Eales's dump across the harbor. Taking the marble-floored elevator to the twentieth floor, Kay could feel the anger steaming off Finn. It was even more palpable when he brought his fist to the double doors of the Web designer's condo. And as they waited, Kay knew there was more behind Finn's mood than Arsenault's site. Her inclusion in the site's content had really put Finn over the edge. He hammered on the door again.

Arsenault was smiling when he answered. He was handsome: lean but well muscled under the crisp oxford shirt with button-down collar, tucked into a pair of pressed linen pants. Except for the trimmed goatee, he had an adolescent's face, with the kind of features and good skin that would likely have him mistaken for twentysomething even into his forties. Kay thought he had a pleasant face.

"You Scott Arsenault?" Finn asked, showing his shield, waiting for the nod. "We need to talk to you."

"Can't this wait, Detective? I'm with a client."

"A client?"

As if on cue, a large, heavy-jowled man stepped into view at the head of the foyer, his tailored suit looking as though it had been fitted forty pounds ago. "Is there a problem, Scott?" the man asked.

Finn moved into the doorway. "You a serial killer too?"

"Excuse me?" Arsenault's face darkened. The smile gone. When he moved to block Finn's entrance, Finn countered and managed to gain another two feet into the overly air-conditioned suite. "I'm in the middle of a meeting here. Do I need to call security?"

"Not necessary, Scotty. Security already knows we're here." And then addressing the suit: "You can go now, sir. Meeting's over."

But not until Arsenault gave the man a stiff nod and apologized did he gather his briefcase and brush past them.

"I don't know what this is about, Detectives," Arsenault said as Finn invited himself into the front hall, "but I trust your superior officers are aware of and approve of your intrusion today?"

"You can call our sergeant, Scotty. I'm sure he'll handle any complaints you have with the utmost expediency, especially given his recent interest in your website," Finn said as Kay followed him past the foyer.

The main room of the open-concept condo was immaculate. Sun flooded through floor-to-ceiling windows, reflecting off polished wood and chrome, glass and mirrors. Bookshelves lined the east wall, banking in a tight arrangement of black leather furnishings. Past the immaculate kitchen bar, Kay saw the stainless-steel appliances and gleaming white tiles. It took a moment for her to decide what was absent from Scott Arsenault's suite. The place had absolutely no sense that someone lived there.

"I'm sorry, I didn't catch your names." Arsenault stood with his arms crossed over his chest.

"I didn't give 'em," Finn said, moving past the Web designer. "Finnerty and Delaney."

Arsenault looked squarely at her this time, his features softening with an ingratiating smile. "Delaney? From Homicide?" When he extended his hand, she took it— warm and dry—into hers. "I didn't recognize you." She thought of the *Sun* photo on his website as his hand held hers just a little too long.

"It's a real pleasure to meet you, Detective Delaney."

She sensed Finn watching as Arsenault ran his gaze over her. The designer's smile broadened unabashedly, and Kay couldn't decide whether she should be insulted or flattered.

"What do you do for a living, Mr. Arsenault?" Finn asked, casually moving through the condo, lingering at the wall-to-wall bookshelves.

Arsenault fingered back a shock of blond hair. "I develop software. Why?"

"Pays well, huh?"

"I'm certainly not in it for the adventure." He smiled, but only to Kay.

"So why all the books then? Criminal law. Forensics. True crime," Finn asked, following the precise line of texts with one finger, like a stick to a picket fence. He removed one of the hardbound books, leafed through it, then replaced it, shoving it too far back.

"It's just an interest," Arsenault answered. "As a kid I wanted to be a cop."

"So what happened?"

Arsenault let out a quick laugh. "I heard the pay's shit. Won't you sit down?" he asked Kay, guiding her to the seating area.

She obliged, feeling his hand against the small of her back for the briefest moment. Passing the windows overlooking the Inner Harbor, she tried to ignore Arsenault's stare. She watched a tug break the surface of the Patapsco far below.

"Can I get you anything, Detective Delaney?"

"No. Thank you."

"So what is this about, Detectives?" Arsenault angled toward the bookshelves that Finn had abandoned.

"We're investigating a homicide," Finn said.

"Really?" Arsenault reached for the book Finn had

pulled and edged it forward so the spine was once again flush with the others. "How interesting. For me at least. Death investigation has always been a fascination for me."

"We know."

On the glass coffee table in front of her an orchid arched in full bloom, and yesterday's *Sun* was squared perfectly with the table's edge. Kay couldn't tell if it had been read. When Finn passed her, he nudged the paper off-center.

"So I take it you're here about my websites. And given Detective Delaney's presence, I'm suspecting it's the Eales site."

"There're others?"

"I've designed several." Arsenault moved in to straighten the paper, his eyes already tracking Finn's next maneuver.

"How many?"

"Eales. Clarence Gossard. Eddie McCleester. Willy Tarleton."

Kay recognized all but one of the names.

"So you develop websites for killers then?" Finn asked.

"I develop websites for men arrested and convicted of murder." Arsenault straightened a couple architectural magazines Finn had shifted. It had become a dance: Arsenault following Finn through the suite, righting whatever he'd messed with. "I think it's important that the public has the opportunity to view both sides. Come to their own conclusions."

"The public already made a decision on those other cases, Mr. Arsenault," Kay said. "They're called a jury."

"Forgive me if I don't have an undying faith in the judicial system. And, please, call me Scott, Detective." Another flirtatious smile.

"So do you know Eales personally, Scotty?" Finn asked.

"No." Arsenault had given up. Sitting on the sofa now,

his spine stiff, his hands fisted in his lap, he kept an eye on Finn. "I've never met the man."

"So where do you get the information for your site then?" Finn asked.

"Everything on the site is public domain. It's all procured from the media."

"Really?" Finn turned. "Are you sure about that?"

"Yes." But there was a tremble in Arsenault's arrogant self-confidence.

"And what's in it for you, Scotty, mounting these websites? Is it money? Or do you just get off on it?"

"I receive a modest compensation."

"Ah, the Eales Defense Fund. Are you the beneficiary of that?"

Arsenault stood now, clearly on edge.

"Excuse me, do you mind if I use your bathroom?" Kay asked, and caught the flash of approval from Finn. Keep Arsenault scattered. Keep him on his toes. And while Finn was busy playing bad cop, she could nose around a bit.

Arsenault waved toward the hall. "Second door on your left."

Heading down the corridor, she heard Finn continue with his questions. "So is that how these sites work, then? People donate money thinking they're aiding some asshole's defense . . ."

Kay slowed at the partially open first door. In the shadows she discerned the outline of several computers and steel shelves of electronic equipment. She heard the hiss of computer fans and the squelch of a police scanner, then an electronic chirp as though e-mail had come through. Or possibly posts on the Eales message boards.

Back at the office, while Finn nailed down Arsenault's address, she'd started reading the hundreds of archived posts. Several from the designer himself. Often his appearance on the board was to correct someone on the Bill of Rights or to direct members to links regarding police procedures or other "wrongfully convicted" felons.

"I said the second door." Arsenault's voice came from behind her. She jumped. Standing squarely at the head of the hall, backlit by the windows of the living area, she couldn't read his face.

"Sorry."

"The money, Scotty, where does it go?" she heard Finn ask.

"The fund goes to Bernard's attorney. You can talk to Mr. Grogan yourself."

Kay could feel Arsenault's eyes still on her as she passed two more closed doors to her right and finally groped for the light switch inside the bathroom.

The room was as sterile as the rest of the place. Pristine white and crimson tiles, gleaming brass fixtures, and plush towels hanging squarely on their racks. And in one corner, an enormous Jacuzzi tub in red marble.

Arsenault had a maid, Kay guessed as she closed the door.

She gave a cursory exploration of the cupboards and drawers, finally sliding open the medicine chest over the sink. Studying the prescriptions that lined the middle shelf, Kay recognized half of them as OCD and anxiety meds from varying dates. Enough to start a small pharmacy. But nothing screamed out as suspicious.

Flushing the toilet and running the faucet for effect, she left the room and found Finn still hammering Arsenault about the money.

"Come on, Scotty, we're not the fucking IRS here. I don't give a donkey's ass if you take people's money and don't claim it. Who's behind Eales's goddamned website?"

Only two feet of tension-filled air separated the two men. "Who hired you?"

"I don't believe I have to divulge that, Detective."

"No, you're right. But why the hell wouldn't you unless you're hiding something?"

"I'm not hiding anything."

"No?" This time when Finn closed in, Arsenault took a step back. "Oh, come on, Scotty. You don't feel threatened by me, do you? Cuz that sure as hell isn't my intention. Trust me, you'd *know* if I was threatening you."

"Right. I'd end up looking like Bernard Eales did after you guys arrested him."

Finn ignored the comment. "Where are you getting your information?" he asked again.

"I already told you. The media."

"Yeah, yeah, yeah. And you already told us that everything on your website is public domain. But that's where you're wrong, Scotty. See, the thing is, you got shit posted on your site that *no* one knows about. Well, no one except us and Eales. But wait, how can Eales know about it, since your site says he *didn't* kill those women?"

Finn was on a roll. He stopped Arsenault before he could interject.

"Man, Scotty, do you see where I'm confused here? If Eales didn't kill those women, like your bullshit site implies, then he couldn't know some of the details that you've got on your site about those murders. Which means . . . well, you see where I'm going with this? I just gotta wonder where you're getting your information."

Arsenault looked to Kay then, a kind of pleading in his eyes, as though they were suddenly longtime friends and she could bail him out.

"So when you refuse to reveal your source," Finn went on, "then I'm left figuring you don't really *have* one, see?

And I gotta say, Detective Delaney and I, we're jumping to some pretty quick conclusions here, Scotty."

But it was too heavy-handed. Kay saw Arsenault square his shoulders, confident again. "It's time for you to leave, Detective."

One final hard stare passed between the two men. "Then I guess we'll have to talk to Patricia Hagen, won't we?"

Kay couldn't be sure of the change she saw flicker in Arsenault's face then, but there had been something.

"I have nothing else to say," he said to Finn. And then to Kay: "It was a pleasure meeting you, Detective Delaney. I hope we'll see each other again sometime. Perhaps under less hostile circumstances."

As Finn watched Arsenault's smile, Kay could see the irritation in Finn's eyes. It simmered there long after they left the suite and took the elevator to the polished lobby. Only when they reached the car did Finn finally speak.

"If that son of a bitch didn't get the information from Hagen, we're going to have to hit him again," he said, "only next time with a grand jury subpoena."

Kay didn't disagree.

"What do you make of that mope?" Finn asked her as he unlocked the Lumina.

Kay shook her head and looked up at the high-rise, imagining Scott Arsenault at his window looking down on them. "I don't know," she said finally. "But I do find one thing curious."

"What's that?"

"He never asked *whose* murder we're investigating."

20

ALONG THE SOUTH SIDE of the asphalted yard, Bernard tapped out the last Camel from the pack the bitch had given him.

Delaney. He hadn't known her name until after his arrest. Today he couldn't get it out of his head.

At the other end of the pen, Dante Gallant and his "road dogs" beat a track along the west fence. Bernard eyed the automatic cigarette lighter mounted on the wall behind the big black man. Dante eye-fucked him, and Bernard tucked the Camel away. Cigarette wasn't worth going through that bunch of spooks.

Delaney. He hadn't recognized her right away yesterday. That night on his porch, the crystal meth and booze had blurred things. He remembered the banging at the door, then standing on the porch looking down at the bitch's gun. The rest wasn't clear, but he'd been ten feet tall and bulletproof, and some bitch with a badge wasn't about to fuck with his high.

But she had. And now she was fucking with him again. She'd go see Patsy, and he worried what the bitch'd tell his girlfriend.

Bernard leaned into the chain-link and closed his eyes, as sweat crawled down his body under the damp jumpsuit. His head was clearer these days without the booze and the drugs. A year ago that wasn't the case. Him and Roach getting high together, driving around till they scored. Then back to the house to chase the dragon's tail. The heroin burning in a piece of foil.

He remembered Annie Harris, greedily sucking back the curling smoke. He'd had to shove her away a couple times, worried they'd run out. Taking her fill, then not even letting him fuck her.

He'd tried to kiss her. On the couch, feeling up her big, soft tits, fumbling with her zipper. Then his own. Next thing he knew, she was standing over him, pointing at his limp, heroin-numbed cock. Laughing. Her dull brown hair tossed over one shoulder as she howled and choked on her own spit. "And what the hell you gonna do with *that,* Bernie?"

He'd never hit a woman before. Not that hard. She'd reeled back and gone down. And he'd left her there on the floor.

He wasn't sure about much after that. Wasn't till the early-morning hours that he found her. Freaked the shit out of him. He'd figured she'd up and left after he'd passed out on the couch. But then he'd gone to take a leak, caught her reflection in the mirror, and ended up pissing down his own leg.

He knew she was dead. He'd seen enough stiffs at the funeral home. Her skin gray-white. Her eyes dried open. Then he'd seen her mangled wrists and the blood.

The water in the tub had drained through the brittle stopper, leaving pale red rings around the porcelain sides. At first he figured she'd fucking killed herself, and damned if he'd have a bunch of cops poking through his place. So he'd started cleaning, mopping up what blood hadn't gone down the drain, gathering the skank's clothes and purse, its contents scattering across the linoleum floor. He'd been on his hands and knees, fishing for her lipstick behind the toilet, when Roach had come in.

Roach had pointed out the box cutter on the ledge of the sink clear across the room. No way she'd killed herself.

But Bernard didn't remember doing it. He kept telling Roach, over and over, he couldn't remember. Roach had called it an alcoholic blackout. And Bernard had tried like fuck to remember.

Roach had stayed to help him clean. Through the rubber gloves, Bernard had felt her cooling flesh as he'd lifted her out of the tub. And as he held her body against him, carrying her downstairs to the tarpaulin Roach had spread out in the hall, Bernard had finally gotten a hard-on.

Out in the alley, Roach had popped the Strat's trunk and Bernard had argued that they should use Roach's car, not the vintage StratoChief. But Roach refused.

He'd double-checked the tarp when he shoved her in and prayed nothing leaked out. He couldn't get rid of her fast enough. Roach kept him calm, though, kept him from speeding. They drove west, to Harlem Park, where a midnight walk constituted suicide. Bernard didn't care. He wanted the skank out of his Strat. And as he hauled her from the trunk and through the busted-down back door of the empty row house, Bernard swore he'd never lose it again.

But he had . . .

21

"I SHOULD BE OVER this shit now, shouldn't I?"

"Why do you think that?"

"It's been fourteen months."

"And that's too long?"

"It is when it still feels like it happened last week."

"You've always known it would take time, Kay."

Kay wanted to light up. It was during these sessions with her therapist that she craved cigarettes the most.

"Everyone's healing processes are different." Constance

O'Donnell's voice was its usual soft, level calm. That voice pissed Kay off some days. Today it only made her want a smoke all the more.

Kay left the leather sofa and crossed to the window. Through the half-louvered blinds the courtyard of the Towson Medical Center baked under a relentless afternoon sun. Behind her, in the quiet cool of the therapy room, Constance was silent. Kay hated when the therapist used silence as a tool. It was a classic interview technique, one Kay had used herself countless times. Silence made people feel obligated to fill it.

But it didn't work on Kay. In the year she'd been driving up to Towson for her weekly sessions, she'd let long silences settle between her and Constance. It was a game. One that Kay relished winning.

"So how have the nightmares been?" Constance asked. "You haven't mentioned them in a while."

"They're getting better."

"They're not as frequent?"

"No. I'm still having them. They're just better."

"How do you mean?"

"Now *I'm* the one shooting Eales. I'm guessing that's good."

More silence. A glance over her shoulder and Kay saw Constance jot a note. She often wished the shrink would say more, especially when Kay was fishing.

"Well, *I* think it's better," Kay said eventually, and returned to the sofa. "I saw him, you know. Yesterday."

"Who?"

"Eales. I interviewed him at the prison."

If Constance was surprised, she hid it well. "Why? Do you suspect he's connected to this new case you told me about?"

"Let's just say I'm not a strong believer in coincidence."

"And seeing him isn't a conflict of interest?"

"Technically, perhaps. It's a gray area."

Another pause. She watched Constance reach for her cup of tea. Several months ago Kay had decided she liked the therapist, in her flowing Chanel pantsuits and her Fendi shoes. Of course, in the beginning, when a pysch profile was required to deem her fit to resume work, Kay hadn't cared for the entire process, *or* Constance. She'd hated the drive, the wasted time, but mostly she hated the therapist's probing.

Now Kay came because she wanted to. She paid for the sessions herself, in cash, so it didn't show up on her benefits, so the Department wouldn't know. Constance O'Donnell had become her refuge. Her weekly dose of reality, where she could mentally check her shield and her gun at the door and be herself. It was the one place, other than sitting in the dark of the symphony hall, where Kay could shed the job and feel hope.

"So how was it? Seeing Eales?"

"Fine." Translation: *a subject not open for discussion.*

Constance took the cue. "What does Finn think about you having seen him?"

"He'd rather I hadn't. He wanted to be there."

"Why?"

"So he could protect me."

"Sounds natural."

Constance scratched another note in her book. Kay hated the note-taking too. It reminded her of the notes she made in her police pad, documenting evidence and pieces of the case. Only here *she* was the case, and every word Constance recorded was evidence against Kay's state of mind.

Countless times Kay had had to remind herself that her evaluation was over. Constance had—by some stroke of luck—given Kay a clean bill of mental health months ago, otherwise she'd still be on desk duty.

These sessions were for her. None of those careful notes would ever go to the Department. Unless she really did go postal one day.

"So how are you feeling about Finn? About working with him?"

"He's a good partner," Kay said. She'd actually enjoyed watching him play Arsenault earlier today, liked the way she and Finn could read each other.

"And on a personal level?"

"Well, the jury's still out on that one." Kay picked at a cuticle, wondering why the topic was so difficult today, when in the past she'd been an open book to Constance regarding Finn.

Beyond Constance's shoulder, Kay looked to the clock, watching the last few seconds slip away. When the timer buzzed softly, she thanked Constance, gathered her jacket, and verified next week's appointment before leaving out the back exit.

She'd parked in the shade, but the Lumina was still an oven. Kay turned over the engine and cranked the AC. She sat in the cooling unmarked for a while, breathing in the stale air. Her decompression time.

She thought about things Constance had said. And she thought about Finn. She remembered Scott Arsenault's flattering smile and his pristine bathroom. And she pictured Valley's body, the warehouse, and Eales, the images sparking like rapid fire.

And as Kay finally steered the Lumina south into the city, she considered the irony of its taking a murder investigation to make her feel alive again.

22

PATRICIA HAGEN asked to see their ID a second time.

When Finn had pulled to the curb across from the compact stone house in the quiet neighborhood of Mt. Washington, Kay figured he'd written down the wrong address. The century-old residence, tucked behind two sycamores, was tidy, with manicured flower beds and lush window baskets.

Through the iron grate of the heavy wood door, Hagen inspected their shields. "How do I know you're police?"

Kay pushed her ID up to the bars, irritation grinding at her nerves. The woman was dating a goddamned serial killer and she doubted police would be knocking at her door?

"I'm sure Scott Arsenault has called you by now," Kay said, her photo ID still pressed to the open grate.

Finally, they heard the dead bolts.

Cool air greeted them, wafting around Hagen as she stood in the open door. She looked midthirties, with a simple but pleasant face, marred only by heavy glasses. The stylish frames did little to conceal that the prescription lenses were only one level shy of Coke bottles. Behind them the pale hazel eyes looked too large for her head.

There was the scent of flowers as she ushered them stiffly into the foyer and through the house. Cut roses filled several crystal vases positioned throughout, and a sitting room overlooked an immaculate garden. A stone path led past fountains and a birdbath, to dense cascades of rose vines climbing the board fence. Kay counted four cats basking on the narrow deck.

Hagen was a sturdy woman, with boxy hips and a flat

chest. The casual pantsuit she wore was off-the-rack Target. It was a size too large and didn't hang right on her frame, and her bare feet looked swollen in a pair of strappy sandals. A plain woman trying to come off as elegant. It didn't quite work.

She gestured to a grouping of rattan furniture. Sitting, Kay spotted the photo of Eales next to another vase of roses.

"Scott said you'd been asking about the website. Is there a problem?" she asked.

"There could be." Finn pulled out his notebook. "How exactly do you know Scott Arsenault?"

Kay let Finn take the lead. Not only would he likely get farther with his smooth demeanor, but Hagen clearly recognized Kay. Contempt and distrust came off the woman in waves.

"My only association with Scott is through the website."

"Well, how did you find out about him? Do you follow his kinds of websites on the net?"

"No. Actually, it was Scott who contacted me."

"He called *you?*" Finn asked.

Kay studied Hagen, surprised. Both she and Finn had assumed *Hagen* had initiated the site, seeking out Arsenault's assistance.

"Yes. He explained what he does and asked if I thought Bernard would be interested."

"And you didn't find that a little odd?"

"No. I think he took an interest because Bernard is local."

"Did you ask how he got your name?"

"He'd spoken to one of Mr. Grogan's clerks, asked if there was any family to contact. She gave him my name."

"Because you're paying for his defense?" Finn guessed.

"No, Detective, because I'm Bernard's fiancée."

For the first time Kay dropped her gaze to Hagen's hands. They looked rough, the nails chipped and stained, no doubt from tending her garden. Kay noticed the diamond before Hagen—perhaps self-conscious—folded her hands in her lap.

"When Scott first called," she said, "he suggested I check out his other sites. He told me about their success in raising awareness. In getting the truth out there."

"And where do you get these 'truths'?" Kay could no longer be silent.

"Pardon me?"

"The information on the site, where does it come from?"

Hagen shrugged. "Most of it from Bernard, through me."

"So you've discussed the murders with Mr. Eales?" Finn asked.

"Of course not. How could we discuss something Bernard knows nothing about?"

A good dose of delusion was probably the only thing that kept Hagen coming back for visitations, Kay thought.

"Those women were killed in Mr. Eales's house, Ms. Hagen. You *are* aware of the evidence in the case, are you not?"

"I'm aware of what the media tries to sell the public, as well as the kinds of things police will do to close a case."

"So you don't believe Mr. Eales killed those women?"

"I believe in the things I see, Detective. And for all the years I've known Bernard I have always seen in him a gentle person. Someone who cares about other people. Someone who embraces life. Not death."

So, Hagen's tunnel-vision view of life wasn't a purely clinical condition.

"Then if not from you, how *does* Mr. Arsenault know about the details of the murders?" he asked.

"You'll have to ask him that. I'm sure he has his sources."

"All right. We'll do that." Finn flashed Kay a look before turning to a fresh page in his notebook. "And how long have you known Bernard?"

"Going on twenty years. My father handled his mother's funeral."

"And that's when he hired Bernard?"

"Shortly after that. Yes."

"What did he do for your father?"

"Ran errands, cleaned. Sometimes he'd assist in the basement."

"The basement?"

"The embalming room. If things were busy, he'd have to help prep the bodies for interment."

"And how long did he work for your father?"

"That first time it was a year. I don't think Bernard could have handled much more. But then, five years later, while I was away at Norfold State, my father took him on again."

"And how long did that last?"

"Less than a year."

"Is there a reason his employment stints were so short?" Finn asked.

"Bernard and my father . . . they had issues."

"What kinds of issues?"

Patricia Hagen shifted and the rattan armchair creaked under her. "I never got the whole story, but there were accusations."

"Of what?"

Hagen chewed her bottom lip. "Improprieties," she said at last. "But that's not the reason Bernard left. Truth of the matter is, Bernard couldn't handle all the death." She was addressing only Finn now, doing her best to ignore Kay's presence. "Like I said, he's a gentle soul."

Kay watched Hagen: her hands twisting in her lap, lips pinched. She was a flake but she wasn't stupid. Kay wondered how Bernard had managed to charm her. She imagined Hagen as a teenager, a pretty but simple girl with thick glasses. The undertaker's daughter. No doubt there were stigmas attached to that. And maybe dumb-ass Bernard had been the first boy to show interest.

Kay could picture Hagen in high school, working for the grades that would get her into college. Or maybe just applying herself to avoid helping out in her father's shop of horrors. And then, a part of Kay understood Hagen. Hadn't she done the same growing up? Turned to her books as a means of escaping her father? Escaping the bitter cold docks and the ragged nets of drowning fish, their guts spilling out across the stained deck of the boat. She'd never wanted any part of his world. So she stayed in her room, with her homework and her books, listening as her mother taught violin lessons in the parlor.

Kay studied Hagen's profile and wondered how different she and the undertaker's daughter really were.

"Did you date Bernard while he worked for your father?" Kay asked.

"We were only sixteen."

"Did you sleep with him?"

Hagen's eyes fixed on Kay. Angry, saucer-shaped hyperbolic eyes. For a second Kay imagined the woman would terminate the interview, but she turned to Finn instead. "I don't see how these questions can have any bearing on whatever it is you're investigating."

"We're just trying to establish some background on Bernard, Ms. Hagen. You were . . . *are* clearly close to him, but if you're not comfortable discussing your relationship . . ."

But she was. What Kay saw in Hagen was a lonely woman, devoted to her garden, her cats, and Bernard—a relationship not many could understand. And with Finn, Hagen seemed almost eager to share the details of her bizarre existence.

"Bernard and I were . . . close. We lost touch after I left for college," she said to Finn. "When I found out he'd been arrested, I came to his aid."

"By paying his legal fees?" Finn asked.

"Yes." And as though she sensed judgment from him: "Look, Detective, I don't expect you or others to see the truth as I do. I *know* Bernard. He's a pacifist. He's simply not capable of doing the things he's been charged with."

Kay couldn't bite her tongue any longer. She nodded to the *Sun* on the table beside Hagen's chair. "You read the paper, Ms. Hagen?"

"Yes."

"You watch the news on TV?"

"Of course."

"Then I don't know *how* you missed what your pacifist boyfriend did to my partner and me last year."

"Bernard was acting in self-defense."

"What he did, Ms. Hagen, was *not* self-defense. And I can also say with complete confidence that your Bernard is *absolutely* capable of having killed those women."

Hagen stood from her chair, her lips a thin red slash across her pale face. "I think it's time you left, Detectives."

They followed Hagen to the foyer in silence, and Finn thanked her before falling in step with Kay down the walk.

"I might have gotten more out of her," he said, his irritation evident as they reached the car.

"Like what, Finn? Eales hasn't told her a thing. Why on earth would he? He's got her wrapped up like a sweet little meal ticket. He's not going to jeopardize that." She opened the car door a little too hard. "How the hell did he even convince a woman like that to marry him? It doesn't fit."

"She's lonely, Kay."

"Yeah, and the irony is, she's probably waited her whole life for her Prince Charming to rescue her from Daddy's funeral parlor. And when the day finally arrives, she's standing alone in some jewelry store paying for the damned ring herself."

Kay got in and slammed the car door behind her, looking out the driver's-side window at the groomed house. "There's something not right about her and Eales."

Finn got in. "Yeah. And there's something not right about her friend Arsenault either," he said. "I for one am not done talking to that little asswipe. There's a lot he's not telling us."

Kay started the car. "Don't worry. He'll talk. And he'll come to us to do it."

"Why would he do that?"

"Because he's a homicide junkie. He gets off on being close to an investigation. I think for now, we need to break the news to Mr. Hagen about his daughter's engagement. Something tells me he doesn't have a clue. *And,* while we're there, I want to know just what kinds of improprieties are really going on at the family business."

23

THE CYBER CAFÉ on Charles Street was crawling with teenagers. Sipping cinnamon-dusted lattes, they hung in congested cliques, drifting from one terminal to the next. Boys in their frayed, low-riding jeans; girls flaunting their pierced navels in skimpy T's.

From the back bank of terminals, he struggled to block them out. When a boy took up the station beside his, he spared a glance. The kid used one hand to navigate the mouse while the other picked feverishly at a rash of zits flaming across his ravaged chin.

He tried to ignore the kid, focus on his own terminal. The message boards had been busy. He looked for any post about Regester's murder, but the morons hadn't put two and two together. He flirted with the idea of starting a new thread himself, to point out that the witness in Bernard's trial was now the subject of a homicide investigation. Headed by Detective Kay Delaney, no less.

But he refrained. Better not to raise any flags. Still, he needed to post a few responses to the various threads using his screen name, or other members would wonder where "Roach" had gotten to. It was all about balance. Blending in. Camouflage.

Roach wasn't blending in at the Cyber Café though. Not anymore: the din was rising as the average age of the clientele dropped. A friend of the zit-picker sidled up, his backpack sliding off his shoulder and bumping Roach.

"Oh, sorry, man." The kid barely afforded him a glance and Roach looked into the half-lidded gaze. He imagined the feel of the two-and-a-half-inch blade of his Spyderco lock-back sinking into the soft depression of the kid's pale temple. A quick upward jab with the knife and a firm twist. Give the little shit a lobotomy to match that lifeless expression.

Roach's hand clenched around the mouse. Out of curiosity he Googled Detective Delaney for anything new. The search engine came up with the archived articles and accompanying photos from the *Sun,* showing the aftermath of Bernard's meth-induced freak-out on her. The picture sparked something in Roach.

He'd dreamed of Regester last night. Then Delaney.

He blamed Bernard for the dreams, and for the desire he felt steadily rising since killing Regester.

All because of Bernard's letter. The man was a worrier: maybe the bitch had seen them both in Leakin Park when they'd dumped the whore's body. Roach doubted it. Wearing Bernard's raincoat, several sizes too large, he'd helped Bernard get the body out of the trunk. Then, as the rain hammered the car's roof, he'd slouched in the dark behind the wheel while Bernard hauled her off.

The moment he'd approached Regester four nights ago in the college lot, Roach knew she'd never seen him before. There'd been no panic in her eyes. In fact, he could simply have walked away, left her there with her broken shitbox of a car, knowing she had no clue who he was. But the plan had brewed too long. A Technicolor fantasy. There was no way he could *not* have gone through with it.

And now, it wasn't just the dream of Regester that kept Roach company. It was the memories from even farther back. Of that first time, in the cool stillness of the embalming room. It hadn't been about power then, but comfort. Comfort in death's embrace. It had been like coming home.

He never knew her name, that first one. But she'd been beautiful, in spite of the dissecting Y-incision left by the coroner's scalpel, and the crude stitches drawing the puckered flesh together. The final incision that would never heal.

He'd slid his hand along her cold, tight skin, followed the line of her rib cage, her round hips, and the swell of her buttocks pooling against the table. He'd pressed his palm along her belly, past her hardened abdomen, until his fingertips touched the triangle of coarse, red-blond hair.

He remembered breathing in the calm air of the

embalming room: the chemicals and the harsh soaps, the damp-stone scent of death. And in that cool, quiet stillness, he'd touched her in a way he'd never touched another human.

It had marked a turning point in his life. For Roach, it was the day he had become a man.

24

THEY'D HAD TO WAIT to see Alexander Hagen. A conference had taken him to Ocean City, and Finn hadn't been able to book with the funeral director until Monday morning.

The Parkview Funeral Home stood as an impressive terra-cotta mammoth on Fort Avenue, a mere half dozen blocks from Eales's Gettings Street home. The Queen Anne–style structure, with its soaring brick chimneys and high-pitched slate roof, loomed over a shallow lawn bordered by an imposing iron fence.

Finn had sensed Kay's unease entering the perfumed interior of the home. The weekend seemed to have done her good. She seemed rested this morning, Finn noted when they sat down in the director's office. Still she was fidgety. Hopped up on caffeine or just pent-up anxiousness about the case, he couldn't tell which. As they sat in the high-backed, leather-upholstered wing chairs in Hagen's office, Finn tried to ignore Kay's fingers' drumming against her notebook, and he focused on Patricia Hagen's father.

Hagen was a tall, angular man with long, square fingers and a firm handshake. His tapered face was accentuated by a centered strip of balding and two slicked-back tufts of dark hair on either side of his narrow head. His nose looked as though it had been broken once, and deep lines bracketed his serious mouth. Still, he had an air of solace. It was his voice, Finn decided: resonant and calm. Every word carefully calculated. Finn wondered if they taught that in mortuary classes.

"It's a location issue," Hagen explained as he filled a packing box. "People don't feel safe coming down here anymore, so I've bought a building up in Overlea. I'm hoping to be out of here by the end of the month." He closed the box and hoisted it on top of several others with apparent ease. Finn imagined the man handling the stiffs in the basement embalming room, wondered if Hagen still did the work himself.

"So this Regester girl," Hagen asked, starting a new box, "the murder you say you're investigating, why would you think I'd know her?"

"We don't necessarily. But we think her death is connected to Bernard Eales," Finn said.

The man's spine stiffened visibly. A fleeting reaction, there and gone as he shuffled papers. "I haven't seen Bernard in years."

"Oh. We assumed you had at least *some* contact with him, given his relationship with your daughter." Finn had waited all weekend to see Hagen's reaction to the news he doubted Patsy Hagen had shared with her old man.

"Pardon me?" What little color there had been in Hagen's cadaverous complexion bled out.

"Your daughter is seeing Eales," Kay said, clearly going easy with the news.

"But he's incarcerated."

"That apparently hasn't stopped her from visiting him. Twice a week."

Hagen shook his head. When he turned his gaze out the window to the shaded grounds and the street beyond, Finn watched the man's heart-rate rocket, his pulse beating wildly along a purple artery that snaked across his temple.

"Actually," Finn said, "from what we understand, your daughter and Eales are engaged. It also appears your daughter's been paying Eales's legal fees. Any idea where she's getting that kind of money?"

"Her inheritance, I suspect." Hagen's deliberate voice sounded broken now. "From her mother."

"Do you know if your daughter was seeing Eales prior to his arrest?" Kay asked.

"Clearly, I'm not the one to ask." The old man's prominent Adam's apple lifted and dropped sharply several times. "What do you want from me, Detectives?"

"We're trying to establish some background on Eales, and since he worked for you—"

"That was a long time ago, Detective."

"You fired him, is that right?"

"The first time he quit. The second time that I was foolish enough to hire him back, I fired him."

"And why's that?" Kay asked.

"I'm really not comfortable discussing that."

"We heard there were accusations of impropriety," Finn said.

"Impropriety? Not at my funeral home." But in Hagen's voice, in the flash of his milky blue eyes, Finn knew the man was lying.

"So you never, say, caught Mr. Eales doing anything—"

"I resent what you're implying, Detective." In light of the accusation, Hagen's apoplexy rose and his shoulders squared. "This home has been in my family for three generations. To even suggest the presence of anything untoward is an insult."

Finn held up both hands. "That wasn't my intent, sir. I do apologize."

"Mr. Hagen"—Kay's voice was soft now as she drew herself to the edge of her chair and closed her notebook—"we're going to need a list of your employees."

"What? Why?"

"Past employees, sir. Especially anyone who was here around the time Mr. Eales was. It's just as part of our investigation into Mr. Eales. I hope you'll accommodate us."

"I don't see how that's going to be possible, Detective." Hagen waved a hand over the room of boxes and taped-up file cabinets awaiting the movers. "It could be weeks before I get to unpacking up in Overlea."

"I'm afraid we'd need those names sooner. Perhaps you could point us to the appropriate boxes and we can save you the trouble?"

"I can't authorize that. There's confidential information—"

"Sir, we need those names." And in Kay's firm tone, Finn knew Hagen had to have heard the words *court order.*

"You're asking for two decades of employees."

"I understand. And the Department appreciates your cooperation." When Kay stood and extended her hand, Hagen looked forced to accept the handshake.

They left him then, his formerly straight and proud silhouette looking suddenly withered. Finn wondered how long it would be before Hagen called his daughter and what the outcome of the confrontation would be.

Finn had to hurry to catch up to Kay as she steered herself down the carpeted corridor, past the showrooms of polished caskets, and out the front doors.

"He's hiding something," she said even before they'd reached the bottom of the wide stone steps.

"Agreed," Finn said.

"We might have to get a subpoena for those records."

"If we have to, we will. But I say give the old man a

couple days. Let him digest the news we've just thrown at him. I think he'll come through with the list. In the meantime, we oughta go over Eales's records again. See if there were any police reports filed in connection with this place."

Kay was shaking her head. "I've been over those files so many times, Finn. I've never seen Hagen's name."

"Well, maybe it's time we looked into Mr. Hagen then. After all, his daughter didn't exactly tell us *who* was accusing who, now did she?"

25

FROM THE PARKVIEW FUNERAL HOME, Kay drove them to Headquarters. Leaving the Lumina in the last available spot on the top floor of the Department parking garage, she and Finn walked down through exhaust fumes, the smell of old grease, and cigarette smoke to the battered steel door that served as the back entrance. Still, she couldn't shed the pall that had crept into her very pores while in Hagen's funeral home.

The air had been musty and cloying. Perfumed decay wafting through the floor vents, choking her with the memories of her mother, laid out in a casket with what few trimmings her father could afford. Eleven years old, and what Kay remembered most about her mother was that she looked as though she were made of plastic before they put her in the earth.

Kay hated the lies of funeral homes: the catalogues of caskets and trite verses on headstones. None of it had anything to do with the reality of death.

When they reached the sixth floor, Gunderson caught

them at the elevators. His tie hung loose and sweat stains marked his shirt.

"Your pretty boy Arsenault's here," he said, shoving a thumb at the closed door of Interview Room One as they followed him.

"Already?" Kay asked.

"You sure were right about this guy." Finn lifted the sheet of paper permanently taped over the eight-by-ten-inch reinforced window of the door and snatched a glimpse.

"I need an update when you're done," Gunderson said, then turned down the corridor. "I've got the captain all over my ass on this one. At least pretend you're onto something," he added, disappearing into his office.

Behind her, Finn let the paper settle back over the window. "It's your move, Kay. You predicted this wiseass would come in. We'll play this your way."

"Let me just grab a couple files."

When she returned, she gave Finn a nod, straightened her jacket, and opened the door.

Arsenault looked crisp. In his crease-free pants and his starched shirt, he paced the length of the narrow room, hands in his pockets. His suit jacket hung precisely over the back of one of the three vinyl chairs. He looked relatively calm until he spotted Finn behind her.

"Hello, Scotty. Nice to see you. Have a seat." Finn gestured to the chair against the back wall.

Arsenault hesitated. His eyes went from Finn to the chair, as though aware of the psychological warfare of interrogation rooms. Whether or not Arsenault saw the iron holds bolted to the underside of the table, he knew the offered chair was reserved for suspects. Kay wasn't surprised when he pulled the chair around to the side of the table.

"Thanks for coming in, Mr. Arsenault," she said, setting the files down.

"Scott. Please." He flashed her a tense smile, but Kay sensed the wariness behind it.

"So what can we do for you today?" she asked, sitting across from him, in the chair with his jacket. She noticed the Armani name on its label.

Arsenault held his breath for a moment. When he let it out, Kay smelled alcohol. She imagined him in a bar, tossing one back to loosen up before coming in. "I saw the papers," he said. "You didn't tell me you were investigating the murder of Valerie Regester."

"Did you know her?"

"Only that she was supposed to be a witness in Eales's trial."

"Ever meet her?" Kay asked.

"No. But I know you're probably looking at me as a suspect."

"And why's that?"

"Because of the website. I know it doesn't look good."

"It might help if you had an alibi, Scotty," Finn said. He leaned against the opposite end of the table.

"That's why I'm here." Arsenault reached into the breast pocket of his shirt and took out two business cards, slid them across the table. "These are two associates I was out with Wednesday. The night the girl was killed."

It was too easy. Kay saw Finn's suspicion.

"Check it out," Arsenault said, giving the cards another shove in Finn's direction.

"And these buddies of yours," Finn asked, "are they expecting my call?"

"I warned them you might be contacting them, yes." Arsenault was bouncing his foot, his knee jiggled up and down.

"So why exactly do you think we'd be suspecting you, Scott?" Kay asked.

He took in another breath, seemed to weigh options she could only imagine. "Like I said, because of the website. And the information on it."

"But you get the information from Patricia Hagen, don't you?"

"Most of it."

Kay wasn't ready to push him. Not yet. Play him slow. Scatter him. "You know anything about Ms. Hagen's father?"

"Not really."

"Patricia told us there'd been conflict between her dad and Eales. She ever mention anything about that?"

"Maybe."

"Look, Scotty"—Finn's voice was gruff—"you actually *want* to help us here. Trust me."

"All right, yes, Patsy did mention there'd been a falling-out the last time Bernard worked for her dad."

"Accusations. We know. Any idea what they were about?"

"Apparently Bernard called the cops on Hagen."

Kay shared a glance with Finn.

Arsenault saw it. "What? You two thought it was the other way around, didn't you? That it was the old man calling the cops." He shook his head. "Patsy told me Bernard accused her father of doing stuff with the bodies. Knowing Bernard, though, he probably did it just to stir up shit for the old man. But it's not like I know Hagen. Who knows what his game is?"

Arsenault picked lint from his pant leg. From there he seemed concerned with his fingernails. The foot-bouncing, the grooming—all signs Kay would normally take as indicators of a lying suspect. But with Arsenault she couldn't be sure it wasn't just part of his obsessive-compulsive nature.

"And what's your take on Patsy and Bernard?" Finn asked then.

"What do you mean?"

"Come on, Scotty. A woman like that with someone like Eales? It doesn't exactly jibe, know what I'm saying?"

"I agree, but it's not like I've got that one figured out either. Though, sometimes I get the feeling Eales might have something on her, you know?"

"Like what?"

"I have no idea." Arsenault checked his watch, then eyed the business cards he'd tossed on the table, clearly anxious to have his alibi verified.

Kay picked up the cards, handed them to Finn.

"Guess I'll go check these out," Finn said.

When the door closed behind Finn, Kay knew Arsenault's eyes were on her. She shed her jacket and laid it across the end of the table. It was about body language now; show him she was relaxed. Keep it informal. Non-adversarial.

His voice was different now that they were alone. Softer. Relaxed. "So how are you doing these days, Detective? I mean, since Bernard?"

"Fine, thanks," she said, surprised at the odd sense of ease she felt with him.

"I bet it's not easy though, being a woman on the unit. On the force," Arsenault went on. "I mean not just the whole old boys' club, but on the streets. You're only what, five-five? That must be a bit of an impairment in some situations."

"I hold my own."

"Still, you've taken more than most. From what I read, Bernard almost killed you."

"I'm still here." Kay couldn't tell if it was something in Arsenault's tone then, or in his eyes, but she sensed a genuineness in his words.

He studied her for a long moment, then sat back in his chair. "So Finnerty, he's your new partner now?"

"We're working this case together, yes."

"He really does like me for this, doesn't he?" Arsenault asked, and Kay suspected he used the cop lingo to align himself with her.

"Well, you gotta admit, Scott, you've given him good reason." Kay opened Valley's case file then. Reports, evidence logs, Jonesy's protocol. As she flipped the pages, she was aware of Arsenault leaning into the table for a closer look.

She stopped when she came to one of the pages she'd printed off his website and added to the file: a detailed documentation of the case, the investigation, and a summary of the evidence, as well as a chronicle of Bernard Eales's insipid life. "These lists of yours," she pointed out, "they're very precise."

"I do my research. Like I said, it's an interest. There's no crime in that, is there?"

"No. But come on, Scott, be honest. You don't actually believe these guys you've got websites for are innocent, do you?"

"In a couple of the cases, after going through court documents, statements, testimony, I did question some aspects of the investigations and trials. Clarence Gossard, for one. And Eddie McCleester. I'm not sure how familiar you are with the cases, but in both of them their lawyers really mangled their defense."

"So they're innocent because they didn't get a fair trial?"

"No. In McCleester's case, sure, the evidence is circumstantial. Still, I'm sure he did it. Gossard too."

Kay wondered if Arsenault was merely indulging her.

"And what about Eales?"

He shrugged casually, but she could tell he chose his words carefully now. "From everything I've heard, the evidence is strong. And you can't argue evidence, can you?"

"Well, there's evidence. And then there's intuition."

"And what's your intuition tell you, Kay?"

She shrugged. "I have my own theories."

He seemed to recognize he wasn't going to get more from her. "Well, I think if there's any doubt in Bernard's guilt, it lies in his character. I mean, he's not some mastermind serial killer. The way I see Bernard, he's more of an opportunist. Sees something he wants and simply takes it. He's not a planner, so one has to wonder, how *could* he have pulled off those murders? At the same time, maybe there's more to Bernard than meets the eye. I'm sure people underestimate him all the time. Even you did."

She tried not to flinch, and she caught a glimpse of sympathy in his eyes then. Regret that he'd brought up the memory for her.

"But you've probably talked to Bernard yourself," Arsenault said. "What do you think?"

When she held his stare for a moment too long, a nervous smile twitched at the corners of Arsenault's lips. He knew he'd pushed the boundary.

"Look, Scott"—she drew his website pages from the file and slid them over to him—"we've got a big problem here."

The smile fell.

"It's about some of this content. You know you've got certain details here, details that were never made public, were never in the media. In fact, they were our hold-back. Can you explain that?"

The wheels turned behind Arsenault's quick eyes.

"You gotta come clean, Scott. You keep silent on this and life's gonna get real messy real fast for you."

When he dropped his gaze to the pages, he appeared to scan them, but she knew he wasn't. Scott Arsenault knew exactly what detail she was referring to.

"It's the cuts to the victims' chests, isn't it?" he asked finally.

"Bingo."

"Oh, Christ." He pushed away from the table. Stood, and paced the back wall of the room like a lab animal in its cage.

"Listen to me, Scott, you're not in trouble if you've got a source. Just tell us who it is. Tell us how you knew about those injuries, especially since you say you've never spoken with Eales."

He wouldn't look at her, and Kay worried she'd lost him.

"Scott?"

But then he stopped, his expression drawn taut when he turned on her. "Wait a second. These are old cases. If this is about those cuts to Eales's victims' . . . Did Valerie Regester have the same marks on her chest?"

Her lack of response gave him the answer.

"Oh, man."

"Come on, Scott, talk to me. No one knew that detail except the investigating detectives and the ME who did the autopsies. And, of course, the killer. So unless—"

"No. There *is* someone else who knew." He'd started pacing again, shaking his head. "Christ."

"Who is it, Scott? We need a name."

Kay watched him pace, his hands clenching into fists, his knuckles white.

"Andy Reaume," he said finally.

"And who's he?"

"She's a friend."

"Girlfriend?"

"No. It's not like that."

"So she's a source. What is she? Is she on the job? A crime-scene technician?"

More hesitation. Then: "She's with the medical examiner's office."

Of course.

"She cleans up after the autopsies," he explained. "Preps the bodies for viewing, organizes personal belongings, that sort of thing. She told me about the cuts to the victims' chests."

"Working at the ME's, she'd have signed a confidentiality waiver."

"That's why I didn't want to say anything when you came to my place Friday. I really don't want to get Andy in trouble."

"Well, it's a little late for that."

When Finn came through the door, Arsenault stiffened visibly. "Have a seat, Scotty." Finn kicked out a chair and motioned for him to sit, then tossed the business cards back onto the table. " 'Fraid your alibi doesn't check out."

"What do you mean?" Arsenault's voice was thin as he sat.

"I mean, your story doesn't wash. You weren't at any bar Wednesday night."

"You talked to my friends?"

"Oh, sure. They said you were at The Cosmo with them down in Fells Point from nine till one a.m. Lied just like you asked 'em to."

A muscle along Arsenault's jaw went crazy.

"You forgot about your doorman, Scotty." Finn planted one hand on the table and leaned across it into Arsenault's personal space. "I did some checking. Guess you figured the doorman didn't notice you when you snuck out at nine thirty. And he says he never saw you come back in."

"I *did* come back. He mustn't have been at his station when I did."

"So you *did* lie."

Arsenault snatched up his friends' business cards and worried them between his fingers. Kay saw the sheen of sweat along his forehead.

"Okay, look, I was home that night," he said. "But I was alone, so what the hell kind of alibi is that, you know? I *did* go out at nine thirty for some takeout. That's all. A half hour. I was back by ten."

But Arsenault must have seen that Finn wasn't buying it.

"Look, I was supposed to meet up with the guys at the bar that night anyway, but I wasn't feeling well."

"So you figured you'd lie."

"Hey, is it my fault the doorman wasn't at his post when I came back?"

Finn shook his head. "Doesn't look good when you lie, Scotty."

Arsenault's chair scraped back against the linoleum as he stood. He turned to Kay. "Look, I've told you everything I know." He reached for his jacket. "Unless there's something else Detective Finnerty wants to harass me about, I think I'll be going."

"Well, actually . . ." Finn stepped back from the table and opened the Interview Room door. "Before you go, Scotty, there's someone here wants to say hi."

"Who?" Tension flared.

"Maureen Greer. You remember her, don't you? From the Rape Unit?"

And Scott Arsenault's face blanched.

26

MO GREER HAD BEEN WORKING Rape for ten years and somewhere along the way had acquired the not-so-flattering nickname Bulldog. Kay never knew if it came from Mo's stout figure or because once she got her teeth into someone she didn't let go.

When Mo stepped into the Interview Room, Arsenault remained standing. His face tight, his back straight.

"Hey, Mr. Kelly." Mo swung her stockiness around with the same ease she did her confidence. She pulled out the last free chair, slapped her own file onto the table, and sat. "Or wait. Detective Finnerty tells me it's Arsenault now? How you been doin'? Why don't you pull up a chair and take a load off, huh?"

Kay watched the Web designer. He didn't move.

"How long's it been?" Mo asked. "Six years, right? I thought I recognized you when you came off the elevator. You had me a little confused though with the name change. No wonder Detective Finnerty couldn't find anything on you. Arsenault. That's your mother's maiden name, isn't it?"

"You have a good memory, Detective Greer," he said stiffly.

"So why the change?"

"My mother passed. I took her name out of respect. Is that a problem?"

Mo shook her head. "Only if you did it to escape this rape charge." She slid the dog-eared folder to Kay.

"The charge was dropped, otherwise I wouldn't have been able to change my name, now would I? And that file should have been expunged."

"Aw, I know. I'm just such a pack rat though. Finnerty here says you're helping them out on this murder case of theirs. Of course, he was pretty shocked to find out about your record."

Kay opened the folder and perused the six-year-old aggravated-assault and rape charge. She knew Arsenault was watching.

"There *is* no record," he said.

But Mo ignored him. "Mr. Kelly here got a little heavy with a girl in college," she said for Kay's benefit. "A real he-said, she-said. She claimed he raped her. Used a knife on her too, didn't you, Mr. Kelly? Only, you said she'd done those cuts to herself after you'd left, to substantiate her story. What was it you said about the girl?" Mo reached across to flip the pages for Kay. "That's right, 'She liked it rough.' You said *she* was the one who brought the knife into the sex act but you refused to use it and left."

"That's right." Arsenault's anger sharpened his words. "Besides, you have no evidence."

"He's right. No prints on the knife. Nothing concrete. Only Ms. Neuwelt's statement. But then, last minute, she recants. Drops everything. Then I find out later she's pregnant. Was it a boy or a girl, Mr. Kelly? And what *does* she get for child support from you anyway for dropping those charges?"

Mo was pushing Arsenault's buttons like an ATM machine. Kay saw his jaw clench, and his movements were brusque as he straightened his jacket.

"I bet she's cleaning you out, huh?" Finn asked, coming around behind Kay. When he reached over her shoulder, he flipped through several pages of the case file himself, stopping at the color photos of Missy Neuwelt. They'd been taken at the hospital: close-ups of her swelling eye and cheek, and one superficial cut to her jaw. There were more cuts though, to her palms and wrists, red slashes across her abdomen, and finally, Finn stopped turning photos when he reached the close-up of Missy Neuwelt's chest. Several red lines crisscrossed the pale skin between her breasts.

Finn let out a low whistle. "Wow, you sure went at this girl."

"No, Detective, she went at herself. The girl's certifiable, especially when she's not on her meds."

"So you're saying she gave herself that shiner?"

"No. I did that, when she attacked me. The rest is her own work."

"Sure do have a way with the ladies," Finn added.

But Arsenault was finished. "If you have any more questions, Detective, I'd like to call my lawyer. Otherwise, I'll be on my way."

Kay sensed the disappointment behind Finn's false smile as he stepped back and made a broad gesture to the door. "That's all right," he said. "We know where to find you."

Arsenault's hard-soled oxfords clicked against the linoleum as he headed out. Kay felt Finn's hand on her shoulder, understood his nod. But she didn't need his cue. She was off the chair and after Arsenault in a second.

She caught up with the Web designer at the elevators. "Listen, Scott, I'm sorry about my partner."

"It's not your fault."

Kay punched the lobby button for him.

"I didn't do that to Missy," he said, staring at the doors.

"I believe you." But she didn't. Not entirely. Not until she'd heard both sides of the story. She waited until he turned to her, and for a second Kay felt sorry for him. If he *was* telling the truth, it wouldn't be the first time some poor sap got framed for rape. And Arsenault had mentioned the girl had been on meds.

"We're still going to have to talk to her." Kay kept her voice soft, needed to remain on his good side. Needed to be trusted.

"Fine. I just don't see how digging out an old fabricated rape charge helps to catch whoever killed Valerie Regester."

"You're probably right."

When the elevator arrived, the car was empty.

Kay held the door as he stepped inside. "Listen, if you think of anything else or . . . if you just want to talk—" She handed him her card from her pocket. "You can call."

Arsenault took the card with a thin smile. "Thank you. I will."

27

KAY PARKED HER 4RUNNER in the graveled lot of the Bridge Marina and sat in the dark silence of the SUV, wondering why she'd agreed to come.

A new moon hung over the water. Like a giant ball being held up by the masts, it bathed the fiberglass decks in an eerie pallor. Beyond them, the concrete vaults of the Hanover Street Bridge looked like black caverns.

It felt strange being back.

Locking the SUV, she crossed the lot to the maze of slips. A nighthawk dipped, squawking as the air whistled through its wings. She followed the east pier to *The Blue Angel*. Finn was one of the marina's few permanent residents and paid no docking fees because the owner liked having a cop on the premises.

He'd bought the *Angel* after Toby's death, after his marriage with Angie had fallen apart, the grief and self-blame eroding what little love had been left between them. He'd moved out, making the boat his permanent residence and leaving the house in Hunting Ridge to Angie and his teenage daughter, Maeve. Kay had never met either of them and suspected Finn preferred to keep his two worlds separate. From what Kay could tell, the relationship with his ex had always been civil but strained. She wondered if Finn had managed a reconciliation over the past year.

The lights of his forty-three-foot Slocum cutter were on. Over the dull slap of riggings, the drone of a saxophone played out over the airways. Kay stopped at the head of the gangway. She didn't want to be here. Didn't want to face the memories.

Finn must have felt the boat's lilt as she stepped onto the wide deck. When he appeared in the companionway steps, he was shirtless, wearing khaki shorts and a pair of stained deck shoes.

Inside, he took out two Dr Peppers and slid one across the galley table for her. He did look good, Kay thought again. His body was firm. Solid. He'd been working out. Refusing to surrender to that rapid creep toward middle age.

As though sensing her gaze, Finn pulled on a T-shirt bearing a faded Habitat for Humanity logo. Past him, the sheets of the queen-size bed in the aft cabin had been roughly straightened. Memories twisted deep inside her. The boat hadn't changed. The sounds, the smells, the feel of the space and the intense vibrations she'd always felt between her and Finn. It was as if no time had passed. And being here made her realize how much she missed it.

"So how'd you make out at the ME's office?" she asked, determined to focus on the case.

"Shearmur and I met with Arsenault's friend, Andy Reaume."

"And?"

"The girl folded. She admitted talking to Arsenault about the cases, even showing him photos. It all started when he saw Chisney's body."

"How the hell did that happen?"

"She swears it wasn't planned," Finn said, almost sounding sorry for the girl. "Says they had a date, and Arsenault met her at the morgue. Apparently he only wanted a peek, but after that Scotty took a special interest in the case."

"And the website?"

"She knew about it, but says she wasn't aware he'd published the details of the autopsies."

"What's going to happen to her?" Kay asked, even though she didn't doubt the OCME's director had made short work of terminating the girl's employment.

"After we finished, Shearmur had her escorted out."

"She worth pursuing for more background on Arsenault?"

"Probably not. The girl doesn't know much. They went out only a couple times. She's never even been to his condo." Finn reached for a pack of Marlboros at the end of the teak bar, appeared to think twice, then dropped them into a drawer. "He's part of this, Kay. And I don't just mean the website. He's connected."

Kay took a long gulp of soda, her eyes watering at the burn of carbonation. "I'm not so sure. I don't know what his story is, but I think you're wrong if you're liking him for Valley's murder."

"He knew all the details."

"Yeah, and so does everyone else who's ever seen his website." Kay shook her head. "If Arsenault killed Valley, he wouldn't have done it the way it went down."

"What, now you're so close to this mope you know how he thinks?"

In Finn's sharp tone there was no mistaking his aversion toward Arsenault. Kay wondered if it stemmed from Arsenault's possible connection to the case or a more personal element. She'd seen the way Finn looked at Arsenault whenever the Web designer softened to her or directed a smile her way.

"No," she answered. "But I think I know Arsenault's type. He's too precise, too careful. He wouldn't just burn Valley up like that. This guy knows how to get rid of a body. If it was him, I doubt we would have found Valley for months, if ever."

"And what makes you think he didn't want Valley found? Maybe he wants the attention. Maybe he wants *your* attention."

"Oh, come on, Finn. Give me a little credit. You think I'm falling for his smooth talk?"

But Finn turned away, crushing his empty soda can in one hand and tossing it into the trash. "Well, maybe you didn't take a close enough look at the photos of Missy Neuwelt after he raped her."

"Allegedly raped, Finn. We have no way of knowing who's telling the truth about what happened six years ago."

"Well, what did she have to say?"

Kay had gone to see the girl this afternoon. Rape victims seldom warmed up to male detectives, so Finn hadn't put up an argument about being left out of the loop. "Story she gives reflects the initial reports," Kay said. "Only now she admits she recanted in order to get more child support out of Arsenault."

"You honestly think she could have cut herself up that way?"

Kay thought of the overly primped young woman who'd offered her pink lemonade, twirling a limp ringlet of chemically treated hair around one finger the entire time

Kay sat with her in the stuffy apartment. Something about her had been not quite right, but Kay hadn't been able to put her finger on it. "My gut feeling? Yeah, I think she could have."

Finn turned to the galley bar and gathered his marine maps. When he reached for one by her elbow, Kay felt the brush of his hand. The contact was too close. Too intimate.

Kay sat back, needing space. "I submitted a VICAP search," she said.

His look was hard when he met hers. "The nicks in Valley's chest were copied, Kay. This isn't the same killer."

"Maybe not." She'd run the MO through the FBI's Violent Criminal Apprehension Program, the national clearinghouse for unsolved violent crimes, where a series of computers and analysts in Quantico, Virginia, ran comparisons against crimes from other jurisdictions.

"Any matches?" he asked.

"No."

"Eales killed those women, Kay. Besides, if it wasn't him, how do you explain that it's been over a year since the last murder? With a signature like his, you would have gotten hits on VICAP. There's no such thing as a yearlong cooling-off period."

"Maybe this guy's been incarcerated."

"Yeah. He's been incarcerated all right. He's down at the State Pen right now. This is someone else, Kay. Give Eales credit where credit's due. He killed those women. All you gotta do is look at the evidence, think about what the hell he did to you."

Kay tossed back the last of her soda. "Thanks. I'd rather not." But the memories came anyway: Eales barging through that door, the look in his eyes as he started swinging.

"It wasn't your fault, Kay." Finn moved around the bar

beside her. He attempted to settle his hand on her shoulder, but she stood, tried to pace in the tight quarters.

When she met his gaze, she could see his frustration.

"I shouldn't have drawn my gun," she said. "I know that's what everyone on the unit believes."

"And what were you supposed to do? Use attitude to stop Eales?" Finn shook his head. "The son of a bitch was so hopped up on crystal meth, he probably thought he was fucking Superman. You didn't stand a chance, so stop second-guessing it."

"So you think I was right in drawing my nine?"

His pause diluted any conviction his reply might have had. "I wasn't there, Kay."

"Sounds like a no." She felt her jaw clench tighter.

"Look, all I can say is, when you draw your weapon, you gotta be prepared to use it." The softness in his tone didn't make the words any less harsh.

Just back off, Bernard. We only want to talk.

Eales's eyes had been slow, his smile listless, as he'd sized her up. And yet, she'd never known a man to move that fast. The thought of actually using her gun had barely entered her adrenaline-laced mind before the first blow caught her wrist.

"That was *you* on Eales's porch, Kay. No one else. No one has the right to judge you. Not even me. Only *you* can decide if what you did was right. And then you have to live with that decision."

"No, Finn, we were *all* on Eales's porch that night. Every uniform, every detective. There's not a single cop in Baltimore who didn't mentally put themself on that porch after I got beat. But you're right about one thing. It's *me* who's got to live with my decision. And there isn't one man on the unit now who would dare partner with me because of it."

"Well, they're going to have to. It's Department policy. You need someone watching your back."

"Trouble is, they gotta trust me to watch theirs."

"I do." There was a bare honesty in his face then. A sincerity that made her actually believe him.

"I don't want you to," she said, seeing Spencer's blood on Eales's lawn. She rounded the bar, heading to the salon doors. "I gotta go."

But Finn caught her wrist. She didn't want this conversation. It was too dangerous. The last place she needed to end up was in that aft cabin. And it would be too easy. Too easy to throw herself into the emotions and the lovemaking they'd shared, to accept Finn's sympathy and turn it into the kind of sex that made her forget everything.

"It's late," she said.

But Finn held her wrist tight. "Damn it, Kay, talk to me. Tell me what you're going through."

She shook her head, again trying to escape his grasp.

"Is it Valerie Regester? You're not responsible for her death. It's not your fault."

"I made her come in, Finn. *I* persuaded her to testify."

"You were doing your job."

"I got her killed." Kay broke free and this time made it to the steps. Still, Finn came after her.

"Kay, what's going to make it better? Tell me." He wanted to comfort, to be the solace she needed, but Kay wasn't ready for it.

Valley was dead. Because of her.

"I don't know." She shook her head. "Maybe . . . maybe I want to bury her."

"You don't have that kind of money."

"I'll figure something out. She deserves a proper burial."

He stared at her a long time. At the bottom of the companionway steps, Kay fidgeted under the close examination.

"Fine," he said at last. "I'll make some calls. I know a couple people."

She wanted him to hold her then. Standing in his boat, a cool breeze curling down from the deck, it would be so easy to step into Finn's embrace, to accept the comfort she knew he was too eager to give. They could make love. She could feel alive. Even if just for one night.

Old habits . . .

But she wasn't sure it would be for the right reasons. And Finn deserved more.

"Thanks," she whispered, and took the steps up to the cockpit before it was too late.

Finn offered his hand as she stepped over the line and onto the slip.

"I'll see you in the morning," she said, her voice broken.

He stopped her before she reached the end of the slip. "Kay?" His voice ebbed into the stillness of the marina, and when she looked back at him, he was only a silhouette against the helm of *The Blue Angel*. "Just so you know, I'll always have your back."

She wasn't sure if he saw her nod.

"And I know you've got mine," he added as she headed inshore.

28

THE CALL CAME IN AT 8 A.M., as the city's sanitation trucks crawled through cluttered back alleys and plastic-wrapped Baltimore *Sun*s sat on lawns, collecting dew. Finn and Kay weren't summoned until nine. Kay was silent on the drive up to Woodberry in the Northern

District, and Finn couldn't decide if it was because of the anticipation of the call or their talk last night.

Rockrose Avenue was already a snarl of Department vehicles. And with the WBAL and WJZ TV stations only just over the hill, the news crews crowded the curbs as well.

A chain-link fence surrounded the rough grounds that lay at the base of the towering antennas broadcasting both local signals. TV Hill—as it was dubbed—was a quiet hamlet where the borders of Druid Hill Park and the Jones Falls Expressway kept crime at bay, and where the sudden flurry of police activity drew a fast crowd.

Finn left the car at the end of the street and they walked the half block to the narrow alley. A turquoise trash truck rose above the postage-stamp backyards with their ragged fencing. Laundry on short lines barely swayed in the stagnant heat, and the water had evaporated from sun-bleached kiddie pools. From the top of the alley, Finn could smell the trash compacted in the truck's hopper.

"Figured I should route this one through you." Fred Worden—a detective from the other shift—looked disheveled after a long midnight tour. "Your sarge caught wind," he said, leading them down the alley. "He's on his way."

Finn saw her from yards away: her nude body splayed across the cracked concrete of the back alley, her skin white in the morning sun. She lay faceup, her arms flung out. Deep gashes ran the length of each pale forearm.

"Sanitation crew found her when they grabbed the top bags." Worden gestured to the shadowed airway between the two sheds where the trash had been stacked. "She musta been wedged in there under some bags."

Worden hung back as Finn stood over the girl. There was the faint odor of decay. She looked early twenties, with dark hair and a pretty face. The eyes had already gone milky, and a thin line of fluid leaked from her mouth and trailed across her cheek, attracting a half dozen green blowflies.

She was childlike in stature: small, neat breasts, jutting hip bones, and evenly curved ribs that showed beneath the translucent skin. There were no track marks on her arms, but that didn't mean she wasn't a junkie.

Finn felt Kay brush against him. Above the low buzzing of the flies he heard her mutter, "It's him."

His eyes, as well, were drawn to the wounds on the girl's chest. The flesh of exposed muscle glaring red in contrast to her colorless skin. "She a Jane Doe?" he asked Worden.

"Actually, no. We got an ID on her." Worden waved over one of the uniforms. "Miller here says he knows her."

The patrolman was a muscle-bound brute, his shoulders drawing the uniform shirt snug across his barrel chest. "B. J. Beggs," he said. "Bobby Joe. She hooked down on Wilkens. I brought her in a few times when I worked out of the South-West."

"She have a file?"

"Yup. Mugs, prints. Good kid, though." The big rookie shook his head, clearly disappointed. "From Wisconsin, I think."

"Long way from home," Finn said. "You know any of the girls she worked with down on Wilkens?"

"A few." Miller shrugged.

"You mind going with us tonight? Talk to some of them?"

"Not a problem."

"In the meantime, I need you and your guys to start a canvass. Find me someone who saw something out here."

Finn watched Kay circle the girl's body, then survey the row houses that backed onto the alley. She'd taken off her jacket back in the car. The sleeveless mock-turtleneck she wore gathered around the butt of her Glock and revealed the angry scar along her left arm. Finn remembered the two-hour surgery required to fix the shattered elbow after Eales's attack. One of several during which he'd paced the corridors of Johns Hopkins.

Past her, Finn noted the sanitation workers: Larry, Curly, and Moe, dressed in stained coveralls, leaning against their truck, gawking. "Worden, get whatever you can from those three and cut 'em loose, will ya?"

Finn joined Kay. "So what are you thinking?" he asked.

"We gotta get this bastard." Kay squatted, scrutinizing the girl's body. "Two in one week. He's moving fast. Like killing Valley gave him a taste. And now he's hungry for more."

With one gloved hand she lifted Beggs's wrist, turned it over, then nodded at the rest of her. "No way she was out here yesterday. With the heat we had, she'd be bloated and putrefying."

"So he put her out with the trash last night."

"That's my guess," she said. "He played with her for a while though, then tossed her before she'd start smelling."

"How do you figure that?"

"She's out of rigor. Rigor doesn't start releasing for thirty-six hours, and it takes a good twelve to twenty more to be completely gone. This girl's at least forty-eight hours dead."

"Well, that doesn't make sense. There'd be more decomp."

"Not if he kept her cold." Kay stood, the intensity rippling off her as she paced the tight alley. Finn saw her stiffen and followed her gaze to the top of the alley, where Gunderson gave Jane Gallagher the brush-off and ducked under the police tape.

When the sergeant reached them, he stood over the

girl for less than ten seconds before dismissing Worden. "I want you two on this." Gunderson's eyes never left Beggs's exposed body. "It goes up on the board under your name, Kay, but you're partnered with Finn still. Any idea who she is?"

"Hooker from down on Wilkens," Finn said.

"This one have any connection to Eales?"

"We'll dig around. Talk to her friends on the street tonight."

Gunderson cleared his throat as he surveyed the scene. "We need a connection between this girl and Eales. Because if there isn't one, we've either got us some son-of-a-bitch copycat taking his blueprints off that mutt's website or . . ." He shook his head.

"Or we got the wrong goddamned guy," Kay finished for him.

But Gunderson looked too tired for theorizing. He backed away, wiping the sweat off his balding pate with the back of his hand. "Tell me what you get on this girl." Nodding to the crush of media at the police tape, he added, "I want this SOB before those jackasses give him a name, hear me?" With that he lumbered back up the alley, straightened his tie, and met the camera crews head-on.

"Someone had to have heard something out here," Kay said, doubt in her voice.

"It's more likely he drove her here." Finn unbuttoned his shirt collar against the heat. "Probably used the cover of the garages, backed in off the street and hauled her out of his car, then buried her under those bags." He nodded to the trash bags close by. One was torn, leaking a fish tin and vegetable matter.

Kay waved to a tech. "Do the bags," she said. "Those two over there."

"You're kidding, right?" The technician scowled.

"Yeah, I'm just full of jokes this morning. You can either do them here or take 'em in. I don't care how. I want them dusted."

"It's a long shot, Kay," Finn said.

"Maybe long shots are all we've got. But when we do get this guy, I want his prints on those bags so we can nail his coffin."

She paced, then nodded to the rear of the row houses.

"He could be right here, Finn. He either chose this spot because it was outside his zone, or the son of a bitch is here. Watching us right now."

29

IT WAS THE KIND OF NIGHT when people killed. Not just the homeys slinging their drugs on the corners with their semis jammed into their shorts. There'd be steak knives and baseball bats, tire irons and anything else brandishable. In the heat of the summer, a late-night argument could go real wrong real fast. In the heat, the homicide rate always jacked up. As much as 20 percent.

Kay drove with the window down, guiding the Lumina along the side streets of Wilkens Avenue, scouting for any hookers who might be working just off the main drag. She felt more connected this way, smelling the city, hearing its pulse.

The unmarked stood out, and Kay took her share of eye-fucks from the neighborhood dealers. Crack-selling crews known as bomb squads broke up in the Lumina's wake and regrouped in her rearview mirror, confident she wasn't Narcotics.

The canvass of TV Hill this morning had been fruitless.

The residents who hadn't already gone to work had seen nothing. She and Finn had left by noon, knowing they'd have to recanvass the unanswered doors tomorrow. At the offices they'd pulled B. J. Beggs's record. It didn't surprise Kay that the girl had wriggled out of two prostitution charges. She'd looked like the kind of girl that had a way with the circuit court judges.

Finn had located Beggs's family in Wausau, Wisconsin, called local authorities to have them inform the girl's parents. Then they'd gone to her apartment. A technician met them there, but it was immediately clear they were wasting their time. Although dingy, nothing in Beggs's one-room, basement dive indicated any foul play. They'd gone over every scrap of paper in Beggs's apartment, searching for any link to Eales or Hagen or Arsenault. But after three hours, Finn had called it quits. They'd taped the door and left to meet up with Miller from the Northern District.

For two hours they beat the pavement with the Wilkens Avenue hookers. With their sweet talk and good looks, Finn and the young officer had fared better with the girls. Still, all they got was a vague description of the car Beggs had hopped into three nights ago. A big, black, shiny number. "New, like, with the fancy grill and all," they'd been told by a hooker named Daisy. "And the driver was blond, clean-cut, with a real white smile."

Now, behind the wheel of the police car, Kay let the steam of the city wash over her and steered east onto Pratt. Finn was still on Wilkens, milking the last of the girls for information. It was Finn who'd sent her home. "You look half-dead," he'd told her, and she'd thanked him for the compliment.

Kay was already imagining a shower and her cool sheets when her cell phone went off in the passenger seat. She caught it on the second ring, expecting Finn.

"Good evening, Detective Delaney." Scott Arsenault's voice was smooth and collected. "Did I catch you at a bad time?"

"I'm on the street, Scott. What's up?"

"It's about the victim they found this morning. I wondered if we could talk."

"You have something you want to share?"

"Possibly. Can we meet?"

"Sure. You could come by the office tomorrow morning."

"I was thinking tonight."

Kay stopped at the light on Greene. It would take only ten minutes to loop back and get Finn.

Checking for traffic in her rearview, she was about to put the Lumina into a U-ey when Scott said, "And not with your partner. I don't have anything to say to him."

When the light turned green, Kay still sat at the intersection. Deciding. She wouldn't go to Arsenault's condo. Not alone. And then she heard voices and music, background noise over the Web designer's cell. "Where are you?" she asked him.

"I'm at The Cosmo in Fells Point."

She knew the bar. "Good. I'll meet you there," and she disconnected before he could object.

Fifteen minutes later, Kay parked the Lumina in a tight spot along Fleet Street. The Cosmo had once been O'Toole's, a crowded sports pub and a regular nighttime address on the Western District radios until it had been converted into the retro-swanky lounge-bar. Now, with its hip lamps shaped like giant martini olives, with its electric-blue walls and piercing halogen microlights, The Cosmo catered to a hipper clientele: young professionals and rich college kids, with only a handful of patrons left over from the bar's rowdier days.

Three of those beer-guzzling O'Toole's castoffs occupied the tall-backed booth diagonal to Arsenault's. They
looked out of place in Fells Point. Billy-Bob, Billy-Bob,
and Billy-Bob. Kay met their slack-jawed stares as she slid
into Arsenault's booth.

"So why am I here, Scott?" she asked, arranging her
jacket over her holster, and wondering why all of a sudden
she felt as though she were on a date.

"Would you like a drink, Kay?" He lifted his empty
cocktail glass toward their waitress.

"No, thank you."

"Another one of these," he told the girl. "Only this time
could you tell the bartender I asked for it stirred. The gin
was bruised."

"I'll let him know. Anything for you?" the girl asked
Kay.

"Just a soda water."

When the waitress left, the three Billy-Bobs continued
to gawk at Arsenault's back, whispering and sniggering,
clearly mocking him. Kay wondered if Arsenault had
already said something to piss them off while he'd waited
for her.

"Why am I here?" she asked him again.

"You should order the mussels. Or the calamari.
They've got great seafood here."

"I didn't come to eat." Her words were strained. She
tried to temper her voice. "What's this about, Scott?"

Arsenault dragged a used olive skewer through spilt salt
across the black tabletop, tracing an abstract design. When
he met her gaze, he smiled. There seemed a shyness behind
those green eyes then. Or maybe it was flirtation. And Kay
questioned whether she'd really been called here tonight
because of the case.

"Scott?" she prompted again. "Why did you call me?"

He shrugged casually. "I've just been thinking."

"About what?"

"You and me, Kay." He looked at her as though searching for a reaction to his suddenly intimate tone and the evocativeness of his statement. "You know, we're not that different really."

"How do you mean?"

"Well, for one, there's our mutual fascination with murder and psychopathology."

Kay nodded, but doubted Scott Arsenault had any idea what she saw day in and day out. It was one thing to look at photos of dead bodies in textbooks, quite another to stand over one in a back alley. She thought of Beggs this morning.

Still, if Arsenault had something to share . . . "Okay," she said, "let's talk about that. Your interest in this case is obviously more than just a passing diversion. I mean, you've really done your homework with this one. Hell, I bet you know more about Eales than I ever could."

Arsenault seemed to lap up the compliment.

"So why don't you give me your take on these latest murders?" she asked.

"Aha, I'm right then. The girl in the trash this morning *is* related." His face lit up, reflecting a pride in his acumen.

Even without acknowledging the accuracy of his observation, Kay knew she was tiptoeing through a minefield. "What's your take, Scott?"

He obliterated his design in the salt and sat back. "Well, come on, Kay, how can I possibly comment on murders I know so little about?"

His eyes never left hers, and Kay had trouble reading them now. But she knew Arsenault was pumping her, and she knew how to pump him in return, get his take on the new murders without ever crossing the line.

"Forget these new ones, Scott. Focus on the first three. The women Bernard killed," she said, even though she had problems believing it now.

"So these new murders *are* related."

"I didn't say that." But he understood.

"All right then. I think you have to start with motive. You have to understand this guy. Get in his head."

"Okay. What about motive then?"

"There are lots of potential motives. Fear. Mental illness. Greed. Honor. Jealousy. Power. Revenge. Self-defense."

Kay was aware of the Billy-Bobs watching. She lowered her voice. "And what's this guy's motive?"

Arsenault paused, giving the question consideration. "I think, based on the fact that the vics were all washed, and kept for some time"—his tone was suddenly flat—"I think maybe he likes them cold."

"What do you mean?"

"Necrophilia."

Kay thought of Alexander Hagen and the accusations Bernard had made years ago.

"And what about the bleeding?" she asked. "Why do you think he bled them?"

"Maybe he's wanting to stall the decay."

"I don't understand."

"The organisms that cause decomposition actually use the blood as their conduit. So a body that has been bled won't putrefy as quickly. You won't get the normal rate of gases and bloating."

"You learned this from your books, I hope."

"Of course, Kay." He smiled.

With the arrival of their waitress, Arsenault sampled his martini, then spat it back into the glass. "Did you even tell him I wanted it stirred?" he asked the girl, handing the glass back.

From the other table Billy-Bob One silently mocked Arsenault behind his back. Kay overheard the word *fag*. Arsenault must have heard it as well; she could see the tension notch up in his face in spite of the outward calm he struggled to maintain.

Kay waited for the waitress to leave with Arsenault's rejected drink. "So do your books give you any other reasons why a guy like this bleeds his victims?" she asked, realizing too late that she'd slipped into the present tense. "Or how?"

"How? Well, they'd have to be unconscious when he bled them, right? You don't bleed if you're dead. But you're on the right track by asking *why*. It's the bloodletting that's going to give you answers. You need to figure out *why* he's draining their blood."

"Any suggestions? Besides this decomposition theory?"

"Could be anything. Some bizarre cleansing ritual, maybe. Or maybe he keeps the blood."

"You think he drinks it?" She'd heard of such things.

"Possibly. I've even read a case where some psycho artist used human blood as an additive for his paints. There are all kinds of possibilities. But if you can figure out his reasons, if you can come closer to understanding why he kills, I think it can lead you to the who. So you're thinking Bernard didn't kill those women, aren't you, Kay?"

She shrugged, sipped at her iced soda water. "What do *you* think?"

"Like I said before, Bernard's probably more than capable of murder, but to pull off such perfect disposals? Face it, if he hadn't gone off on you and your partner a year ago, he may never have been caught. You had nothing on him until then."

"So what if he had help?"

Arsenault appeared to consider this new angle for a

moment. "If Bernard did kill those women," he said finally, "then, yeah, maybe someone could have helped him clean up. Someone with brains. Someone who knew what he was doing."

"You know," Kay said, sitting back in the booth, "my partner thinks it's you."

"Me?" Arsenault allowed himself a smirk then. "And what do *you* think?"

She gave him another shrug. "For procedure's sake, maybe I should ask where you were Saturday night."

"Is that when this last girl was killed?"

"Best guess."

"I was home. Alone, of course. I just don't seem to have much luck in the alibi department, do I?"

"Guess not. Do you have a girlfriend, Scott?" The question had been professional, but the second Kay asked it she realized the suggestiveness of the query—sitting in a bar with a man who was clearly interested. "It's just that given your lack of an alibi, I was only curious."

Kay's attempt to recover set a smile on Arsenault's face. He leaned forward again, his hand sliding across the table to where she held her soda.

"I work long hours," he explained. "And I love my work. But I don't need to explain that to you, do I? You know the toll of dedication, I'm sure. Of course, with the right person, I'd have no problems making adjustments. Making time."

When she felt the caress of his finger against the back of her hand, Kay lifted the soda to her lips.

"Are you seeing anyone, Kay?"

But she didn't have to answer. Their waitress appeared with Arsenault's martini. Regret passed over his face as he sat back to make room for the drink.

This time the girl didn't stick around for the taste test.

Arsenault eyed the bartender across the room as he brought the thin-stemmed glass to his lips.

The rest happened too fast. Kay had barely registered one of the Billy-Bobs standing up from the neighboring booth and starting past them when Arsenault swung the glass out.

"Oh, for crying out loud," Arsenault shouted, "are you putting it through a fucking blender?" But his last words faded as his hand collided with Billy-Bob's groin behind him. Gin and vermouth sprayed out, soaking the faded denim of the man's crotch.

"You little pansy-ass fag."

Arsenault's surprise was momentary. "What did you call me?"

"You heard me, asswipe."

Arsenault shot out of the booth. So fast that even Billy-Bob seemed temporarily stunned. There was the sound of shattering glass, and as Kay stood, she saw the broken cocktail glass in Arsenault's hand, the bowl gone and the jagged stem now pressed into the brute's throat.

"Scott, leave him."

Billy-Bob's eyes were wide, his head thrust back to escape the pressure of the sharp stem. In her peripheral, Kay was aware of the other two Billy-Bobs clambering out of their booth.

"Scott, he's not worth it," she said. "Let's go."

But there was no breaking through the red rage. A muscle twitched wildly along Arsenault's jaw. There was a fierceness in his whisper. "I could open you up right here," he said. "What do you think about that, you ignorant fuck, huh?" The stem pressed tighter and a bead of blood broke the skin at the tip of the stem.

The music in the bar droned on, but the din had lowered. Kay sensed the eyes on them.

Then, Billy-Bob One swung at Arsenault, sucker punching him from below. Arsenault folded. And Kay moved in.

"Come on, guys, it's over." She angled herself between the brute and Arsenault, almost knocking him off his feet as she did. Somewhere behind her she was aware of a bouncer moving in, but not before Billy-Bob swore and went to throw another punch.

Kay made a grab for him before realizing she was too close. His upward swing clipped her, his elbow connecting sharply with her lip. For a second she saw stars, felt the rush of endorphins. Then Kay felt the heat of blood. She sucked at it as the bouncer muscled in, hustling the boys back. Jostling and shoving. Swearing.

Arsenault was still heaving for air as she escorted him down the row of booths and to the door. "Put it on his tab," she said to another bouncer on the way out.

"What the hell were you thinking in there?" she asked him once they hit the street. "Christ, did you seriously think you could take on those three Neanderthals?"

He didn't answer.

"I hope you don't do that on a regular basis," she added, "or one of these nights it'll be your body I'm standing over."

"I'm not a fag." Arsenault wheezed the words.

"And why would you think I'd even give two shits?" But Kay knew why.

He coughed several times, hacked up a wad of spit and sent it to the cobblestones. In the dim light, Kay didn't see any blood.

"Come on," she said, guiding him into the side alley that led to Fleet Street.

He coughed some more, this second fit preventing her from hearing the Billy-Bobs coming. One moment Arsenault was at her side, the next he was on the ground.

It was the same brute Arsenault had doused with the

martini that started the kicking, his heavy, military-style boot driving into the Web designer's side at least once before his buddies joined in.

"Hey!" Kay groped under her jacket for her shield. "Hey!" She yelled this time, grabbing the shoulder of the closest Billy-Bob and spinning him around.

From the wildness in the brute's eyes she knew he wouldn't have thought twice about taking a swing, but Kay shoved the shield into his face.

"Back the fuck off. All of you! Now!" Her jacket brushed back, she had one hand on the butt of her nine. The shield was up and steady in her hand as the three goons backed away from the gagging heap that was Arsenault.

"You're a fucking cop?" the first one muttered, a small trickle of blood still marking his throat.

"Damn right. And you guys can consider this the biggest fucking break of your lives that I'm not going to haul you in. Now get the fuck out of here."

Before the three of them had even hit the end of the alley, she was at Arsenault's side, hauling him up.

"I'm fine." He brushed off his ruined chinos and straightened his hair. "Really."

But Kay knew the bruises he'd have in the morning would not be restricted to his ego. She walked him out to Fleet Street then, his arm over her shoulders as she guided him to the Lumina. In the glow of a streetlamp she checked him over.

"I'm all right, Kay," he assured her again.

"You're damn lucky. Those guys could have really messed you up. I don't know what the hell got into you," she said, remembering the flare of rage that had come over him. She thought she'd had Arsenault pegged.

She unlocked the Lumina and fetched a tissue and pressed it to her bleeding lip.

"I know it was wrong," he said. "It's just guys like that . . . I'm *not* gay."

"So you said."

She wasn't sure what prompted him then. One moment he was staring at her, the next he'd taken the tissue from her hands and was dabbing at her cut lip. The boldness of his move caught Kay off guard.

When he leaned in, one hand braced against the roof of the Lumina, the other lifting her chin to the light as though to inspect it, Kay wasn't entirely sure of his intentions. But then Arsenault moved in, and she knew he was going to kiss her.

His advance didn't surprise her. What *did* surprise Kay was that a part of her wanted him to. It had been a long time since someone had shown interest. A long time since she'd let someone close enough. And she was only human, after all.

In the dim glow of the streetlamp she saw the desire in Arsenault's face, but in her mind's eye there was Finn.

Pushing him back, Kay ducked under his arm. Behind her, Arsenault groaned, and when she looked at him again, she saw his disappointment.

"Come on," she said, realizing she was shaking. "I'm taking you home."

30

THE SUN HAD SIZZLED the dew off the shallow front yards of the row houses sloping up to Television Hill. There was the smell of mulch, the lingering of yesterday's garbage, and—for Kay—the memory of B. J. Beggs's body splayed out in the back alley.

Kay knocked on her sixteenth door of the morning.

She'd been recanvassing the neighborhood since seven. Not knowing how late Finn had been out on Wilkens last night, she hadn't wanted to wake him. She'd left a message for him on his desk, then drove to the district office on Cold Spring, where she enlisted the help of two uniformed officers.

On the concrete porch a plastic planter hung from the rail, the contents dead. Several editions of the *Sun* lay in the weather-bleached recycle bin. She rapped against the screen door's lower panel, loud enough to wake the dead, let alone the living late for work. In the second-floor windows, closed blinds hung askew.

A strange déjà vu twisted in her gut then. Licking the tenderness of her lip, Kay pushed the memories aside and instead thought of Scott Arsenault.

He'd been silent during the short drive back to his building from the bar last night, and when she'd said goodnight, he'd turned in the passenger seat, and again she'd wondered if he would try to kiss her. She'd actually felt flattered by the Web designer's interest last night. For the first time in longer than she could remember, it made her feel alive, part of the real world.

Knocking again, Kay eyed the flyers that jammed the misshapen tin mailbox mounted next to the door. Perhaps the house was a rental, sitting vacant between tenants. She moved to the bow window on the main floor, cupped her hands to shield the daylight, and peered through the crack in the curtains. There was little to make out. Dim outlines of scant furnishings. An oval mirror on the opposite wall reflected what little light bled through the drapes.

She was about to knock a third time when her cell went off.

"You still on TV Hill?" Finn asked over the digital connection.

"Yeah." She turned down the steps of the empty house. "What's up?"

"I'm at the ME's. Jonesy's starting on the girl. I thought you'd want to be here."

"I'm on my way."

Leaving the two uniforms to finish the canvass, it took Kay almost twenty minutes to battle morning traffic across the city and find a parking spot on Penn Street. Finn was waiting for her outside the OCME, crushing a cigarette into the sidewalk.

"I thought Jonesy wasn't doing her until later," she said as they took the elevator down to the autopsy suite.

"Guess he figured he'd get an early jump on things. He's just wrapping up. What's with the lip?" he asked, pointing.

"I'll tell you about it later." She swung open the steel doors of the main suite and crossed the floor. "Sorry I'm late, Jonesy."

"Wow, who clipped you?" the ME asked.

"It's a long story. What have you got on our girl so far?"

"Ketamine hydrochloride." Jonesy handed her the tox results across Beggs's body. "A dissociative anesthetic. Manufactured by Parke-Davis, marketed as Ketalar, and related to phencyclidine."

"PCP?" Finn asked.

"Yeah, only ketamine's safer, and much shorter-acting. It was originally created for children and was the anesthetic of choice in Vietnam. Works as a hallucinogenic. Causes the patient to feel dissociated from their body, making it possible to carry out surgical procedures. It's still used in third-world countries, but here it's mostly utilized in veterinary medicine."

"So how does someone get the stuff?" Kay asked.

"You can buy anything on the streets. Illegal ketamine's usually stolen from vet hospitals in its pharmaceutical form. Users either inject it intramuscularly or cook it down into powder."

Jonesy half-rolled Beggs's body on the cutting table and pointed to a perfectly round bruise circling a puncture mark behind the prostitute's left hip. "Given the injection site, it's not likely she did it herself."

"When you say short-acting, what are we talking about?" Kay asked as Jonesy let the body slide back.

"Depends on the dose. Full onset can take anywhere from one to four minutes, with the total trip lasting twenty or thirty. Residual effects can linger for an hour or more."

"Trip? So people do this stuff recreationally?"

"Ever since the sixties. It was called Vitamin K back then. Resurfaced in the last few years on the rave scene as Special K."

"And what does it do?"

"Blocks the nerve paths, impairing motor skills, often simulating paralysis, but without depressing pulmonary or circulatory function. It's also used as a date-rape drug."

"So you're saying it paralyzes them?" Kay asked, her mind reeling at the possibilities.

"Depending on the dose, yes."

"So how much did our girl have in her system?"

"Can't say for sure. Not without a time of death. Putrefaction was likely delayed because of the blood loss. Blood provides a channel for the spread of putrefactive organisms within the body. Plus I think he kept her cool ..."

But Kay was hearing Arsenault's words now. . . . *he's wanting to stall the decay.* So Arsenault had been right.

"But the ketamine didn't kill her?" Finn asked.

"No." Jonesy held up one of the girl's slashed wrists. "Exsanguination. The radial artery was sliced. Very clean. He knew what he was doing. This girl bled out till there was nothing left."

"So definitely not a suicide?"

"Not with the ketamine in her system. I doubt she could have held a knife." Jonesy leaned back, surveying his morning's work. Beggs had been opened and emptied, her individual organs examined, packaged in red plastic bags, and returned to the body's cavity to be closed up again.

"What about the bruising?" Kay pointed to the marks on Beggs's arms and legs. They were more noticeable this morning than yesterday. "How old are those?"

"Most, I'd guess, were sustained just prior to her death. These"—he pointed to the backs of Beggs's wrists and arms—"these look like handprints. Like she'd been grabbed. The rest are random."

"She struggled then?"

"I'd say yes."

Kay looked again at the girl's remains, willing them to provide her with the answers. *What did he do to you?*

"She's also been washed," Jonesy said. "Some kind of industrial soap. There's not much evidence on her. Trace or fiber."

"Prints?"

"We fumed with cyanoacrylate and hit her with the lasers. Nothing."

"What about inside her? Did you find anything?" Kay asked.

"Traces of spermicide. But no seminal fluids. She made sure her trick used a condom. But who knows if it was the same guy that killed her?"

"Nothing forcible?"

"Doesn't look like."

"Any way of knowing when she'd had intercourse last?"

"Hey, I'm a good cutter, Kay, but I'm not psychic." Jonesy shot her a smile. It faded when she didn't reciprocate.

"Any ideas why he'd bleed her?" she asked eventually.

"I'm not a forensic psychologist either."

"Come on, Jonesy, you've seen a lot. Anything come to mind?"

"Bleeding a victim . . . I don't know. Could be anthropophagy."

"What's that?" Finn asked.

"Vampirism. Drinking of blood. Or it could be a cult thing, or maybe he's reenacting some scenario."

"Funeral homes drain the blood from the bodies," Kay said.

"Sure. But they use an embalming machine. A Portiboy. Pumps a formaldehyde-based fluid in through the carotid while forcing the blood out the jugular. They don't cut open the wrists." Jonesy snapped off his latex gloves. "It would probably help if you knew what this guy's goal was. The body or the blood."

"There're easier ways to get blood." Finn began untying the paper gown he wore over his suit.

"Then maybe it's the process he's after." Kay looked down at Beggs's wrists, seeing the white glare of bone and tendons that lay beneath the muscle. Beggs's life had pumped from those gashes while she'd lain unconscious. *Is that what you're after? You want to see the life drain out of her?*

"I wish I had more for you," Jonesy said. "But given how clean she is, she's not telling me much."

They thanked him and left the cutting room. Out in the corridor they tossed the paper gowns in the bin.

"So you gonna tell me about the fat lip?" Finn asked again.

"Bar fight." She caught his side glance. "It's not what you think. I wasn't drinking. I was with Arsenault."

"Last night?"

Kay nodded and punched the up button of the elevator.

"He called me. On my way home from Wilkens last night. Wanted to talk, so I met him at The Cosmo."

She saw Finn's jaw tighten. "You could have come got me."

"Yeah, but he wasn't going to talk with you there."

"He's a suspect, Kay."

She didn't argue, even though she didn't agree.

"It was a public place, Finn. I had the situation under control." She thought of Arsenault leaning into her, her back pressed against the Lumina. "Nothing was going to happen."

"Nothing except for that fat lip of yours."

"It was an accident. Really. A couple drunk Neanderthals looking to pick a fight on a hot night."

"Uh-huh." He didn't sound convinced. "So did you get anything from Arsenault?"

The doors opened to the lobby and Kay had to squint against the glare of the sun on the marble panels of the OCME's foyer. "I don't know how much stock to put in this, but he suggested a necrophilia angle."

Finn shook his head as though considering and dismissing the theory in the same breath simply because it came from Arsenault. "The guy's not right, Kay. Don't let him fool you."

"He's not fooling me." She sensed Finn's possessiveness again, only this time she wasn't sure if she should find it insulting or charming.

"He's connected to all this, Kay. Somehow."

"I agree, but the more I talk to him, the more I'm convinced it's not him we should be looking at." Still, Kay couldn't forget the spontaneous rage she'd seen explode from Arsenault last night. She could still see the brute's head snapped back in fear, the jagged edge of the martini glass's stem jammed up against his stubbled throat, and the thin line of blood that sprang from its point. And she could still feel the crawling suspicion she'd had last night when she'd actually contemplated the possibility of Scott Arsenault killing.

31

IT HAD BEEN A LONG DAY of chasing down names and addresses and anything else connected to B. J. Beggs. Still, they wound up with nothing. Whoever had picked up the young prostitute three nights ago was not a Wilkens regular. No one recognized the late-model sedan, had noted even a partial tag number, or remembered seeing it before. Finn and Kay had hit a wall.

It was late when Finn pulled up to Kay's front door, and he was surprised when she invited him up. Now, as he listened to her shower running down the hall, he wondered if the only reason she'd asked him up was to discuss the case.

"Maybe we need to rule out Scott Arsenault," Kay shouted from the shower.

Finn made his way down the hall to the open doorway. He watched her blurred silhouette behind the tempered-glass stall doors, unable to avert his gaze. "How do we do that when the genius can't even come up with a decent alibi?" he asked.

"What about prints? The Mobile Crime Lab came up with all kinds of latents from Eales's house, right? What about running those against Arsenault's?"

"You mean, from his rape file?"

"Exactly. The charges were dropped, but he's probably still on Printrak. If there's a match, then we can put him in Eales's house."

"And if there isn't, that doesn't exclude him from being there either." Finn sipped the glass of Wink she'd poured him. The soda was flat. He pushed away from the doorframe and wandered to her office.

Kay's monitor glared red and white. Finn recognized the Eales website message board. He didn't doubt Kay read the messages every night, searching for anything that might resemble a lead.

"What about this website of his?" he asked, heading back to the bathroom. "How about subpoenaing the wiseass for a list of the dipshits on his chat group?"

"Sure, but it's probably not going to help. When I dropped him off last night, I asked about getting a list. He said most of them use non-server-based addresses. Almost impossible to track," she said over the pounding water. "He's going to try though. I also asked him to remove a lot of the details on the site."

"And?"

"And he agreed."

"Guess you do have a way with him, huh?" he said, coming back to the bathroom door.

But if Kay heard his remark, or the jealousy in his voice, she chose to ignore it.

Through the textured glass and the steam, Finn watched her soap herself and wished he'd never come upstairs.

"The list I really want," Kay said, tilting her head back to rinse, "is Hagen's."

Alexander Hagen hadn't proven cooperative. They'd called the funeral director twice already for the list of employee names.

They'd also pulled the fifteen-year-old police reports corresponding with Eales's accusations against the old man. It had been nothing but bullshit. No evidence. No other complainants. The case had been dropped within days by the investigating officers. But Finn couldn't escape the feeling that there was more behind Eales's accusations than a simple case of a horny teenager being denied access to Hagen's only daughter.

And then there was Kay's theory, spawned by Arsenault. Necrophilia. The connections to the Parkview Funeral Home were too obvious to ignore.

"Well, if you ask me," Finn said, still watching Kay, "Hagen's got to have the mother of all hate-ons for Eales. First the accusations. I mean, something like that, if it had gone public, the old man would have been ruined. And then he's got Eales pawing all over his daughter."

"What are you thinking?"

"Just that if anyone actually wanted Eales locked up, it'd be old man Hagen."

"You mean, set Eales up?" Kay turned off the water and Finn turned his back. "Look, Finn, I agree, there's something wonky about the Hagens. And the old man's definitely hiding something. But to set someone up as a serial killer . . . come on, it's a bit of a stretch."

"Yeah." Finn left the doorway and wandered back down the hall. "I think we need to talk to Patsy again," he called over his shoulder. "She's too involved. I don't for a second buy that she came to Eales's rescue *after* his arrest. Nobody, I don't care how fucked-up, does that. She's probably been seeing him all along. And I'm sure she knows more than she's letting on."

"Like maybe if Eales had help."

Kay had posed the theory earlier today, and Finn agreed it had merit.

When she came out of the bathroom, she was wrapped in a light terry robe, the sash snug around her small waist. "Patsy would know who his friends were at least. If someone helped Eales get rid of those bodies a year ago, maybe the guy's still keeping the fantasy alive. And maybe Hagen knows him."

"Or . . . maybe we really *are* looking at a damn copycat," Finn said, trying to get them back to the hard facts of the case, rather than on wild theories and hypotheticals. "I don't see anything about Beggs's murder that isn't on Arsenault's website. And the ketamine's new too."

Kay's face was tight. She looked as overwhelmed by the rampant possibilities as he was. Fingering back her wet hair, she shook her head. "I need a drink."

When she came back to the living room to join him on the couch, her beer was already half-drunk.

"Why did you ask me up here, Kay?" He needed to know.

She said nothing for a moment, then: "I didn't want to be alone."

Their silence then was uncomfortable. He wanted to say so many things but didn't know how. As he stared at Kay, a year of waiting hit him. A year of sitting on the sidelines of her life, waiting for this day.

And now that it was here, Finn felt powerless.

Kay caught his stare.

"I worry about you," he told her, admitting the truth at last.

"I don't want you to."

He washed down his laugh with the last of the bitter soda. "Trust me, it's not something I can control. I've tried."

"Finn, listen, you're a good friend. The best I have. I—"

"You know something? I don't want to be your god-damn friend." He set his glass down on the coffee table a little too hard, and when he stood, he saw the surprise on her face. "I should go."

"Finn, wait." Kay caught him at the door.

He already had it open, one foot out.

"Damn it. Wait." Her hand closed around his wrist.

But when he turned, she only stared, the rush of emotions behind her eyes too scattered for him to interpret.

"Don't you need anything, Kay?" he asked finally. "Don't you ever need *someone* in your life? Someone who gives a shit about you?"

She was struggling. Biting her lip. Searching for an answer. "Yes." The word caught in her throat. "Yes. I do. Okay? I do. Now just close the door."

Finn did.

"Listen, I'm sorry," she said. "I should never have shut you out."

She looked small then, standing there in her robe, the rawness of her emotions unraveling in her voice.

"It wasn't fair of me, Finn. I know that. I was only thinking of myself. I'm just . . . I'm fucked-up, okay? And—"

He didn't let her finish. When he pulled her to him, he felt her body trembling. His kiss was frenzied. Desperate. Driven by a year of missing her.

He wasn't sure who locked the door then. He heard the dead bolt drive home, felt her heat press against his body. He drew her close, devouring her. And when she started to pull away, he held her tight. In that moment, if she'd said no, Finn wasn't sure he would have been able to stop.

But Kay didn't say no.

The path to her bed wasn't straight. Staggering and stumbling down the hall. Past her office and every tacked-up memory of Bernard Eales and Joe Spencer. Pulling at each other. Tearing at each other's clothes. The familiar dance. Just the two of them. Not Eales. Not Spencer. Not the job.

He threw aside the comforter. Fumbling with the sash

of her robe, then pushing back the terry. His hands took her in, sliding across damp skin, over familiar planes and curves. Her small breasts fitting in each hand.

She unzipped his slacks, slid her hand beneath. And she held him as a moan slipped from her mouth and into his. When he lowered her to the bed, she pulled him with her. Arching. Clutching. Drawing away briefly, he reached for the nightstand where he knew she kept the condoms. He slid open the drawer and heard the thud of something heavy shift inside. In the dark, he could just make out the lines of her old Glock, and he knew why she kept it there.

He felt Kay stiffen beneath him, worried the reminder might cause her to withdraw. When he looked into her face, the pale glow from the streetlamp outside washed over her confusion.

"I don't know what I'm doing anymore, Finn," she said, a bare and uneasy honesty in her whisper.

"Then just let me love you," he said.

A half nod. Her legs circled him, urging him into her rhythm.

It had been too long. He wanted to have her hard and fast, in the way their sweaty athletics had often been. Driving and all-consuming. The kind of exhausting all-out physicality that could—even if only for a few moments—block out the job, block out everything they saw and dealt with daily.

But tonight was about passion. A passion Finn prayed was mutual. It had to be slower this time. It had to last. Tonight he needed to lower the volume on Kay's need and his own. Draw it out. As long as he was making love to her, as long as he was inside her he could at least imagine they were together again.

Kay was frantic though. Her hands, her body, her heat, urging him on. Driving him to a climax he dammed back as long as he could. But when she came, when her tremors clenched around him, Finn couldn't hold back any longer. He emptied himself deep inside her and fought back the disappointment. It was everything he'd wanted, everything he'd imagined for months. And still, it wasn't enough.

It wasn't until later, as the sound of traffic down on the Key Highway ebbed, and the city quieted, that Kay spoke, her voice thin in the dark. "I'm sorry, Finn."

"For what?"

He heard a car pass by the end of Hamburg Street. A breeze blew the sheer curtains inward, then sucked them out again.

"For everything," she whispered eventually.

And Finn held her tighter.

32

"So you're seeing Finn again?"

"I guess so."

"Well, you said you're sleeping with him."

"Yeah, but . . ."

"But what, Kay?"

"But it's going to take more than one night of sex to repair the damage I've inflicted on this relationship, isn't it?" Kay shifted on Constance O'Donnell's couch, the leather cool under her palms.

She'd woken at 2 a.m. from the same old dream. The memory of it clinging to her like a thin sweat. She'd thrown back the sheets and stared at the ceiling, listening to Finn's breathing. When he'd woken, he'd reached for her and she'd turned his comfort into sex. Only this time she let him take his time.

Slow or fast, Finn was a skilled lover. The best she'd had. But making love to Finn slow made Kay feel like a better person. When he came inside her, she felt that she was giving instead of just taking. That she was his lover. His partner.

Sex for them had always been an attentive give-and-take. But last night had mostly been about "taking" for Kay. Selfishly, she'd answered her own needs above Finn's. She'd needed to feel consumed. To find that sweet oblivion once again.

But that wasn't what she wanted from Finn. Not ultimately. She *wanted* to give the way she had before. She wanted to be that better person Finn deserved.

"So do you think you're ready for a relationship again?" Constance asked. "A few weeks ago, when you admitted to missing Finn, you said you didn't think seeing him would be a good idea. That you didn't want to use him as a crutch, and you needed to heal first. Do you feel you're beyond that now?"

Kay nodded. "I think so." But the truth was she *didn't* know, and now she regretted having brought up the subject.

She eyed the soft leather briefcase she'd dropped next to the coffee table—the real reason she hadn't canceled her appointment this morning.

"I need your help," Kay said, feeling the gears shift.

"That's what I'm here for."

"Actually, it's on a case." Kay nodded to the bottom two shelves of a cherry bookcase that dominated the south wall of the room. She'd noted the texts' spines on her second visit a year ago. "I know you've got an interest in psychopathology. Sexual deviance, homicide."

"It's only ever been an extracurricular interest. I'm certainly not qualified to give advice on a police investigation, if that's what you're after."

"Then how about an unqualified opinion? I'm allowed to talk about anything I want in these sessions, right?"

"Of course. But you know any input I offer won't hold up in court."

Kay nodded. She'd already considered this, *knew* she'd have to move carefully on anything Constance gave her, since it could be challenged down the road by a defense attorney. "I just need a sounding board."

Kay reached for the briefcase. Sliding out the files, she fanned the photos across the glass coffee table. Annie Harris. Roma Chisney. The Jane Doe. And now Valley and Bobby Joe Beggs.

Constance took them in, silently examining the five-by-sevens, before pointing at Beggs's: "Was she posed like this?"

"No. She fell out of the trash."

"And what about her?" She picked up the photo of the Jane Doe—her nude body laid out in Leakin Park.

"We don't think she was posed either. It looked more like he chucked her body down this slope." Kay indicated in another photo the steep embankment that chiseled down from the roadway above. "And there was no indication he went down with her."

"But she's clean. No debris from the trip down the slope?"

"We had rain that night."

"So none of them were posed?"

"No. It looked more like they'd been dumped."

Constance set her clipboard onto the table next to her chair. Kay saw the flash of notes in elegant penmanship. How many times had she wondered what Constance wrote in that notepad of hers? And now, with the notes in full view, Kay didn't care.

Constance leaned forward, elbows on her knees, and skimmed through more photos.

"Can you tell me anything about their killer?" Kay asked when the silence became unbearable.

"I thought you had Bernard Eales for these?"

"These two are new. We're trying to establish whether they're copycats, or if . . ."

"If you got the wrong guy?" Constance finished for her.

Kay nodded. "I need an objective opinion on this. You don't know Eales like I do. You're not biased."

"So I'm to profile your killer and you'll see if it fits?"

Kay shrugged. That was exactly what she was hoping for. *And then find something I missed.* Because the thought that a year ago she could have missed a critical detail was too tough to swallow.

"Kay, I'm not an expert. Why not take all this to the FBI? Get a real profiler?"

"Based on my own experience, a profiler's not going to tell me anything you and I can't figure out on this one."

Kay remembered the Randal Hinch case, early in her homicide career—a pedophile whose carnage was a string of young boys' bodies, left strangled in abandoned buildings. It appeared the twenty-five-year-old had heard voices most of his adult life, and their volume had been increasing, leading him to murder his victims instead of simply scarring them for life.

Overenthusiastic, Kay had pushed for a profiler on the case, in spite of Spencer's loud disdain for the process. Three suits had descended upon the unit, sitting in the cramped and hot boardroom, and at the end of the day she and Spence had gotten nothing more than a plate of hard-shelled crabs down at Cross Street on the FBI's tab. In the end, it had been Kay's own intuition and Spencer's doggedness that had figured out Hinch.

"All right," Constance said at last. "I'll offer what I can."

Kay spent the next half hour briefing her on the five

cases, ending with Arsenault's website and the details that had been laid out for all of cyberspace to see.

"So do you think these could have been committed by the same person?" Kay asked after Constance had examined the photos and autopsy reports.

"Sure. But that's an unprofessional opinion."

"So what kind of person are we looking at? To have pulled these off?"

"You're wanting me to assume we're looking at one killer for all five?"

Kay was going with her gut now, even though she didn't like what it was telling her. "Yes."

"Well, I'd have to say these are definitely well-orchestrated crimes. You say all the victims had been cleaned?"

"Meticulously. Even their hair."

"And no one witnessed these girls' abductions?"

"All but one worked as prostitutes. They were easy targets."

"Still, he managed to avoid witnesses. And he kept this last body a couple days. He definitely falls into the category of organized offenders."

Psychological theories. Sociopathic versus psychopathic. The kinds of hypotheses that rarely came into play while on the job in Baltimore City, where homicides were predominantly drug- or gang-related. Kay had read the differences between organized and disorganized, the principles of sexual homicide. She let Constance give her version.

"He plans these abductions," Constance said thoughtfully. "Probably takes his time to choose his victims. All these girls are similar in stature and age, even if their looks vary slightly. Most likely he stakes out an area in advance. With this burned victim, the witness, her abduction on campus took careful planning. The fact that she was burned, that she wasn't kept for a couple days like this last one, suggests her death may have served more than one purpose. Eliminating her as a witness could have been his primary goal.

"But all of these are organized. Premeditated. He's got a pattern he's following. With a *dis*organized offender, you're often looking at at least some form of psychosis. That's not present here. These aren't frenzied or blitz-style attacks. These are planned. He's fantasized about these beforehand."

Constance pulled out the photo of the Jane Doe lying in the leaves of Leakin Park. "Overall," she said, "he's got control of the situation. He transports the body. There's an absence of weapons and evidence, removal of the body from the primary crime scene. These are all signs of an organized mind. Also, his choice of victims points to his need for control. These women are all small. He doesn't want a struggle. He needs to be able to handle them through every stage of the fantasy as he plays it out."

"And that's why he drugs them?"

Constance nodded. "And the stun gun you mentioned with this burned victim. And the use of heroin with the first three victims. It's all about maintaining control so the fantasy can unfold as accurately as possible. Fantasy and ritual dominate the organized offender's way of working. You often see obsessive-compulsive behavior in these individuals and in their crime-scene patterns."

Kay's mind flashed to Scott Arsenault's medicine cabinet. The OCD prescriptions lining the shelves. Was it possible she was wrong about Scott?

"In the case studies I've read," Kay said, "it's usually the *dis*organized offender who keeps his victims' bodies." Wackos stashing body parts in their freezer, keeping them for years. Some even burying their victims, only to dig up body parts after the spring thaw to have sex with them.

"Your guy's different," Constance said. "He keeps them under controlled conditions, otherwise you'd see more advanced putrefaction. He uses them after they're dead but gets rid of them before they start decomposing."

"So we might be looking at a necrophilia angle?"

"That would be my guess."

"And the cuts to the chest?"

"If they were made postmortem, I'd say they were mutilation as a substitute for sex or as a way to demonstrate his control over them. Or maybe they're the result of a deep-seated anger that's playing into his fantasy. Were there any foreign objects found in any of these women? Inserted into their body cavities? Any mutilation of the genitalia?"

"No. So you're saying these murders are sexual?"

"Definitely. Control and sex."

"Even though we found no indicators of rape?" Kay asked.

"Just because there's no penetration doesn't mean you don't have a sexual act. He could be masturbating. The homicide triggers a sexual reaction or fantasy, and if he has a history of solo sex or has difficulty with interpersonal relationships, he'll revert to masturbation rather than pene-tration."

"Even when the victim's dead."

"*Especially* when they're dead. That's when he has the ultimate control over them, when he feels the most empowered."

"And then he washes them because he's ejaculated on them?"

"That's one possibility. He's getting rid of evidence. Maybe he's educated himself on forensics. He knows about trace evidence, fibers, prints, DNA coming back to him." Constance gestured to the photos. "These are all secondary crime scenes. Even if you had the primary scene, I doubt you'd find much evidence. This guy's probably a clean freak."

Kay had more questions but the session timer went off, its muted click marking the end of her fifty-minute hour with Constance.

Kay gathered the photos. "So, based on all this," she asked, "on the fact that he's just leaving them to be found, do you get the impression this guy wants to get caught?"

"Eventually most serial murderers do," Constance said. "I'd say this killer's actions certainly point to a desire to be discovered, especially with the last one left in the trash. At the same time, I wouldn't say he appears to be in any hurry to get caught."

33

"JUST WHEN I THINK all the killable people in Baltimore are either dead or locked up, we get another murder." Over the phone Kay heard Vicki snap open a can of soda and imagined her sitting behind the towers of files that generally occupied her desk over at the State's Attorney's Office.

"They just keep falling," Vicki went on, exhaustion in her voice. "All the little drug boys on their corners. Barely scrape one up off the pavement and another takes his place."

"Is Finn still over at the courthouse?" Kay asked.

"Last I saw. Judge Reager hadn't adjourned by the time I left my trial."

Kay leaned back in her chair and looked through the sixth-floor windows of Headquarters to where traffic downtown began to congest. While Finn was in court on another case, she'd spent most of the afternoon at her desk, reviewing reports and compiling the Beggs file.

"So, you're calling for an update?" she asked Vicki.

"No. I caught up with Finn already, warming the bench outside Reager's courtroom. He told me about the comparison you had Latents run on this Arsenault guy's prints against Eales's house. Seemed a little pissed that there were no matches. Finn really does have a thing for this guy. Just itching to get into his condo. What's your take on him?"

"I'm not sure yet."

"Well, like I told Finn, until you guys get me some probable cause, I can't help you with a warrant."

"I know."

"Listen, if you want to get together earlier on Saturday, before the symphony, we can chew over some of this stuff. Maybe come up with a new angle to get this guy."

"Sure, Vick." But Kay knew that if there was any way for Finn to have gotten into Arsenault's condo, he would have found it by now.

As Kay hung up, she wondered if she *should* talk to Arsenault again, this time with Finn. Based on the informal profile Constance had given her today, Kay wondered if she *was* wrong about the Web designer. Or maybe her doubt came from a different place.

Kay's gaze dropped to the photo propped on the windowsill. She'd never gotten around to framing the snapshot, and now a film of construction dust dulled its colors. A technician had taken it of her and Spence—at Spence's request—on the scene of her first arrest in Homicide. She looked dour, half-shaken and half-victorious after the Quick Response Team had busted down several doors to flush out her suspect. But Spence smiled, still pumped with adrenaline in his Kevlar vest and backward Orioles cap.

This one's for you, Spence. I'm getting this son of a bitch for you.
But what the hell was she missing?

Kay looked again at Jonesy's autopsy reports, studying the injection site, the bruises, the cuts to Beggs's sternum.

What was she *not* seeing?

A good investigation had direction. Focus. They had neither.

In a perfect world, a good investigation was linear. Cause and effect. One witness leading to the next, until a suspect emerged.

And a good investigation flushed out a suspect quickly, then focused on the accumulation of enough solid evidence to nail the bastard when it went to trial. But here . . . they had no direction. No answers.

Just trees, Kay thought. Too many trees to see the goddamned forest. Scott Arsenault. The website. Patricia Hagen. Alex Hagen. The funeral home. Bernard Eales's accusations of necrophilia.

Kay closed her eyes and mentally pushed everything aside. When a case got this messy, Spencer would have told her to go back to the beginning. Back to that first crime scene. To where it all started.

Eales's house.

Three women had died there. That was indisputable. Of course, he'd never confessed to the murders, regardless of the evidence against him. Kay recalled the transcripts of Eales's interview five days after the beatdown, after he'd already been grilled by Gunderson and Sergeant Lutz on Spencer's shooting.

Varcoe and Holewinski had worked as a tag team, running Eales in circles over the prostitute murders. Around and around, trying to trip him up. Fourteen hours and he'd given them nothing incriminating. In the end, the evidence would have to convince the jury.

Throughout the interview Eales had maintained he suffered from alcoholic blackouts. Didn't remember how the women had died in his house. He remembered nothing between the time he brought the women home to when he found them dead.

He'd always maintained the women must have slashed their wrists themselves, even though he couldn't explain the coincidence of all *three* of them committing suicide in his house. No, he didn't wash them, he said. He'd found them in his tub. Guessed they'd taken a bath. All he did wrong was dump their bodies because he didn't want a bunch of cops ripping through his house.

Yes, the house.

Pushing aside the reports, Kay flipped through her case notebook, looking for the number. Then, after dialing, she listened to the hollow rings bleed out across the long-distance line until Billy Coombs answered. His voice sounded thin and thready.

"You want what exactly?" he asked after she explained the reason for her call.

"Permission to enter your brother's house," she said. "We could get a warrant, Mr. Coombs, but it's a lot of paperwork and signatures. I was hoping you might save me the labor. I'm assuming the house is in your name?"

"Yes, it is."

"All I'm after is a quick look around. I promise nothing will be removed or disturbed."

In the background she heard a voice over a PA system. Guessed she'd caught Coombs at his car dealership. When he didn't answer her right away, she debated lying, telling him whatever it took to get permission. But she didn't have to.

"Yeah, sure," he said. "I don't see why not. I don't know if anyone's been in the house since Bernard's arrest. In fact, maybe you can let me know if there's been any damage or vandalism?"

"Certainly."

"I guess I really should sell the thing. I just haven't had the time to go down there and clean the place up. You don't happen to know of any companies that do that sort of thing, do you, Detective? Clean up ... you know, houses where—"

"Actually, yes, there is a place I can put you in touch with." She searched her Rolodex for the number of the crime-scene detail company in Forest Hill that often came in after they'd finished with a scene. But only seconds after giving Coombs the number, Kay regretted the decision. Maybe it was too soon to have the house emptied. After all, there were still stones obviously left unturned.

"You'll want to talk to Jerry Bates," Coombs said then.

"That's your brother's neighbor, right?" Kay remembered the man's name from the file.

"Yeah. He lives a couple doors down. I'm sorry I don't know the number. I think he's got a key. He can let you in. That way you won't have to break any locks."

"Thanks, Mr. Coombs. By the way, how well do you know Mr. Bates?"

"Not at all."

"Do you know if he and your brother are close?"

"They're neighbors. That's all I know."

Neighbors. But it was from Bates's house that Eales had finally surrendered to police after the beatdown. Maybe Bates and Eales were *more* than neighbors.

She should have thought of Jerry Bates sooner. If they *were* looking for someone who might have helped Bernard ...

"Just let me know if there's anything else I can help with, Detective," Coombs said as the echo of the PA system blurted behind him again.

"Actually, have you had any contact from the press, Mr. Coombs?" she asked before he could hang up.

"Pardon me?" The connection crackled.

"The press," Kay repeated. "I'm just wondering if they've tried to reach you at all."

"No. Why? Have there been more developments?"

"No," Kay lied. "I was just checking, since you said you'd had a problem in the past." But she wondered how long it would be before the media started connecting the dots and rang Coombs's doorbell again.

"Before you hang up, Detective." There was a hesitation over the line. "Have you seen Bernard?"

"I have."

"How is he?"

How did she answer that? "He's fine, I guess. The preliminary motions of his trial start next week. If you wanted the court dates—"

"That's all right, thanks."

"Is there a message you'd like me to get to him?"

A pause. "No. I have nothing to say to Bernard."

Kay sensed a sadness in his voice. Or maybe it was resignation.

"No," he said again. "I guess, as far as I'm concerned, Detective, I really don't have a brother anymore."

34

ANY SUSPICION KAY might have had of Bernard Eales's neighbor assisting him with the meticulous disposals of his victims' bodies was dashed the second Jerry Bates answered his door.

Bernard Eales's friend was on the verge of being what

the guys on the job called a skel—a long-term heroin addict so strung out he resembled a skeleton. Bates's hair was a grown-out buzz cut that stood up and back, making him look as if he stood in a perpetual gale. His narrow chest was hairless and paper white, and his ribs shot out from beneath his translucent skin as he scurried through the hot, cluttered row house. From the stained sofa he snatched a wrinkled T-shirt sporting a peeling Harley-Davidson decal and pulled it on.

The living room smelled sour. Past it, on the kitchen table, along with a stack of empties, Kay spotted drug paraphernalia. Getting high was clearly Bates's life calling, not murder. Kay doubted Bates had enough sobriety to take out the trash, never mind the bodies Eales had found himself stuck with.

Bates's movements were twitchy and spastic as he searched for Eales's key. Kay guessed there was deceiving strength in those pale, thin arms. It was always the small, wiry ones, she thought, the ones who looked as if they'd never win an arm-wrestle with their own mamas, who gave you the biggest fight out on the street, their unpredictable strength exploding from those lean junkie frames.

When he finally handed her the key, Bates informed her he'd been looking after the place and no one had been inside except him. He wanted the key back, he told her with a degree of claim that made Kay wonder if Bates used the place himself somehow.

Down the street, Eales's two-story corner row house looked different in the daylight—tall and tapered, with a sagging front porch. Built in the early 1900s for dockworkers and cannery employees, the old Formstone row homes had seen better days.

Kay paused at the head of the walkway, unable to set foot on the cracked cement path that had led to her personal hell over a year ago. She felt Bates watching her from down the street and closed her grip over the key. The wire twist-tie looped through it bit into her palm.

Get a grip, Delaney. It's just a house.

But a part of her wished Finn had come along. She'd reached him on his cell phone, still pacing the hall outside Reager's courtroom, and he'd agreed she should take a walk through the house herself. "I don't need to see that dump again," he'd told her when she'd asked if he wanted to come. "If you give me an hour though, I can meet you there."

But it was better this way. She didn't need her hand held. Besides, going alone would give her a better feel for the place, for what had gone on behind those walls.

Drawing a fortifying breath, Kay took the walk and climbed the steps to the narrow, cluttered porch. It was even tighter than she'd remembered. In the daytime, she would never have drawn her weapon here. No room to extend her shooting arm, to distance herself from anyone coming out the door. In the daytime, she would have gauged reasonably and taken a step back.

Only it hadn't been daytime.

The key was dry in the lock. Flyers had banked against the door. She rolled one into a tube and used it to brush away the cobwebs that crossed the frame. The door was snug, and she drove her shoulder into it twice before it opened.

The smell hit her before the heat did. Mothballs and a sweet staleness, like the stench of beer bottles left out in the sun.

It was dark in the foyer. Even darker up the staircase. Kay swiped her hand over the light-switch plate. Nothing. She should have known the power would be cut.

Leaving the door ajar, she sidestepped a mound of junk mail. The house *felt* dead. She could almost taste the long absence of life, of air, movement, and sound. The heat washed over her, and she wondered how many showers she'd need to scrub away the sensation that slid across her skin.

In the living room, she pulled aside the yellowed sheet hanging over the window. She coughed against a rain of dust as several slow cluster flies beat themselves against the gray panes. Dozens more lay dead on the sill.

Dust motes danced in the light as she turned several times in the center of the room. Taking it in. Everything was as she remembered from the case photos: the threadbare sofa with its sagging cushions, the green Naugahyde recliner, the veneered coffee table, the grimy banister and railing. All of it covered in black smudges of Magna fingerprinting powder. Magazines flowed from a shelf in the corner: vintage cars, hot-rodding, and porn.

At the back of the house was the kitchen. Light streamed through the warped slats of an acrylic blind. More carbon dust here. The sink was jammed with crusted dishes, and when she neared it, there was a sudden burst of scurrying. Cockroaches. Kay shuddered, wondering how many generations had lived here with no human contact.

Over the wall phone, a calendar from a South Baltimore garage featured antique cars and big-busted blondes. It still hung on last July. Kay looked at the empty box of the twenty-first, as though there should be something there, some indication of the horror of that night. There was nothing. The only entries on the calendar were pay dates every second week and the word *roach* scrawled on the twentieth. Given the state of the kitchen, she wasn't surprised Eales had had a pest-control problem prior to his incarceration.

"The guy's probably a clean freak," Constance had said.

It didn't fit.

Kay headed upstairs. The back bedroom had been used for storage. Car parts, dash gauges, even a couple of old vinyl-covered seats. In the corner sat a twin-size bed with an unmade mattress.

Taking a final survey of the room, she crossed the hall to the bathroom. The blind there had come off one bracket. This room was relatively clean. Still, the linoleum was scarred and lifting in places, the enamel of the tub and sink dull. The toilet seat was up, the bowl dry and ring-stained. Most of the evidence had been documented from this room. But nothing spoke to Kay.

The second bedroom to her left was larger. And darker. Kay discerned the outline of the low bed, a chair, and a dresser along the east wall. She crossed to the window overlooking the street. The heavy roller blind spun up slowly, the vinyl cracked, the springs gone slack. It stopped partway up.

She'd barely turned in the half-light to inspect the room when instinct drove Kay's hand to the grip of her nine. First fumbling with the safety strap, then fighting with the hem of her blazer. She drew the weapon and went into a crouch, and only when the Glock's muzzle cleared the leather holster did Kay comprehend what she was seeing.

With her heart still in her throat, she studied the dim outline in the corner of the bedroom. The figure against the back wall didn't move. And when Kay stepped away from the window, allowing the light to reach the corner, she recognized it as a mannequin.

She swore, crossed the room, and squatted before the fiberglass figure. A blond wig sat askew on its bald head, and the fuchsia-colored bra was at least two cup sizes too ample for the pert plastic breasts. Kay remembered Roma Chisney's panties logged into evidence and wondered if it was a matching set.

Nothing else was on the mannequin except black smudges left by the Crime Lab, where the carbon powder had come in contact with the oils no doubt left by Eales's hands. The son of a bitch sure loved his mannequin. He must have stolen it from Dutton's years ago when he'd worked there, taken her with him when he moved.

Standing over the mannequin and the sunken mattress on its low metal frame, Kay felt disgust. The sheets had been stripped, and the faded blue polyester of the double Beautyrest was stained—one spill overlapping the next. Blood? Urine? Semen?

This is where he slept. The man who almost killed you with his bare hands. This is where he spent his nights. Maybe sometimes with his mannequin. Maybe others with Annie Harris's body. Or Chisney's.

Kay stepped away from the bed. In the corner, next to a shadeless lamp, were more porn mags and an overflowing ashtray. She imagined Eales smoking in bed. If only he'd accidentally set the old mattress on fire one night. Roasted himself while he slept.

She thought of Valley's burned body. One smoldering butt on Eales's bed and she might be alive today. Along with the others.

Kay crossed the red and orange shag. The carpet had been vacuumed, but not by Eales. The Mobile Crime Lab had gone over the entire house with the 3M vacuum, sucking up trace evidence too small for the naked eye.

The wallpaper here was floral—wide, luscious poppies—faded and nicotine-stained, peeling back at the seams. A vintage-car poster hung lopsided over the veneer dresser. It was an old ad, a painted image of a green-and-white sedan with whitewalls and heavy chrome bumpers. "Pontiac's Beauty Is Pontiac's Alone!" It was selling the 1959 Canada-made 7100 StratoChief. Kay guessed it was the same model as Eales's, sitting in the police impound off the Fallsway.

The top of the dresser was clearly where Eales emptied

the contents of his pockets at the end of each day. Small change, half-used matchbooks, pay stubs, and ATM print-outs. All covered in a dense dust.

Past a box of tissues, a man's ring, and a crucifix on a chain, Kay's eyes stopped on a worn copy of Webster's dictionary.

"You think I never owned a dictionary?" Eales had asked her. "There's more to me than you think, Detective."

Kay picked up the battered volume, blew a layer of dust off its cover, and opened it. The purple-inked stamp from the Francis Scott Key Middle School inside its cover didn't surprise her. Fanning through the pages, Kay imagined Eales's slow brain taking in the words. She stopped at where a folded sheet of lined paper had been inserted between the pages.

Kay removed it, unfolded it. And in the dim light, she scanned the mangled words in the teetering handwriting. Clearly Eales had struggled with the phrasing and grammar, painstakingly crossing out words and battling with his punctuation as he'd composed the letter.

However, its content was chillingly clear. And when her cell phone chirped at her belt, Kay was already feeling the thrill of long-needed answers.

35

FINN MET HER ON GETTINGS outside Bates's house ten minutes after he'd called her cell. She was still shaking as she returned the key to the junkie, and her hands clenched the steering wheel as she drove the six blocks to the Parkview Funeral Home.

With Finn following in her rearview, she turned the

Lumina into the manicured grounds. The place looked deserted. Only one hearse was parked outside the old carriage house where there'd been three before. Kay took several calming breaths as she parked; Hagen *had* to be there.

The front doors were locked, and Hagen took a long time to answer. "I'm on my own," he explained, leading them back to his office. "I have that list for you."

As they followed the carpeted corridors, Kay's excitement thrummed along every nerve.

"That's everyone," Hagen said in his office, handing her the list off his barren desk. Only a few remaining boxes and the larger furnishings awaited the movers. "I trust that should satisfy you?"

"Actually, we did have a few questions, Mr. Hagen," Finn said, and Kay saw the old man's shoulders stiffen.

"Then you're going to have to join me downstairs. I'm in the middle of something."

It was the last place Kay wanted to go. Still, they followed him down the narrow stairwell with its velvet-textured wallpaper and formaldehyde stench. Kay heard a motor and saw the glare of white tile through the open door at the end of the hall.

Hagen had an embalming in progress—a woman spread out on the stainless-steel prep table, its drainage channels brimming with watered-down blood and body fluids. She was young, and as with all deaths in the city of Baltimore that hadn't been signed off by a medical doctor, she'd already been to the ME's. If the autopsy hadn't been violation enough, her remains were now subjected to Hagen's desecration.

Two thick tubes ran from the girl's body, one of them carrying dead blood to a three-gallon glass tank, suctioned out by the pump that whined in the corner. Kay guessed it was the Porti-boy Jonesy had mentioned, replacing the blood with a pink formaldehyde solution.

Hagen donned a rubber apron and gloves and flipped off the pump. Kay watched him remove the hollow metal tubes from the body and plug the holes with beveled plastic screws. She made a mental note then to tell Finn she wanted to be cremated.

Unlike the rest of the place, the embalming room was only partially gutted. Amidst the sinks and workbenches, Kay surveyed the shelves of brightly colored fluids and the horrific apparatuses of the trade.

When she looked to Hagen again, he was massaging the dead girl's arms. There was nothing tender or deferent about the action, and Kay envisioned the man working late into the night, alone in his embalming room.

"She's my last," he explained. "We'll be operational at the new location after the weekend, but I don't have the prep room there functional yet."

"And all the equipment down here?" Finn asked.

"I'm selling off most of this older stuff. So what is it, Detectives?" Hagen was done with the small talk. Impatience seemed to make his movements brisker now.

Kay bit her tongue. She'd agreed to let Finn lead. After all, he had a daughter himself, and she knew that his abhorrence of the implications of Bernard's letter would get them farther in the interview.

Finn took the letter from his pocket then, but didn't open it. "When exactly did Mrs. Hagen pass?" he asked.

There was an inappreciable pause in Hagen's work. "My wife passed twenty-four years ago."

"So your daughter would have been how old?"

"Nine. What's this about?"

Finn ignored the question. "And so that's when you started molesting Patricia? Or did it start even before that?"

Hagen froze, his expression as cold as the girl's flesh he held in his gloved hands. "Where the *hell* do you get off coming in here with such—"

Finn unfolded the ragged letter and held it over the embalming table for Hagen to read. Kay watched the old man's yellowed eyes take in Bernard's accusations.

Patsy told me everything, Bernard had written in the letter addressed to Hagen, then called him a *sorry-ass diddling fuck. She's not yours to diddle anymore,* he wrote. *I told you before, I'd do whatever it took to keep your hands off her. . . . Just because you fired me doesn't mean I still can't get you. I'll let everyone know about you. I'll tell the media . . .*

But in the end it was money Eales was after. How much though, he hadn't figured out yet. In the final paragraph of the letter he'd asked for $10,000 then scratched it out and written $20,000.

Hagen stepped back from the letter. "Bernard would do anything to get money. In fact, this doesn't even really surprise me." He waved a hand at the letter, dismissing it as he might a parking ticket. "I've never laid a hand on my daughter, Detective."

Finn refolded the letter, then nodded down to the dead girl on the table. "Right, but the corpses can't talk back, isn't that right?"

"I would never—"

"The way this looks to me," Finn went on, "is that Bernie came and took your daughter away from you. And when you didn't have her anymore, you turned to your *clients* here in the basement."

"Please. More unfounded accusations from Bernard."

"Accusations that would have ruined you," Kay pointed out.

Hagen's anger was peaking now. She could see it in his eyes, even though his face maintained that funereal calm.

"Do you mean to tell me that you believe the rantings of a man who's presently sitting in prison for killing three women and a police officer?"

"So, then, Bernie just made all of this stuff up?" Finn asked, waving the letter. "I gotta tell you, he doesn't strike me as being that imaginative."

"Of course he made it up."

"And why would he do that, Mr. Hagen?"

"Because I wouldn't let him see my daughter. When I knew him, he was a kid with a temper. Nothing but a bully. Besides"—Hagen nodded at the letter that Finn was pocketing—"I didn't see any date on that. Bernard could have written that fifteen years ago, after I fired him and told him to stay away from Patricia."

"Sounds to me like he just wanted you to leave your daughter alone."

"I told you, Detective Finnerty, I never touched my daughter. Why don't you ask her? In fact, why don't you show *her* that letter, so she can see exactly what kind of reprobate she's got herself tangled up with. Now, if you'll excuse me . . ." The old man turned back to his work, massaging the dyed formaldehyde through the girl's dead veins, bringing an artificial color to the pale flesh.

The subject was spent. Kay turned to the employee list Hagen had handed her upstairs. Unfolding it, she scanned the almost three dozen names, then stopped on one. "Wait a second, Jerry Bates worked for you?"

"Yes. For twelve years."

"Jerry Bates who lives over on Gettings Street?"

"If that's where he still lives." Hagen's words were crisp and he refused to make eye contact.

Kay studied the list. "He quit a year ago?"

"I let him go, last August."

"Why?" Finn asked. "I mean, twelve years is a long time."

When Hagen looked across the table this time, the lines in his face seemed to relax marginally, as though he was relieved he was no longer the subject of their interview. "Jerry developed a drug habit."

"When exactly did Mr. Bates start using?" Kay asked.

"You'd have to ask him that. All I can say is, he was one of my best employees, and then he wasn't."

"And what did he do for you? Did he help out down here?"

"No. He kept my books, organized inventory and supplies, and managed all the accounts. He used to be extremely competent."

"Did you know he was friends with Bernard Eales?"

Hagen moved to the girl's legs, rubbing the gray skin vigorously under gloved hands. "No, I didn't. But it doesn't surprise me. It was probably Bernard who got him addicted."

"What else can you tell us about Mr. Bates?"

"Nothing. Like I said, he was good at what he did. Smart. Organized. Punctual. I wouldn't have kept him for twelve years if he wasn't. Now, if you don't mind, Detectives—" Hagen reached behind him and took up a long steel tube. Except for the heavy silicone hose attached to it, he looked like a fencer brandishing his foil. "I do have work to do here." He threw the switch on the pump then, and it whirred back to life.

Touching the honed tip against the girl's abdomen, immediately below the ME's Y-incision, Hagen paused and looked across at them. "You might want to show yourselves out now."

And as she and Finn left the embalming room, Kay heard the distinct suction of fluids as the motor of the Porti-boy whined.

36

"**YOU GOT A WARRANT?**" Bates scowled at them as they stood on his porch.

Hagen's former bookkeeper had clearly been about to shoot up when Kay and Finn knocked on his door. With his hair spiked straight up and his eyes a little wild, Bates wedged himself between the door and the jamb. Finn noticed the fresh impression of a belt across the scrawny biceps of his right arm. Below this, on the inside of his arm, was what looked like a relatively new tattoo—a pachuco cross, used by addicts to conceal their injection sites.

"No," Kay answered. "We don't have a warrant."

"Then you can't come in. I know my rights." He tried to close the door but Finn propped it with his foot.

"I'm sure you do, Jerry. But we just want to talk," Kay said, her voice soft.

" 'Bout what?"

"Bernard Eales."

"And you need four of you to do that?" Bates nodded at the two uniformed officers who shared the porch with them. With the possibility of a deviant conspiracy between Bates and Eales, and not knowing what to expect from the junkie, they'd called for backup.

"I don't gotta let you in," he said again.

"That's right, Jer." Finn snagged the skel's arm fast and yanked him onto the porch. "So why don't you come on out and talk?" He gave a quick nod to the uniforms, dismissing them back to their radio unit parked across the street, and tried to swallow his impatience.

Wasting an entire day at the courthouse always put Finn

in a mood, especially when there was a case to work. He'd wanted to be there for Kay when she went through Eales's house, and that she'd had to go alone pissed him off even more. And now this—pussyfooting with a junkie—was the last thing Finn had the patience to tolerate.

"Come on, Jer. Just relax." Finn squeezed Bates's shoulder a little too hard. "Unless of course there's something you *need* to be nervous about."

Bates's eyes flitted back to his door. Kay pulled it shut.

"See?" Finn said. "We're not interested in what you've got going on in there, okay? But if you don't cooperate, we *could* be."

Leaving the Parkview Funeral Home, they'd swung by HQ to check Bates's record. It didn't surprise Finn to see two counts of drug possession, but the solicitation charges surprised him. If Bates was a true addict, sex would be the last thing on his mind.

"What do you want from me?" Bates whined.

"Just wondering what you've been doing with yourself since leaving the Parkview Funeral Home."

Bates chewed frantically at his bottom lip. Finn followed his gaze to the adjoining porch. One neighbor sat on a rusted lawn chair; past that, another cooled herself on her stoop.

"Okay, listen. Let's go to the car and have us a chat, all right? Nice and private." Finn escorted Bates firmly across the street and to the unmarked Lumina at the curb. When he opened the door to usher Bates into the backseat, Bates balked.

"Come on, Jer, don't piss me off here. We just wanna ask a few questions." Finn tried to keep the antagonism out of his voice. "Now scootch over," he said, and slid in after the junkie.

From the front seat, Kay remained silent, letting Finn

have this one. She switched off the police radio and turned in the passenger seat to watch Bates.

"So, d'you take an early retirement, Jer?" Finn asked. "You didn't like working for Hagen anymore or what?"

"Maybe."

"You worked for the man a long time. You ever see anything hinky at that place?"

"What do you mean?"

"The old man. He ever do anything weird?"

"I don't know what you're talking about."

"Your buddy Bernard called the cops on Hagen a long time ago. You know anything about that?"

"No. That was before I ever worked there. All I heard was rumors. And frankly, what the old man does in his basement is none of my business, right?" Bates winked.

"And what the hell does *that* mean?" Finn asked, imitating the junkie's wink.

"Nothing. Nothing. Forget it."

"You ever see anything? Ever go down to the basement?"

"No. That's not my thing." Bates cleared his sinuses with a sucking noise, then wiped the corner of his mouth with the back of one shaking hand. When his eyes darted to Kay briefly, Finn could see the whites were bloodshot, but the pupils weren't dilated. Bates was jonesing but he wasn't high.

"What about Hagen and his daughter?" Finn asked him. "Anything untoward going on there ever?"

"Don't know what you mean."

"Come on, Jer, quit pissing around."

"I'm not, man. Seriously, I don't know what you're after." Under the stained and threadbare sweats he wore, his bony knees had started bouncing, and again he sucked at his sinuses.

"So how well do you know Patricia Hagen?" Finn asked.

Bates showed no reaction to the name. "I only know her through the business. Even then, she weren't around much."

"Any idea if she and Eales dated? Before he was arrested?"

"I don't know. Bernard said no though. I asked him once, a long time ago when I seen her leave his place."

"So he *was* seeing her then?"

"I don't know. I only seen her twice leaving his house."

"Did she ever stay over?"

"How should I know?"

"Come on, Jer. You're four doors down."

"Yeah, and I ain't no Peepin' Tom neither. I mind my own business."

"You have a girlfriend, Jer?"

"No."

"So what do you do for fun then?"

"I don't know. Watch NASCAR."

"Well, you weren't watching any races on May tenth of last year," Finn reminded him. "You remember that night?"

Bates shook his head, eyed his front door across the street.

"That's the night you got picked up for patronizing a prostitute. Remember that? And I guess there weren't any races September eighth either, because they nailed you then too."

"What's that gotta do with anything?"

Finn gave him a shrug. "You ever pick up hookers with your friend Bernie? Go over to his house, do a little two-for-one?"

"No. Bernie and I'd get high once in a while. Maybe five or six times, total. That's it."

"What? Come on, Jer. You never shared a bit of ass with your best buddy? Or do you keep them all to yourself?"

"Look, man, I don't do that kinda thing."

"Do what?"

"Share ass. Now come on, quit hassling me. I already told you we'd get high. That's it."

"So while the two of you were getting high, did Bernie ever talk to you about the murders?"

Bates flicked his middle finger against his thumb repeatedly, and when his gaze went to his front door again, he eyed it as if it were the portal to an eternal high that he couldn't get to fast enough.

"Just a few more questions, Mr. Bates, and you can go home," Kay said from the front seat. "Annie Harris. You know about her?"

His eyes went back to Finn, and he ran his fingers through his buzz cut, scratched at his scalp.

"Answer her, Jer."

"Okay. Okay. She's the girl they found in that Harlem Park row house, right?"

"A plus, Jer." Finn wondered if there was any substance to the clarity of Bates's memory on that point.

"Did Bernard ever talk about her?" Kay asked.

Bates shrugged.

"What did he say, Jerry?"

"Said he knew her. This was after it was in the paper."

"That's it?"

Bates hesitated enough that Finn knew there was more, but the junkie had clammed up. He'd always hated interviewing addicts. The only thing on their minds was the next fix, the next score, even beyond self-preservation. He'd interviewed enough of them to know they'd say whatever it took to get to that next high. And if you pushed too hard, especially when they were needing a fix as Bates was tonight, they'd shut down. But Finn's patience had been tapped.

"Okay, look, Jerry"—Finn moved to get out of the car—"we may as well take you in." He shoved his thumb at the radio car parked behind them. "I'll just get these guys to run you downtown while we get a warrant. How much smack d'you figure we'll find on your coffee table tonight, hmm?"

"No. Wait. Shit, man, give me a break."

"Then give us something, Jer," Finn said. "It's not like we're not askin' pretty."

"Okay, look. Yeah, Bernie did say something, okay? We were getting high together, a week or so before he got arrested. He was acting all stupid. Asked me if I ever seen a dead body, other than at Hagen's place. Then he asks me if I ever seen anyone die before, like while it was happening. And then he starts saying shit about how he killed Annie. Christ, I didn't actually believe the son of a bitch. I thought he was just blowin' hot air, you know? Joking around."

"You always joke about killing people, Mr. Bates?" Kay asked.

"No. But I didn't think he'd killed her. Now, honest, I don't know anything else." The whine in Bates's voice had become irritating.

"We know Bernard came to you when he was wanted," Kay said. "He surrendered from your house. So was it you who talked him into turning himself in?"

Bates nodded.

"You must have a lot of influence over Bernard, huh?" Kay asked. "Convincing him to turn himself in on a multiple murder charge."

"Maybe." Suspicion marked Bates's whine.

"So where were you Saturday night?" Kay asked, shifting the direction of the interview like a pro, deliberately keeping Bates off-balance.

"I don't know. I'll have to check my social calendar."

"Hey, don't be a smart-ass, Jer," Finn warned.

"I'm home just about every night, okay? So I'm guessing I was Saturday too."

"Come on, Jer. Where were you? Cuz if you don't give Detective Delaney here a good alibi right now, I'm thinking we'll have to haul your skinny ass downtown."

Bates inhaled and sat up straighter. "Fine. Take me the fuck downtown." His voice was suddenly stronger. The whine gone. "And then I'll be needing to call my lawyer."

Finn backed off. It wasn't worth it. They'd only spend the night dancing with a two-bit defense attorney. They needed more first.

"Never mind." Opening the door, Finn ushered the junkie out. "We'll be in touch," he said, and watched Bates scurry across the street.

"I want a car on his house," Finn told Kay after Bates disappeared behind his front door.

Kay was silent, leaning against the roof of the Lumina, staring across the street.

"This mope's not as helpless as he seems," he said. "Plus he had access to Hagen's funeral home. Probably even had keys to the company van. If you're thinking someone may have helped Eales ditch the bodies"—he shoved a thumb at the skel's closed door—"he's the most likely candidate so far."

"He's a junkie, Finn. Do you really think he could pull off something like that?"

"Hey, it didn't sound like he was so strung out while he was working for Hagen."

"But what about now? What about Valley? And Beggs? Look, I agree, he's mixed up in this. Somehow. But"—she nodded to the house—"do you really see this guy pulling off these murders?"

Finn shrugged. "Who knows? There's a big difference between an occasional skin-popper and an all-out main-liner. I don't think Jerry's there yet. I think we caught him on a bad night. Who knows what he's like when he's not jonesing. I don't get the feeling his only hobbies are smack and NASCAR."

Kay shook her head, her gaze finally leaving Bates's house to pan four doors down to Eales's.

"What is it, Kay?"

"It just doesn't feel right," she said at last, shoving away from the car and pacing the sidewalk.

"You're saying we shouldn't put a car down here?"

"No, let's get a car on Bates."

"But what's your gut telling you?"

She shook her head again, and Finn could see her mind working at the possibilities. "I don't know," she said finally. "I think we need to find out more about Patricia and Eales, and what really went on in that funeral home."

37

SHE BROUGHT HIM A FRESH PACK THIS TIME.

The smoke spiraling from the tip of the Camel enticed Kay. She watched him flick a long ash to the concrete floor and imagined the smoke curling down into her own lungs, sedating her nerves.

She'd come to see Eales alone again. Finn had con-ceded, begrudgingly agreeing that she'd likely get more out of Eales on the subject of Hagen's molesting his daughter. The topic required sensitivity and the kind of familiarity Kay hoped she already had with Eales.

But the bigger reason Kay hadn't wanted Finn along

was his anger. She recognized the hatred he had for Eales, the man who'd almost killed her, and she couldn't afford to let it get in the way of the answers they needed.

As predicted, Eales had again waived his right to have James Grogan present, doing so with a hint of amusement on his ugly face. And as he stared across the narrow table now, Kay was beginning to doubt the bargaining power of her cigarettes. Patricia Hagen probably stocked Eales with enough to outfit his entire cellblock.

Kay kept an eye on Eales's hands, free of the irons this time. In his left, the burning ash of the Camel sizzled down to his nicotine-stained fingers. His right was under the table. Kay saw a slight rhythm of movement in that forearm and hoped he was only scratching his crotch. When he tossed the last of his cigarette, he squashed it under the sole of his sneaker, his ankle swollen and pink, bulging with spidery veins.

Kay drew her gaze up. She could tell Eales was eyeing the cut on her lip from her bar brawl the other night. Curious, but not bold enough to ask.

"That's a nice watch, Bernard," she said.

He'd been reaching for the smokes again, paused, checked the time, then grabbed the pack. The watch looked expensive.

"Patricia give you that?"

"Maybe."

Kay wondered how long before he traded it for drugs. "She sure takes care of you, doesn't she?"

He ignored the comment, tapped a cigarette out onto the table. When it rolled toward Kay, he left it. Slow revolutions gaining momentum. Only as she was about to reach out to stop it from spilling over the edge did Eales make his move.

She'd forgotten how fast the son of a bitch was.

His meaty hand shot out, slammed down on the cigarette, nearly catching her hand. She jerked back, but not quickly enough. Kay felt the moist heat of his palm. The thickness of his fingers.

He smiled, brought the cigarette slowly to his lips, and lit it with the easy grace a high-society dame might afford a cigarillo.

Don't let him get to you, Delaney.

"I bet Patsy brings you lots of things, hmm?" she asked.

He shrugged. Examined the lit cigarette between his fingers.

"After all, she owes you, doesn't she, Bernard? Owes you a hell of a lot."

"Wadda ya mean?" His eyes narrowed.

"I saw the letter."

"What letter?"

"The one you had tucked in your dictionary."

When he lurched forward, it was more the sudden clatter of his leg-irons than his movement that made Kay jump. She kicked herself mentally for the reaction.

"What the hell you messing with my shit for?" His words hissed through crooked teeth and his sour breath spilled over her.

"I didn't mess with your stuff. I'm trying to find answers. Your brother gave me permission to enter your house."

"He shouldn't have done that. It's not his house."

"We talked to Patricia this morning. I showed her the letter." She and Finn had pulled up to Patricia Hagen's home just as she'd been stepping out of a Yellow Cab at 10 a.m. They'd followed her up the walk, but this time Patsy refused to let them in.

"She said it never happened." But Kay remembered the tremble that had taken over the woman's hands as she held the letter. "She says her father never touched her."

Eales's mouth was a red slash.

"That's why you never sent the letter, isn't it, Bernard? You knew that, even if her father did do those things, Patsy would never have supported it. But she owes you, doesn't she? It's because of you that Hagen stopped molesting her, isn't it?"

There was a distant look in Eales's eyes then, and Kay imagined he was reliving the day he'd confronted Hagen. She pictured the old man's throat in Eales's big hands.

"I think it's a good thing what you did, Bernard. What Hagen was doing to his daughter, to Patsy, that's just wrong. No man should get away with that. And you stood up for her. You saved that little girl, didn't you?"

She hoped to see his expression soften. But there was nothing.

"Is that why you made the false allegations against him?" she asked.

"You mean about the negro-feel-ya?" he pronounced it. "They weren't false. Cops just didn't prove it. Didn't want to."

"So they're true then?"

"And *you're* gonna believe me?"

"Yes, Bernard, I will."

"Great. So what are you going to do about it?"

"I don't think there's anything I can do. Necrophilia isn't a crime in the state of Maryland. We might have been able to go after him for defamation of a body, but that was fifteen years ago, Bernard. I can look into what the statute of limitations is, but—"

"Forget it. You ain't gonna do nothin' about it."

"Sure I would, Bernard. If you help me."

When he looked at her then, Kay finally saw interest

spark behind those blue eyes. The connection she'd been waiting for.

"I need to know who helped you dump the women," she said. "The night Valerie Regester saw you in Leakin Park, who was with you?"

"No one." His voice was flat. The spark gone as quickly as it had appeared. "I was dumping my trash. Why don't you go to the park and check it out, huh? No one ever did that. Why don't you go there, 'stead of sittin' yer skinny ass in here wasting my time."

"Bernard, you've got nothing *but* time. I think you can afford a half hour. Now, we both know you dumped Roma Chisney's body in the park. Those women were killed in your house. Who helped you get rid of them?"

"I didn't kill nobody."

"Oh. Right. They committed suicide. Sorry. Then who helped you dump those suicide victims, hmm?"

The tip of the Camel flared.

"Was it Jerry Bates?" she asked.

"You been talkin' to Jerry?" The flicker of worry in his eyes was so fleeting Kay wasn't sure she'd seen it or if her desperate need for answers had put it there.

"Jerry's a good friend of yours, huh?" she asked. "You two spent a lot of time together. Getting high together."

"So?"

"Did you ever do anything else together?"

Eales offered no reaction.

"Was Jerry with you the night you brought Annie Harris home?"

"Which time?"

"The time she ended up dead."

"I don't remember."

"Was he there the night you brought Roma Chisney home?"

"Dunno."

"Maybe *he* killed those women, hmm, Bernard?" she suggested, offering him some wiggle room.

"Yeah, maybe."

"Maybe it was *you* helping *him?*"

But even given that out, Eales wasn't biting. His lips made a smacking sound around the Camel.

"Was it Jerry who was with you when you dumped them, Bernard?"

With the pinkie of his cigarette hand he picked at some dirt under a nail, then tore a hangnail from his thumb with his teeth and spit it across the holding cell.

"Was it Jerry who helped you get them out of your car trunk?"

"Hey, where *is* my car anyway?"

She considered not allowing the divergence, then said, "Police impound."

He shook his stubbled head, his eyes going to the floor. For a second Kay could have sworn she saw genuine sadness behind those blue eyes. "That was my granddaddy's car, you know. He drove her all the way down from Canada in '62. Only made 'em up there. Nineteen fifty-nine Pontiac StratoChief. Best damn car. My mother let it rot in the back alley for years. I put a lot of work into that beaut, and now she's stuck in some fucking police lot."

Kay could almost see him withdraw, as though his mind had taken him back to the alley behind his Gettings house, polishing the big, black Pontiac.

"Who helped you, Bernard?"

She watched him withdraw from the memory.

He took a deep drag on the cigarette.

"I know you couldn't have done it on your own."

His reply was a cloud of blue smoke.

"Okay." Kay backed off. Eales wasn't interested in any

"outs." "So what if I told you I think you're too stupid to have pulled off those murders by yourself?"

The half-smoked Camel hit the floor, instantly crushed under his sneaker as his leg-irons dragged across the steel-cased chair. When he leaned over the table now, Kay couldn't be sure if he hoped to intimidate or impart a secret.

"Oh, yeah?" His whisper was laced with spent smoke and sarcasm. "Well, what if I told you I thought you were so fucking smart that you shoulda bin able to figure all this out yourself by now?"

Kay stood, needing space.

From her briefcase she removed the folder of photos she'd prepared. She hadn't known if she would use them, if she'd give Eales the opportunity to get his rocks off, but she was running out of avenues.

The photos hit the table one after the next. Five in all. Beggs in the alley—pan shots, close-ups. One from Jonesy's camera at the OCME. "So what can you tell me about these?"

Eales's eyes feasted on the images. Again, Kay wondered if she saw worry flicker in his features. Then something resembling a smile touched his dry lips. Then: "Nothin'."

"Her name's Bobby Joe Beggs. She worked along Wilkens Avenue. You know her?"

"Nope. Am I supposed to?"

"What about the way she was killed? Anything look familiar?"

"You mean the way she hacked up her wrists like that?"

"Yeah. The same way those women did in your house. Is there anything you want to tell me about her, Bernard?"

"How the hell you figure I know anything about this?"

"I think you do. I think whoever helped you with those other women, I think he did this." She gathered the photos. His gaze followed each into the folder. "Either that, or you have one very enthusiastic fan out there."

"Well, how 'bout that."

"I want to know who helped you."

"Nobody."

"Come on, Bernard. Was it Jerry?"

No response.

"No. Wait, maybe it was Patsy. How badly *does* she owe you, hmm, Bernard?"

This time when he exploded across the table, even the guard at the door jumped. This time, though, Kay was ready. She didn't move.

"You leave her out of this."

"So was it Patsy?"

"Fuck no."

"Then who?"

With his big arms crossed over his chest, Bernard Eales appeared finished. But she couldn't let it go. Not yet.

"I tell you what. If you answer my questions, maybe I can do something about your car. Get it out of impound. Maybe get it up to your brother." She lay one photo onto the table again. "If you won't tell me who, then at least tell me this: Whoever helped you, whoever was there for you when you had to get rid of those bodies . . . could they have done this?"

She could almost see the answer forming behind those clamped lips, sense the desire to give her something in return for his car. It was right there, as if she could reach out and take the answer from him.

But he was silent.

"Did you ask this person to take care of Valerie Regester so she couldn't testify? Or maybe he thought Valerie saw him and now he's protecting himself. Is that it?"

Nothing.

She slid the photo closer. "Do you think that person could have done this?"

The silence swelled, broken only by gates slamming and a warning buzzer bleating into the wing's hot, stale air. It was useless. He'd shut down. She'd come close, but now she'd lost him.

"Fine," she said at last, gathering her briefcase. "I'll tell you what I think, Bernard. I think you *didn't* kill those women. I think someone else did and you blacked out. Then, when you found them dead in your tub, you were willing to believe *anything,* including the ridiculous coincidence of three women committing suicide in your house. I'm thinking there's someone else who's behind those murders, *and* these new ones. And you're too fucking stupid to have even figured it out yet."

The feet of her chair grated against the polished concrete.

Only when she started for the door did he speak again. "Why you doin' this?"

"Doing what, Bernard?"

"Talking like I didn't kill them women."

"Did you?"

He grunted. When he stood, his hands habitually came together at his groin, aligning with the steel rings on the leather waist belt. "Why you tryin' to prove I'm innocent?"

Kay crossed the shallow room. Stopping three feet from him, she stared into the merciless eyes that had looked down into her bloodied face a year ago. "I'm not, Bernard. And you're hardly innocent. I'm only after the truth. That's my job. Even if it means getting your lying ass off the hook."

38

"SO NOW YOU'RE THINKING this mutt Bates was working with Eales?" Gunderson leaned back in his chair, dry metal springs groaning beneath him.

"Well, the guy certainly fits the bill," Finn said. "We have a car on his place right now."

Kay watched a vein pulse along Gunderson's temple. Within fifteen minutes of her returning from the Pen, Sarge had called a meeting. Vicki had already been seated in his office when Kay and Finn filed in. And as an old, steel-bladed fan thumped rhythmically in the corner, rustling the papers across his desk, they'd caught Sarge and Vicki up on Beggs, Bates, the Hagens, and Kay's interview with Eales.

"And what exactly do you have on Bates?" Sarge asked. Behind his desk he looked weary and pasty. Broken. As if retirement were no longer some vague notion.

"Enough to make us want to get in his house," Finn said. "A search warrant might produce a connection to Regester or Beggs."

"And what's Eales got to say about his buddy?"

Kay shook her head. "I can't read him. I pushed him on Bates, but . . . either Bates isn't involved or Eales is a good bluffer. So, I agree with Finn, a search-and-seizure would help."

"Any way you can put him with this last victim Beggs?"

"We've got a vague description of the car she got into on Wilkens the night she was killed," Finn said. "And it could vaguely match the '96 Impala Bates has parked in the back alley. His license was suspended, but that doesn't mean shit."

"Anything else?"

"Not unless you count personal impressions and gut feelings." Finn looked tired, and every bit as frustrated as Kay. "This guy's got hinky written all over him, Sarge."

"Well, hinky's not enough." Vicki shifted in her chair, tugging at the hem of her midthigh skirt, clearly feeling the heat as well. "I'm going to tell you the same thing I told you about Arsenault. You need more probable cause. You're already skating on thin ice with the radio car you've got parked outside Bates's house. I'm surprised he hasn't gotten a lawyer screaming harassment already."

Vicki stood and moved for the door. "Get me something on him, guys. Anything. Put him with Beggs somehow. Get his picture down there on Wilkens, see if any of the girls have seen him. Connect him to Regester. Find out where he was those two nights. Hell, if you can find something from the past murders to link to him, I could probably get you into that house. But right now, with no PC, you're not setting foot through his front door."

"Not to mention," Gunderson said, nodding for Vicki to stay, "we got the brass to worry about."

"What's going on, Sarge?" But Kay knew what was coming. Her chest tightened and the room got hotter.

"I'm taking a lot of heat on this one, Kay. I hate to say it, but they're talking task force."

"Oh, for Christ's sake." And if Vicki hadn't already been at the door, Kay would have stormed through it.

"Listen, Sarge," Finn argued, "Kay and I are all over this investigation. You know we're working it harder than anyone can work a case. We're going to get this guy."

"And maybe a little help won't hurt," Gunderson added.

But he was wrong. "This is bullshit," Kay said then, no longer able to contain herself. "You get a half dozen other detectives on this, trampling our evidence, pushing suspects the wrong way, yapping about it to their buddies down at the bar, and you're going to turn this case into one huge cluster fuck real fast."

"Kay, look, my hands are tied." Impatience twitched at Gunderson's already tight jaw. "All I'm doing is warning you there's rumblings, and honestly, I got no idea how long I can keep those dogs at bay."

Kay shook her head and stood at last. "Fine. Well, I guess we've got a case to put down. Is there anything else you want to warn me about?"

Sarge shook his head, and Kay blew past Vicki, out the door, before he could change his mind.

"Sons of bitches," Finn said under his breath, joining her at her desk where she was furiously rearranging case files. "You okay?"

"Fucking great." She shoved several files aside, in search of the list Alexander Hagen had given them. "At the rate we're going, by next week we'll have a three-fucking-ring circus all over this case. And as soon as the media gets wind there's a task force, we'll be spending most of our time dodging cameras and mikes. That is, when we're not running circles with our heads up our asses delegating tasks and typing up ten-page reports in triplicate to justify to the brass why they're paying overtime to a half dozen detectives."

Finn was silent for a moment. She didn't need to look at him, could tell by his breathing that he was trying to bring his anger in check. When he put his hand on her shoulder, he gave it a squeeze. "We'll get him, Kay, I'm not letting the brass take this case from us."

And Kay wished Finn actually had a say in it.

"I *know* we can get this guy, Finn," she said finally. "We don't need a task force. We need a goddamn break."

39

FROM HIS PARKED CAR across the street he watched her windows, the warm yellow glow pushing out into the steamy Baltimore night. She'd drawn all the blinds but one, and he caught glimpses of her passing the bare pane. She was pacing. Or maybe cleaning. He couldn't tell from the angle.

He'd watched her leave the Pen today from where he'd parked outside the gates on Madison. He'd thought of Bernard, wondered if he'd heard yet about the dead prostitute he'd left in the trash. If he knew it was him. Well, Bernard would certainly know about this next one.

When she passed the window again, Roach felt a quickening in his groin. The sensation surprised him.

Lifting the can of Tab, he tossed back the last of the sweet soda. It had gone warm and flat, and the car smelled of onions from the steak hoagie he'd bought earlier at the Cross Street Market.

He and Bernard had had hoagies the night they killed Annie Harris. Or rather, the night *Bernard* had killed her. Bernard had picked her up, brought her to the house to share their high. Bastard thought he'd get lucky, and when he didn't, he'd hauled off and nailed her square in the face. She'd gone down like a sack of wet laundry. But it had been the crack of her skull against the coffee table, and the perfect twist of her head, that had ended Annie's life. She was dead before she hit the floor.

There hadn't been any blood. Nothing more than a trickle from the skank's nose. Even once he'd dragged her dead weight to the bathroom and slopped her into the tub, filled it with warm water, and taken out his knife . . . even then she hadn't bled much. Not with her heart already dead in her chest.

He'd learned from that first one. From Annie Harris.

The next couple he kept alive. Passed out from heroin. He'd watched the thick blood pump from their opened wrists. Could almost feel his own heartbeat fall in sync, the drumming in his chest keeping cadence with the steady rhythm of the blood's flow until the pulse faded and the bathwater turned crimson.

She passed by the window again. Her hair looked wet and he imagined her in his bath.

He could take her tonight.

But better that she come to him. It would be more thrilling that way. To see her step through his front door, then the gradual look of shock as realization hit. That was worth the wait.

40

KAY WASN'T TAKING THE THREAT WELL. Finn had seen the beginnings of it in the office earlier, after Gunderson had warned them of the possibility of a task force. But now, when she opened her apartment door for him at ten o'clock, the idea of her investigation being taken over was clearly exerting a toll.

Her hair was wet from a shower, and she wore a T-shirt over an old pair of his boxer shorts. She didn't smile. Didn't invite him in. Just turned back into her apartment, expecting him to follow.

Last night, after leaving Jerry Bates on Gettings Street, they'd come back here. Both discouraged, both wired. They'd made love, and even though Finn wondered if

Kay's motivation in bed had more to do with countering her frustration, he'd stayed the night.

He wasn't sure whether she'd been expecting him tonight, but after fruitless hours of going over Hagen's list of employees back at the office, Kay had disappeared and Finn had started to worry.

Now it seemed that his worry was warranted.

Kay was drunk. "Lightly drunk," his mother would have called it. Still, drunk was drunk.

"I'm in the office," she said, heading down the hall and leaving him to close the door. When he caught up with her, she'd settled in behind the cold glow of her computer monitor. At the corner of the desk, amidst texts and papers, Joe Spencer's tabby crouched under the single lamp, soaking up the heat.

"I swung up to Pikesville after you left the office," Finn said. When he set the cardboard box from the crematorium onto Kay's desk, he saw her stiffen. He'd called in a favor from a friend of his ex-wife's, making arrangements to have Valerie Regester's remains picked up from the OCME when Jonesy was done with her earlier in the week. Cremation had been the only realistic option, and it had saved Kay money as well.

"I also called up to Dulaney Memorial and they've got a spot reserved for her in the mausoleum whenever you want to take her up."

Kay nodded stiffly, staring at the box on her desk. Then, as if the subject was too sensitive, she pointed to her computer monitor. "I was just checking Scott's website for messages."

Finn hated that she used Arsenault's first name. The image of the Web designer's smug face bloomed in his mind, and as he remembered the way Arsenault looked at Kay, Finn's hatred grew more.

"Finding anything?" he asked.

"No. Unless Scott's using a screen name, it looks like he's keeping a low profile."

"And the details he said he'd remove?"

"They're gone."

"Yeah? I wonder for how long." He stood over her, watching her click through the links.

"They've caught on to Beggs now. A lot of messages about her."

It was all speculation though.

"And the site's up to almost nineteen thousand hits," Kay said. "Of course, not all the messages on the board support Eales." She read several of the posts, but Finn wasn't listening. Instead, he was taking in what had become of Kay's life. The texts. The photos. Copies of case reports. She'd surrounded herself with Eales. With death.

"Kay."

She continued reading messages.

His eyes went to the half-drunk bottle of Silent Sam on the desk and the empty tumbler. Nothing wrong with a drink now and then. Most of the guys on the unit drank. Often too much. It helped to blur what they saw every day. Made them forget. But Finn suspected Kay was dulling far more than the job now.

"Kay, come on. Why are you reading this bullshit?"

"Because he could be on here, Finn. Whoever killed Valley, and Beggs, he'd want to see what people are saying about his murders."

"All right, well, why don't you take a break now?"

She read another post out loud. Someone speculating on how long it would be before the next victim.

"Kay."

Her hand froze over the mouse. She looked up at him.

"Why don't we go for a coffee?" he asked.

"It's late, Finn."

"It's never too late to be sober."

"Oh, for God's sake, Finn. I've had a couple."

"More than a couple." He reached past her shoulder, took the bottle of vodka. "How can you do this?"

"Do what?" The edges of her anger were dulled by the alcohol.

"Christ, Kay, you're the one who got *me* into AA." Finn turned from the office. She caught up with him in the kitchen as he tipped the neck of the bottle into the sink.

She was too late to save it and swore at him.

His mother had been a drunk. Worse than him. And as the last of the vodka splashed down the drain, Finn felt as if he were twelve years old again. "You gotta stop this, Kay."

She held up one hand to silence him. When he took her by the shoulders, her eyes came up. They were slow.

"Look, I *know* you've been through a lot. I've had to sit back and watch all of it." He tried to temper his tone. "But it's time to get past it, Kay. It's time to see that you've got the power to do something here, that *you* control your life, not Eales. If you're serious about putting this case down, this isn't the way to do it. Trust me, I know."

He brought the emptied bottle down onto the counter a little too hard. The noise made Kay start. When he turned from the kitchen, she caught his arm.

"Don't go."

Finn shook his head. "I want to support you, Kay. Really, I do. I want to be there for you. I want to be *with* you, but I can't when you're like this. Don't you see that?"

"Finn—"

"Damn it, Kay, I love you."

He hadn't expected her kiss then. Didn't have time to back away. She was too close, and the smell of her too enticing. When she took his mouth, he tasted the vodka on her lips. It was the closest thing to a drink he'd had in months.

The desperateness in her response, the yielding, assured Finn he could stay the night if he wanted. But not this way.

If Kay needed help, it couldn't come from him. Not when he wanted her so badly. Not when he wanted to pour himself a drink right now and join her.

"No, Kay," he said, withdrawing. "I'm not doing this. Not like this."

She caught him at the door. He couldn't tell if it was the vodka that caused her loss for words then or if she truly didn't know what to say. And this time when she kissed him, she pulled him close. He felt the heat of her body, and then her hand, moving to the erection already pressing against the zipper of his jeans.

"Please stay," she whispered against his mouth.

It would be so easy.

"Kay, I can't."

"Why not?" She didn't get it.

"Why not?" He pushed her back, holding her at arm's distance. "Because, damn it, I'm not someone you can just fuck once in a while when you have the sudden urge to let loose. I can't be that for you, Kay. I can't help you." And when Finn turned this time, he thanked God she didn't try to stop him.

41

HE'D COME LOOKING FOR ANSWERS.

Finn choked up on the aluminum shaft of the Maglite and swept its beam across the front of Eales's house. He hated this place.

After leaving Kay, he'd sat in his car outside her apartment for a long time, torn between going back upstairs or heading to O'Reilly's, bellying up to the bar, and ordering himself a Jack Daniel's. He'd never been closer to wanting a drink than he was tonight.

Dangerously close.

He'd actually taken up his cell phone and debated calling his AA sponsor for the first time in months. In the end, he hadn't. He knew that Terry Degan, the retired desk sergeant who'd acted as his sponsor for almost two years now, would only lecture him about how it wasn't up to him to help Kay. It didn't matter to Degan that Kay had been there for Finn when he'd been so far in the bottle he was risking losing his job the same way he'd lost his marriage.

So Finn had driven away from Kay's tonight. Left her, even though it was the last thing he wanted.

He'd focused on the case then, on Kay and Eales. If there was one way to help Kay, it would be to close this case, help her put it behind her. Eleven o'clock at night, and he'd come here. To Eales's house. To where their end had begun.

From the moment he'd pulled up to the curb, Finn's memory had flooded with the images from fourteen months ago. He'd been on duty that night when the call came in. Like every other available detective, he'd raced to South Baltimore. No idea who, or what, to expect. Only knowing that two of their own were down.

At Cross Street he'd passed one ambulance hurtling north to Johns Hopkins. Then a second. Lights and sirens shattering the night. He hadn't known one of the ambos was carrying Kay until he arrived on scene.

He'd stayed only long enough to see Kay's blood on the gray, cracked asphalt. Hurling the cherry onto the dash of his Lumina, he'd left some rubber along Gettings that night.

Finn could still feel the fear that had consumed him back then, when he'd followed the ambulances carrying Kay and Spencer.

To his right, a door slammed. Four houses down, he saw the dark silhouette on Bates's porch. The junkie's lean frame was unmistakable as he took the front steps down to his bare yard.

Bates stopped only five strides down the sidewalk, frozen—it seemed—upon recognizing Finn.

"You going somewhere, Jer?" Finn called out.

"Uh, no." Bates pinched his nose once, then turned on the heels of his flip-flops and scuttled back up the steps and into his house.

Down the block, across from Bates's house, the Southern District officer on watch had stepped out of his radio unit. Finn gave him a wave, then turned back to the porch. His gaze followed the beam of the Maglite, sweeping across the tangle of junk: rusted lawn-chair frames, tires, a discarded fridge.

How had it gone down that night?

He'd read the reports at least a hundred times, pouring over every detail, enough that he'd started to feel as though he'd been on the porch with Kay.

She and Spence had expected Eales to bolt out the back, Kay had told investigators. But he hadn't. And when he'd come through the front door, he'd knocked the gun from her hand. From then, Kay had stated, Eales started beating on her—from the moment he'd smashed the gun from her hand to when she heard the gun go off. *Yes, the whole time,* she'd told the IAD investigators. *The suspect was on me the whole time.*

And when they'd questioned her on how Eales had fired

the gun while he was still beating her, Kay had admitted she was confused about the events, that her memory was scrambled, and she may have blacked out briefly. According to the transcripts, the interview had gone downhill after that.

Finn stood at the top step, imagining Kay's position as she'd banged on the door. She would have moved aside then, not knowing whether Eales was armed, not exposing herself to the possibility of a round or a shotgun blast coming through the door. Finn mimicked what must have been her movements that night, his back against the porch pillar, his arms extended.

Barely enough room.

The gun in her right hand, Eales stepping out at her left.

There'd been no porch light, Kay had reported. Dark, just like tonight. Finn panned the beam of the flashlight down the walk, then back across the junk-filled porch once more. Taking it all in. Calculating.

The suspect was on me the whole time.

And then, slowly, a chilling realization took hold.

42

"COME ON, KAY. ONE MORE TIME."

"Christ, Finn, I don't want to do this."

"I know, but it's important. You'll see what I mean."

Kay had still been in bed when Finn called the next morning. He'd given her fifteen minutes to get dressed and honked the car horn from the street. Handing her a coffee from Starbucks, he'd driven them down to Gettings Street.

She'd wanted to apologize for last night, but Finn

didn't give her a chance. He was too pumped about his latest theory.

As the sun broke through the dense haze over the Northwest Harbor and baked the parched yard outside Eales's house, Finn had led her up the walk. A solitary cicada buzzed over the clatter of the Locust Point rail yards behind them.

Now at the base of the steps, Finn prodded her. "So you came up here while Joe went to the back, right?"

"Finn, please."

"Damn it, Kay, just do this."

She conceded, again going through the motions of that night. She heard little of Finn's narration this time, allowing him to lead her through the murky memories of Eales bursting through the door, Spence coming around the side, and finally the gunshot.

"So you ended up here." Finn had steered her back to the spot along the walkway, barely five yards from the street, where she'd at last surrendered to Eales's assault. "And that's when you saw Joe come around from the back, right?"

This time when he pointed to the section of lawn at the corner of the house where Spencer had died, Kay stared at the swath of sun-burned grass and dried weeds. She wondered about spirits, if somehow Spence was here. She hoped not. For someone who saw so much death, Kay had never clung to any notion of an afterlife or heaven. Dead was dead. But for Spencer's sake, she hoped there was some kind of heaven, a place far away from this desolate strip of squalor.

Finn was heading back to the porch, dragging her with him. "Don't you see it, Kay?"

"See what?" Kay rubbed at the headache that had started at the base of her neck.

"Okay, there was no porch light on, right?"

"Right."

"And Eales was on you the entire time."

"From what I remember, yeah."

"Well, look at this mess." He waved a hand at the trash-cluttered porch, then stood at the door facing her. He brought her hands up, as though she were holding her gun. "You said he smashed the gun from your grip like so?"

He brought one arm up, connecting with her wrist. She nodded.

"So where'd the gun go, Kay? Huh? Where did it land?"

"I don't know. I'm sure I heard it hit the porch."

"Well, where?"

"I said I don't know. Probably somewhere to my right. But it was dark."

"Exactly. So how the hell did Eales find it? *Especially* when he was busy beating the shit out of you, huh?"

"I don't know," she murmured. "Maybe I'm not remembering it right."

"No, I think you are. And I think you're absolutely right about Eales. I think he *did* have help getting rid of those women's bodies, and I think he had help that night."

Kay could feel Finn's intensity.

"Think about it," he said. "The only latents they lifted off your gun after it was recovered were Eales's. Not even a partial print from you. Why?"

"Because he wiped it at some point."

"Or the *shooter* wiped it. Then dumb-ass Eales carries the piece around for two days until he turns himself in. Kay, I think someone was with Eales that night, and *they* picked up the gun on the porch. *They* shot Spencer, not Eales."

Kay shook her head and left the porch. Her knees were weak as she took the steps and headed down the walk. She focused on the Lumina across the street, needed to get to it, to get away from the memories, from the implications.

But Finn came after her. "Kay." He caught up with her at the hood of the unmarked, took her wrist, and pulled her around. "Why's this so hard for you to believe?"

She felt sick. "Because it means that Spencer's killer is still out there. And it means that because of *my* fucked-up memory his killer's been free all this time." She yanked her wrist from his grasp and turned so Eales's house was behind her. "Besides, how are you going to prove this theory, anyway, when the only proof is locked in here," she said, pointing to her head, where the throbbing magnified now.

"Not the only proof. You're not the only person who was there that night, Kay. Bernard Eales knows who shot Joe."

"Yeah, well, good luck trying to get it out of him." She opened the passenger door and got into the Lumina. Glancing across to the driver's side, she checked the visor where Finn usually kept his cigarettes. If there'd been a pack, Kay was sure she would have lit up then.

Finn was silent as he got in behind the wheel. Staring out the windshield.

"Listen, Finn, I'm sorry about last night."

"You don't have to apologize, Kay. I've been there. I know how drinking blurs the edges. But I also know how tempting it is to keep those edges blurred permanently."

"I'm not a drunk."

"I know."

She sensed that he wanted to take her hand then, so she kept them in her lap. She thought of the cardboard box on her desk back home. Valley's ashes. She'd spent what felt like hours last night staring at it, pondering the unfairness of a young life, so filled with hope and promise, reduced to a small, plain cardboard box. "I'm just . . . I'm dealing with stuff," she said to Finn at last.

He started the car but left it in park. "So come to me, Kay. Talk to *me.*"

"I'll try." She really meant it. She *wanted* to lean on Finn, to let him in as she had before.

When he turned to her, he looked skeptical.

"I will," she assured him, and if he'd intended to push further, she'd never know. From her jacket pocket, her cell phone trilled.

It was Gunderson.

"You two might wanna come in," Gunderson said. "It's about Eales. Vicki just stopped by looking for you and Finn. Left an audiotape for you."

"What is it? *Eales's Greatest Hits?*"

But Gunderson didn't laugh. "Better than that. He just sang us a full confession."

43

THE REALIZATION HAD BEEN SLOW COMING. Or maybe he'd known all along.

Bernard shuffled down the north corridor between two guards, the irons biting into his ankles. He was tired. Hadn't slept good last night. Lay on his cot, hearing Delaney's words loop in his head. And when he'd rolled over, he'd started rehearsing his own words, over and over, getting the story straight.

What exactly had happened a year and a half ago? Back then he'd lost whole nights, passed out in front of late-night TV ads selling specialty knives or big-busted bimbos. Back then he'd never been real sure what had gone on those nights the women died. He'd believed Roach. Let Roach convince him he'd done it.

And why not? Roach was always so chilled out. *He* didn't have the kind of anger that had smashed in Annie Harris's face.

Besides, why would Roach lie to him?

But Detective Delaney, she didn't believe he'd done it. And if *anyone*'d wanna nail him with them murders, it was that harpy bitch.

After she'd left yesterday, he'd had cleanup duty in the can off the cafeteria. Pushing the gray mop head between each urinal, he'd stewed over her suggestions. Gone through his shredded memory, searching for the truth about those nights.

Somewhere between scrubbing the last stall and returning the equipment to the guard, he thought he had it figured out. And he knew what he'd have to do.

He'd gone back to his cell, smoked his last coke-laced cigarette, and got only half-mad at Roach for letting him take the fall. He wrote Roach a letter then and finally called Grogan.

His defense attorney hadn't agreed with his plan, of course. Grogan had spent an hour humpin' his ass, trying to convince him to take the weekend to reconsider. And he'd still been working Bernard this morning as he sat shackled in a room at the State's Attorney's Office downtown, waiting to give his confession.

The SA had been smug as shit when he'd signed the waiver for her and told her three times how he'd killed the women. And the whole time the blond bitch in her pink dress smiled as if he'd just handed her his dick on a silver fucking platter.

He'd said nothing to Patsy when she visited at lunch. If he had, she wouldn't send the letter for him. So he'd sat on the other side of the grimy Plexiglas, nursing a headache, and listened to her yap through the receiver. Her old man was pissed. Razzing her about coming here to see him. Delaney had obviously gotten to the old fuck, probably told him just to raise shit for Patsy.

Bernard had never seen Patsy so upset, rubbing the diamond on her finger, her voice getting higher and higher till he thought his head was gonna bust open from the headache. But she always sent through the cigarettes at the *end* of her visit. So he'd had to sit through it all today just to see the three packs of Marlboros come through the slot. Waiting like a goddamned lapdog doing tricks for a Milk-Bone.

As he rounded the last corner, Bernard could see the interior of the holding cell in the convex mirror. He'd thought it might have been Grogan. Or maybe Patsy had found out about his confession and had come back.

He should have known.

Delaney stood in the middle of the room.

Without thinking, Bernard slowed. Almost to a full stop.

"Come on, Big Man," one of the guards urged. "Move."

The end of a nightstick nudged his ribs. When he reached the door of the cell, the bitch turned. Her face looked sour, and he could tell she was pissed.

Bernard realized one of his greatest mistakes then. One of his few regrets: not killing Delaney when he'd had the chance.

She nodded to his irons. "Leave 'em on," she told the guard.

No pack of cigarettes. No friendly chat. Not after he'd pulled the rug out from under her investigation.

She yanked out the far chair. "Sit, Bernard." When he settled onto the hard steel seat, she started to pace, trying to look tough.

Her jacket hung over the back of the other chair, and her shirt was stuck to her back. It was wrinkled and the fabric bunched around the empty holster where the butt of her gun would have ridden all day. When she crossed to the table, she spun the chair around and straddled its seat.

"I listened to your taped confession on my way over, Bernard."

"Yeah?"

"Yeah. And you are so full of shit it's a wonder it doesn't stink even more in here."

"You think so, huh?"

"I only *guessed* you hadn't killed those women last year, but after hearing your taped performance today, I *know* you didn't."

"Are you sure I'm supposed to be talking to you?"

She grunted a laugh. Shook her head. "You're a piece of work, Bernard. You want your lawyer here? I'll save you the quarter and call him myself. I'm sure he's got nothing better to do right now after you've already wasted half his weekend."

He met her stare. Amusement gave way to reason. Sure, he didn't owe the bitch anything, but what were his options right now? Back to his cell, where Darnell was nursing a case of the shits?

"No. I'll talk to you," he said. "But you gotta get my car."

"No deals. There's nothing you got that I want."

"You sure about that?"

He studied her. Except for the butch haircut, she wasn't too hard on the eyes. Not *his* type, with those small tits and her tight, little ass. He liked more meat on his women. More curves. But she was definitely in line with Roach's tastes, even though she was probably a pussy-eating dyke.

"No jury's going to buy your confession, Bernard. You got too many holes in your little story."

He shrugged. "State's attorney didn't seem to think so."

"She will once she takes a closer look at the evidence."

"So I forgot a couple things. I told you, I had them alcoholic blackouts. Forgot a lot."

She shook her head. "Too many holes."

"Like what?"

"Right. And I'm gonna tell you where you fucked up in your statement so you can prep some lame-ass retraction?"

"You talking 'bout them cuts to the chest? I covered that."

"Oh, right. 'I heared their hearts beat-beat-beating in their chests and had ta cut 'em out.' " She looked ugly when she mimicked him. "Are you planning to have Grogan present an insanity defense?"

"You think that'd work?"

"Don't hold your breath." She paced again, two lengths of the holding cell, then returned to the table. "Why the false confession, Bernard, hmm? You afraid someone's going to steal your limelight? I mean, Patsy's paying for that flashy website for you, bringing in money. Even got people out there believing you're a worthy cause. Can you believe that? Sorry sack of shit like you."

"I can't help it if I got fans."

"I tell you what I think, Bernard. I think you got scared when I started talking about looking at someone else for the murders. I think you're worried someone's gonna prove you're just a dumb-ass Bawlmer billy-boy with a bad temper, so you figured you'd better give the SA's office what they want. Nail down that fifteen minutes of fame, huh?"

"Well, you got that wrong."

"I doubt it."

"So what about my car?"

"What about it?" she snapped. Impatience narrowing her mouth.

"I want it released from the impound."

"Yeah? And who's gonna want that piece-of-shit antique?"

"Patsy's gonna take it."

Kay laughed. "I've met Patsy, and there's no way she's gonna take your car. The girl's blind as a fucking worm."

He choked on a laugh because he knew Delaney was right. "She can still use the car. Have someone else drive her around."

"And where's she gonna ride, Bernard? In the trunk? Does she know you chauffeured dead women around in there?"

When he didn't answer, Kay shook her head. "Fine," she said at last, "you want your car? Tell me who killed those women."

"You're looking at him."

"You really are dumb as shit, aren't you? Are you even remotely aware that if you *do* convince a jury you killed those women, you're getting the death penalty? Ever heard the term *capital crime?* Cuz that's what you've got coming, Bernard. Those girls were murdered in the commission of a felony."

"What felony?"

"You robbed them."

"Like hell."

"Their belongings were in your house. Jewelry. Clothes."

Grogan hadn't said anything about that. He'd have to talk to the moneygrubbing prick.

"But I guess that doesn't really matter though, since shooting a cop is what's gonna stick that needle in your arm anyway. And don't count on some trumped-up self-defense argument, because I was there. I identified myself at the door. You *knew* I was police. Who do you think the jury's gonna believe?"

When she leaned across the table, nailing him with those angry eyes, he felt the lick of adrenaline quiver through him, the muscles in his legs and shoulders twitching.

He could clear the table in a quarter of a second. Come down on top of her and have her throat in his shackled hands before she ever knew what hit her. And by the time the guard swung his stick, he'd at least have crushed her windpipe. Maybe even snapped the bitch's neck.

But then one link of chain on his leg-irons rattled.

It was the only warning she picked up on. The bitch backed away. The opportunity passed. Another regret settled in.

When she lifted her jacket from the back of the chair, he was glad she was going. But not soon enough. "Unless, of course," she added, "you're going to start saying it wasn't even you who shot my partner."

She was fishing. He knew it. No way he was taking the bait. He watched her shrug on her jacket, pace a few more lengths of the cell, before returning to the table.

"Who was there that night, Bernard? Who else was in your house when I knocked?"

She couldn't know, otherwise she'd have questioned him a lot sooner.

"There was someone else there. I know, cuz when you were beating me, he found my gun on your porch. It was him who shot my partner. Not you."

"First those three skanks, and now you're thinking I didn't shoot that cop either? What? You gonna try 'n' prove me innocent on all the charges now? Hey, maybe I should be payin' you instead of that shit-for-brains attorney of mine."

When she leaned in that last time, there were daggers in her whisper. "Trust me, Bernard, I'm sure as hell not doing it for you. I want whoever it is that shot my partner, whoever you're covering for. And I swear to God I'm going to get him."

44

"SHOULDN'T WE SAY SOMETHING?" Kathleen Koch whispered.

Valley's best friend had worn black. Standing between Kay and Vicki in the mausoleum sanctuary of the Dulaney Valley Memorial Gardens, the girl looked wan as she wrung her hands.

"You can say some words if you like," Kay said.

Koch stared at the marble niche that now housed Valley's ashes. Its front was marked with a piece of cardstock bearing nothing but a number, soon to be replaced with an engraved bronze plate, the director of the cemetery had promised.

"I don't know what to say." Koch held back tears, and Kay suspected Valley was the first loss the girl had experienced in her young life.

"Then you don't have to say anything." Kay touched the girl's hand. It was cold. "It's what you feel that's important."

An early-evening breeze swept over the seventy acres of grounds, lacing through the granite benches and pruned hedges. It ruffled the pink and yellow blooms in the rows of flower vases designating the flat grave markers and found its way to the shade of the mausoleum. Kay welcomed the coolness.

After leaving Eales, Kay had gone over the disappointing interview with Finn. She'd left him at the office and gone to the gym. But even a strenuous workout and a shower hadn't cleansed her of the visit with Eales. Vicki had picked her up at five and they'd battled traffic north through the city and up to Timonium. Kathleen Koch had already been waiting for them.

Now, in the quiet shelter of the mausoleum, Kay tried to rid her mind of Eales. Past Vicki's shoulder and beyond the arch of the outdoor sanctuary, Kay looked to where the grounds leveled down to a small man-made lake. Beyond it lay the Fallen Heroes section of the Gardens. It didn't feel like fourteen months had passed since she'd stood on that slope, Gunderson holding her up. A full police funeral with honor guard, a mile-long motorcade halting traffic along the beltway, and the mounted unit leading the procession through the cemetery grounds off Padonia Road. Kay remembered flinching at each round of the twenty-one-gun salute, watching numbly as taps played and Grace was handed Spencer's departmental hat.

Kay hadn't been back since. Hadn't been able to face the guilt.

She turned to Valley's unmarked niche. Now she had two reasons to come here. She made a silent vow to do so.

"We should get going," Vicki said, then slid her arm around the girl's shoulder. "Are you going to be all right, Kathleen?"

Koch nodded.

"And you're okay to drive back?"

"Yeah." Koch forced a smile and let Vicki guide her to where they'd left the cars on the cul-de-sac.

Kay followed, but not before laying her palm against the

smooth marble of Valley's niche. "I'm sorry," she whispered, but didn't feel better for saying it.

As the sun lowered into a haze of smog, they left the grounds and drove south from Timonium. In the passenger seat of Vicki's blaze red Del Sol, Kay had lost sight of Koch's Chevy long before the city limits. She thought of the girl, going home alone.

With only enough time for a quick change, Vicki waited while Kay slipped into her dress and heels. Kay had tried to get out of their symphony date, but Vicki had argued that the night out would do Kay good. Take her mind off things.

They parked in the Mt. Vernon cultural district and walked the three blocks to the $24 million brick-and-glass hall on Cathedral and Preston, and by the time they took their seats in the center orchestra section of the Joseph Meyerhoff, Kay tried to shed the job and her frustrations.

Sitting in the elegant, wood-appointed interior of the hall with its sculpted box seats and modern sound-baffles, with the din of decked-out concertgoers buzzing around her, Kay felt the excitement rise. Wearing suits all day, she loved putting on the tight black dress and rubbing elbows with the elite of Baltimore, even if she did feel slightly misplaced. She didn't feel like herself in this place, and she liked that. Liked the escape. Liked pretending to be someone else just for one night.

Still Eales was with her. And Patricia Hagen. Kay closed her eyes, tried to block them out, but found herself strategizing.

"I'm going to call Hagen in the morning," she said, leaning over to Vicki.

"The old man?"

"No. Patsy. Maybe I can get something out of her if I

sympathize with her, convince her that I believe in Bernard's innocence. If she *does* know anything about the murders, maybe she'll be more willing to give it up if I promise to help her get Bernard off. If I play her right, I might get a name."

"You really think he had an accomplice?"

"More than ever." Given Eales's confession and his attitude this afternoon, Kay was almost certain of it.

"You said Bates implied to you that Hagen was seeing Eales *before* his incarceration, right?" Vicki asked, taking out a compact from her purse and checking her lipstick.

"Yeah, which means Patsy Hagen might know who helped Eales."

"Then talk to her." Vicki snapped the compact shut and tucked it away. "It can't hurt. Now, are you going to listen to some music or keep chewing at this case all night?"

The din in the hall hushed as the orchestra tuned. Kay tried to focus on the concert program in her hands, but her mind was crashing.

Patsy Hagen . . . Eales was covering for someone. Kay pictured Patsy, standing in the doorway of her Mt. Washington home, distrust in her eyes. The woman had lied about her history with Eales. What else would she lie about?

Maybe it was Patricia Hagen who'd been at Eales's that night, Hagen who'd found Kay's gun on the porch while Bernard beat the shit out of her.

It made sense that Eales would cover for Hagen.

The orchestra settled and the lights dimmed then.

In the darkness of the symphony hall, Kay conjured up Patricia Hagen—the calloused hands and strong shoulders. She imagined the woman's childhood; Hagen admitted to being numb to the death that pervaded her life as an undertaker's daughter. What better person to help Eales dispose of a body? Or three? A woman blinded by love with a stomach for death.

It took the first quarter of the first movement of Corigliano's *Red Violin* Concerto for the last traces of the case to seep from Kay's thoughts. There was no escaping the power of the music. The strains of the strings swelled over her, reflected off the soundboards overhead, and filled the hall, consuming her entirely.

It swept her away. Away from Eales and Hagen, the dead women, Valley and Beggs. Away from Spencer, the job, the streets. The clean vibrations of the violin solo took her home again, to the most vivid memories of her mother. She'd spent many afternoons sitting at the top of the stairs, listening to her mother administering violin lessons to the children of Jonesport. It helped pay the bills, but Kay had always suspected her mother would have done it for nothing. And after the lessons were done, after the last student had left their weather-beaten clapboard house that overlooked Chandler Bay, Kay would sit and listen to her mother play.

If she were still alive today, Kay would have liked to bring her here. She imagined her mother sitting next to her, breathing in the beauty of the music.

It was Kay's pager, vibrating in her lap through her handbag, that startled her out of the abstraction of memories. In the dark hall, she dug out the unit and angled its display.

"Shit."

"What is it?" Vicki whispered next to her.

"It's Finn. nine one one."

45

FINN HAD TO LOOK TWICE before he recognized
the two women getting out of the two-seater sports car
that turned onto Gettings Street. He identified Vicki first,
in her figure-hugging red dress and stilettos. Kay's heels
were shorter, but the little black number she wore was
every bit as sexy as Vicki's.

He let out a breathy whistle as they crossed toward him.
"Whoa. What did I drag you two away from?"

"Girls' night out," Vicki said, smiling in spite of the
interruption. "This better be good."

"Well, just my luck to get both of you down here." He
pointed to Bates's house. "I want inside."

"What's going on?" Kay asked.

Seeing her standing there in the soft amber glow from
the streetlamp, he tried to take his eyes off her, but wasn't
having much luck. He remembered the dress too well,
remembered the Habitat benefit they'd attended less than a
week before the beatdown. And he remembered how he'd
peeled that black number off Kay later that night, back at
her place.

Leaning against the front fender of the radio car, he gestured to Bates's house, the windows dark. "Seems our boy
was on the prowl tonight. He's home now though."

"Where'd he go?"

Finn nodded to the uniform next to him. "Mikey here
caught him slipping out the back." He gestured for the
Southern District officer to fill them in and wondered if
the rookie could stop ogling Kay long enough to string a
sentence together.

"Mike McNally," he said, extending his hand first to

Kay, then Vicki. "I didn't actually see him exit the back, but I saw headlights in the alley. Then Bates's car comes round, he's got his hand up against the side of his face, like he thinks I won't recognize him or his ride."

"You're on your own here?" Kay asked.

"Yes, ma'am. We're short-manned. So I called it in, then tailed him. He took me up to Hollins Market, tried to lose me, but I caught up with him on Wilkens and Fulton."

"Wilkens Avenue?"

"Yes, ma'am. I hung back at first so maybe he figured he'd ditched me. Then he starts cruising the ladies." He smirked. "Didn't get too lucky though, with my unit glued to his ass. Girls'd take one look and move on. He led me around again for a bit, trying to lose me, then ended up back on Wilkens. Finally he pulls over, gets out, and walks back to my car."

"What did he have to say?"

"Not much besides cussing me up one side and down the other about his rights."

"Do we know for sure he was trying to pick up a girl?" Kay asked.

McNally shrugged. "When I threatened to take him in on a john charge, he claimed he was only trying to score a little H for personal use. Said he prefers dealing with the ladies. I followed him home after that. He parked out back again, and his lights came on inside. There's been movement, and now it looks like he's either gone to bed or he's sitting in the dark watching us."

Kay studied Bates's dark windows, assessing. Finn couldn't help thinking she looked out of place down in this dirty end of Baltimore.

"So what are you thinking?" Vicki asked Finn then.

"I want in that house, Vick. Tonight."

She was already shaking her head. "You've got nothing, Finn." She turned to McNally. "Did you see Bates go into his house with a possible victim?"

"No."

"Anyone else enter the premises?"

"Nope."

"Then you've got no exigent circumstances to warrant an immediate search," she said to Finn.

"What about the fleeing-felon rule?" he asked.

"It doesn't apply here, Finn. Sorry."

"But we *can* get a warrant, right?" Kay asked. Finn could hear the edginess in her voice, knew that if she could bust through Bates's door right now, she would, sexy dress and all. "If Bates is trying to pick up prostitutes, from Wilkens Avenue where Beggs was picked up, we've got our PC right?"

"Along with everything else, yeah. I think I can get a warrant signed. Not till Monday though. Yes, the probable cause is there, but it's shaky. I'm not going to push a judge with anything less than solid on a Sunday."

"All right, in the meantime, Mike"—Kay turned to the rookie—"you'll stay here, right?"

"All night."

"And can you see the back from in your car?"

"Not really."

"What about getting a second unit down here?" she asked Finn.

"We're lucky to have this one," he told her.

"Look," McNally interrupted, "I've got the place covered. If he tries again, I'll see him. There's only one way out with his car, and it's past me."

"And what if he heads out on foot? If he goes out the back, he can hoof it over to Decatur and hail a cab down on Fort Avenue. I don't like this, Finn."

Finn walked several yards down the street, studied the angles, and returned. "Just pull your unit up a hundred feet or so," he said to McNally. "You should be able to see if he comes out the back then."

Still, Finn could see Kay wasn't satisfied. "You need another coffee?" she asked the uniform.

"Detective Finnerty's already taken care of me." McNally tipped the oversize take-out cup at her.

Kay offered the rookie a parting nod. "All right then. Have a good night."

"So Monday morning, right?" Kay asked Vicki as Finn walked them back to Vicki's sports car.

"First thing."

"Good, cuz I wanna hit this guy before reality does," Finn said. He held the car door for Kay as she folded herself into the tiny car.

Vicki nodded, no doubt considering the work that lay ahead of her, and the judge she'd have to bat her blues at for a predawn signature on Monday. "All right. Let me see your paperwork tomorrow and have a team ready to go. We'll see what this slimeball's all about."

46

JERRY BATES NEEDED A HIT. He paced, beating a path the length of his foyer between two uniforms, his fingers drumming his hips, his eyes blinking spasmodically. Kay almost felt sorry for the junkie as the search team flipped his house.

Bates must have been sleeping when they arrived at 6:30 a.m. Or he'd been hiding his stash because, when the ram busted through the front door, the team found Bates shaking in the middle of the living room. Kay thought he was going to piss himself.

For over an hour they'd gone through the narrow row house. And in that time Kay had tried to get a read on Bates. If the former funeral-home employee had been capable of helping Eales a year ago, she couldn't say. Any evidence of his once-organized life had decayed into the chaos of drugs.

For Kay—thinking of Valley and Beggs, both murdered in the past eleven days, both conscientiously disposed of— nothing fit.

From upstairs the thud of boots marked the progress of the uniforms as they dissected the place, and beside her, Finn foraged through papers littering the kitchen table.

Kay moved in next to him. "He's not our guy." She kept her voice low.

"Why do you say that?" he asked, but she guessed he already knew.

"He'd keep souvenirs. There's nothing here. Where's Valley's driver's license?"

"I don't know. Maybe he's got it stashed someplace else. Maybe he got rid of it." Anger had crept into Finn's voice, sharpening his words. "Maybe he doesn't kill them here. This place is a fucking sty. How the hell do you live in this shit?" But he didn't expect an answer from Bates.

When Finn pushed aside more junk, a six-pack of empty Milwaukees fell to the floor, several rolling away across the old linoleum.

"You got no right, man. No right," Bates chanted from the door. "Bustin' in here like this. Messing with my shit."

"Do I need to come over there and show you the warrant again, asshole?" Finn's patience had worn thinner than Kay's. "Now just shut the fuck up."

They'd worked long into Saturday night and most of

Sunday morning putting together the search-and-seizure warrant for Vicki to process. Then Finn had surprised Kay with lunch on the boat. He'd taken her out onto the bay after, wrapped her in one of his wool sweaters as the sails of *The Blue Angel* unfurled to catch the crisp, autumn gusts that whipped around Wagners Point. For a few hours, she'd been able to forget about Bates, Hagen, and especially Eales. Finn too seemed to relax as they sailed, and Kay had felt the shift in their relationship, the beginnings of normalcy.

But this morning, assembling the team outside Bates's house, faced once again with the case, Kay had shared a mutual frustration with Finn. It had only intensified when each room they searched produced nothing. There were no ties to Eales, to Valley or Beggs, or any of the three previous victims. And Kay knew the task force weighed as heavily on Finn's mind as her own.

"Here." Finn held up three fat blunts, pinched between his gloved fingers, and dropped them into the evidence bag Kay provided. "And we've got more."

He pushed aside magazines and flyers to reveal hypodermics, a burned spoon, and several dime bags of heroin.

"Christ, Jerry, I don't know *why* you thought you had to score the other night. Look at all this shit," he said.

Kay handed the evidence to one of the uniforms and turned her attention to a small chest of drawers in the alcove between the living room and kitchen. She pulled one drawer, but the catch was broken and a mess of bills, pens, coins, and other junk clattered to the ground.

"Jesus!" Bates worked his nails into his scalp, then tugged at the ends of his buzz cut. "You gotta trash everything?"

"Then make it easy for me, Jerry. Tell me where you keep your stash of ketamine," Kay said.

"My what?"

"You heard me. Your Special K. Vitamin K. The stuff you use to shoot them up with."

"I don't know what you're talking about," he whined.

"Fine." She pulled out the next drawer, letting its contents spill around her feet as well.

"Fuckin' bitch. You did that on purpose. You—" He started to come at her, but Finn was across the room in an instant.

"What did you call her, Jerry, hmm? Did I hear you right? Did I just hear you call a decorated officer a 'fucking bitch'?" He smacked Bates on the back of his head with his open palm and the junkie teetered a couple steps. "Now, unless you're gonna cooperate here, just shut the fuck up. You're giving me a headache with all that whining."

Only when Finn's cell phone rang did he turn from the junkie. He took the call in the kitchen, listening intently, and finally his eyes went to Kay.

"We'll be there," she heard him say, and he snapped the phone shut. "We might have another one," he said to her.

"What?" Kay dropped the papers she'd been searching.

"Leakin Park." He spun to face Bates again. "Where the hell were you last night, Jerry, huh? Where'd you go?"

"I was right here, man. The whole night."

"Bullshit. You're a lying fucking asshole. Where were you?"

"You got a goddamned car on my house, you *know* I was here."

"D'you go out the back, Jerry? Is that what you did? Fuck." Finn turned to Kay. "Come on. We have to roll." And then to the uniforms: "Everything in this place gets taken apart. Everything!"

At the door Finn borrowed a set of cuffs off one of the officers and spun Bates against the wall. "I want you to take this lying piece of shit downtown and book him," he said to the uniform.

"On what?" Bates squealed as the cuffs snapped.

"Oh, I don't know, Jerry. But with all the smack and the reefers you've got lying around your crib here, I'm sure we can drum up something, huh?"

"This is bullshit!"

"Yeah, right, Jerry." Finn grappled with Bates again, pushing him aside, maybe a little too hard, to make way for Kay. "We'll talk to your lying ass later," he told Bates.

At the car, Kay could still hear Bates screaming profanities.

"Let's go see what they've found," Finn said as they got into the car. "And pray to God this one isn't related."

47

THE BODY IN LEAKIN PARK had come to rest at the bottom of a dry ravine, surrounded by decaying leaves and rotting stumps. By the time Kay and Finn arrived, several radio cars crouched in the mist along the shoulder of Franklintown Road, which cut through the three hundred acres of park.

She'd been discovered by a jogger, her white skin a beacon between rain-blackened trunks. She'd been dumped sometime in the early-morning hours and didn't have a name until Kay stumbled down the steep pitch with Finn and looked into the mangled face.

"Jesus Christ, are you sure it's her?" Finn asked.

Kay nodded, as shocked as Finn. Squatting over the body, she pointed to the diamond on Patricia Hagen's muddied finger.

"What the hell happened to her face?"

Rain pooled in one of Hagen's hazel eyes; the other had been mashed in. The left side of her head had been crushed, and her hair was matted with blood and brain matter.

"You think that happened on the way down?"

Kay gauged the embankment. "No. Looks more like he kicked her face in. Must have done it after she was dead. There'd be more blood otherwise. But it's him."

Water had also settled in the shallow knife wounds on her chest and in the long gashes that ran halfway up the inside of her arm. Kay guessed that this morning's heavy rains had washed away most of the dirt and leaves that would have collected on her body during her long tumble down the slope.

The uniforms had given way to Kay and Finn, and other than the distant squelch of police radios up on the roadway, the ravine was silent. Water dripped from the golden leaves still clinging to the branches overhead and drummed the carpet of spent foliage.

Kay stood and surveyed Hagen. Her right arm was pinned beneath her at an unnatural angle. And plastered on her hip, a flame-red maple leaf was brilliant against her colorless flesh.

Kay felt embarrassed for the woman—exposed, splayed out before everyone. There was no dignity in death. Certainly not in murder. Here, and then at the OCME, Hagen's body would be laid out, picked apart, examined, and dissected with little regard for privacy. Kay always hoped she'd never die in Baltimore City, lying on a slab for Jonesy and her fellow detectives to see.

"He wasn't worried about her being found." She shuffled one duty-shoe in the dense leaves underfoot. "He could have covered her, and she wouldn't have been found for months."

Kay thought of Valley. And Beggs. He *was* trying to get their attention.

She pointed to the wounds on Hagen's chest. "There're more this time," she said. "How many do you count?"

"Eighteen. Twenty, maybe."

"Almost twice as many. Why?"

"She's bigger than his last two. Stronger. Harder to sub-due."

"Not if the wounds are postmortem." She pointed to the ligature marks circling Hagen's outstretched left wrist. Similar marks scored her ankles. "He tied her. That's a first."

"I don't get this, Kay." Finn circled the body once, shaking his head. "If we're looking at Bates for these murders, how the hell did he pull this one off under our noses?"

"Maybe he *did* get out the back." Kay breathed in the damp forest air and watched ants trail lines across Hagen's damp skin, marking routes over their new landscape. "Or maybe we *are* off base with Bates. This is someone smart, Finn. Someone who's got it together, knows what he's doing."

"Like Arsenault?"

She let out a breath. What if her fleeting attraction to Arsenault *had* impaired her judgment? "I wish I knew. This just doesn't make sense to me."

On the road some thirty feet above them, the OCME's white van pulled to the shoulder. The crowd had multiplied: joggers and dog walkers, drivers rubbernecking. A Mobile Crime Lab technician was making the treacherous descent into the ravine, her camera around her neck, as she gripped the guide rope patrol officers had strung around the rain-slick tree trunks.

Kay scanned the area and the slope cutting farther down to Dead Run, the river that snaked to Gwynns Falls. This was all too familiar. Last year, after she'd caught the Annie

Harris case, she'd come here, the Jane Doe long gone, the crime scene weeks old.

She turned several times now, gauging her bearings, then pointed west. "We passed a T-intersection back there, didn't we?"

"Yeah. Lazear, I think. About a hundred yards back."

"Son of a bitch."

"What is it, Kay?"

"Varcoe's Jane Doe. She was found right around here. Maybe a little farther down. It's the same spot."

"This guy dumped Hagen here just to fuck with us?"

"Either that or he's fucking with Eales." She nodded to Hagen's body, stark and white amidst the leaves. "This guy might have been doing Eales a favor by killing Valley, but he's just taken out Eales's meal ticket."

"Or maybe this is a favor too. Guess it depends on how Eales really felt about his inside-outside."

"I don't think Eales asked for this one, Finn." Kay's stomach clutched around the coffee and muffin she'd eaten on the way to the search-and-seizure at Bates's. "This one makes things way more complicated."

"I wanna talk to Arsenault." Finn scanned the crowd above them as though he expected to find the Web designer there. "Even if this isn't him, he's responsible. Him and that goddamned site of his. *And* I want to know if good ol' Jerry was really home last night."

The Crime Lab technician was a hard-faced girl with a weak smile. She shuffled through the leaves, stopping several yards back from the body, and unhitched her camera. "Where do you want me to start?" she asked.

"Shoot her first, I guess." Finn pointed to Hagen.

"No," Kay interrupted. "She's not going anywhere. Start with them." She nodded at the spectators crowding the yellow tape. "You got a wide-angle or a zoom on that thing?"

"Of course."

"Good. Get as many of them as you can before they start disappearing. I need to know if the son of a bitch is watching us."

48

WHILE THE EYES of the morbidly curious sought out Hagen's body down in the ravine, Roach watched Delaney.

Seeing Patsy only reminded him of the frustration, of the need going unquenched. He had hoped for so much more from the cow.

Two nights ago when she'd knocked on his door, he'd been giddy with anticipation. Absolutely exhilarated when he'd nailed her in the thigh with the needle. She'd shoved him away, grappled uselessly as her glasses went spinning across the floor, and she blubbered profanities he'd never expected from Daddy's good girl.

She'd gone down fast though.

He'd dragged her to the bathroom then and peeled off her clothes. And all the time, her eyes wide and gawking.

Only after he'd managed to get her into the tub did Roach allow himself a smile. Staring down at her blank gaze, her head slumped onto one shoulder and her white flesh pressing against the porcelain sides of the tub.

"Patsy. Earth to Patsy. Stay with me now," he'd crooned.

A thin moan. Her eyelids fluttered. He slapped her cheek and wondered if he'd given her too much of the ketamine. Or maybe she was faking. He checked the bonds. Ankles. Wrists. Her flesh swelled around the knots as the end of the rope was secured to the old pipes under the basin sink. The last whore had taught him the importance of ligatures; he wouldn't make the same mistake twice.

He'd undressed and folded his clothes on the toilet seat. When he returned, the sour stench of her vomit hung in the air. It must have been the ketamine. He'd washed the puke off her, all the while worrying he wouldn't be able to get it up after that.

Naked, he straddled her in the big tub. The AC blasted against his sweat-slicked skin, and he shivered as he looked into her half-lidded eyes, the irises barely pale rings around her dilated pupils.

"There you are. How you feeling, hmm, Patsy?"

When her eyes threatened to close again, he jostled her. "Come on, old girl. Don't you wanna play with Roach?" He wondered if a shot of cold water might bring her around. He needed to see the realization fill her eyes. That's what got him hard.

Planting himself over her ample hips, he took one breast in his hand and kneaded it between his fingers, pinching the stiffened nipple. When that didn't rouse her, he squeezed harder.

Her eyes widened then, as the blood rose to her tit, revealing the imprint of his hand.

"Ah, you're awake now, aren't you?"

He twisted over her and reached for the lock-back knife on the sill. Showed her the gleaming blade. He'd worked on the Spyderco Police Model for an hour the night before, honing the small blade until he'd had to take his hard-on into the shower. But with Patsy for company, he wouldn't be jacking-off solo. No, sir.

He leaned forward, his erection pressing against her belly. The heat of her body did nothing to excite him. Instead, it was the knife. The feel of the thin handle in his palm, the anticipation of its blade loving her. But the best was always later, when she'd cooled. For now though, her fear would be his prize.

"How're you doing, Patsy, hmm?" He caressed her cheek with the blade. This time her moan was louder, her paralyzed body shifted weakly under his, and if not for the pink panties he'd wadded into her mouth, he knew she'd be screeching.

Reaching up with the knife, he traced its tip from her wrist, down the inside of her arm, all the way to her pit. He lowered his face and inhaled. Just under her rose-scented deodorant, the smell of her sweat was intoxicating.

A couple days' growth shadowed her armpit. He'd expected she'd have kept herself better. He brought the Spyderco's blade to the pale mound of stubbled flesh.

The blade was sharp enough, and her deodorant acted as a lubricant. He stroked the knife across the porous skin and watched the small black hairs accumulate along its blade. The hunger grew. Its pressure boiled under his skull, snaked deep in his groin. And when she stiffened weakly beneath him, and he heard her gurgled moan, Roach figured Patsy would be one to remember.

In the end, though, she'd been a huge disappointment. Long after she was dead, after her flesh had started to cool, he'd tried to haul her upstairs to the bedroom, wanted to lie with her as he had with the hooker. But Patsy was heavier than he'd counted on.

To top it off, she'd been a pain in the ass to get rid of. It had been a long night. His muscles had burned as he'd dragged her to the new tarp in the hall. Only then, securely wrapped, had her dead weight slid more easily across the worn linoleum flooring to the back door.

The porch had been a challenge, and getting her into the trunk of the Park Avenue had really pissed him off.

Then, in Leakin Park at 2 a.m., as spikes of rain pelted his hooded jacket and drove past the glare of the headlights like shiny nails, he'd worked up a sweat getting her back out of the trunk. The nylon cord had cut his hands, and he'd cursed as he hauled her to the side of the embankment.

And there, in the dark silence of the forest, Roach had vented the enormity of his anger on Patsy. Over the drumming rain, he heard his own satisfied grunts as he brought his heel down hard and square onto what he imagined was her face under the tarp. It had felt good, and he'd done it again, and again, before—exhausted—he'd unfurled the tarp and let her body loose, listening to it tumble and come to rest somewhere in the blackness.

Still, in spite of the hassle, it was good Patsy was dead. Sooner or later she would've slipped up. Delaney and her partner had already talked to her. And even though Patsy wasn't the sharpest tool in the shed, she might've figured everything out and pointed the finger.

So, it was business. He wondered if Bernard would understand.

Now, Roach watched Delaney as she stood over Patsy's body. He wondered if her partner recognized the life force in her. Her determination and her will to live. Delaney's drive for survival was high. He'd witnessed it himself the night Bernard had kicked the living shit out of her. Anyone else might not have survived it. Anyone else would not have hung on the way she did.

And he hoped, in his hands, she would show that determination again.

49

THEY GRABBED A COFFEE on the way up to Overlea and found Alexander Hagen in his new Parkview Funeral Home. Amidst the ostentatious trappings of death, the man's stoicism endured. It wasn't until they'd taken him to the OCME—at his insistence—to view his daughter's remains that he'd finally broken down.

Finn had intended to ask the old man for an alibi. But witnessing Hagen's breakdown, Finn had refrained from asking. For now.

Supplying them with a spare key, Hagen had found his own way home, and by four o'clock Finn and Kay let themselves into Patricia Hagen's Mt. Washington home.

"Well, he didn't snatch her from here," Finn said as they pushed their way past five yowling cats. "No forced entry. Nothing out of place."

The air in the small stone house was stale and reeked of litter boxes. The flowers in the vases drooped, but there were no signs of foul play.

The cats followed them into Hagen's office and Kay dumped a sixth off the chair at the computer. While Kay fired up the PC, Finn took stock of Patricia's devotion to Eales.

"Jesus, will you look at all this?"

Corkboards mounted on either side of the office window boasted photos and Post-it notes, all painstakingly tacked up, perfectly spaced. Their content: Eales. Photos of Eales as a teenager, photos of him with what looked like his mother, his baby brother, and others Finn didn't recognize. Several shots had captured him with his vintage car. Finn recognized a few snaps from the website. But none were of Eales and Hagen as the happy couple.

"Welcome to the shrine of Bernard Eales."

To the left of the photo wall, a bookcase was wedged into the corner. The spines of the texts reminded him of Arsenault's condo, but Hagen's collection lay predominantly within the realm of law. Finn imagined Eales's girlfriend had become a major pain in Grogan's ass as the trial loomed, no doubt grasping at angles to save a man she probably figured she owed her life to.

"We're not going to get much from this," Kay said from behind the computer's monitor. "Her in- and out-boxes are practically empty. Her recycle bin has been deleted."

"Any emails to Arsenault?"

"Several. The last one she wrote offers him a higher cut from the defense fund if he can arrange some national exposure."

"So the bastard's been getting a percentage all along." Finn shook his head. "What about documents?" He waited as Kay perused the user files. Together they scanned the short list. Letters to Grogan mostly. Several love notes to Eales.

"Fucking nutcase," Finn said, backing away from the computer. "I say we pack this up and take the whole mess in. Let the computer guys go over it. Maybe they can salvage some of the deleted shit."

He ferreted through the letter trays on the desk. Articles and photocopies from law journals. Online pages printed from other sites developed for "innocents," and letters to and from national organizations supporting the "wrongfully incarcerated."

"And all this garbage too," he said, indicating the stacks.

He scanned the desk again, and the red flashing digit

on the answering machine caught his eye. Finn hit the play button and heard the satisfying whir of tape rewinding. Old technology. Far more accessible than voice mail, and no need to subpoena the phone company for messages.

They listened to the half dozen messages. One from Kay asking Patricia to call, three hang-ups, then one from Arsenault:

"Patricia, it's Scott. Saturday night. Ah . . . ten forty. Listen, I know it's late, but I need you to call me. Something's come up." There was a rustling in the background that Finn couldn't identify. "I may have lined up something with one of the networks, but we should talk. They're calling me in the morning, so I think we should meet tonight. I'm at home."

"Sounds like bait to me," Finn said.

After Arsenault's call, there were two more hang-ups, then nothing.

"I want a dump on this line," Finn said. "We need to find out who's been calling, and who the hang-ups are. I'll have the subpoena ready tomorrow."

"What about outgoing?" Kay asked.

Picking up the receiver, Finn jabbed the redial button.

"Checker Cab." The voice over the line was laced with phlegm.

"Yeah, this is Detective Finnerty. Baltimore Police. I'm trying to trace a call you would have gotten from this number. Can you check your logs?"

He heard the tapping of a keyboard. "Nineteen Wetherburn?"

"That's right."

There was another burst of keyboarding. "Yeah, that call went out Saturday night. Ten fifty. Fare went to three-eleven Keystone."

"Keystone? You're sure about that?"

"System doesn't lie. But I can check with the driver and get back to you."

Finn gave the dispatcher his number and hung up. "You're gonna like this," he said to Kay. "Cab took Hagen to an address up on TV Hill. *After* Arsenault's message."

50

KAY WAS THE FIRST ONE UP the concrete steps of 311 Keystone, a queasy déjà vu sweeping over her. Just last week she'd banged at this very door, hoping to find a witness to the disposal of B. J. Beggs's body in the back alley.

How had she been this close and missed it?

On the drive up, Finn had radioed for backup. Then he'd gotten a call from the cabbie who'd actually seen Hagen go into the house Saturday night after dropping her off.

Three-eleven was a narrow row house three doors down from where Keystone ended at the top of TV Hill. There were no lights behind the blinds in the upstairs windows or on the ground floor. The last tinges of daylight reflected in the dark panes.

On the covered porch, Kay swung open the dented aluminum screen and hammered on the door. Nothing. As she had the other day, she moved to the main-floor bow window and cupped her hands against the grimy middle pane, peering through the narrow slit between the heavy curtains.

Finn beat the butt end of the police radio against the door. Then waited.

On the street, a radio car pulled to the curb behind their

Lumina. The two uniforms took the first set of steps to the walkway, adjusting their equipment belts and assessing the quiet neighborhood.

"Might be nothing, guys." Finn beat on the door again.

Turning back to the window, Kay thought she saw movement in the soupy darkness beyond the parting of the curtain. It had been quick. A fleeting shadow. Or nothing at all.

"I think I saw something," she said, and pressed tighter against the window. But the phantom—imaginary or otherwise—was gone.

"What was it?" Finn already had his gun's holster unclipped.

"I think the son of a bitch is in there." She pushed Finn aside, hammered on the door herself as the first wave of adrenaline lashed through her. "Baltimore Police. Open up."

"Go around back," she instructed the uniforms as she tried the handle, found it locked.

"Kay, I don't think there's anyone in there."

She kicked at the door one last time before letting the screen slam shut. "I could have sworn I saw something."

Taking the steps back to the sidewalk, Kay studied the dark windows. "I want in this house, Finn." *Was she the only one who felt the electricity in the air? Did Finn not have the same deep coil in his gut that she did?*

"We need a warrant," Finn said.

"Then let's get one. We've already got the cabbie saying he saw Hagen go in. That should be enough PC."

Kay scanned the street. It was getting dark now; only a thin line of dusk clung to the top of the tree line skirting Druid Hill Park. It smelled like more rain.

At the bottom of the block a screen door slammed, and a tall figure descended the steps of the other porch. She watched the man gimp in a calm, long-legged shuffle up the hill toward them. Finn followed her into the street to meet him.

"I help you with something?" the man asked, taking an easy drink from his can of Natty Boh, his docile eyes swinging from them to the radio car and back.

"Yeah." Kay nodded to 311. "Can you tell us anything about this house?"

"Sure I can." He tipped his beer at its front door. "It's mine."

51

HIS NAME WAS LEON GAINES.

Gaines had been renting out 311 Keystone for the last eight years since his uncle passed and left him the place.

"It comes furnished," he said, walking them down the block to his own house. "Easier 'n having to get rid of all the furniture. And I can charge more."

As they mounted the steps of his porch, Finn felt the exhaustion in his bones and guessed Kay did as well. Since Bates's house this morning, they'd gone nonstop, but the new rush of adrenaline had offered them both a second wind. Now, Finn shared Kay's raw excitement.

"This about that girl they found in the alley?" At his door, Gaines turned to face them. He was a tall, rawboned man with deep-set eyes that were spaced too close together. His jeans were tattered and his T-shirt stained. "Cuz if it is, you guys already talked to me. Twice." He crushed the can of Natty Boh in his fist and tossed it in a recycle bin. It clattered against a dozen other beer cans. "I already told the uniformed guy the other day I didn't see nothing."

"What can you tell us about your tenant, Mr. Gaines?" Kay asked.

"He's quiet. Not around too much from what I can tell."

"He moved in recently?"

"Yeah. 'Bout a week ago. Not much to move in, but he did install an AC unit, so I'm hoping he figures to stay a bit."

"Do you have a tenancy agreement?" she asked.

"Yeah."

Kay nodded toward his door. "Can you show it to us?"

"Sure." Gaines turned into his house and probably hoped they'd stay on the porch. But Kay invited herself in.

Inside the stuffy house, Finn offered a cursory nod to a woman sitting on a plastic-covered sofa, an open bag of Utz potato chips in her lap. Her bifocaled gazed flitted briefly from some country-western music video, then back again. Gaines had disappeared somewhere in the back of the house. When he returned, he held a stained manila folder in one hand and a fresh beer in the other. He handed Kay the folder and Finn scanned the contents with her.

The rental agreement was a photocopy of a standard, and Finn's eyes passed no farther than the renter's name.

"Son of a bitch," he said under his breath.

"Can you tell us what your tenant Mr. Arsenault looks like?" Kay asked.

"I dunno. Average, I guess. Clean. A bit of a pretty boy. Wore a nice suit when he came around to see the place."

"What else? Size, build? Hair color?"

"Like I said, average. Shorter 'n me, and skinny. Pale too, like maybe he doesn't get out much."

"Blond hair?" she asked.

"I guess. Dirty blond."

"Yeah, and he had a bit of a beard."

"A goatee?"

"Dunno. Maybe, but honestly, I don't pay attention to that sorta thing. Guy looks decent and pays the rent, I mind my own business."

"How did he pay?"

"Cash. Four months up front."

"And what's a clean-cut suit doing renting a dump from you?" Finn asked.

"Not a dump. 'Sides, you think I'm gonna start counting teeth in a horse's mouth? But he did say something 'bout looking for a place to buy and needed a short-term rental."

"Have you ever seen anyone else with him?" Kay asked.

"Like I said, he ain't around much. Low-key. Kinda tenant you want."

Kay closed the folder and tucked it under her arm. "I'll get this back to you, Mr. Gaines. In the meantime, we need access to the house."

He seemed to take a mental stumble. "What's this about?"

"Mr. Gaines, please, we're not at liberty to say."

"Well, you can't. Get in the house, I mean. Not tonight anyway. I have to give the tenant twenty-four-hour notice."

"You won't need any notice when we show you the warrant," Kay said, turning out the door then. "We'll come get you when we have it so we won't have to bust up your doors."

Gaines lifted his sweating beer can in a limp toast. "Appreciate that," he called after them as they headed back to the street and up the hill to 311.

"I'm having problems seeing Scott in this," Kay said when they reached the car. She opened the driver's-side door and tossed the folder onto the dash.

"Gaines's description matches."

"Only vaguely." She nodded to the house. "This isn't Scott's style."

"And why not? Why wouldn't he keep a place up here? At his condo he's got a doorman, he's got neighbors. No easy way to get those victims in and out without being seen. This dump's perfect. Pretty much a dead-end street up here, and he's got the alley in the back."

"Anyone could have thrown that form together, Finn. Besides, it's all fiction. The address listed as his last residence . . . I worked the Northwest. There *is* no nine hundred block of Booker Street."

"Why Arsenault's name then? If it's not him, how would this mope even know it?"

"He reads everything written about his murders. Including Eales's website. He's fucking with us. He's using Scott's name because he knows we're sniffing around the guy. He could have put any John Henry on that form. Cash up front, Gaines isn't going to verify any of it. He's using Scott's name to throw us a curveball."

"Well, fiction or not, that form is all a judge'll need to sign a warrant for us to toss Arsenault's condo. And I am *not* going to pass up that opportunity."

Kay was silent for a moment, her eyes still on 311. "Fine. But I want a warrant for this place first." She looked at her watch in the twilight. "I want inside that house before the night's done."

52

Fearing an overreaction downtown, Kay asked Finn to keep the latest development quiet as he went to arrange for the warrant. Last thing she needed was a Quick Response Team busting down the door of 311 and a descent of brass trampling the crime scene she knew must lie beyond its front door.

It had been an hour since Finn had caught a lift to Headquarters with Giordano, one of the Northern uniforms, while the other—a wide-shouldered slab of a kid named Madjarian—kept Kay company. They'd sat in the Lumina, positioned on Rockrose, allowing a full view of 311's front porch as well as the mouth of the alley. She and the kid had exchanged shoptalk, but Kay's attention was on the house, the alley, on every car that passed the bottom of Keystone and every moving shadow.

With Giordano's return, Kay instructed the two uniforms to park their unit out of sight and go on foot to record tag numbers of the vehicles parked in the neighborhood. In the past twenty minutes, she'd radioed them twice for progress reports as they worked the five blocks south of the Hill. It was raining now, and she imagined them taking cover on someone's porch.

Through the open window, the smell of wet asphalt was heavy. A nighthawk squawked softly overhead, and a weak breeze stirred a bamboo wind chime somewhere down the street. To her left, the lights of the TV towers blinked red into the night, refracting into shattered patterns across the rain-beaded windshield.

She looked at the house again and wondered if she'd really seen movement inside earlier. It could have been her own reflection. She remembered the mirror she'd seen hanging on the opposite wall when she'd peeked through the drapes last week.

Focus on the street, Delaney. The alley. If he comes back, you've got to be ready. The radio lay in the seat next to her, its channel open to Giordano and Madjarian in case she needed backup.

She thought of Scott. They'd have to talk to him about his phone call to Patricia. And his name on the tenancy agreement. Could she have been wrong about him? Had it been Scott who'd lured Patricia out here?

Kay eased her head back and listened to the rain drum the car's roof while mentally reviewing the day. From Leakin Park to the funeral home and finally Patricia's house. All day she'd struggled to find a possible motive for Hagen's murder.

Had her killer known her personally? Had she simply been a convenient victim? Or was there more behind her death? Patricia Hagen had been more than vocal on Scott's website. *Had she said too much? Or had Hagen known the truth all along?*

Kay imagined Hagen's body now, lying in the OCME's admissions cooler in a white plastic bag, awaiting autopsy in the morning. Another victim. Another possibility for answers.

But it was the house, 311 Keystone, that was going to give them answers that no victim could. Kay was certain. Her eyes fixed on the darkened windows, imagining what might await them inside. She took a breath. Tried to relax.

Then she spotted the headlights behind the block of houses. The beams panned across the asphalt on Keystone, then disappeared. At first she figured it was a car parking down the block, until she saw the light stretch down the alley, reaching the top street only yards from where she sat.

She waited for the vehicle to emerge from the alley.

When it didn't, she grabbed the radio: "Giordano, do you copy?"

There was a crackle of static, then: "Yeah."

"I've got a vehicle in the alley. I need backup and I need someone on the front." She swung open the car's door, blinked away the drizzle that hit her face. "Where are you guys?"

"We're on our way."

"I need you here *now*. I've gotta check it out." A last burst of static, then silence. Only the rain and the hollow clicking of the chimes.

Rounding the Lumina's hood, she paused at the top of Keystone, watching the light spilling out of the alley, then searching for any sign of the two officers. The car in the alley idled.

And then she was moving. She crossed the wet lawn of 315, the end row house, and followed its brick side to the fence. The mortar was rough under her palm as she felt her way to the corner. At the fence she stopped, taking in the damp air. Her heart hammered as the darkness settled on her.

She clipped the radio to her belt and took another shaky breath. She dried her palm on her hip, drew her nine, and stepped beyond the corner of 315.

For an instant the headlights blinded her. In the harsh glare, the alley looked foreign, even though she'd spent hours here last week when Beggs's body was discovered. She couldn't remember the layout, which porches were covered, which were open. Which had sheds or fences.

Three houses down, the car sat roughly parallel to the rear of 311. Kay could make out only shapes and silhouettes in the alley and backyards. No movement. The only sound was the car's engine, and some hip-hop tune pulsing from its stereo.

Past it, several of the houses at the end of the block had their lights on. But up here, at the top of the row, the porches were dark. She struggled to decipher 311's yard, a narrow, fenced-in chunk of concrete. The headlights caught the edge of the four-foot fence, but reached no farther. And the partition that separated 311's back porch from its neighbor blocked any view she might have of its rear door.

With her free hand she brought the radio up: "Where the hell are you guys?"

"We're almost on Keystone." Giordano sounded out of breath.

"The front's wide open. I need you there."

She didn't like leaving it without surveillance, but she had no options. Drawing in a stiff breath, Kay stepped into the flood of headlights. No cover. No way to conceal her approach.

Squinting, she searched for any movement beyond the glare. Was there someone past the dark windshield, behind the wheel? Ready to gun the engine and hurtle up the alley at her?

Kay held the gun tight, barrel down, pressing the sidearm to her thigh as she moved past the rear of the first row house, then the next, her senses spiking.

She focused on the car. Through the blaze of headlights she thought it might be a hatchback. The engine sounded small. Four-cylinder probably, and something rattled under its hood.

And then Kay heard a screen door slap in its frame. Training made her bring the nine up. Fear made her flinch. The hip-hop tune on the car's radio ended. There was a four-second break, then a rapper assaulted the airways. And in those four seconds of silence, Kay spotted the figure on the concrete porch of 311.

53

Average height. A lean build. Just as Gaines had described his tenant.

He must have come home, spotted the uniforms in the neighborhood, and figured he'd use the alley, clear his things out of the house, and make a quick getaway.

Kay inched toward the back of 311. The rapid-fire rhythm of her heart pulsed inside her iron grip on the Glock. She held the nine high now. Ready.

He could be armed, Delaney. Watch. Had he already seen her?

He came down the back steps casually in a half-skip and headed to the car. He was carrying something. Not a gun. Something big, tucked under one arm.

Removing evidence from a suspected crime scene. She could take him *and* the evidence. Didn't need any warrant.

Kay moved steadily along the fence. Fifteen feet from the car now. Twelve. How could he not see her?

He adjusted the cap on his head, pulling it lower over his eyes. In the dark there was no discerning the man's features. *Scott?* No. But she couldn't be sure.

Crossing the shallow yard, he kicked at the already open gate, stepped into the alley, and reached for the driver-side door. Then he saw her.

"Baltimore Police. Stay right there!" She stood firm, bringing the gun into position. "I want both hands on the roof of the car."

He stopped two feet from his vehicle, frozen. The haloed edge of the headlights' beam caught his blue jeans and the bottom of a dark red Windbreaker. What little she could make out of his face was ashen.

"Up against the car. Now!" *Could he see the nine shaking in her hand?* She hated that she couldn't see the bastard's face.

The rapper on the radio kept belting. Under her shirt she felt herself sweat. She took three steps forward. "Put the package on the roof and get up against the car. I swear to God, I'm not going to ask again."

This time he complied. The package hit the roof, and the second he turned to the car, she lunged. Grabbing a fistful of his jacket, she spun him hard into the side of the vehicle. The air came out of him in a rush and she ground his chest against the car's roof molding.

Pinning him, she holstered her nine and patted him down. Her hand slid expertly into his jacket pockets, coming up empty. And when she reached his denimed waist, she saw the decal stuck to the side of the panel of the old car. She stopped. "Christ." The word came out on her breath.

"What the fuck's going on?" He sounded young. Blubbering.

"What's your name?"

"Don. Donny Hansen. What the hell d'I do wrong?"

"What are you doing here?"

"What's it look like?" he nodded at the package on the roof. The insulated pizza-box pouch smelled of cheese and pepperoni. "Deliverin' a motherfuckin' order." He was trying hard to sound gangsta tough, instead of scared shitless with a cop pulling a 9mm on him in a back alley.

"Somebody ordered a fuckin' pizza." He tried to look at her over his shoulder.

Kay relaxed her grip, allowing him to turn cautiously, arms coming down. He tilted the beak of his cap to block the rain, and she wished she'd brought her flashlight. Wanted to see his face more clearly.

"He home?" she asked, nodding to the house.

"Naw. Boss musta got the wrong goddamned address again. No wonder the fucking moron's going outta business."

"So you didn't make the delivery?"

"Naw. Like I said, nobody's home. G'on. Bang on the door yourself if you don't believe me. I bin hammerin' for two goddamned minutes now. So much for a fuckin' tip. What's this about anyway? Somethin' goin' down?"

"No."

"You on a stakeout or somethin'? You with Narcotics?"

Kay stepped back, straightened the edge of her jacket around her holster. "Nothing's going down."

"You can tell me. My cousin, he's a cop with the Southern." His tone changed. Softer, more conciliatory. "Still uniform, but he wants to be a narc. Maybe you know him."

"I doubt it." Kay surveyed the rear of 311. Blinds drawn. Windows closed.

"I tried out for the Academy myself. Didn't pass the physical though. Got a fucked-up knee . . ."

His yapping faded from her awareness as realization took slow hold. Too slow.

"This guy who ordered the pizza," she interrupted him, "did he specifically ask for you to deliver it to the back entrance?"

"Yeah. That's what my boss—"

"Son of a bitch." Kay spun and sprinted down the alley. Groped at her belt for the radio. "Giordano, where the hell are you guys?"

"We're just coming up the front."

"You see anyone?"

"What?"

"Do you fucking *see* anyone?"

"No. Nothing."

"Hey! You done with me?" Behind her, the pizza boy stood next to his car, his arms at his side, the delivery pouch still on the roof. "Cuz I got more deliveries here. If you don't need me—"

"No. Get out of here." She waved him off and started across the side lawn of the corner house.

When she reached the street, Madjarian and Giordano were on the sidewalk in front of 311. "What the hell's going on?"

"The son of a bitch might've gone out the front," Kay started to explain just as Finn's Lumina turned onto Keystone. Another radio car followed, then stopped at Gaines's house.

"I don't know if it was a setup," she told Finn once he joined them and she'd filled him in. His tie hung loose and he smelled of cigarettes. "Or if it was really a wrong address."

"Well, let's get inside and see." He handed Kay the warrant. "And let's hope we find more than they did at Bates's house. I checked while I waited for the warrant. Nothing."

To her right Kay was aware of the pizza-delivery car coming around Rockrose. She heard the engine whine as he geared down and passed them. Rap music pulsed into the night. Giordano waved him on, and Kay watched the taillights disappear.

"Come on," Finn said. "Here's Gaines."

The landlord's shoulders bowed inward against the rain. "Gotta go round back," he told them. "Only key I got's for the back."

"Does your tenant have a key for the front?" Kay asked him.

"Yeah. But I think he's been using the back."

Kay mentally flashed an image of Patricia Hagen being

dragged down the rear steps and shoved into a car trunk. She stopped at her car for her Maglite, then led Gaines and Finn, along with one of the uniforms, to where she'd frisked Don Hansen only moments ago.

Through the gate, across the concrete yard, and up the steps, Kay tried to pace herself. *Take it slow. Expect the unexpected.* Easier said than done with the frustration of three open murders weighing on her.

Gaines turned the key in the lock and the bolt slid free with a muted thud. Wordlessly, she ushered the landlord aside. In the tight confines of the porch, she felt Finn behind her. She slid her nine from its holster for the second time tonight, steadied the short-barreled Glock, and aligned it with the flashlight in her left hand as she nudged the door with her toe.

She didn't like the dense silence that greeted them. She liked the smell even less. Recognized it. Like damp stone and copper.

The gun's black muzzle went in first, following the sweep of the Maglite's beam across the small kitchen and into the maw of hell.

Behind her Finn whispered, "Sweet Jesus."

54

THERE WAS NOTHING to describe the smell of that much blood, the miasmic odor of a fresh kill.

His name had been Jason Beckman. They got it off the wallet in his jeans. He was seventeen, his teeth still in braces above the wide gash that had opened his throat. The killer's blade had left a swath of exposed muscle, tendons, and severed arteries. According to the ME's investigator, the kid had bled out in a matter of seconds or, more likely, asphyxiated on his own blood, inhaling it through the opened trachea and drowning. Even if Kay had known what lay beyond that dark porch, even if she'd gotten there the moment the fatal slash had been delivered, there would have been no saving the kid.

Gaines had taken one look into his rental unit and thrown up his beer into the bushes out back. Kay had almost joined the landlord. The thought of the teenager having died on the other side of the door, less than thirty feet away from her, as she'd let his butcher drive away, sent Kay's stomach reeling.

She'd had him. The bastard had looked her in the eye. She'd felt the heat of his breath. And she'd let him go.

While the Mobile Crime Lab began their painstaking work, Kay tried to remember anything she could about the guy she'd pinned against the car, tried to recall the bastard's face, but couldn't. A sketch artist would be useless. It had been too dark. Too fast.

And staring into the dead teen's fixed gaze, Kay guessed that he too had probably gotten no real look at his killer.

The bastard was slick. His escape smart and controlled. He wouldn't have risked throwing on any lights, even for a second. He'd probably cajoled the boy into the dark kitchen, or . . .

Kay circled the pool of coagulating blood. Its edges had thickened, ridging up almost a quarter inch from the floor. She squatted next to the victim, his body acting as a dam against the spill of blood. Snapping on a fresh latex glove, she took the boy's chin between her thumb and index finger. Her stomach lurched when the kid's head slopped to one side, all connective tissue ravaged.

"I need some light on this," she instructed a technician. And then Kay saw it. On the back of his neck. The same two circular contusions Jonesy had found on Valley. The guy must have lured the boy in, then hit him with the stun gun.

She surveyed the cramped kitchen again. Clean dishes sat in a wire dry-rack, a Baltimore phone book lay on the counter along with the pizza, still warm in its box. There'd been no struggle, and he wasn't a small boy. In fact, Jason Beckman was bigger than the man she'd had up against the car. It would have been impossible to slit the boy's throat while he was standing, not without some struggle. And there should have been more blood on his assailant.

Kay didn't remember seeing any. Sure it had been dark, but she'd seen his jeans in the edge of the headlights. She didn't recall any spatter.

Kay studied the arterial spray against the humming ice-maker. *You didn't cut him until he was already down.*

So much blood.

You knew the kid wouldn't have been able to ID you, but you killed him anyway. Pulled your knife while he was unconscious. Stepping back from the body, she stood over the boy as she imagined his killer had. *You knew I was watching.*

If she hadn't been parked outside, the kid would still be alive. *You killed him for me, didn't you, you son of a bitch. You had to show off.*

"It's not your fault, Kay." Finn stepped into the kitchen behind her. "You couldn't have known. Guy comes out the back with a pizza sack under his arm, tells you there's no one home. I'd have let him go too."

She felt his hand on her shoulder. Normally she'd rebuff any public show of affection, especially in front of other cops, but tonight she welcomed Finn's support. If she could, she would have let Finn hold her while she cried for Jason Beckman.

"They found the kid's delivery car," he said. "It was ditched down on Clipper Road. Other side of the expressway. No way to know if the killer hiked from there or if he had his own vehicle down there on Clipper. If we're lucky, maybe he parked up around here, closer to the house, and the uniforms got his tag number."

"I don't know if you've noticed, but luck hasn't been beating on my door lately," she said, hating that she sounded sorry for herself. "Who the hell is this guy, Finn? Cuz that sure as hell wasn't Jerry Bates or Scott Arsenault I slammed up against the car tonight."

There was a beat of silence, then Finn gave her shoulder a final squeeze. "Come on," he said. "We got lots of work here. There's more."

55

IT HAD BEEN SHEER BRILLIANCE.

Roach steered the Park Avenue into the sweep of Jones Falls Expressway that curved under Preston Street. Traffic was thin, trickling south into the city. His heart still raced, and his knuckles were white around the wheel.

Divine opportunity. That's what it had been. Not impulse, but providence. As if the Angel of Death had just handed him a freebie.

And Lady Luck too. He might have parked his Buick closer to the house, but after his trip back from Leakin Park this morning he'd needed to unwind, needed the six-block walk. So, he'd left the car down on Clipper Road.

And if necessity was the mother of invention, then, tonight, necessity had bred absolute genius.

The whole thing had taken no more than two, maybe

three, minutes from the moment the delivery boy arrived to when Roach finally stepped onto the back porch. The kid had barely knocked when Roach opened the door. "Sorry, my power's been out." The kid lapped up the lie and stepped into the dark kitchen. That's when Roach nailed him.

Kid had barely hit the floor before Roach was emptying the delivery pouch; it was still warm as he'd slid in his laptop and the few belongings he'd gathered from the house. Using the penlight on his key chain he'd grabbed the kid's cap, taken one last look around, and drawn out his knife.

He'd thought twice before doing it. But the temptation to leave something for Delaney had been too great. The Spyderco's blade had gone in to the hilt. Clean and smooth, nicking once across bone.

It had been almost as exhilarating as the moment in the alley, standing right there, in front of Delaney, looking her in the eye while he boasted the kid's blood on his red Windbreaker. And Kay Delaney had no fucking idea.

Roach didn't realize he'd been smiling until a horn blasted next to him. He jerked the wheel to the right, bringing the Park Avenue square into his own lane. The SUV passed him, and Roach caught the guy's hand gesture in the light of the truck's dash.

Then, in his side mirror, Roach spotted the radio car in the left lane behind him.

Careful, you brilliant son of a bitch. Last thing you need is to be pulled over on some traffic violation.

But it was too late. The cruiser tucked in behind him, its light-bar flashing in his rearview.

56

KAY KNEW THEY'D FOUND the killing house.

Although the threadbare furnishings had seen years of use, nothing in 311 Keystone indicated anyone actually lived there: no soda can on the coffee table, no ashtray or *TV Guide,* no shoes by the door. Even the fridge sat empty, except for grease-stained containers of leftover takeout.

Finn turned on the TV, flipped through snowy channels. According to Gaines, the basic BG&E usage and phone were included in the rent. But the tenant hadn't hooked up the cable. Why? Kay couldn't imagine the killer not following the local news coverage. Did he live somewhere else? With a girlfriend? With his mother?

Kay turned several times in the middle of the living room, trying to conjure up an image of the man who, only a short time ago, had probably stood on the same spot and devised Jason Beckman's slaughter as his escape.

And why this house? Anonymity was the obvious reason. But why this dump when the bodies he left were so clean, his crimes so organized? Was this all he could afford? Was it a retreat from his real life? Was the house significant? Or merely convenient?

Through the living room and past the foyer, the smell of bleach and Lysol intensified, becoming almost overwhelming as she moved once again to the full bath at the bottom of the stairs.

When she'd first stepped into the bathroom, she hadn't been surprised to find it scrubbed clean. The 1930s honeycomb tile on the floor and partway up the wall gleamed. Even the faded enamel of the claw-foot tub sparkled, and what little chrome wasn't tarnished on the old fixtures held a sheen it hadn't probably seen in years.

She'd sent in Lenny DeSousa, one of the best techs with the Mobile Crime Lab. Now he crouched over the tub, angling a high-intensity light.

He shook his head. "There's nothing here."

"Anything in the sink trap?"

"Nothing earth-shattering. Looks like your guy shaved recently. Got some stubble out of the drain. No good for DNA though without the roots. But we found a couple head hairs that should give us something."

"And what about the tub and surrounding area? You getting anything there?"

"I'm not seeing anything."

Kay imagined the killer on his hands and knees, scouring each tile with a toothbrush.

"Can you tell me why we're going over this room when the body's in the kitchen?" DeSousa asked.

"This is a separate scene," she said. "Separate crimes."

The scent of death was here, beneath the bleach and the lemon cleaner. Kay wondered if anyone else could smell it. If they could taste it in the air the way she did, feel it crackling in the room around them. It reminded her of Eales's house; sitting empty for a year, but still she had felt the death there.

"This is where he killed them," she whispered to Finn, standing next to her. She scanned the pristine room again. Again, no evidence of anyone living here. No toothbrush or glass on the wall-mounted sink with its exposed plumbing. No magazine on the back of the ring-stained toilet. No meds in the cabinet. Only a single bath towel hanging perfectly folded over the rack by the sink.

She nodded to the new AC unit mounted in the high

window behind the tub. "He kept them cool," she said to Finn.

"So what exactly are we looking for?" DeSousa asked.

"Blood." The blood of B. J. Beggs and Patricia Hagen for sure. Kay prayed there weren't others.

"You want us to luminol then?"

"Luminol the whole damn room," Finn said before she could. "Every inch. I want to see exactly what happened here."

"All right then. Give me a few minutes to set up."

"Wait." Kay stopped DeSousa at the door. "You've taken samples, right?"

"Of what? I can't see anything to sample."

"Do the drain traps. The sides of the tub. The sink and the grout. Just swab. Do it before you spray. I'm not going to have the luminol destroy what little DNA evidence we might have here."

DeSousa gave her a nod. "I'll call you when we're ready."

"We'll be upstairs," she said, and Finn followed her.

The air on the second floor was stale. Kay thought she could sense death up here as well. The back two rooms didn't appear to have been used. Bare mattresses in battered bed frames, dressers with their drawers pulled out, closets empty. It was the master bedroom, overlooking Keystone, that the tenant had used. The sun-warped vinyl blinds were drawn. A lamp on the nightstand had been switched on by one of the officers who'd cleared the house for the team. In its dull glow, Kay saw evidence of the killer.

He'd left clothes: several shirts and a couple pressed khakis hanging on dry-cleaner hangers, a pair of loafers and folded socks. On the top of a small desk in the corner was some loose change. All precisely stacked. The single drawer of the desk was empty.

Finn found the phone line. The five-foot cord was plugged into the wall socket, the unused end lying behind one desk leg.

"What do you figure? A modem?" he asked.

Kay nodded. Of course he'd have a laptop. He'd probably followed the coverage of his murders through the WBAL news site. Maybe even lurked on Eales's website, chatting online. Could she actually have read his posts on the board?

There was little else. What few personal belongings he'd had in the house, he'd no doubt stuffed into the insulated pizza pouch along with the laptop.

At least they'd get lots of prints. The Crime Lab had lifted several dozen cards' worth already from the kitchen alone. Kay scanned the room again, turning, wishing for more light and knowing she'd have to come back in the daytime.

"The guy's a fucking nutcase," Finn said, looking at the bed, the corners of the sheets tucked squarely like a hospital bed's. "Probably did some army time."

"Or prison."

From downstairs, Lenny DeSousa called for them. When they reached the bathroom, the tech handed them each a vapor mask. "You ever done this before?" he asked.

She and Finn both shook their heads.

"Once the spray hits any trace blood, the luminol reacts with the iron in the hemoglobins. The proteins are the catalyst to the chemiluminescence—in other words, the glow you get. Same principle as those light sticks you buy at rock concerts."

"Yeah, like I go to those every weekend," Finn said. "How long does it take?"

"If there's anything there, you should see the reaction within a few seconds." DeSousa ushered them in, fastening his own mask and closing the door. His assistant was already standing by with a video camera, and between the four of them, it was tight quarters.

"So what's in this stuff?" Finn nodded to the spray bottle.

"Three-aminophthalhydrazide and a little sodium carbonate."

"Sounds healthy." Finn snugged the mask firmly over his nose.

"If there *are* any trace blood patterns," DeSousa explained, "we'll get lucky in here. These pebbled tiles and this old grout hold more than the newer stuff. Where do you want me to start?"

"The tub area." Kay took a solidifying breath, already imagining what awaited them.

"All right then." He reached past Finn's shoulder to the switch plate on the wall. "You ready?"

"As I'll ever be."

With a faint click, the room pitched into black. The darkness swallowed her. She felt Finn behind her, used him for support.

She heard the first pump of the spray bottle. Then another. DeSousa mumbled instructions to his assistant. Another few sprays, silent seconds, and then the eerie blue-green luminescence began to grow. With each pump of the spray bottle there was more, as though Lenny DeSousa were pumping out blue glow-in-the-dark paint directly onto the tub and wall.

The glow intensified. The entire wall, the edges of the tub, the floor around it. Everything glowed.

"God, all that's blood?" Finn's voice sounded thin in the hollow room.

"Doubtful." Lenny's voice. "It's probably a false positive. Happens a lot. Luminol reacts to any kind of protein. My guess is it's the bleach." He sprayed more, revealing the entire outline of the tub. "Just give it a while. The proteins in blood are a stronger catalyst than bleach, so if there is any blood residue you'll get a longer reaction."

They waited. Kay could hear her own heart beating, could feel Finn's behind her, as the seconds slipped away into the eerie, glowing silence of the bathroom.

"Here it comes," Lenny said at last.

And finally Kay saw it.

57

IT HAD BEEN A BLOODBATH.

They spent almost an hour in the cramped bathroom. One spray after another, one savage luminescent smear leading them to the next. The fine mist filled the black air. Kay's eyes had begun to sting, and her skin felt as if it were crawling.

The luminol's reaction to the bleach gave way to a display of violence that rendered even the technicians silent as they worked. The wall behind the tub glowed with luminesced blood: spatters and thick arches, handprints and streaks fanning across the old tiles in frenetic patterns. With his assistant videotaping it all, Lenny DeSousa had worked his way around the room, past the sink and to the toilet. There, Finn had cursed as the chemical revealed a crude smiley face drawn across the tiles, chest high. Kay imagined the killer pausing to relieve himself, then finding amusement in an impromptu sketch with a bloody finger.

But always, Kay's eyes came back to the tub wall: the partial handprints and wild smears. Now she knew what she'd only imagined. There *was* a reason he'd tied Patricia.

It was because of Beggs. Kay remembered the prostitute's bruises. The blood across the tub wall had to be from Beggs, thrashing in her final bid for survival.

You didn't expect that, did you, you sick fuck? The drugs wearing off, and her coming to. She saw you, saw herself bleeding, and she struggled. That's why you tied Hagen. You didn't want her flailing like Beggs had.

Even in the dark, Kay could picture him standing over Beggs, then Hagen. Each paralyzed by the ketamine, each aware of her life ending. Every heartbeat forcing the life out of them through their opened wrists.

"He wants to see them die." She hadn't meant to say it aloud.

"What?" Finn asked behind her.

"He watches them bleed. Only, he wants *them* to see it too. He wants to witness their fear as they're dying. That's part of the thrill for him."

The pump of DeSousa's spray bottle continued while the gleaming red button on the video camera pierced the blackness. More spray. More fluoresced blood. This time a partial footprint in blood. Then another. Bare feet across the tile floor from the tub to the toilet, then the sink. Had he been naked?

"Get close-ups of those," Kay said. "Maybe we can get a patent print."

DeSousa had come full circle in the small room. The luminescence was dying now as the chemical compound of the luminol ate up the proteins in the blood.

"That's it." DeSousa's voice was muffled by his mask. "We've hit everything."

Kay felt shaky, wanted to blame the chemicals, but knew it was much more than that. She groped for the door. "I need some air."

"Go on," DeSousa said. "We'll finish up."

She was vaguely aware of Finn following her as she left the damp room, crossed the foyer, and pushed her way out the front door. The night's heat felt cool compared to the thick air of the bathroom. She filled her lungs, steadied herself at the porch's railing, and surveyed the crush of response vehicles. Farther down Keystone, the media had arrived with their satellite trucks. She spotted Jane Gallagher from WBAL under a huge, black umbrella.

Kay turned her back to the circus. In the flashing blue strobe of the radio cars, Finn's face was unusually pale. And he looked older. Clearly he'd been as affected by the visuals in the bathroom as she had. This wasn't the kind of stuff a murder cop in Baltimore saw daily.

Finn patted his jacket for cigarettes, reconsidered briefly, then withdrew the pack anyway. Tapping one of the Marlboros out, he offered it to her. "You probably could use one too," he said.

She could almost taste the sweet, rolled tobacco. She looked at the cigarette, wanted it, then pictured Eales: his moist lips pinching the unfiltered end of her stale Camels.

"No, thanks," she said.

Leaning against the porch railing, Finn lit up. He took in several long drags and scanned the sea of crime-scene vehicles and personnel. But his gaze seemed unfocused.

"How the hell do you do it?" he asked eventually.

"Do what?"

"What you did back in there? It's like you can see this asshole work or something."

"I just look at all the pieces. Let the evidence tell me."

"Naw, there's more to it than that, Kay. I look at evidence every day and I can't do what you just did in there. You're inside this guy's fucking head."

"I guess you just gotta think outside your own box, your own set of perceptions of the world and the way it should work. Letting go of who you are and how you view things. You have to see it through their eyes, think like them."

Finn gestured with his cigarette to the front door. "But this guy? How can you think like *him?* He's a fucking nutcase. Probably hears voices in his head."

"I doubt that."

"After what you saw in there?"

"The guy's not psychotic. If he was, he couldn't have pulled it off. He's smart, Finn. Organized. His pattern is based on his needs, and he's following it with passion. But he's also cool enough to mastermind what he did tonight, killing that kid."

"So, where do we go from here?" Finn asked.

"I don't know." She was too exhausted to think. "What I *do* know is that we've got all the evidence we need to build a case against this guy. It's all in there." She nodded at the open door of 311. "We're fucking buried in evidence. We've got this guy's prints, we've got possible DNA. Once the lab gets through with this house, we've probably got Hagen *and* Beggs in there too. And we can't do shit with any of it until we get someone to match it all to."

Finn finished his cigarette, then squashed it out against the porch rail and pocketed the butt.

"Come on. I want to tear this house apart. There's gotta be something."

58

BUT THERE WASN'T.

They worked long into the night, side by side with the Mobile Crime Lab, going over every corner of 311, but found nothing to point them in any direction. Gunderson had made an appearance, then left sometime after midnight. Kay and Finn didn't head out until the last technician had packed up, leaving the house under surveillance. Even then, Finn had sensed Kay's reluctance to leave.

At Headquarters, they'd typed the twenty-four-hour reports and Kay had sifted through the disappointing results from the search on Bates's house. It was almost 3 a.m. before Finn steered them up Hamburg Street and parked outside Kay's.

Inside, the apartment felt good—a sanctuary from everything they'd seen tonight. Kay looked wrecked, and Finn could sense the weight of the kid's murder still on her as she handed him a soda from the fridge. He watched her grab for a beer, then opt for a soda as well. They sat on the couch, drinking in silence. Being home seemed to relax Kay, take the edge off, and Finn hoped she would be able to let go of the case for even a few hours.

He should have known better.

"Patricia Hagen knew him," she said. "Ten forty-five at night, she's not going to some stranger's house. Somehow she knew him. And she had to have trusted him to some degree."

"We've gone through Hagen's employee list and there's nothing there. No one connects to Eales except for Bates."

"What the fuck are we missing?" Kay's grip on the soda can threatened to crush the thin aluminum. "I feel like we're spinning our wheels, Finn. I mean, where the fuck *are* we with all this? What are we doing?"

"We're doing the legwork, Kay. We're getting the evidence that's going to guarantee the son of a bitch gets a needle in his arm."

"Yeah, well, we gotta get him first, don't we?" She settled her head back on the top of the couch and stared at the ceiling.

Finn knew she didn't care about evidence. Not after tonight. Now, more than ever, Kay wanted the man who'd slipped through her fingers. The man who'd killed Jason Beckman and three women, maybe more. The man who may have shot Spencer. The man who was probably laughing at her right now.

Tonight, the hunt had become far more personal for Kay.

And it was becoming personal for Finn too. All he had to do was imagine Kay in the alley behind 311, standing with the man who'd so coldly slaughtered the kid tonight for no other reason than sport, and Finn wanted him in his own hands.

"It's Eales." He heard the exhaustion in Kay's voice. "He's the common denominator."

"Then let's get some answers from him. I want to talk to him myself this time," Finn said, finally voicing what he'd been thinking all night.

Kay closed her eyes. He thought she nodded.

There was only the rattle of the AC unit in one of the tall windows overlooking Hamburg Street and the Hill. Spencer's cat stalked into the room, regarded them briefly, then took to an empty sill to watch the street below.

Finn's thoughts went back to the bathroom in 311. The big tub. The fluoresced blood.

"I just can't let go of the cuts to the girls' chests," Kay said eventually. "Even the premortem ones, they're not about subduing his victims. He's using the ketamine for that."

"Subduing them for what though? Sex?"

"I think it's more about power."

"Well, what if it's both, Kay? What if part of it *is* sex. I know there hasn't been any evidence of penetration, but what about masturbation? What if . . ." He didn't like the images that flashed in his brain then.

"What if what, Finn?"

"What if he . . . let's say he gets into the tub with them. The wounds were inflicted before *and* after the women were dead. So what if he's jacking off on them, Kay? In the tub? Before he bleeds them? Then again after they're dead?"

"Okay. Go on."

"And maybe he's a breast man. Maybe he's jacking off on their breasts, and while he's doing that, he's got the knife . . . I don't know, maybe he's holding it against his dick."

"Jesus, Finn."

"Look, after Jonesy told us about the knife, I checked the internet. Searched single-edged lock-backs. Some of these knives are pretty narrow-handled. Even Jonesy said it's probably the kind that'd fit in the palm of your hand.

"I may be completely off base, but I think, maybe, the blade's making contact when he's actually coming. That's why there are sets of marks in one direction, and others at slightly different angles. He's doing it more than once, using the knife. Different sessions. This guy, Kay, maybe this guy's in love with his blade."

When Kay stared at him then, Finn imagined her thoughts were back at 311.

"I'm going to take a shower," she said suddenly, as though needing to wash away the images Finn's theory had provoked. "You hungry?"

"Yeah, you got anything?"

"No. But you could go get something. Bring it back."

He left her to shower and drove to the Sip-and-Bite on Boston Street, serving up the only twenty-four-hour gyros. He ate half of his on the way back to Federal Hill and tried to let go of the mental images from tonight, as well as the ones his own brain had created.

What he'd seen at 311 had spooked him. Years of working drug murders had a way of dulling you to the violence. Drug shootings started to make sense after a while: a kid getting killed over a $20 pack of rock or for crossing onto someone else's corner became commonplace. But this . . . the man who'd slashed the kid's throat was a butcher, a psycho with a warped agenda. It went beyond the usual framework.

The water was still running when he dropped the take-out containers onto the kitchen counter.

"Kay?" He called several times, but got no response.

In the open doorway of the bathroom, the steam washed over him. Through it he could just make out her figure behind the textured glass of the shower door. She stood, leaning against the front of the stall.

"Kay? You all right?"

She didn't move, even as he crossed the room.

"Hey. You okay?" This time Finn slid the door open an inch. With her head bowed under the pounding water, she looked lost. When she turned to him, her eyes were swollen from crying.

"What's wrong?" he asked.

She reached for him then, saying nothing. Her hand was hot against his arm, her skin red from the scalding water. She drew him closer.

The water flowed off her, drowning their kiss and drizzling to the floor. One wet hand pressed against his cheek, while the other moved to his belt, fumbling with the buckle.

"Damn it, Kay," he mumbled against their kiss, and tried to push her away.

"What?" She didn't let him go.

"I worry about you."

"I know."

"I want to be there for you."

"You are, Finn. I promise." And in her kiss, Finn believed it at last.

Later he didn't remember undressing, only the hot needles of water stinging his back and the heat of her skin
against his. Even as he kissed her, he could feel a shift in
Kay's need. A sense that this, tonight, was more than they'd
ever shared. It was more than sex for the sake of feeling
alive, for escape and for blocking out the job as they had in
their past.

They made love in the shower. An intense but gentle
union. And later in Kay's bed, as they made love again, Finn
felt a softness return to her. A vulnerability. A giving of
herself at last. She looked at him when they came together,
and afterward she cried.

Only much later did Kay speak, jarring him from the
first stages of sleep. "I had him, Finn," she whispered. "I had
him."

"I know."

"I keep trying to see his face. To remember anything
about him."

He kissed her breast, then found her lips in the dark. But
she didn't return his kiss this time.

"I had him," she murmured again. "Do you know what
that feels like?"

"We'll get him, Kay."

"If he kills again . . . it'll be on me."

"No."

Traffic noises from the Key Highway filtered through
the open window. A salt-tinged breeze, smelling of yeast
from the H&S bakery, billowed the curtains. He listened to
Kay's heart, knowing she would find no peace in his words.

"He killed Spence," she whispered into the darkness. "It
wasn't Eales. It was him. And I had him."

"You'll have him again," he told her. And the day she
did, Finn hoped he was there to stop her from murdering
the bastard.

59

THE VACANCY SIGN for the motel on Pulaski flick-
ered red into the early-morning hours. The place was a
dive. That's why Roach had chosen it. He knew the lard-
ass at the desk would barely look at him when he asked for
the room, wouldn't notice his hands shaking as he pushed
the cash through the slot.

The encounter with the trooper on the JFX had left
him agitated. He'd tried to talk his way out of the speeding ticket, but the wide-necked ape might as well have
been deaf. Roach tossed the ticket on the nightstand
now.

The room stank. He'd thrown open one of the
unscreened windows and let the night's heat and exhaust
fumes from the parking lot waft in. With the vomit-green
bedspread thrown to one side, he sat on the sagging mattress and studied the spider that shared his room. Her web
spanned the far corner, and for the past ten minutes she'd
set about repairing the damage left by a moth an hour ago.
Now she hung, idle, her work done. Waiting for the next.
Patient. Confident more would come before she'd return
to feed on the silken sack.

He liked the company. Felt a kinship with her, as though
their lives paralleled. Certainly more than the roaches of his
youth. He remembered the ones he'd kept as a kid. The
big-ass tropical ones that filled the palm of his hand with
their cool bellies, their barbed feet tickling his skin as they
climbed his bare arms.

He'd always marveled at the creatures' resilience. He'd
read about how a roach could survive a microwave. How
it could live nine days without its head before it starved to

death. Johnny Newcomb from next door had tried to prove the latter theory once, tearing the head off Roach's biggest specimen. That was the first time he'd ever pulled a knife on someone. Ten years old. He'd pressed the blade tight against Johnny's screaming white throat. He'd never been sure what he would have done, since Johnny managed to wriggle free and run home to his mama. And Roach had turned the blade onto his pet instead as it made frantic backward circles across his bedroom floor. With one swing he'd ended its suffering.

Still, he'd gotten even. Little Johnny never saw that flea-bitten dog of his again.

Roach looked away from the spider and fingered the three plastic cards in his lap. Valerie Regester's and Bobby Joe Beggs's driver's licenses. Their photos did them little justice. Weak smiles for some overpaid MVA worker. Still, the cards offered enough visual reference for him to conjure up the women's last, splendid moments.

The third card was Patsy's State of Maryland ID.

Hers had been a calmer death than the whore's, flailing and gasping in her final throes, smearing the blood everywhere. But to see Patsy come around like that, to watch her horror and the sheer disbelief at her own death, had been exhilarating. A real learning experience.

Each was getting better. But the best was yet to come.

Roach perched at the edge of the bed, rocking, letting the plan take hold, already craving the sweet oblivion he would find in Kay Delaney's dimming eyes.

60

THE PLASTIC SPOON threatened to snap as Bernard stirred milk onto the congealed slab of cold oatmeal. Hunkering over his breakfast tray at a back table in the cafeteria, he ignored the conversations buzzing around him.

He'd gone to sleep in a pissy mood and woken up the same. A headache jangled behind his eyes. Made him miserable, then made him twitchy. He'd recognized the nicotine withdrawal yesterday when he'd run out of smokes.

Three days since he'd seen Patsy. And not a word. In spite of all the bitching about her father, all the yapping about her damned cats, he sort of missed her. At least she was a break from the routine. And of course, there were the cigarettes.

As he pushed the oatmeal around his bowl, he toyed with the notion of calling her. He could have fresh smokes by the afternoon. But he wouldn't call. He was starting to feel guilty about taking advantage of her. He'd always figured that Patsy's taking care of him the way she did was some form of payback for him having saved her from her father's mauling hands. But now he was starting to suspect she might actually love him.

He didn't usually think lovey-dovey thoughts. Just wasn't in him. It was Patsy who'd asked him to marry her. She said it would make her happy. Bring "substance" to her life, she'd said. At the time he'd said yes mainly because he didn't want to lose the good thing he had going with her, and because he'd have conjugal visits to look forward to. A man got lonely.

Before Patsy, whenever he'd wanted a piece of ass, he'd have to either buy it or beg for it, and sometimes he'd just take it. He'd never had to buy or beg from Patsy. She actually *wanted* to be with him, even if it meant only two times a week behind a Plexiglas wall.

Now with his confession, he was sure to get life, probably a death sentence if that bitch Delaney was right. Either way, he wasn't getting out, and he needed Patsy. He didn't want to be alone. Certainly didn't want to die alone.

Then, as he chased the last lump of oatmeal around the bottom of his bowl, Bernard entertained a paralyzing thought. What if Delaney had already gotten to Patsy? What if she'd told her about his confession and that's why she hadn't come to see him? Maybe Patsy was pissed. She would be. From day one she'd held faith in his getting off, getting out, and being with her. Patsy had come up with the self-defense angle for shooting that cop. As for the prostitutes, she avoided discussing them.

But if Delaney had gotten to her before he could explain . . . A twinge of panic followed the last bite of oatmeal into his gut.

No. Patsy would be here. She loved him, and she'd come around eventually. And maybe one day, he'd even tell her the truth.

61

IN THE HANDS OF A SKILLED ME, a body on the cutting-room table could resemble little more than a rack of ribs in a matter of minutes. But in Patricia Hagen's case, Eddie Jones took his time. With each piercing whine of the Stryker saw, each smooth slice of his scalpel, Jonesy seemed to find satisfaction in his morning's work. For him, Hagen was one piece of a larger puzzle.

By 10 a.m. Patricia Hagen's body lay before Kay as a shell of muscle and bone. Her skin resembled marble, waxy and translucent.

Beside her, Finn sipped his coffee and watched Jonesy work.

Nothing about the body on the table resembled the woman they'd first interviewed a week and a half ago. Hagen's skull had been sawn open, the brain and dura removed for tests, and her face sagged like a rubber mask, partly concealed by the overturned scalp. Patricia Hagen had become another faceless casualty in Baltimore City.

"I figured you'd want me to run a preliminary tox screen for ketamine," Jonesy said, his latex gloves covered in a gory slick of body fluids.

"And?" Kay asked.

"Same as your last girl. We've got an injection mark on her outer thigh here. Can't be sure how much she had on board, but it must have been enough because, other than the ligature marks, there're no signs of significant struggle.

"Also, the cuts to her chest"—he flipped back the breast plate, and the overlying skin—"there are more this time. And deeper too." He pointed out the notches in the long, flat bone of Hagen's sternum. "Half of them were made premortem while the rest were post. There's soft-tissue hemorrhaging in half of these. The others, none. And the premortem ones are a little more ragged."

"Implying what?" Kay asked. "A different knife?"

"No. Same blade. I'd say she flinched, like she was conscious when the first cuts were inflicted."

Jonesy detailed the other findings—the ligature marks, the exsanguination, the time of death set sometime over forty-eight hours ago.

When Kay glanced up from Hagen's dissected shell, she studied Finn's profile. As he watched Jonesy work, Kay felt the urge to touch Finn, to ease the deep lines of worry that had set in his face, to be there for him as he'd been for her.

In the dark of morning, Kay had finally put herself out there. Let herself free-fall. And Finn had caught her. In his arms, Kay had realized that only Finn could have done that for her. Only Finn could comprehend what she experienced and felt, because he saw the things she did, day in and day out. Last night he'd seen the evidence of the slaughters that had taken place in 311. His reaction had been different, but he'd seen. He knew where her mind was at, and he was the only person who could come close to understanding what haunted her.

And if anyone could be that for Finn in return, Kay realized she could. After their lovemaking last night, for the first time, Kay started to believe she *could* be that person Finn deserved.

"Got something here." Jonesy's voice snapped her gaze back to the table where he prodded Hagen's pelvic area like an overzealous gynecologist. In moments, he withdrew a small packet. "Lodged up in the vaginal canal. He sure didn't do that with your other vics."

"What the hell is it? This girl wasn't a crack whore." Finn moved in as Jonesy set the packet onto the table behind him.

"No, it's not drugs," Jonesy said. "Looks like a piece of paper." He took out two sets of forceps and gingerly began working at the moist edges of the tightly wadded ball.

Constance had suggested the murders were sexual. *Were there any foreign objects found in any of these women?* she'd asked in Kay's last session. *Inserted into their body cavities?*

Kay herself had read the textbook cases. Bottles, broom handles, umbrellas, hairbrushes . . . anything that was handy could act as the killer's substitute for penetration sex. But this was different. This wasn't some item jammed into a victim out of lust or as a penis substitution. It was a message. Just as Hagen's murder was some kind of message.

She watched Jonesy peel back the edges of the stained paper, as handwriting appeared. And when Finn angled one of the lamps, Kay saw something else. "What's that inside it?"

For Kay, Jonesy couldn't work fast enough, bit by bit unfurling the paper until it lay spread out before them, and in its center lay a crucifix. Jonesy removed the pendant.

"That's Eales's handwriting," Kay said, recognizing the stumbling scrawl from the letter he'd drafted to Hagen. "And it's dated the day before his confession."

Some of the words were indiscernible, the blue ink having bled from the vaginal moisture. It was addressed to someone named Roach, and between the smudged letters Kay managed to decipher the gist of the note's intent.

"This is it," she said, feeling charged now. "This 'Roach' is our guy. Look, Eales is telling him to leave town. '. . . don't know what's going on, but if it's you, get out. I'll take care of things at this end,' " she read. " 'Like we arranged.' If Eales mailed this, it wouldn't have gotten to him in that time frame. Someone delivered it, and the only people who visit Eales—"

"Hagen," Finn finished for her.

"He sent this out with her. That's why she went to 311 Keystone. She hand-delivered it."

Kay turned to the crucifix. The cross was three inches long, made of gold and silver metal, with inlaid wood. The bottom upright post was worn, as though a thumb had worried it over the years. Borrowing Jonesy's forceps, Kay turned the pendant over. On its back, centered at the cross's articulation, was a medal boasting a robed figure and encircled by Latin words.

"It's a St. Benedict crucifix," Jonesy said.

Finn nudged him. "Didn't peg you for a churchgoer."

"Take my mother every Sunday. According to St. Gregorio, the cross was used by the patriarch against the assault of demons."

"Oh, great," said Finn. "Here comes the insanity defense. 'The demons told me to kill all them whores.' "

"I've seen this before." Kay stared at the piece. "And not at church. It was in Eales's house. On his dresser. I'm sure of it."

"Well, I'll send it to Latents." Jonesy snapped his gloves off. "But something that size, don't get your hopes up for anything more than a smudged partial."

"No," Kay said. "I'll sign it out. I'll take it to Latents myself. I'm putting a rush on this one. What about the note?"

"It's too contaminated. You won't get anything from it. I'll have it dried and processed, but right now I've got other customers rolling in." Jonesy nodded to the next case being wheeled into the bay beside them.

Kay bagged the crucifix, signed Jonesy's form, and followed Finn out to the main corridor.

In the elevator, Finn asked, "You sure about seeing that cross at Eales's house?"

"Yeah. Or one very much like it. Time to go through the crime-scene photos again."

In the polished copper of the elevator's interior, Kay stared at her distorted reflection, but in her mind she was seeing Hagen, in the tub at 311. "Roach" standing over her as she bled out. "Why does he cut their wrists, Finn?"

"To bleed them."

"Is that all? Or is there more to it? I mean, is it a staged suicide? Is it fantasy, or is he reliving something?"

She caught Finn in her peripheral, saw the frustration set in his jaw. They were both feeling it. When the elevator doors opened to an empty hallway a floor too soon, Finn jabbed at the lobby button again. "We gotta find out who this Roach guy is."

Roach. And then Kay remembered Eales's kitchen, the filthy sink, the infestation, and Eales's calendar by the fridge. "He was there," Kay blurted out.

"Who?"

"Roach. He was there the night we banged on Eales's door. Eales had the word *roach* written on his calendar on that weekend. It was him, Finn."

"That's it. We're seeing Eales now," he said. "And this time *I'm* doing the talking."

62

FINN AND KAY waited in a dim holding cell on the fourth floor of the MTC while the guards brought Eales up. They hadn't stopped for lunch, running from the OCME to Headquarters, then the crime lab, and finally the State Pen.

Finn's stomach tightened around the half dozen coffees he'd poured into himself since this morning as he heard the rattle of chains and saw Eales's ugly mass come around the juncture in the corridor. The man paused momentarily. The cold blue eyes caught his, perhaps searching for recognition, and finding none, he shambled through the door. Sweat stains marked the underarms of Eales's jumpsuit.

Finn shook his head when the guard motioned to remove Eales's cuffs.

"Have a seat, Bernard." Kay laid her briefcase on the table.

Crossing his arms, Finn hid his fists and watched Eales watch Kay. He felt the hate move through him.

"What the fuck you want?"

"Nice to see you too, Bernard."

"And who the hell's he?"

"This is Detective Finnerty. I don't think you've met." She pulled out the chair across the table from the big man and sat as Eales glared. "He wants to talk to you."

Locked in his cold gaze, Finn couldn't escape the image of Eales standing over Kay on that filthy sidewalk fourteen months ago.

"I don't got nothin' to say to him." Eales started to stand, the clatter of his chains filling the cell.

Finn saw Kay about to move, but he was there first. Circling the table, he reached Eales before he was a foot off the seat of the chair. When Finn forced him back down, Eales swore and nearly toppled the chair.

"Get comfortable, Eales. You're not done here."

Circling the table, Finn returned the man's scowl.

"I got something that belongs to you," he told Eales then, his hand going to his jacket pocket and feeling the plastic evidence bag.

He and Kay had gone through the old crime-scene photos from Eales's house, verifying the presence of the crucifix on Eales's dresser top. After an hour of cross-referencing the entire inventory log, they knew the piece hadn't been seized in the original search.

From there they'd made a quick visit to the Crime Lab. Kay had stood over Walt Currie's shoulder, watching him dust the crucifix. As Jonesy had predicted, no usable prints were on the piece.

Finn withdrew the bag now and opened it, shaking out the contents. The St. Benedict's pendant clattered onto the table.

"Recognize that?" Finn asked.

Eales picked it up, the fingerprinting powder already wiped from it. When he looked up, his glare was reserved for Kay.

"You been in my house, you bitch." He almost came off the chair again, but Finn gave him another shove.

"Are you sure it's yours?" Kay's voice was surprisingly calm.

"Damn right. Was my mother's. Why you messing with my shit?"

"We didn't mess with your shit," Finn said. "We found that."

"Like hell."

"Don't you want to know where, Eales?"

Eales strangled the crucifix in his thick hands.

"We found it on your girlfriend," Finn told him.

"What the fuck you talking about?"

"Actually, it was more *inside* your girlfriend. Patricia's dead, you shithead. She was murdered two nights ago."

Eales shook his fat, shaved head. The confusion Finn saw in Eales's face in that moment seemed authentic.

"He cut her wrists, Bernie. Bled her to death. Then he threw her out when he was done with her, for everyone to see." Finn opened Kay's briefcase and pulled out a photo taken in Leakin Park yesterday morning. He slapped it down on the table.

Eales turned away.

"Look at her, shithead."

Eales refused. His knuckles whitened around his mother's cross.

"Look at her!" Finn slid the photo closer, the print buckling when the edge of it caught Eales's arm.

He looked then, but his expression remained hard.

"There's your meal ticket," Finn said. "She's dead. Now

what are you going to do, huh? Who's going to bring you smokes now?"

More silence. Finn imagined the big man was scrambling to put the pieces together, to make sense of it.

"She loved you, didn't she, you schmuck. Did you love her?"

Eales averted his gaze.

"Did you *love* her?"

But Eales wasn't answering. Finn removed the photo and watched the man's eyes. The raw confusion was gone, and now, any emotion that might have lain behind the glazed expression was unreadable.

Next, Finn took out the note. Dry now, and pressed flat in an evidence bag. "You recognize this?" He laid it on the table.

Eales stared blankly at the tattered and stained remains.

"Who the hell is Roach?" Finn asked.

But Eales was mute.

"Should I tell you where we found the note, hmm, shithead? Maybe you'll start talking then. We pulled it out of Patsy too. Roach killed her, then he used your letter to wrap up your mother's crucifix and shoved both of them into your girlfriend's twat. You ready to talk *now?*"

Eales clutched the cross. Swung his ugly head from side to side.

"Tell us who you're covering for." Kay spoke at last, her voice soft, compensating for Finn. "I *know* you didn't kill those women, Bernard. But whoever this Roach is, he let you believe you did, and then he helped you get rid of the bodies, didn't he? *He's* the one who killed them though. Not you. And now he's killed Patricia."

There was a shift in Eales's expression, but Finn couldn't read it.

Kay leaned in closer. "If you tell us who he is, Bernard,

we can get the state's attorney to cut a deal. I'm sure of it. You'd be looking at an assault charge and obstruction at most. The rest can go away. With the time you've already served, you're ahead of the game." But she might as well have been pleading to a deaf-mute.

"Come on, Bernard," she said. "Help us out. Help yourself. I know you didn't ask him to kill Patricia. He's operating on his own now, isn't he? This wasn't part of the game, was it?" She gestured to the crucifix. "He's telling you to fuck off, that he doesn't care if you rot in jail or take a needle in your arm. Tell us who he is, Bernard."

But the dumb Bawlmer billy-boy had shut down. Too stupid even for self-preservation. His blue eyes half-lidded and fixed, his mouth hanging open as his sour breath seeped out.

Finn couldn't take it. "Answer her!" When he brought his open palm down on the metal table, the resounding slam reverberated through the cell, but Eales barely flinched. His gaze slid from Kay to him.

"Who is he, shithead?"

Eales's lips curled back, revealing crooked, yellowed teeth, and Finn knew they weren't going to get what they'd come for.

"Fuck off" was all he said. But there was little weight behind the words. Eales was deflated. Resigned.

"Fine," Kay said quietly. She tucked the bagged note back into her briefcase and slid one of her cards across the table. "Call if you change your mind."

Finn recognized the tactic. Leave gentle. Let Eales absorb the news, maybe he'd soften. Let him believe Kay was on his side and maybe he'd roll over on Roach.

When Kay held out her hand for the cross, Eales choked it tighter.

"I'm sorry, Bernard. It's evidence." She motioned for it again. "Maybe I can get it back for you after."

The big man moved fast. The clatter of chains was the only warning, but by the time Finn registered the movement, Eales already had Kay's wrist in his big hand.

Finn was about to launch himself across the table when Kay put up her free hand to stop him.

"You be careful now, Detective Delaney," Eales whispered then as he slid the crucifix into her palm.

"And what the fuck do you mean by that, asshole?" Finn demanded.

Eales released his grip on Kay, and this time when his gaze drifted over, Finn knew it was a look he'd never forget.

Nor would he forget Eales's parting words: "Just that she's Roach's type."

63

THE CRIMINAL INVESTIGATION BUREAU'S boardroom was dusty and airless, with half the fluorescent bulbs overhead either burned-out or flickering. Kay's headache had started around her eyes, and after three hours of sorting photocopied reports, compiling copies of photos, and mounting case stats on the four whiteboards, the pain had graduated to her temples. She needed a coffee. And she needed sleep.

But she stayed, for Gunderson. With Hagen's murder, he'd been unable to hold off the brass any longer. Kay's worst fear had come true: by the end of the week a team of six detectives would be working the new murders. Gunderson was still conferring with other sergeants in the unit deciding who would make up the task force, but it would be up to Kay and Finn to bring the new detectives up to speed, to organize and delegate. And while they wasted precious time kissing the asses of the brass upstairs, Roach would be cutting up his next victim.

The resentment was hard to swallow. Twelve days ago Valley's body had been lifted from the floor of the burned warehouse. They'd worked the investigation less than two weeks, and already it was being taken away from them.

To her right, Albert Arbor, one of the Department's systems experts, sat behind a smudged monitor wired to Hagen's computer for the past hour. As he worked the keyboard, the CPU chirped, and the technician himself let loose the occasional blurt of victory as he undeleted yet another series of files.

Finn sat at the far table, sorting through the papers taken from Patricia Hagen's house. The woman had written dozens of letters to organizations across the country: the Innocence Project, the Center for Wrongful Convictions, even the National Association of Criminal Defense Lawyers. All contacted with the same plea: assistance in Eales's defense. Kay had been ready to light a match to the whole ludicrous pile until Finn had taken over.

"I thought I'd find you two here."

Kay started at the sound of Vicki's voice. When she looked up, the assistant state's attorney crossed the boardroom.

"I heard about the task force," Vicki said. "How long before the reinforcements ride in?"

"Sarge is trying to hold them off till the end of the week." Kay rubbed her temples and leaned back in her chair.

"So what's all this?" Vicki nodded to the papers Finn was sorting through.

"Patricia Hagen's attempt at exploitation. I can't believe

how many people this woman tried to milk money from for Eales's defense," Finn said. He didn't look up from the letter in his hands, and when he sat forward, the chair's springs squealed. "You ever heard of someone named Adele McClurkin?" he asked, reading from a letter.

Vicki nodded. "The name's familiar."

"Eales's aunt?"

"Right. I remember. We talked to her after Eales's arrest. I think Varcoe did the interview. Tried to get more background on Eales," Vicki said. "She was a dead end though. She took him and his brother in briefly after their mother's death, but then Eales apparently moved out. Took his brother with him. Varcoe didn't get much out of McClurkin. She hadn't spoken to Eales since he was eighteen. Why?"

"Patricia Hagen wrote her a letter. Asking for money."

"Any response?"

"Not that I've been able to find." Finn indicated the stacks of paperwork while the portable laser in the corner spit out even more letters that Arbor was printing from the recovered files off Hagen's hard drive.

"Well, maybe a task force *will* help," Vicki suggested then. "Help you go through this stuff."

"It's not more detectives we need," Kay said. "It's a concrete lead."

"Looks like you've got a mess of those." Vicki nodded to the boards.

"Yeah, and they all go nowhere." Kay followed Vicky's gaze to the photos mounted on the whiteboards, and the notes in different colored markers surrounding them, indicating possible links.

"Maybe it's time to start eliminating some of them," Vicki suggested. "Any word yet from Latents on the results from the Keystone house?"

"They ran the print cards already, and they didn't get any hits on Printrak. But we *did* get several corresponding prints between three-eleven Keystone and Eales's house. Whoever was operating in three-eleven *was* in Eales's house over a year ago."

"Well, that's good. And what about Scott Arsenault's prints?"

"A couple partials had similar points, but not enough for the technician to classify them a match," Kay said. "Like I told you, too many leads and no solid suspect."

"But you don't think it's Arsenault anymore?"

From the corner of her eye, Kay caught Finn's look. She ignored it and shook her head.

Vicki seemed to study the boards. Then: "You've still got to eliminate him. And Jerry Bates too. You've been investigating these guys, and I know you've seen Grogan work a jury on reasonable doubt. He's going to make sure those jurors know you were targeting Bates and Arsenault as suspects, and unless you give me ways of absolutely eliminating each of them to those jurors, Grogan's going to succeed in casting enough doubt in their minds. We need alibis for these guys. Solid ones. *Something* that proves neither was involved."

Vicki was silent for a moment, and Kay knew she was visualizing her prosecution. "You've got Arsenault's name on the tenancy agreement for three-eleven, correct?"

Kay found Gaines's landlord form and handed it to her.

"Good. I can get you a warrant on this. I want you to check out Arsenault's place. Rule him out. You want it for morning?"

"That'd be great," Finn said.

Vicki looked across to the boards again. "And Bates? Where are you at with him? Is he still being held?"

"He lawyered up and they cut him loose before we

could get to him," Finn explained. "We crossed his prints with the Keystone house, and there's no matches."

"Get an alibi too," Vicki demanded.

"Kay and I are going to talk to him again tonight. The weasel's gotta know something about this Roach guy."

Vicki nodded, seemed satisfied. "All right. Let me know if you get anything from Bates."

Her gaze lingered on the five-by-sevens: Valley, Beggs, and Hagen. Kay wondered if Vicki noted the space Kay had left below them. The space she hoped she wouldn't have to fill with more photos of victims.

"Get this guy," Vicki said to both of them finally. "You've got me all the evidence I need to put him away. Now all you have to do is bring the son of a bitch in."

64

"I DON'T KNOW NO ROACH. And I was damn well here the other night." Jerry Bates was twitching for his second, or maybe third, hit for the night.

They knocked on Bates's door at nine thirty and pushed him hard for fifteen minutes, forcing him to sift through his heroin-rotted brain for names of Eales's associates. He gave them a couple, but on "Roach" he drew a blank.

"Come on, Jerry, think. You never heard Bernie use the name?"

"No. I already told ya, Bernie and I didn't hang out. We got high a couple times. That's it. I don't know his friends."

Bates paced. Kay watched as Finn followed him, clearly amused at the effect his presence had on the junkie. Bates scratched his arms, his neck, then worked his nails into his scalp.

"I swear, I don't. And I was right here Saturday night." He was whining now and nearly tripped over a toppled stack of magazines to get away from Finn. The living room was still a wreck from the warrant team's sweep. Apparently, getting a fix after a night in jail was a higher priority for Bates than straightening up.

"Look," he said, "I'm sorry Patsy's dead. Really. I like the old man."

"You mean Hagen?"

"Yeah. I know what you're thinking. That I had something to do with Patsy being dead. That I was pissed at the old man. But I wasn't. I'm not. It's my own fault I got canned. And I hope whoever killed Patsy rots in hell."

Kay couldn't read Bates's wild, darting eyes, but suspected there was truth behind them.

Finn met Kay's gaze. Shook his head. "All right, Jerry, we're done. For now. Now where's the key to Bernie's house?"

Bates waved to a hook near the door. The key hung from its twist tie. Finn grabbed it.

"You be good, Jerry," Finn warned him as they left the house. And Kay guessed the junkie was still nodding long after they left.

In the street, Finn dismissed the marked unit parked across the street and took two Maglites from the Lumina's trunk. He nodded to Eales's house four doors down. "Crime Lab must be running late. You want to wait for them or go in and take a look around?"

They'd called the Mobile Crime Lab an hour ago, asking for a van to meet them at Gettings Street. With Bernard's crucifix obviously stolen from the house, Vicki had agreed they should have the house processed. And even though Kay felt that deep, familiar twist in her gut as she looked at Eales's front door, she hoped they'd find answers beyond it tonight.

Finn must have sensed her apprehension. "Come on." He handed her a flashlight and gave her a reassuring nudge. "Let's just have a look-see."

Mounting the steps to the front porch was easier this time with Finn at her side. She took one last galvanizing breath as he unlocked the door and followed him into the blackness of the foyer.

"What's that smell?" she heard Finn ask beside her in the dark.

Kay inhaled. "Cleaner." She grappled with the Maglite's switch and panned its beam across the living room.

The place was empty. The old recliner, the sagging couch, the cigarette-burned coffee table with its porn magazines . . . all of it gone.

"When the hell did this happen?" Finn moved through the hollow living room, stopping at the kitchen.

"Everything was here last week," Kay said, her sinuses stinging from the industrial cleaner. "This smells recent."

"Why didn't Bates tell us?"

"We didn't ask," she said. "Maybe he figured we knew."

"Well, there goes any evidence."

"Son of a bitch. This is my fault." Kay scanned the empty room again, the shadows of Eales's belongings still engraved in her memory. "I gave Eales's brother the number of the detail company. I guess he's finally decided to get rid of the place."

"Well, I don't blame him." Finn was at the back window, overlooking the alley. "Looks like they parked a Dumpster out back. I guess they're not finished."

Finn directed the beam of the flashlight back to the foyer, and Kay raised her hand against the glare. "You okay to check the upstairs?" he asked. "I want to look over things down here. See if the back door's been jimmied or the basement window's busted out. This guy had to have broken in before they cleaned."

He waited for her nod, and when his flashlight turned away from her, Kay felt her heart kick into overdrive. She aimed her own Mag up the stairs. Took a breath and clamped down on the slow brew of emotions inside her.

She took the stairs quickly, chest tight, nerves jangled. She passed the back room after a cursory scan and took the corridor to Eales's bedroom. Empty as well. Even his mannequin was gone. Kay imagined it in the Dumpster out back with the rest of his crap, with the dresser on which she'd seen the crucifix. The dresser that she'd hoped to get prints off tonight.

From downstairs she heard Finn heave open the basement door. Heard his boots thump down the wooden steps.

Then, Kay felt the subtle displacement of air. At first she wondered if Finn had the back door open and the night air was filling the empty house. Then she heard a car drive by out on Gettings.

Somewhere a window was open.

A burst of adrenaline fired through her. Kay killed the flashlight. *Was there someone else inside the house?* Cautiously, she moved to the door, unclipping her holster, her eyes adjusting too slowly to the darkness.

Kay tasted her fear now, dry and metallic in her mouth, as she moved into the corridor. Listening.

She felt the hot draft from the bathroom. Her bones felt cold and her muscles were heavy. *Relax, Delaney. Use reason. One of the cleaning crew had left the window open to air out the place.*

But as she neared the doorway of the bathroom, something deeper than reason made her reach for her nine.

Instinct, or maybe paranoia.

She was too late. The Glock was barely in her hand when the dark blur came from just inside the room.

There was no making out his face. Barely enough time to register his size, as he exploded from the shadows. Silhouetted briefly by the gray light of the open window, he didn't seem big, but he hit her like a Ravens linebacker.

Kay reeled back, down the short corridor and through the bedroom door. Her left arm pinwheeled, grappling for the support of the jamb. But she had no stopping power against his speed.

When she hit the floor, pain knifed through her ankle. Her head snapped back, and her skull struck the floor with the force of their combined weight. Her ears rang, and she saw flashes of light she knew weren't there. She tried to yell, but her breath rushed out of her as he came down on top of her.

"You son of a bitch!" But the words caught in her throat.

Surely Finn had to hear their struggle from downstairs.

And then Kay felt her empty gun hand. With a panicked glance behind her she saw the semiautomatic nestled in the shag rug. A sliver of light from the street snuck under the roller blind and gleamed dully against the gun's black slide, the grip inches from her outreached hand.

Kay braced her heels and thrashed beneath him, trying to buck him off, trying to reach her gun. His knee dug deeper into her gut, and in the struggle she thought she felt his hand on her throat.

Only this time . . . this time she'd die before she lost her gun.

One more buck and a sharp twist, and her fingers closed around the gun's grip. But he went for the nine too. His hand skimmed down her arm. In the thin shaft of light she saw the tapered fingers, the skin smooth and polished, the knuckles bulbous.

Not this time.

His nails clawed at her flesh, and when she didn't give up the piece, his fist came down hard. It smashed against the delicate underside of her wrist, bruising bone and muscle. A second strike, and pain flared up her arm. Kay cried out. Finn *had* to hear them.

She could barely feel her fingers on her gun. And the next time he struck, she dragged her arm away. He cursed when his fist met the floor.

But her hand was almost useless now. Barely able to grip the piece, she couldn't be sure she'd be able to draw the five-pound pressure of the trigger.

And finally there was Finn. From downstairs he called her name. Then she heard him on the stairs.

Keep your gun, Delaney. Don't let the fucker get your gun.

She felt dizzy, her awareness sliding into a slow spin. Her assailant twisted away from her, and Kay tried to yell. To warn Finn. But her lungs were empty. Her fingers slid uselessly over the slick surface of her attacker's dark bomber jacket.

She heard Finn start up the stairs and felt the churning of air as her assailant plunged through the door. Kay brought her gun up, trying to balance it in her good hand, but he was gone.

There was the sound of a scuffle, of Finn swearing, and finally of running.

"Go!" Her yell was a rasp in her throat. "I'm all right."

Then she heard Finn crash down the stairs. More banging on the first floor, and Kay heard the slap of the back door . . . once. Then again.

It felt like whole minutes before she managed to draw a full breath. Wiping at her lip, she spat out blood and searched the floor for her Maglite. She balanced the heavy flashlight in the crook of her arm and shifted the Glock to her left hand as she staggered down the stairs.

Her ankle felt weak and her head throbbed. She limped through the house. Through the kitchen, to the back. And when Kay kicked at the screen door, she welcomed the fresh night air.

To her right, the sound of running. A steel garbage can exploding across concrete. Then silence. And finally Finn swearing again somewhere in the dark.

He was holstering his Glock when he came back up the alley. "Son of a bitch just turned into the fucking invisible man."

Kay holstered her own gun and leaned heavily against the railing.

"You okay?" Finn asked, coming up the steps.

"Yeah."

"You sure?" He grabbed her flashlight and turned it on her. The beam caught the spatter of blood bright against her hand. "Is that yours or his?"

"That's mine. But *this* is his." And when Kay held up her fist, a half dozen dark blond hairs shimmered in the beam of light.

65

ROACH WONDERED IF SHE WAS DEAD.

When he'd returned to the motel on Pulaski a half hour ago, he'd still been shaking. He'd barely escaped tonight, busting past the cop on the stairs, then tearing down the back alley with him on his heels. He knew he was home free when he ducked into a side alley and ran up Beason to where he'd parked. But he was still shaking twenty minutes later as he'd cruised up The Block, looking for dope.

He looked at her again. The spider hadn't moved from the center of her web. In the diluted light of the motel room, he watched her. Even when a dozy fly snared itself in the strands and the web pulsed and vibrated, the spider hung motionless.

He'd been so close tonight.

Delaney right in his hands. If she'd been alone, she would have been his.

Now he wanted her all the more. He couldn't remember when something had mattered so much to him, couldn't remember a time before the lust and the drive, the plan and its fulfillment. It was as if he'd never known anything else.

He should leave though. Bernard was right. It wasn't safe.

Roach fingered the Spyderco, sending the knife into a slow spin. Letting *it* decide.

Five revolutions and it stopped, the blade pointing at him.

It was time.

He eyed the new vials of ketamine he'd scored tonight, looked up at the motionless spider, then fished out a fresh syringe from the side pocket of his laptop case. Tossing the wrapper to the floor, he pierced the vial's rubber stopper with the needle and drew back the plunger. The clear liquid flowed into the barrel. Fifty milligrams. Sixty. Seventy. *May as well do it right.*

He set the empty vial back on the nightstand, held the syringe up, and flicked the bubbles from the shaft. He hated needles. Still, he didn't flinch when he drove it into the muscle of his thigh and waited for that rush to oblivion.

66

ELIMINATING LEADS. That's what Vicki wanted. Last night it had been Bates. And this morning, Scott Arsenault.

Kay scanned the disarray left in the wake of yet another search team. This one had invaded Scott's condo.

The Web designer sat in one of his fine leather chairs, but he didn't do so willingly. His hands were white around the armrests, and there was panic behind his eyes as he watched the team toss his home.

Vicki had had the warrant ready to go by the time she and Finn rolled into the office at nine.

They'd had a late night. The Mobile Crime Lab had arrived on Gettings Street after Finn's failed pursuit of Kay's assailant. Working with the portable halogens, the technicians had dusted the bathroom, the window ledge, and the back door on the slim chance that he'd left a print.

It was midnight before Finn steered them homeward, where he'd raided the icebox for a bag of frozen peas and iced Kay's wrist. And later, when she'd finally found sleep in Finn's arms, she'd been haunted by the shadowed images of the man she'd almost had in her hands . . . twice now.

Finn had pointed out that they had no real proof the man in Eales's house was connected to the murders, and that they shouldn't jump to conclusions. It could have been some punk spotting the open window and hoping for some quick loot, or a junkie or crackerjack looking for a stash.

Now, sitting in Scott's posh condo, favoring her tender wrist, Kay wished she'd been able to see her attacker. Finn too hadn't gotten any real look at him. The only vivid detail she remembered was his hand reaching for her gun.

From Arsenault's kitchen, there was the sound of shattering glass. Scott flew to his feet.

Finn caught the movement, and Kay saw his smile before he zeroed in on the bookshelves, shoving texts aside, pulling others out. The muscles along Arsenault's jaw went mad as the books started to fall.

"Come on, Scott." Kay took him by the arm and led him through the foyer, out into the corridor. "Listen to me. If you say anything in there, you'll only make it worse."

"How can it be worse?"

Through the open door came the clatter of something hitting the floor.

"Calm down."

But Arsenault looked ready to explode. "What the hell do you want from me? I already told your partner where I was Saturday night."

"Let's go through it again."

"Oh, for Christ's sake. I called Patricia around ten thirty from home. I left a message. Waited twenty minutes. When she didn't call me back, I met up with some friends at Cosmo. We stayed until last call."

"You didn't phone her again?"

"Yes. I tried from the bar around eleven. I didn't bother leaving another message. But I'm sure you're subpoenaing her phone records, so you'll see my cell number there."

Inside, something else fell.

"Good Christ. Just *tell* me what you're looking for and I can help." His voice had risen in pitch.

"They're almost done." Kay felt sorry for him. The team had been working for an hour now, and as she'd suspected, nothing connected Arsenault with any of the dead women or even Eales.

"Don't you think if I knew something, I'd give it to

you? Look at what they're doing to my place." He gestured through the doorway, and Kay turned him away.

"Then give me something, Scott. Help me out."

"How?"

"Get inside this guy's head. I know you can. What's he doing?"

Arsenault stared at her for a moment, those *GQ* looks tight, his expression uncensored.

"These murders are getting closer to home, Scott. Why Patricia? What did she know? What was her association with this guy?"

"I have no idea."

"Do you think he's targeting Eales?"

"How should I know?"

"You do, Scott. I know you do. All those books in there, the websites you design, you *know* how these guys think. Where they live in their heads. Help me out."

He appeared to consider. Then: "Look into Bernard's past."

"We have."

"Look harder. Killers aren't born overnight, Kay. All this started years ago."

67

"**THERE HAVE TO BE OTHER VICTIMS,**" Kay said. "Ones we don't know about. Bodies that haven't been found."

The afternoon sun slanted across Constance O'Donnell's therapy room and touched the photos Kay had spread across the coffee table. There'd been plenty to do back at the office: prepping the boardroom, typing reports. But Kay refused to miss her appointment. She needed Constance. Today more than ever.

From the moment she sat down, the case was the only subject on Kay's agenda. She spent the next forty minutes filling Constance in on Patricia Hagen's death, the Keystone house, and the slaughter of Jason Beckman. When the photos came out, Constance again warned Kay that whatever investigative directions she took, based on discussions in the therapy room, had to be taken carefully.

"It's been fifteen months since the first three murders," Kay said. "If there *aren't* more victims, what's he been doing all this time? And why start up again now?"

"It could be something simple, like maybe he was out of town."

"No. We would have gotten a hit on VICAP."

"Maybe he hid the bodies."

"But that doesn't fit his MO."

"He could have been institutionalized or incarcerated. Or"—Constance worried her pen between her fingers—"maybe he was in remission."

"You make it sound like it's a disease he's got."

"In a way, it is. Often the urges these men experience aren't controllable. He may have been able to *curb* those urges for the past year through counseling or medication. There are drugs to suppress those."

The same ones Constance had tried to push on Kay a year ago. As soon as she'd heard "Prozac," Kay had threatened to walk out.

"But why go on medication in the first place? He got away with three murders."

"He might have sought professional help for depression, anxiety, or OCD. Without intending to, he may have suppressed his deviance with drugs. Or maybe something scared him. Maybe he almost got caught, so he decided he needed to control his urges. Then, if he went off his medication, the inhibitor would be gone and the fantasy would be open to grow again."

"And why go off the meds?" Kay asked.

"Usually with these kinds of killers there's an inciting incident. A triggering factor. Something that pushes them over the edge, begins the cycle again. It could be any number of events: loss of a job, loss of a spouse, birth, death. It could have even been the murder of your witness. You already said you suspected there was more of a motive behind her murder. If you're right, and her death served a purpose, killing her could have started up his fantasies again."

Constance reached for her mug. The coffee had to be cold, but she didn't seem to care.

"And what do you make of his killing so close to home?" Kay asked. "Patricia Hagen knew him."

"She might have simply been an easy target. She came to him."

Kay wanted a smoke. She needed the nicotine to fill her lungs and spark answers in her brain. "Who the hell *is* this guy?" The question was rhetorical, but Constance answered anyway.

"Organized offenders tend to be of average to above average intelligence, and socially competent. You're looking at someone who's probably, at the least, a skilled worker. He owns a car, maybe even his own house. And in spite of how it looks, he's sexually competent, has probably had girlfriends. You already know he's familiar with police procedures and forensics because of his diligence in obliterating evidence."

Killers aren't born overnight, Scott had told her. *All this started years ago.*

"So how does someone get to be like this?" Kay asked.

Constance's face was hard lines now, not the usual soft, muted planes Kay had grown accustomed to. "Profiles start with generalizations. With killers like this you're usually looking at a troubled childhood, often one involving sexual predators and abuse. Having suffered those traumas, the child craves control. You've heard the stereotypes: bed-wetting, animal abuse, setting fires. And then there's the early preoccupation with death, from which the fantasy develops. Once they cross the line and begin acting on the fantasy, the control and power it awards them gradually convinces them that violence and killing are natural. Combine that with their damaged childhood, and they feel their violence and cruelty is justified."

Kay let out a breath. Where was this supposed to take her?

Constance must have sensed her frustration. "If you look at the initial trauma," she explained, "you can often understand the fantasy, or vice versa."

"What do you mean?"

"It's in his childhood that the serial killer typically acquires the scars he will later inflict on his victims. And it's this trauma that is often reenacted in the adult fantasy."

The silence of the room swelled for a time. Kay sank back into the supple cushions of the couch. "So he's not psychotic, right?"

"No. He's psychopathic. A psychotic can't maintain this level of control. Like a psychopath, your killer is amoral and asocial. He craves immediate satisfaction. His personality is characterized by irresponsibility, a lack of remorse, and impulsive or perverse behavior. *And* he feels no guilt for anything he's done. The psychopath is like an infant, absorbed in himself and sating his needs. In fact, more likely he feels entitled to whatever he takes since he believes he lives in an unjust world. His fantasy is his escape from that world, a place where he can express his emotions and his control over others."

"So that's why he uses the ketamine. For control?" Kay asked, needing something concrete to grab on to.

Constance nodded.

"Do you know much about the stuff?"

"Only that it's used more as a tripping medium than a date-rape drug," Constance explained. "With the right dose, users like it for its NDE properties."

"NDE?"

"Near-death experience. Ketamine mimics the conditions which precipitate an NDE—low oxygen, low blood flow and blood sugars, temporal-lobe epilepsy. All of these release a flood of glutamate, which overactivates certain receptors in the brain, leading the user to an altered state of consciousness."

"And people do this for fun?"

"There are worse things out there, Kay. With ketamine, a user can create the typical features of a classic NDE: the sense of timelessness, analgesia, clarity of thought, and feelings of calm. They may also undergo out-of-body experiences and hallucinations of anything from landscapes to people in their lives—alive or dead."

"Sounds like a real trip."

"For many it is. NDEs are classified on a five-stage continuum: feelings of peace, a sense of detachment from the body, then entering into a 'tunnel experience,' moving to a bright light, and finally entering that light. This final stage is called the K-hole, when the user feels completely free from themselves and their life.

"Some relive aspects of their lives, reevaluate things they've done, and simply let go of it all. That's when the body is virtually paralyzed while the sense of self feels removed from the body. And when a user comes out of the trip, they'll usually refer to it as an alien birth or rebirth."

"So you think his victims might have been conscious?"

Constance nodded. "It's quite possible. If they were, they'd be aware of their bodies even though they don't feel connected."

Kay shuddered at the image that had already started to take hold the other night. "I think he wants them conscious," she told Constance. "I think he wants them to witness their own deaths."

"If that's the case, then I'd say you're dealing with someone who's been fascinated with death for most of his life."

When the session timer went off, Kay flinched, then gathered the photos into her briefcase.

"I know a lot of this doesn't immediately help you," Constance said, "but the more you can figure out *why* this guy does what he does, and where he truly comes from, the better chance you're going to have of catching him. I promise you. Serial murderers aren't born; they're created," Constance said, echoing Scott's words. "This killer has a past. People know him."

And then Kay knew where she had to go next.

68

ALL THIS STARTED YEARS AGO.

After leaving Constance's office in Towson, Kay had driven south into the city, with one thought on her mind: *Go back to the beginning.* The *very* beginning.

So she did.

Adele McClurkin had had the unfortunate responsibility of taking in her two nephews after their mother's death. Children's Services records indicated that Bernard and

William had gone to live with their aunt in the West Arlington neighborhood for a short period. With a little cross-referencing, Kay found out that McClurkin was a fifth-grade teacher at Liberty Elementary, had never been married, and had lived at the same address all her life.

As Kay took the stairs to the lit porch of the quaint, cedar-shingled, wood-framed home, she wondered if Finn had gone home yet, or if he was still at HQ preparing the boardroom.

"Whatever he's done, I don't want to hear about it," McClurkin said the instant Kay pressed her shield against the screen door.

She was a small but ample woman, and Kay guessed it was his father's genes that gave Eales his size. McClurkin wore an understated floral skirt and a prim blouse. She looked older than her fifty-two years, with glasses strung from a chain around her neck and a wild toss of black and silver hair.

Kay promised her questions would be brief, and in minutes she was seated at the woman's kitchen table with a cup of herbal tea.

"So his trial starts tomorrow, does it?" McClurkin asked.

"Yes. Preliminary motions. Will you be going?"

"No."

"You don't visit Bernard, do you?"

"Honestly, Detective, I never liked the boy. And don't give me that look either," she said, her voice making Kay feel as if she were one of McClurkin's pupils. "Just because he was my sister's son doesn't mean I have to like him. Bernard is trouble. Always was. I did what I could for the boy."

"What kind of trouble?"

"From the time he started school," she said, stirring honey into her bone-china cup, "there was bullying and fights. Mary, his mother, God rest her soul, had her hands full with that one. Even had to move several times on account of the neighbors complaining."

"Complaining about what?"

"Oh, you know, first it was childish pranks. Then vandalism. Rocks through windows. Cars broken into. Graffiti."

Kay tried to imagine Eales's creative side coming out on the side of a brick wall.

"The police had even been called once, when they lived down on Covington. Neighbors accused him of killing their dog. He was sixteen." McClurkin sipped her tea. "Bernard was always in trouble at school too. Fights. Selling marijuana to other students. Then steroids. And that wasn't his first suspension."

"I thought he dropped out of school to work? To raise his brother?"

"Dropped out? No, he was suspended. But I'll say this, raising his little brother was the one good thing he did in his life. I guess he made a promise to his mama, and he did right by it."

"How old were they when their mother died?"

"Bernard had just turned seventeen. Billy was eight."

"So the boys lived with you then?"

McClurkin nodded, a distant look in her dull eyes as she remembered days she'd clearly rather forget.

"Do you remember any of Bernard's friends? What I'm trying to establish, Ms. McClurkin, is any connections from Bernard's past to a recent homicide I'm investigating." Kay didn't want to alarm the woman with any more details than necessary.

"No. I never met any of his friends. Honestly, Bernard and I barely made it through three months together. He's just like his daddy. A violent temper. He stole from me, lied to me, even threatened me. I didn't feel safe in my home.

"Billy, though, he was an angel. Sensitive, soft-spoken, bright. I offered to raise him, but Bernard wouldn't hear of it. Billy was his family. And then one day I came home and they were both gone, along with every last cent I had hidden in the house."

"You didn't try to get custody of Billy?"

There was regret in McClurkin's eyes. "I didn't have the energy at the time, and I hate admitting it, but I was afraid of what Bernard might do if I did. I kept tabs on the boy. Worried about him, but he did fine with Bernard. Always well-dressed, went to school, had decent grades. And now he's got a successful car dealership, a young wife, and a new baby.

"Bernard did a great job. Really applied himself. I figured the responsibility had changed him. Guess I was wrong."

Kay savored the spiced tea. "So how did their mother die exactly?"

"Overdose." McClurkin shook her head. "Mary didn't have an easy life. Bernard's father was a bastard. He beat her on a regular basis, even prostituted her to his friends. The day he ended up in a wheelchair from an accident down at the docks was the day Mary could finally run away from Eddie Eales. He died a couple years later.

"She was good for a while after that, then hooked up with Billy's father. Harold Coombs. He wasn't much better than Eales. Treated her and Bernard like dirt and got her back on the drugs."

"So your sister's death was an overdose?"

"Yes, but it wasn't accidental. Mary tried to kill herself, and when that didn't work, she went back into her bedroom and pumped herself full of heroin to finish the job. Bernard found her in the morning, called me because he didn't trust the police. When I got there, he was still cleaning up Billy."

"I don't understand."

"She'd bled everywhere. Looked like someone tried to murder her. Blood all over the bathroom, the bed, the sheets, herself, and Billy. Poor boy must have gone to his mother sometime in the night. Bernard found him curled up next to Mary's body in bed, covered in her blood."

Kay tried to process the images in her head as the cold understanding settled over her. *Childhood traumas.*

"Ms. McClurkin, before the heroin, how exactly did your sister attempt to kill herself?"

"She cut her wrists. Poor girl couldn't even do that right."

69

THE FILE ON MARY COOMBS'S DEATH had been left as "pending" for two decades, filed away with the seven hundred other cases per year that were suicides, overdoses, and questionable deaths not ruled homicides. After an hour of searching, Kay had signed out the manila folder and sat at her desk, reviewing the reports and staring at the twenty-year-old photos.

Now, as she steered into the Bridge Marina's lot, Kay could still see the photos in her mind. Mary Coombs's body, the empty syringe, all the blood, and the Spyderco lock-back knife.

Tucking the case folder under her jacket, she sprinted down the pier. *The Blue Angel* listed gently in the dark, the riggings on her mast silent. Finn had the radio on: Creedence Clearwater.

314 • Illona Haus

"We got him," Kay said, clearing the companionway steps.

Finn wore stained jeans and a sweatshirt and was elbow-deep into some kind of small motor. Tools, rags, and grease-blackened parts covered the galley table.

"It's Billy Coombs," she said. "Eales's brother."

"Whoa. What did I miss?" Finn dropped his wrench. "The guy lives up in Pittsburgh."

"Exactly why he'd have to rent the place on Keystone."

"But why here?"

"He grew up here, Finn. He knows these streets. This is where he feels safe. In control." She slapped the file onto the table. "You need to see these."

She opened the folder for him as he worked cleaning gel into his hands over the sink. "Billy's mama, Mary Coombs, didn't just OD," she said, spilling the photos across the table. The bathroom: the tub half-filled with pink water, the sides smeared with blood, crimson footprints on the old, cracked linoleum. And in the bedroom: more blood on the carpet, the comforter, and sheets.

"She suicided," Kay went on. "She hacked up her wrists, only she didn't do it right. The cuts *cross* the radial artery, not follow it. So, when that didn't work, she went back into her bedroom, bleeding everywhere, and shot herself up with whatever heroin she had left in the apartment. Combined with the blood loss, it was enough to finish her off."

Finn listened as she told him about Eales finding his brother in the morning. What was most vivid to Kay about the police photos was the oval-shaped area of unstained bedding in the midst the bloody squalor, a nest where the eight-year-old Billy had huddled against his dying mother. Mary Coombs's left arm had rigored in a position that suggested she'd had it flung over her youngest son, cradling him long after death.

"With each murder," she said, "he's reenacting his mother's death. And think about it—who else would Bernard cover for all this time? Who would he take a possible death sentence for?"

Kay was shivering, but it wasn't from the chill off the harbor. She was pumped. Could barely stand still. "It all fits, Finn. Coombs could have been down here visiting his brother each weekend those first three women were killed, *and* the night Spence and I hit Eales's door."

"But from what they've said, and everyone else, the Bozo brothers haven't spoken in years."

"It's bullshit," she said. "Coombs killed Valley because he was with Bernard the night he dumped Chisney's body in Leakin Park a year and a half ago, and he was scared Valley might have seen him. Killing her is what probably started him up again."

"And Hagen?"

"Patricia Hagen was easy for him. She knew him. When we get the dump back on her phone line, I'm sure Coombs's number'll show up. He probably called her, convinced her to see him."

"But by killing her, he took out the one person hell-bent on proving his brother's innocence," Finn reasoned. "You're saying he wants Eales to take the fall for the first murders?"

"I don't think this guy's even planning that far in the future. I think he's satisfying his own needs. Maybe the brotherly love doesn't run on a two-way street with these two. It's him, Finn. I know it." Unbidden, the memory of the diner on York Road came to her: the burned coffee, the electric train trundling on the rail overhead, and William Coombs's neat smile as he looked at her across his plate of greasy eggs. She'd believed it was compassion she'd seen in his eyes that morning when he'd apologized for his brother's attack. Now she knew better.

"And this mutt doesn't have a record, right?" Finn asked. "We've got no prints to run for comparison?"

"No, he's clean." Kay pulled the photos together while Finn changed into a fresh sweatshirt and joined her at the table.

"So where do you want to go with this?" he asked. "We need something on him before we can make a move."

"I know. That's why we gotta go to Pittsburgh."

"You think he went home?"

"After the scare we gave him at Eales's house last night, that's my guess. And I can't wait to see his face when we show up on his doorstep tomorrow."

70

THEY LEFT BALTIMORE IN FOG. Driving under a gunmetal sky for four hours up the I-70 and west on the Pennsylvania Turnpike, Finn and Kay arrived in Pittsburgh by 1 p.m. Kay had insisted on driving, perhaps believing her lead foot would get them there sooner. She was amped and Finn guessed it wasn't the half dozen coffees she'd downed or that she'd slept barely two hours.

She'd stayed the night on the boat, sharing his bed for the first time in over a year. They'd made love, and later, as he held her, they'd talked openly about their relationship, of being there for one another and trying again. He didn't wake until 5 a.m., to the sound of Kay scrounging the galley for coffee. They'd gone to the office then, sorted through the jurisdictional details of leaving the state, and hit the road by nine.

They found Billy Coombs's car dealership along Baum Boulevard. It was one of the higher-end car lots on the strip, boasting new and used luxury domestics, with a few foreign models thrown in for spice. In the gleaming show-room Coombs's partner informed them Billy had stopped in briefly that morning, then hit the road again, bound for some car auction. Finn had the sudden image of Coombs driving back to Baltimore and envisioned having passed him on the interstate.

They headed north to Stanton Heights then, and when they finally located Coombs's large, two-story brick house and pulled to the curb, Finn could feel Kay's excitement.

"Doesn't look like anyone's home." Finn nodded across the quiet residential street to the house. "Then again, car could be in the garage. How are you handling this if he's in there?"

"I'll tell him we just wanna talk," she said. "Like, he knew Hagen. Maybe he's got some ideas who'd want her dead, et cetera, et cetera. Just a nice civilized visit."

But as Kay reached the wide wraparound porch, Finn saw her unclip her hip holster and adjust her jacket over the duty weapon.

Sheila Coombs was a heavy girl. Quite pretty, Finn guessed, before the exhaustion of having a newborn had taken its toll.

"Billy's not home," Mrs. Coombs said as Finn tucked his shield into his jacket pocket. "Actually you just missed him. He was home yesterday and left again this morning. What's this about? You said you're from Baltimore?"

"Baltimore Homicide. We're investigating the murder of a Patricia Hagen."

"Name doesn't ring any bells."

Finn sensed the girl's sincerity. "It might for your hus-band. We're doing some background work on Ms. Hagen and hoped Mr. Coombs could help."

"You drove all the way up here for that?" A baby cried

somewhere in the house. Mrs. Coombs held her eyes shut for a moment, as though willing the infant to stop. "Excuse me for a second," she said, disappearing into the house.

Kay stepped through the door. "You don't mind if we come in, do you, ma'am?" She didn't wait for an answer.

The front hall was middle-class lavish, boasting antique gilt mirrors and a reproduction Victorian chandelier. A chaise lounge in fake crushed velvet with ornately carved legs might have looked chic except for the baby diapers and toys.

Mrs. Coombs returned, carrying a wailing bundle of pink terry cloth. "So how do you think Billy can help you?" she asked, desperately bouncing the baby in her arms.

"We think he may have known Ms. Hagen."

"Wow. You're going back a ways. Billy hasn't lived in Baltimore in years. And, honestly, I don't remember him ever mentioning her. How exactly do you think Billy knows her?" Finn heard a waver of paranoia in Mrs. Coombs's voice, the kind that came with a new mother's sense of diminished attraction and the worry of a husband's straying affections.

"Ms. Hagen was close to your husband's brother." Kay moved farther into the foyer.

"Then I doubt Billy knew her."

"When was the last time your husband saw your brother-in-law?"

"Not since the bastard was incarcerated." She spat the words as though even the thought of Eales left a foul taste in her mouth.

"So he visited him before then?" Finn asked.

"Yes."

"Oh. We were under the impression your husband hadn't seen Mr. Eales in years."

"And that's what he always tried to convince me of too since he knows I don't like Bernard. But I know Billy used to visit. Every few weekends. He always told me he was going to see friends, but I know it was Bernard he was seeing cuz Billy hasn't been to visit anyone in Baltimore since Bernard was arrested."

Weekends. Finn looked at Kay. She nodded her acknowledgment and then started to wander down the main hall, searching casually. Beyond her, Finn saw the door of a sitting room opened to the left, and sunlight flooded a living room at the end of the hall. Only one door remained closed.

As Mrs. Coombs fussed over her colicky infant, Kay reached for the knob of the closed door.

"Do you mind if I use your bathroom?" Kay asked. "It's been a long drive."

But before the latch could clear the frame, Mrs. Coombs stopped her. "That's not a bathroom." Her suddenly sharp tone started the baby up again, and she rocked the infant harder in her arms.

"I'm sorry," Kay said. "I just assumed—"

"That's my husband's office," Sheila Coombs's voice rose over the baby's crying. "Look, Detectives, if there's nothing else, I'd rather you left."

"Actually, there is one other thing," Kay lied. "We also needed to talk to your husband about Mr. Eales's house. It was broken into the other night."

"Billy sold the house."

"No, ma'am, I don't believe he has. And since he's the owner, we need permission to change the locks." Kay was thinking on her feet. "See, we don't know who your brother-in-law may have given keys to, and we need to secure it since it is still a crime scene."

"Did you try phoning Billy?" The infant's wails were

rising in pitch, in spite of Mrs. Coombs's desperate efforts.

"I've left a couple messages. But it's important we get the house locked up quickly."

"Why don't you ask his deadbeat brother. I assume you know where to find him."

"Yes, but since he's not the actual owner—"

"Fine, then put locks on it. You've got permission from me."

Kay looked to Finn, and he took her cue. "That won't work, ma'am," he said. "It's gotta be done right. Honestly, you'd think we didn't have enough paperwork, but we do need something to take to our bosses. Make sure it's all on the up-and-up. Can't have the department getting sued because we tampered with private property."

"What we'd need, ma'am, is the deed," Kay cut in. "If we had that, showing Mr. Coombs as the owner of the house, then your permission would probably satisfy our legal department."

Sheila Coombs couldn't answer, distracted by the intensifying cries of her newborn.

"Would your husband have a copy of the deed in his office?" Kay asked.

"Look, I just . . . can't this wait for when Billy gets home? He can fax it to you."

Kay shook her head. "I understand it's not a good time, Mrs. Coombs, but if you could just get us that deed—"

"No, you don't understand. I don't go into my husband's office, Detective. I respect his privacy." The woman averted her eyes, and Finn glimpsed an awkwardness that seemed bred of reprimands rather than respect. "You'll have to wait till he's home."

But Kay played it like a pro. They needed to get in that room. Just one more push. "I understand, Mrs. Coombs," she said. "I certainly don't want you getting in trouble over this. But it's a four-hour drive back to Baltimore. Maybe if you have an idea where he keeps it, we could look for it. He wouldn't even have to know. It would be on us. And if he does find out, you can tell him we gave you no choice."

Mrs. Coombs bit her bottom lip, her eyes shifting from Finn to the closed door, then to the bawling infant.

"We promise nothing will be disturbed," Finn assured her.

And finally, as though realizing consent would be the quickest way to get rid of them, Sheila Coombs reached for the door.

71

PAST SHEILA COOMBS'S SHOULDER, the room was dark. A crack of daylight cut through the sliver of space between the heavy curtains over the west-facing window. She reached in to flip a switch that operated three desk lamps placed around the crammed room.

The woman stepped aside, allowing them to enter, but would not cross the threshold herself. Nor would she allow her gaze to pass beyond the doorway. From the hall she pointed vaguely into the room. "There's a file cabinet in the corner. Top drawer. I think that's where Billy puts the bills. The deed should be in there. He labels everything."

And Kay didn't doubt it. It looked as if Billy Coombs had bought shares in the latest label-making products. They were everywhere, on files and drawers, even the bookshelves bore labels indicating the subject matter of the volumes shelved there. The spines of the texts were familiar. Some Kay owned herself, others she'd seen in Arsenault's bookcases.

Behind her, Finn let out a low whistle. "Impressive," he said to Mrs. Coombs. "Does your husband study law?"

"No. It's for his brother. Billy's put hours into his brother's defense. Guess he figures he owes him. Like buying him the house wasn't enough."

Kay crossed to the desk, certain Mrs. Coombs had no idea the real purpose behind the books.

"Like I said," the woman repeated, "it's probably in the file cabinet. And there's a copier there. Don't take the original." She excused herself then, the infant's wails rising again.

"Look at all this, Finn." Kay scanned the top of the desk, sure that Mrs. Coombs was gone. "Newspaper clippings, printouts from the internet about the new murders. He's either doing a lot of commuting or Billy did all this when he was home last night."

She was about to open a desk drawer, but Finn stopped her. "Don't, Kay. You got us in here legal, don't fuck it up. We're allowed a plain sight search. And she gave us access to the cabinet's top drawer."

He opened the top drawer then and began his search for the deed, keeping up appearances in case Mrs. Coombs returned. But he was scanning as well, Kay noted, his eyes washing over the same photos tacked to the walls. Photos of crime scenes from other serial murderers, printed off the internet. And articles from the *Sun* about the victims he'd let Bernard take the fall for. And finally, photos of Spencer and Kay, after the beatdown, then later at the funeral.

It was all here.

"She's never been in here," Kay whispered to Finn. "Coombs's wife hasn't set foot in this room."

"How do you know?"

"She doesn't recognize me, I can tell. And look at these photos."

Kay brushed aside the newer clippings, then jumped back, almost colliding with Finn.

"Jesus!"

In a thick, double-glassed box-frame a huge insect had been museum-mounted. Pinned behind the dusty glass its three-inch body was shielded by long, semitransparent amber wing coverings. They looked brittle, and beneath their gleaming surface, Kay could discern the striped body. Long antennae swept back along the length of the bug, and on its amber-colored hood there was a pattern in black. It looked like a skull.

"What the hell is it?" Kay asked.

Finn picked up the frame. *"Blaberus cranifer,"* he read off the label that floated behind the glass. "Death's-head roach. South America."

"How appropriate." And she fought back a shudder as she wondered if Billy Coombs had mounted the specimen himself. "There better not be any live ones in here."

She continued her search, pushing the framed roach aside and scanning the small piles of papers until she spotted the speeding ticket.

"Here's something." She picked up the ticket. "Son of a bitch was clocked doing seventy heading south on the JFX two exits past Falls Road. Guess when?"

At the file cabinet, Finn shrugged.

"About ten minutes after he drove in Jason Beckman's pizza-delivery car at TV Hill. We got him, Finn."

Her gaze caught the small cluster of personal photos at the edge of the bulletin board: a wedding photo, a couple Polaroids, and several vacation shots tacked up. She studied Coombs's smile, imagining how easily he'd charmed each of the women in the clippings over his desk.

"I got the deed," Finn said, extracting a document from

the cabinet. Keeping up the legal facade, he fired up the photocopier. Only when he returned the document did he root deeper in the cabinet's drawer.

Kay was vaguely aware of his withdrawing a kraft envelope.

"I think we just got more on the bastard," Finn said, bringing it to the desk.

The envelope was stained and dog-eared. Pawed over, Kay thought, and the button-and-string closure looked well-worn. Finn shook its contents out onto the desk.

Cards. Driver's licenses and photo ID cards. Annie Harris. Roma Chisney. And the Jane Doe from Leakin Park.

Kay picked up the third card and looked into the face of the woman who had spent the past sixteen months without a name.

Ellen Roth. Kay ran the name through her head a few times until Finn spoke again.

His voice startled her. "Kay," he said quietly, "there's one more."

72

IT WAS AFTER TWO by the time they left Pittsburgh, bearing east as the sun finally broke through the bank of slate-gray clouds. When the Baltimore skyline came into view, Kay realized she had little memory of the drive. She'd focused on traffic but her mind had spent the hours retracing every step of the investigation, every bit of evidence, cataloging everything against Billy Coombs.

Back in Coombs's office, something deep inside her had turned, something she couldn't put words to. She wanted

Coombs more than she remembered wanting anything in her life.

The plain brown envelope with the IDs of Harris, Chisney, and Ellen Roth lay on the Lumina's dash. But it was the final card that had fallen from the envelope that haunted Kay and caused her gaze to return to it throughout the drive.

The reality hadn't registered when she'd picked up the Fraternal Order of Police card off Coombs's desk and turned it over in her hands. Even as she'd read the name, the truth was slow coming, as if the world around her had suddenly warped. But when she looked at Spencer's photo, she was back on that lawn outside Eales's house. Coombs *had* been there that night. And—as he had with all his victims—he'd taken something of Spence's. He must have stood over Spence, her gun still in his hand while he watched him die. Then he'd removed Spence's wallet and taken the card. No one had missed it.

Kay imagined Coombs moving across the lawn to her. She wondered if he'd held the gun on her as well, if she'd blacked out by then or simply couldn't remember. She'd always figured Eales had left her for dead, but now she knew that wasn't the case. If she'd been dead, her FOP card would have been in that envelope as well.

No, Coombs and Eales had fled. She'd read the police logs: the district units had responded quickly to the report of gunfire. The sirens would have scared them off before Coombs had the chance to finish her.

"You okay?" From the passenger seat, Finn reached across and settled his hand on her thigh. A gesture of comfort. Only, it wasn't comfort Kay wanted. Not now.

"I should have been onto him sooner," she said, steering the Lumina east onto Edmonson.

"And how's that?"

"I had him in the alley. Had him up against the car, Finn. How could I not know that was Coombs?"

"It was dark, Kay. Your adrenaline was pumping. The guy had a good cover story. Besides, you've only met Coombs once, in a neutral setting. It's not like you were out looking for him. Plus, he'd shaved."

Kay remembered the residue from the drain trap of the bathroom sink in 311 the night of Jason Beckman's murder.

"I should have put it together."

"Come on, Kay. No one would have."

"*I* should have." She ran the amber at Fulton. "He was right there, on top of me, in Eales's house the other night."

"It was dark, and he blindsided you."

But Kay didn't want excuses. She just wanted Coombs.

When her cell phone rang, Kay was glad for the diversion.

"Kay? It's Vicki. Where are you?"

"On our way to see you. We need a warrant."

"It'll have to wait." There was a shakiness in Vicki's voice that Kay had never heard before.

"What's wrong."

"It's Eales."

Over the cell, Kay heard an explosion of voices in the background, a door slamming, then shouts.

"We've got . . . we've got a situation at the courthouse. You and Finn need to get down here. Right away. The whole district's on high alert."

"What the hell happened?"

"He's out, Kay. Eales escaped."

73

CALVERT AND FAYETTE STREETS were impassable, blocked by squad cars, QRT vans, and unmarked vehicles with their cherries strobing on their dashes. Kay and Finn left their car in the tangle and sprinted up the two blocks to the Clarence Mitchell Courthouse. Division of Corrections guards manned the entrance, pushing back the media crews as they jockeyed for position, waiting for an official statement.

The foyer was controlled chaos. Past the sea of uniforms, Kay spotted several of the Quick Response Team members in full gear storming the marble corridors.

They found Vicki on the second floor in Judge Leventhal's courtroom. She was at the prosecution table, gathering her papers. When she spotted them, she shook her head, her face flushed.

"Are you all right?" Finn asked her.

She nodded, looking more pissed off than anything. "They figure he went out a window."

"How the hell does that happen?" Finn asked.

"We finished preliminary motions at two, took a recess, then started defense motions to suppress," she explained. "Grogan's trying to have the confession thrown out, claiming Eales is recanting it now."

"I'm not surprised," Kay said.

"Anyway, tension was getting a little high, so Leventhal called a brief recess. Then Eales starts whining about needing to use the bathroom. Says he can't hold it. But Leventhal wanted counsel in place when he resumed the bench, so he instructs the guards to take Eales to *his* chambers instead of escorting him all the way downstairs.

Fifteen minutes later, they come back without him. They figure he went out the window."

"If he did, he'll be hurting." Finn didn't sound anxious about Eales. "That's a two-story drop. He won't get far."

"Still, we're in a semilockdown. QRT's combing the building just in case, and they've got an APB out on Eales. Mass Transit's been notified as well, just in case he tries to hop a bus or the Light Rail."

"The mope's probably home already," Finn said. "They always go home. Send a patrol over to Gettings Street, and you'll probably find him hiding in his closet."

"Already covered," Vicki said.

"We should get someone on Patricia Hagen's address too," Kay said. "Just in case." *Where else would you run, Bernard?*

She thought of 311 Keystone, turned to Finn. "Could Coombs have helped him get out?"

"What do you mean?" Vicki asked. "Eales's brother? What's Coombs got to do with all this?"

Kay took the envelope from under Finn's arm and unlooped the string closure. Vicki watched as each card clattered onto the table.

"These are from Coombs's home office. Consensual search," Kay clarified, then pushed Spencer's FOP card toward Vicki. "It's Coombs who shot Spence."

74

KAY HAD GIVEN IN.

Standing outside, on the eighth-floor terrace at Headquarters, Kay balanced a Camel between her fingers as if it had always belonged there. She studied it for a moment, then brought it to her lips and inhaled. Finn could almost see the tension ebb.

"Should have had one of those long ago," he said.

"You're a bad influence." She smiled, but he could tell it was forced. Her mind was out there, in the streets, searching for Eales, for Coombs. That's where she wanted to be, not stuck at Headquarters pushing the necessary papers and procedural buttons to get the warrant for Coombs.

She shoved away from the picnic bench and crossed to the railing. Pacing the length of the barrier, she looked over the lights of the city. She hadn't sat still since they'd left the courthouse hours ago. But then, neither had he.

They'd had to pull Gunderson off the Eales situation, brief him along with Vicki, then start making calls to the Pittsburgh PD and their district attorney for warrants. Now it was only a matter of time before they had the warrant for Coombs. Just one more call from the DA in Pittsburgh.

A siren from somewhere in the downtown core cut the night. Kay looked west, following the sound. She dropped the cigarette and crushed it under her shoe.

"Where the hell is he?" she asked, grasping the top rail in her hands and scanning the expanse of lights.

"Eales or Coombs?"

"They'll find Eales. He's too stupid to stay hidden long. Where the fuck is Coombs? What's he doing?"

Finn put out his own cigarette and joined her.

"We got him, Kay. It's just a matter of time."

"And how much time does he need to kill another woman?"

"We'll get him before then." Finn reached over and placed his hand over hers on the rail, gave it a squeeze. He saw her tension ease then, but only marginally.

Still, standing here, just as on the night Joe Spencer had

first introduced them on this very terrace, Finn felt a peace he hadn't in a long while. Felt, for the first time in months, that a future with Kay might be possible.

Another siren erupted to the south.

"I can't stand this waiting," she said. "We should call the DA again."

"He'll call." He turned her. "Maybe you should get something to eat."

"I can't eat now."

"We haven't eaten since breakfast. Besides, even when this DA calls, we've still got to wait for Vicki. If you want, I can go get something."

"No, you're right. I'll go. I can't sit around here anymore."

He walked her down to the street. "Hey, you did good today, Kay. We're gonna get Coombs. And you just watch, they're going to give you *another* Bronze Star."

"Yeah, right." She shot him a smile as she headed down Frederick Street.

Finn loved that smile.

75

AS KAY WALKED THE HALF BLOCK to the public parking garage where all the Central cops parked their personal vehicles, she wished she'd bummed a second smoke off Finn. Her nerves felt raw and she was on edge. Another siren blurted at the far end of the one-way street, and Kay's heart jumped.

She wanted this over. She wanted Coombs. She wanted to sit across from him in an interview room, to look him in the eye, feel his energy, and smell his sweat. And more than anything, she wanted to witness that moment when Coombs realized, in spite of all his cleverness, she'd got him. Because only then could Kay begin to forgive herself for Spencer's death.

Entering the ramp of the public garage, Kay gave Manuel, the nighttime attendant in the booth, a nod. She wondered if Coombs had gone home yet, if he knew they'd been there. What would he do when he found out?

And would Eales try to contact him? Kay knew Coombs couldn't have helped with his brother's escape from the courthouse. It had been opportunity, not planning, that had led Eales out that window this afternoon.

Bernard. Where was he? She almost felt sorry for the poor bastard now, and she hoped they'd take it easy on the big, sad fuck when they found him. All this time Billy Coombs had let him take the fall for the murders. He'd convinced Bernard—with his alcoholic blackouts—that he'd murdered three women.

Or had Bernard known all along?

No, Kay didn't believe he had. His confession had been a last-ditch effort to cover for his brother. He probably hadn't thought he'd need to until Kay had enlightened him with the truth.

On the fourth level of the garage, she started down the north row to where she'd parked the 4Runner this morning. She hated that the shadows still spooked her, and in the dim light of the concrete structure, she felt a glimmer of the fear that had haunted her for the past year. Only now, she could process it logically. She knew she had nothing to fear from Bernard, that he wouldn't come after her. Facing him in that holding cell, she'd put that demon to rest, even though the residue of it would probably always be with her.

The 4Runner sat in the back corner, crouched under a burned-out light fixture. Kay flipped through her key ring in the shred of light that filtered in from the street, then unclipped her cell phone. She had the sudden urge to call Finn, to thank him and tell him she loved him.

Only then, as small chunks of safety glass ground beneath the soles of her duty shoes, did Kay realize the lamp mounted over her car wasn't just burned-out.

Valley.

But the thought came too late. Even as she felt the burst of movement behind her and swung her elbow in a wide, defensive arch, Kay felt the prongs touch the back of her neck. No maneuver could have protected her against the stun gun. The surge ripped through her. Her muscles spasmed, and the blood roared in her ears.

And as she went down, Kay had the overwhelming urge to apologize. To Spence and Valley. To her mother, her father. And to Finn.

76

BERNARD DIDN'T KNOW where he was going. On foot, he'd followed the Key Highway, zigzagging down side streets and alleyways until he staggered into the Locust Point rail yards. The suit Patsy had arranged for him through Grogan was ruined; the jacket was split at the shoulders and the pants were torn over his right knee.

All his life he'd never known luck. But today . . . today Lady Luck had handed him the mother lode. Just taking a piss when he'd seen the open window. He hadn't stopped to think. No, sir. Just move. Follow his nose. Nothing to lose. His fly was still unzipped when he'd hit the concrete of the side street and tried to roll, his shoulder cracking under his weight.

He knew instantly that he'd dislocated it. It had happened before, as a kid, coming down wrong after a basket shot. Billy's asshole dad had told him to buck up as he wrenched it back in for him. Bernard fixed the shoulder himself this time, in a side alley off Grant, wadding the jacket under his armpit and smashing his shoulder against the filthy brick wall.

The pain was hot now, shooting down his arm and back. Three hours ago, he'd risked sneaking into a Rite Aid and lifted a bottle of Excedrin. Rattling another four into his palm now, Bernard swallowed them dry.

He hadn't been surprised to spot the patrol car parked outside his house. Another in the back alley behind Jerry's.

Four blocks west he found an unlocked storage shed in a narrow alley running north from Fort Avenue. Inside, he pulled two lawn chairs together, put his feet up, and listened to the rain on the aluminum roof.

Where to go? Even if he had the money for a cab, he couldn't go up to Patsy's house. The police'd be there too. He wondered about her old man. Probably blamed Bernard for his daughter's death. Goddamn Roach. After everything he'd done for him. Kid never had no respect. Bad enough the little prick had led him on about the dead women, but then to kill Patsy. That just wasn't right. Then again, the kid never had been too right.

It was because of Roach they'd had to move those couple times. Once when the neighbors' cat wound up dead in the trash. And again when it was Johnny Newcomb's dog. Bernard had known Billy'd done it. He'd threatened to toss the little bastard's bug collection for getting him in shit. Always creeped him out having them around anyway. Big-ass tropical cockroaches, scuttling around in the old, cracked fish tanks the kid had salvaged.

It was a few years later that Bernard had finally taken care of the lot. After finding one of the roaches in his Cheerios, he'd smacked it with a rolled-up *Penthouse*. Hit it a dozen times, then finally crushed the damn thing under his boot. Billy had come in, started wailing like a girl.

Bernard had had it.

He'd busted into the kid's room, taken every last filthy tank, and smashed them into the street below. Roaches running in every goddamn direction. Kid never forgave him for that.

In the musty silence of the storage shed, Bernard stretched. The lawn chair bowed under his weight.

He'd been thinking about those fucking roaches ever since he'd heard Patsy was murdered.

And then, suddenly, Bernard knew where he could go for the night.

77

"I'VE GOT JUDGE WATTS on call for this." Vicki sounded tired over the phone. "He's ready to sign when you get the paperwork here."

"I have it now." Finn hunt-and-pecked his way across the keyboard and finally hit PRINT. "Pittsburgh's on board in case Coombs has gone home. Just got off the phone with the DA."

The printer in the boardroom whirred to life.

"Oh, and we got the results of the dump on Patricia Hagen's line." Finn pushed aside several reports and pulled out the phone company reports that had come through the fax only ten minutes ago. "One of the incoming calls the night of Hagen's murder is from the Pittsburgh area code. Probably Coombs's cell. I just have to check Kay's notes to confirm."

"All right then. Anytime you're ready."

"We're ready."

"Good. Meet me at my office."

Finn hung up and grabbed the affidavit out of the printer. In the side office, he rifled through the paperwork and phone messages across Kay's desk, searching for anything that might have Coombs's number on it. He knew she'd called him at least once for the key to Eales's house.

He rummaged in her desk drawers until he found her police notebook, and when he removed it, he uncovered a five-by-seven photo. It was a shot of him, two weeks ago, at the burned-out Dutton warehouse, squatting over the shadowed remains of Valerie Regester. Kay must have pulled it from the rest of the crime-scene photos, kept it for herself. Finn liked the implication and left the picture.

Flipping through the pages of careful notes in her police notebook, Finn found Coombs's numbers. His cell was a match.

"Hey, Finnerty." Stan Kimble from the night shift stood in the doorway. "Jane Gallagher's asking for you. Line three."

"Tell her to talk to the spokesperson," Finn said, picking up the phone and punching an open line. "I'm busy."

He jabbed at the number pad, dialing Kay. He'd expected her back by now, and she needed to be part of this. She deserved to have her signature on the paperwork.

Sitting at her desk, Finn listened to the hollow rings stretch across the line, and an irrational fear settled over him. That fear made sense when it wasn't Kay who answered her cell then.

78

KAY FELT THE LISTING of the car first. Smelled fine leather and aftershave. The dashlights glowed pale green, and over the radio Tony Bennett sang Louis Armstrong with k. d. lang. She thought of Jonesy humming along in the cutting room, thought of Valley on the slab. And then she remembered the voltage surging through her body in the parking garage.

Kay swallowed the instant panic. *Assess, Delaney. Look for the out.* Through half-lidded eyes, she saw his fine hands wrapped around the wood-grain steering wheel, saw the stun gun. Then she spotted the hypodermic in his lap. Fear coiled deep in her bowels.

Don't panic.

Her hands were numb, tied behind her. But she felt no bonds on her ankles.

Keep calm. Don't let him know you're conscious.

Moving only her eyes, she looked across the narrow space at Billy Coombs. Streetlamps blurred past, their light making the fierce angles of his clean-shaven face appear to melt in between sweeps of the wipers. She eyed the syringe again, the needle exposed. *Don't let him stick you, Delaney. Whatever you do. He sticks you, and it's fucking over.*

She'd kick the shit out of him before then. *Think. Like any abduction, the longer you wait, the less chance there is of escape.* He would have to get her out of the car. She could run then. But how far would she get? She'd have to take him out first. Somehow.

"I know you're awake." His calm voice startled her. "I bet your head's killing you. It's the depletion of blood sugar you're feeling. Six hundred thousand volts will do that to you. Converts the blood sugar into lactic acid. Fucks with the muscles. You probably know that from the Academy though, huh?"

The dash clock read nine twenty. They'd been driving what, ten, fifteen minutes? They couldn't have come far. She tried to spot a landmark, a building, anything to give her bearing. But it was just another back street. Row houses and cluttered stoops, trash cans and chain-link.

Three more minutes and the big car stopped. Coombs threw it into reverse. Turning in the seat to look out the back, his hand brushed her hair. Kay saw his thin smile.

When he killed the engine, she could make out a concrete overhang. Were they under a bridge? Another garage? She tried to crane her head, her body still quivering from the voltage. She heard his seat belt retract, then the squeal of leather as he turned in his seat to face her.

Where was the syringe? *Keep your eye on the needle, Delaney. Where's the fucking needle?*

"You're making a big mistake," she said, and hated how weak her voice sounded.

"I don't think so." Another smile.

And then, somewhere in the shadows below the dash, she felt his hand. Hot and damp through the thin fabric of her suit pants. *Don't react. Don't give him the satisfaction.* His hand moved up, caressing her thigh. Would he rape her? He hadn't with the others. He inched even higher.

"You son of a bitch!"

And then Kay saw the hypodermic.

Kick him, Delaney. Move! What the fuck are you waiting for? But even if her body could cooperate, he was too fast. She caught the flash of the needle, then heard her own pathetic cry as the tip drove through fabric and into her thigh.

Ketamine. Had to be. It burned going in, the heat spreading through her leg and settling in her hips even as she tried to wrestle herself free from it. Jonesy's words ran through her thoughts: *fast-acting . . . blocks nerve paths . . . paralysis . . . unconsciousness.* How long had he said it took? Minutes? Or only seconds?

Coombs opened the driver's-side door. The dome light glared for a moment. She saw his shadow pass in front of the car's hood, and when he swung open her door, she almost spilled out onto the concrete.

Run! But the world spun. She was floating. She would drift away if he let go of her. Her legs felt rubbery as he guided her up a short ramp to a door. He propped her against the wall, one hand pinning her, the other working a key.

Where the hell were they? She couldn't focus.

When he shoved her through the door, he said something, but she couldn't decipher his words. There was a buzzing in her ears, like a swarm of hornets. He flipped some switches, and lights blinded her. Her throat constricted.

Then he was dragging her, shuffling as he supported her weight. The hornets droned louder, and her lungs felt heavy. She knew this place, but didn't. And when he lowered her, she recognized the smell. *What was it?*

She slumped to the floor, the tiles cold against her cheek. She watched his black Reebok sneakers as he crossed the room several times. In and out of her line of vision. What the fuck was he doing? And then Kay heard water running. Crashing into a tub or a basin, drowning out the hornets in her head.

When he returned, his shirt was off, his skin pale. Trails of light and movement swirled around him, as if a dozen Billy Coombses were coming at her. *Keep your eyes open. Focus.*

She tried to scream, but nothing came out. She wanted to throw up.

His hands wormed beneath her shoulders, grasping her under her arms. The room did a somersault, and she swallowed bile. He was dragging her, grunting and cursing as he did. Then he was tugging at her clothes.

The crash of water amplified, then she felt it—warm and swirling. For a moment she thought he'd stripped her completely, then felt her blouse plaster to her ribs.

When she tried to focus, reality seemed to shift. Light and color changed. She thought of Patricia Hagen. *So this was what it was like?* The embrace of the water, the lull of her own heartbeat in her head, her muscles slackening as the drug flooded her veins.

Her body was numb now. There was only warmth as the water rose around her. Kay wondered if she'd even feel it when he cut her. An easy death. Quiet. Almost peaceful in a way, as the drug annulled any instinct for survival.

And then Kay saw the knife. Small, fitting into his palm. The honed blade trailed reflected light through the air. Dancing before her face.

He lowered it and she saw his smile. Saw his lips move, but the words were lost. There was only the roar of water. And her heart.

She felt him pull at her blouse, and the smooth sweep of the knife as he cut the material away.

When she blinked, she saw Valley. Spencer. Their bodies. Maybe this was how it was supposed to be. Maybe this was *her* death and she should accept it. Accept that fate had, at last, delivered her justice.

"No, you don't."

Were they Coombs's words or her own? When she opened her eyes he was a blur over her, one moment his eyes in focus, the next his mouth. Everything shifting.

"Don't you go down so easy." She read the words off his lips. He wanted a fight. Wanted to see her struggle.

She wouldn't give him the pleasure.

Close your eyes, Delaney. But she couldn't. Like a voyeur at her own death, she was drawn to the violence of it. When Coombs brought the knife to her neck, she sensed the blade caress her throat but didn't feel its slice. Then she recognized the heat of her own blood leaking out, staining the water.

". . . should have shot you when I had the chance," Coombs said. "You were so far gone. Probably don't even remember me being there, do you?"

Close your eyes. Accept.

"That night on Bernie's lawn, you grabbed on to his leg like a fucking pit bull. So where's your spit and fire now, huh? Give me some of that fight."

He shoved her, and her innards jostled deep inside her.

"I should have shot you. Your own gun too. I should have pulled the trigger just like I did on your partner. Do you know what he said before he died? Do you?"

Kay swallowed. Fighting the drug. Battling the assault of colors and light, the urge to vomit.

"Abso-fucking-lutely nothing. The son of a bitch cried. Blubbering in his own blood. Chickenshit cop couldn't even face his own death."

She wanted to say something, but couldn't remember how to form the words. She wanted to struggle but knew her body would only disappoint her. Her auditory bandwidth narrowed, and the blood slowed in her veins. She listened to the air fill her lungs.

"But *you* will," she heard him say as he unzipped his chinos. "You'll look death right in the eye, won't you?" His words whispered in her ear, his steely breath washing over her. And as reality dissolved, Kay wondered if she'd at last find peace.

79

FINN CAME DOWN HARD on the accelerator. The Lumina surged up the base of the JFX, the tires thudding over the joints of the Gay Street viaduct, hurtling north.

It was the attendant at the city garage just down from Headquarters who had answered Kay's cell phone. The kid had found it ringing under Kay's 4Runner and described for Finn the dark-colored sedan that had left the structure shortly after he remembered seeing Kay come in.

Less than a block from fucking Police Headquarters.

Finn had ordered a patrol to check on Kay's apartment, then warned the units covering Eales's house and Hagen's and put out an APB on Coombs's maroon Park Avenue. Then Finn had been mobile, powered by hundred-proof adrenaline.

As the Lumina blasted past the State Pen, the speedometer's needle inched to seventy-five. Finn grappled under the seat for the cherry and threw it on the dash. He didn't know where else to go. He radioed the Northern, ordered more units to 311 Keystone, and demanded they patch through the stationed uniforms to him. Backup would arrive before he did, but if Kay was in that house . . . His mind flashed on the images of Beggs's and Hagen's drained, nude bodies, and his foot came down harder on the gas.

The radio blurted, and a Northern District officer came on.

"I'm on my way but I want you and your partner to go in," Finn instructed the uniform. "Front and back. I need that house secured."

"We're moving in."

"And keep this channel open. Take me with you."

Finn cranked the police radio's volume: car doors slammed, then silence, and finally banging. He focused on traffic, but in his mind he was hammering on the door of 311 with them.

The radio hissed. The banging grew louder. Then: "No answer, Detective, and there's no lights on inside."

"Take the door," he said into the radio.

But even as he listened across the airwaves to the battering on 311's door, Finn knew there was only a slim chance that Coombs would risk returning to the rental house.

Where the hell do you have her, you dirtbag?

Baltimore was Coombs's hunting ground. Kay had said it was because he knew the streets. Because it was where he felt safe. In control.

Where he felt safe. As safe as he'd probably felt in his dead mother's embrace.

The Lumina's wheels almost locked when Finn's foot punched the brake. The vehicle squealed onto the North Avenue off-ramp.

"I know where you feel safe, you son of a bitch." And as he careened into southbound traffic, Finn prayed his hunch was right.

80

KAY HAD NEVER KNOWN such absolute calm.

There was nothing familiar about this place, yet there was comfort here. Time converged into a fourth dimension where past, present, and future were the same. The images came at her in waves. Bernard's lawn. Spencer's blood. Harris the cat. Hagen's nude body in the leaves. Finn's face when he came inside her.

And then there was Valley. The girl sat on the bare mattress in her apartment, boxes and secondhand furniture surrounding her. She laughed at something, the shyness and mistrust gone.

"This is your future," Kay had told the girl. "You can't change your past, but the future . . . you can make something of it."

Valley stood, settled a hand against Kay's cheek, and she felt its warmth. Then Valley dissolved.

Kay turned, looking for the girl, but the room was gone as well. She was someplace else. No ground, no walls, no horizon. Just a churning gray. Then Spencer. There was a light behind him, and she squinted against it. He wore one of his brown, off-the-rack sport coats. The kind that always made cops look like cops—the cuffs frayed, and a patch worn bare above his right hip from years of covering the butt of his nine. His tie was lopsided.

"But you're dead." The words formed in her mind.

Spence was gone.

Kay spun. Searching. The light grew brighter. Pure and white. And he was back, sitting at his desk across from hers in Headquarters, his loafers propped on the corner.

"I killed you," she said.

"Bullshit. Only person you killed was yourself. Don't go all Mother Teresa on me, Delaney. Martyrdom never suited you."

The light pulsed behind him, and then he stood before her: uniform crisply pressed, stripes pinned to his lapel, and his cap under his arm. Just as they'd buried him.

"And now look at you. Ready to throw in the towel. What the fuck are you doing?" She heard his voice, but his mouth didn't move. Were they her own words?

"You're a fucking good cop. You figured this bastard. *You.* Are you gonna let this shit-for-brains win?"

Then he was at the wheel of their Lumina, cigarette smoke curling around him. "Everything I taught you, and you're gonna throw it away on this little dickwad?"

The word *absolution* moved through her thoughts, felt as if it entered her body. As if she could taste its sound.

"The only person who needs to forgive you is you."

The light pulsed weaker this time.

Redemption came to her in a flash of brilliant blue.

"You're a good cop, Delaney."

She hovered in the blue-gray, searching. But Spence was gone. Another voice beckoned her now. Hot in her ear. Words distorted.

The water swirled, and when she opened her eyes, the light hurt. A shadow moved, and Kay struggled not to react. Coombs was over her, in the water with her.

What had he done to her? Why wasn't she dead?

Her pulse pounded against the bite of rope on her wrists. He'd secured her arms back, over her head, muscles stretched, rope taut so she wouldn't slip beneath the water. She watched Coombs's lips move, but still the words were a garble in her ears.

When she felt his hand, she refused to flinch. She let his fingers crawl down her neck, her chest, and finally grasp one breast through her sheer bra. He squeezed it hard, and she guessed there should be more pain.

She heard him moan.

She wanted to spit at him, to scream something, but her mouth couldn't form the words. He smiled, as though sensing her attempt. His Adam's apple lifted and fell several times as he swallowed, and the heat of his shirtless body pressed against her.

And then Kay knew what she had to do.

She held his stare, the blue eyes boring down on her, closer and closer. *Come on, you sick son of a bitch. Just another inch*. She could feel his cheek against hers, smell his breath. His hair tickled her forehead as he inhaled her. And Kay could see his heartbeat pulse through the artery along his neck.

In her mind, Kay lunged then. Her teeth sank into his soft flesh like a dog and ripped out his throat as the hot blood from his lacerated carotid poured over her.

But with a thin, pitiful cry, her body failed her. Her deflated muscles only quivered in an attempt to respond to the electrochemical signals firing through her brain, the drug severing any connection.

Still, Coombs backed off. Inches only, but enough that she could see his eyes. And in them she recognized his understanding, his comprehension of what she'd hoped to accomplish. His thin smile stretched across his face.

81

ROACH HEARD SOMETHING bang upstairs. A second and a third bang. Then silence.

No doubt neighborhood kids looking for a cheap thrill. The funeral home was locked up, a couple windows boarded already. Still, the little thugs would snatch up anything that wasn't nailed down if the Realtor didn't close on it soon.

Lucky for him old man Hagen hadn't removed the spare key stashed over the delivery-bay door. Thirty minutes ago when he'd stepped into the basement, Roach had bathed in the sweet familiarity. The smells, the quiet, the calm lingering of death.

He remembered the first time Bernard had snuck him

down here and dared him to touch one of the stiffs. He'd thought of his mother then, as he'd touched the cold, gray flesh.

He would come after school whenever Bernard worked late and sit upstairs in one of the viewing rooms, staring across a sea of empty folding chairs at some fancy casket with a stuffed body. The whole formality of death had always seemed obscene to him.

The embalming room made the most sense, even at that young age. There were no lies here, among the steel tables and the mortician's instruments. Bernard had shown him some of the equipment once: the Porti-boy embalming pump, the drainage instruments, and the tro-car—a two-foot-long metal shaft, tipped with a razor-sharp point and connected by a rubber hose to an aspira-tor. His brother had explained how Hagen used it to suck out the cavity fluids, to perforate and empty each of the major abdominal organs, sucking it all out like a puree. Roach had always wanted to watch. Just once.

As he looked down at Delaney now, he toyed with the notion. *Maybe later.* Other tasks had to be completed first. The ketamine would be wearing off, and not soon enough. He should have shot her up with less, should have guessed she'd be more susceptible to the drug. Cop had probably been clean all her life.

For now, only her eyes moved. He relished the panic he saw there in spite of her attempts to mask it. It was what lay behind that panic that excited him the most. Delaney's old fire. The spark he'd seen in her on Bernard's lawn. That's what gave him a hard-on now.

The knife in his palm beckoned him. The urge blos-somed. He lowered the Spyderco, at last pressing the streamlined handle along the shaft of his cock, the cool, mother-of-pearl inlay already warmed. He saw her fight back her reaction. Maybe he'd cut her again, just to get a rise out of her.

With her hands tied to the embalming table bolted to the floor, Roach let his gaze trail the pale skin along her inner arms. He brought the blade to her wrist and traced its tip along the blue, pulsing vein. She couldn't move, but beneath him in the stainless-steel service tub he felt her desire to. He celebrated her thin, choked whimper. He wanted to kiss her, but he couldn't trust her.

He guided the blade farther down, caressing her armpit with its tip, and wondered what she'd say if she could actually speak. He let the Spyderco's honed edge follow the lines of her toned midriff, past her navel, and to the top of her panties.

Teasing her with the blade now, he watched her try to move. Her head lolled uselessly to her shoulder. With no strength to right it again, she shifted her eyes, trying to see his hands. Fear, frustration, and anger darkened her face. God, it was beautiful.

He wanted to stand over her, make her see his power, watch her acknowledge her own death. He'd never felt it this strong. But just as he was about to rise in the tub, Roach saw Delaney's gaze move to the door.

82

BILLY COOMBS was out of the service tub in one lithe movement. Like a cat. He was naked, Kay noticed then. His chalk-white skin glistening from the water, his erection meager but blatant.

"Jesus Christ, Bernie! You scared the shit out of me." His voice was magnified in the hollow room.

Bernard shuffled through the doorway, his suit damp and torn. He favored his right leg. Given the useless angle of her head, Kay couldn't see his face clearly, couldn't tell if he focused on her or his brother.

"I heard about this afternoon," Coombs said, going for his clothes. His movements jerky. Nervous.

What did he see that she couldn't?

"Fucking brilliant. But you gotta get outta town. I think I know someone who can help."

When Coombs squatted, reaching for the shirt he'd folded with his pants, Kay could at last see Bernard's face. Pure rage—the kind she'd seen once before.

Coombs came up with the shirt. But he never got the chance to put it on.

Bernard struck fast. Kay barely saw his fist swing before it connected with Coombs's jaw. Coombs's head snapped around, and blood flew from his mouth, splashing the wall.

He dragged a pale wrist across his bleeding lip, the knife still in his grip. "You son of a bitch. You fucking hit me!"

"Yeah?" The second blow, lightning fast, took Coombs under the ribs. Kay heard the vicious crack, and his thin, naked frame buckled. He wretched, tried to turn from Bernard, but the third strike took him in the small of the back.

Coombs reeled into one of the workbenches. She heard his knife clatter to the floor, but couldn't tell where it landed.

Kay flexed her hands, testing the ropes, but still felt nothing.

She could only watch as Coombs turned, wheezing, a red welt already forming along his rib cage. His voice sounded diluted, almost desperate with fear. "What the hell are you doing, Bernie? You on something?"

"You motherfucking double-crosser. Why'd you kill her, Roach?"

Bernard took another swing, but this time Coombs was ready. He ducked. The empty punch left Bernard open, and Coombs hooked him in the gut. The big man didn't even flinch. When Bernard hit him again, there was more blood, and Coombs sprawled into the next bench. Glass and stainless-steel pans smashed across the tiles. The room went thick with the stench of formaldehyde.

Coombs flailed for balance. Another two blows and he hit the floor. He floundered on the wet tiles, slipping on broken glass. When he regained his feet, they were bleeding.

Still, Bernard didn't let up. "Why the fuck d'you kill her?"

Past Bernard's wide back, Kay glimpsed Coombs's panic, but he wasn't giving up. When he tried to defend himself, Bernard laid in even harder. Coombs fell again, his scrawny frame spinning across the floor. Only this time when he came up, he was armed. In one bloodied hand he brandished the two-foot-long steel shaft Kay had seen Hagen use. Coombs jabbed the honed point in the air at Bernard, the gesture impeded by the length of hose attached.

"I'm warning you, Bernie. Just relax."

"Patsy was mine, Roach. Mine! Not yours."

Kay strained against the ropes, welcoming the new sensation of pain as she tried to slip the knots.

Coombs stabbed the air again. "Just back off, Bernie. I'm warning you." And then, as though to emphasize his threat, Coombs reached behind him and flipped a switch.

A muted whirring started up in the corner. The motor of the pump she'd seen Hagen use. And the same sucking sound, like a vacuum. Bernard's next step blocked her view, his mass obliterating Coombs's attempts at defense. She couldn't be sure what happened next as the two brothers clashed. Bernard lurched to one side, and she saw the glint of the polished shaft. Then Bernard twisted. One of them swore. More grappling. Coombs's bare arms flailing in the air. And finally a muffled grunt.

Through Bernard's legs, she could see Coombs. Naked, streaked with blood. He was suspended for a moment, his feet lifting off the littered floor. And then Bernard dropped him.

Kay tried to look away, but couldn't.

Coombs was a pale, convulsing mound. His muscles contracted and stiffened. His eyes were wide, and his mouth gaped. And then Kay saw the steel shaft, sunk deep into Coombs's abdomen, the rubber hose dancing and jerking from the protruding end.

Coombs clutched at the embedded tool. "Jesus, Bernie," his whisper rasped between clenched teeth. "What the fuck . . ."

Bernard stood over him. Silent. The only sound in the room was the wet slurping and the dull hum of the Portiboy. The big man appeared to watch until Coombs stopped twitching. Then Bernard's neck and shoulders straightened. Kay thought she heard a sigh.

And finally, he turned.

Sprays of blood marked his shirt and hands, a few drops on his cheek. When he looked at Kay, he wouldn't meet her eyes. She tried to say his name, break through the trance that seemed to grip him. But she couldn't remember how to form the words.

And then, as Bernard looked from her to her brother's knife on the floor, Kay wished Billy had killed her.

83

IT WAS TOO QUIET.

When Finn had steered into the Parkview Funeral
Home's lot, he worried his hunch had been wrong. With
no sign of Coombs's Buick, he'd gotten out to circle the
building. That's when he'd found the jimmied side door.
Barely inside, he heard the ear-shattering crashes and
exploding glass. Then voices.

He brought the police radio up, opened the frequency,
and ordered immediate backup.

Finn took the same carpeted stairway Hagen had led
him and Kay down only the other day. To the embalming
room and the stench of death and chemicals. He moved
cautiously. *Assess the situation. Know the layout. Know what's
waiting for you down there.*

Two steps from the bottom, Finn made a silent prayer to
God, made promises he doubted he could ever keep. *Just let
her be alive.*

At the bottom now, back pressed against the velvet wallpaper, Finn inched to the doorframe. *Too quiet.* A quick
duck around the corner: all clear. At the end of the corridor, light flooded from the embalming room. Finn edged
toward it, his Glock ready.

Ten more feet. Six. Finn gathered himself. With the
element of surprise he might avoid a hostage situation.
The image of Kay with a knife to her throat galvanized
him. He gripped his nine tighter, already visualizing the
single shot he'd make to take out Coombs.

Assess the situation.

One deep breath, and Finn eased around the doorframe.
First he saw the broken glass, the tossed pans and instru-

ments, a slurry of chemicals and blood spilled across the tiles. Then he saw the body. Male. Nude. Smeared with blood. A steel rod extended from the victim's gut and there was a moist sucking sound Finn didn't understand.

From the angle, he couldn't be sure it was Coombs. There was another voice, a muted mumble. It sounded male. Finn edged farther around the doorframe, his eyes frantically scanning. And then he saw him.

Eales's hulking mass was unmistakable. With his back to the door, he hunkered over a wide steel service tub. Finn evaluated the situation in rapid flashes. Blood on Eales's pants. On his shoes and hands. Then Kay. He could barely glimpse her past Eales: her face pale, and the bright glare of blood along her throat.

And then Finn saw the knife.

"Eales!" Finn lined the big man into his Glock's sight. "Drop the knife, and back away from her. Now!"

Eales's great frame turned slowly.

"Step away from the tub, you bastard, or I swear, I'll fucking shoot you."

And in that moment, Finn hoped the son of a bitch made a move. As he felt the trigger's curve under his finger, he hoped for any excuse to let loose the slug that would drop Eales. For Kay. For her year of hell. And for himself.

"Come on, Eales. Give me a reason."

But the knife clattered to the floor, and Eales took two steps forward, arms coming up.

"Now get down. Flat on the floor."

As he did, Finn kicked the knife away. There was blood on its blade, and he looked to Kay.

Her mouth was open as though she wanted to say something. Then her eyes closed. And in that instant of horror Finn realized he was too late.

84

"KAY? KAY, TALK TO ME."

Finn crouched over her, at first a blur, then clearer. As she focused on his eyes, Kay recognized his fear.

She gave him a feeble nod, felt his hand at her throat, and realized he'd believed her dead.

The world had tilted and spun like the teacup ride at a fairground when Finn had come through the door. And the blood seemed to wash out of her the moment before she blacked out.

"Stay down, you piece of shit," she heard Finn growl at Eales.

Finn had his gun still on the big man where he lay on the floor: belly-down, his face pressed flat against the tiles. But his slow eyes were fixed on Kay.

"Are you okay?" Finn was touching her, his hands moving over her. Her face, her throat, checking each wrist.

Kay worked at a nod, and her voice was shaky. "Yeah." She floundered in the shallow water, trying to push herself up.

She remembered Eales coming at her, the knife in his meaty hand, the vacant look in his eyes. She'd feared the worst when he'd reached for her. But, instead, he'd cut her loose, slicing through the bonds only seconds before Finn had burst through the doorway.

She would never know if Eales had intended to release her or use her as a hostage. And she didn't want to.

"That's him, right?" Finn nodded to Coombs's prone body, his face angled to the far bench.

"Yeah."

"You sure you're all right? Did he . . . he didn't . . ." Finn shook his head as though he couldn't say the word.

"I don't think so."

Eales coughed.

"You just lie there, you hear me?" Finn told him. "You so much as hiccup, you prick, and I'll put a fucking slug through your brain, you got it?"

Eales nodded once.

From outside, Kay heard the sirens. She struggled again, this time managing to sit as the strength returned to her quivering muscles. Finn's arm was around her waist then, drawing her up and out of the tub, his gun's sight never leaving Eales. Even when Finn lowered her to sit on the edge, he switched the Glock to his left so he could remove his jacket and place it over her shoulders.

Uniforms thundered down the stairs, and she heard them moving along the corridor.

"Room's clear," Finn shouted, holstering his nine when they stormed in. He nodded at Eales. "Read this asshole his rights. And call for an ambo. We'll need the ME down here too." Coombs's body still gurgled in the corner.

Finn had found her shoes and helped her with them as she watched the uniforms cuff Eales. All of it so surreal.

When she stood, Finn supported her. He helped her navigate the floor of broken glass, trailing water over the tiles, until she reached Coombs. She stood over him then, surprised that she had nothing to say. Staring down at his frail, deflated body, she was amazed at how small Coombs seemed. How utterly human he looked.

He *was* just a man.

Kay gestured to the Porti-boy, and as she wavered there in the middle of the embalming room, Finn switched the machine off. The sucking sounds stopped.

"Come on," Finn said, returning to her side. "Let's get you out of here."

He drew her away from the spectacle of Coombs's partially drained body and ushered her up the stairs. Someone was reading Bernard his rights. Outside, she shivered when the night air hit her damp body.

"You sure you're okay?" Finn turned her, the fear she'd seen in his face was fading.

She nodded and welcomed his embrace.

Not until Eales was led from the side door did Finn release her. Kay watched the big man shuffle across the lawn and placidly allowed himself to be wedged into the back of the closest patrol unit. When the door closed on him, she sensed his stare. Even in the strobing glare of the radio-car light-bars, she knew Eales watched her.

In some warped sense that she doubted anyone else would ever understand, Kay knew she owed Bernard Eales her life. And as the radio car pulled away and she caught his expressionless nod, she recognized that—like one of those crystal-clear snapshots in time—her mind would never let go of the image of Eales's eyes on her.

This time it was Kay who moved to embrace Finn, holding him tight for a long time as the scene bustled around them.

"The only person who needs to forgive you is you." Spencer's words. No, they'd been her own. She hadn't spoken to the dead tonight, or touched some higher plane. At least, that's the reality she would cling to because, right now, any other explanation was beyond her comfort zone.

And there, on the lawn of Hagen's funeral home, Kay felt the subtle shift. The move toward forgiveness. For Spencer. For Valley. For Coombs's victims. She had a long way to go still, but Kay at last believed in the possibilities.

POCKET STAR BOOKS
PROUDLY PRESENTS

THE NEXT CAPTIVATING THRILLER
IN THE KAY DELANEY SERIES

ILLONA HAUS

Turn the page for a preview. . . .

1

"HE'LL SHOW. IT'S JUST A MATTER OF TIME."
Kay Delaney eased the unmarked police car through the amber at Franklin. Water sprayed the Lumina's underbelly as the tires took a pothole, and, in the passenger seat, Bobby Curran balanced his take-out double latte, saving his tailor-made, crepe-wool suit yet again.

"I tell you, Kay, no dealer in his right mind is dogging the streets this early in the morning. All's we're doing is wasting time and gas."

She ignored his comment. Kept scanning.

Two years as a deputized agent with the special Redrum Unit working with DEA, Bobby Curran knew a thing or two about drug organizations and gangs. But when it came to murders, Kay thought, the former Bostonian and her new partner, as of three weeks ago, was a rookie. A proven investigator, a spiffy dresser, and a flirt. But still a homicide rookie.

"Trust me, he'll show," she said again, making a left onto Edmonson.

Under a gunmetal sky, Harlem Park was a bleak stretch of desolation and despair, owned by dealers at night and haunted by crack-addicted ghosts during the day. Trash cluttered the narrow back alleys, cans toppled and leaking their contents into the slushy gutters.

Last night's freak snowfall had blanketed the city with a pristine but fleeting patina, and now Baltimore was gray again. Kay slowed the car, passing a couple of homeboys, their hoods drawn up for warmth, their breath haloing around them as they blew on their hands and shivered next to a public bench. On the back of the bench, the rampant slogan "Baltimore: the city that reads"—a dying memory of the former mayor's Literacy Campaign—had been altered with spray paint to read: "the city that bleeds."

For two years she'd done patrol here in the Western. A decade and a half ago. Back when the neighborhood wasn't quite as bold. When a shield meant something.

"Look, I know Dante and his crew," Bobby went on, licking foamed milk from his lip. "These dealers don't come crawlin' outta their cribs till after noon."

"With three murder warrants on his head, our boy isn't exactly keeping dealer's hours anymore."

She'd driven through here at least a dozen times in the past three weeks, usually at night, when the streets pulsed with drug activity. She'd cruise it like she was working a grid on a crime scene, the smell of car fumes and pot wafting in through the open window as servers and jugglers—teenage dealers—scowled at the unmarked car and gave the "five-oh" to their hand-to-hand men on the corners to signal police.

"How is it you even figure Dante's still around anyway? You think he's a dumb-ass with a repeat prescription for stupid pills at the Eckert or something?"

"It's not about stupid, Bobby. It's about nature. Dante's a homie. Farthest he ever strayed from west Baltimore was probably the Inner Harbor on a field trip before he bailed out of grade school. When a guy like Dante starts feeling insecure, last place he's heading is out of town."

Rolling onto the first stretch of the three blocks that had become the Western District's hottest corners, Kay slowed the Lumina, casing each narrow side alley. Just past the grounds of Harlem Park Middle School two homeless men shared a shopping cart filled with crushed soda cans and scrap metal, and salvaged damp cigarette butts from the sidewalk. Three boys Kay guessed were no older than seven dragged their sneakers through the slush, fists jammed into their pockets. When they spotted the unmarked, they practiced their own version of the five-oh hand signal. In the rearview mirror, Kay caught the biggest of the three giving her a sneer and the finger.

"Dante needs to feel safe," she said to Bobby. "Needs the security of his own turf. He's here."

"Then let Fugitive flush him out. 'Sides, the longer Dante Toomey's on the streets, the more chance someone else'll pop a bullet into him."

Kay spared Bobby a sideways glance, sitting there in his pressed suit, his perfect hair, and the aftershave that she'd been growing accustomed to for the past three weeks. She knew he would rather have lingered at the Daily Grind with his cinnamon-sprinkled latte, his jacket drawn back to reveal the badge tucked in his belt, charming the med students from Hopkins.

"Besides," he added, "it's not like he killed someone's grandma. Texaco was just another dealer. If Dante hadn't put those .45 slugs in his brain, someone else woulda. Welcome to the lifestyle of death."

The Redrum Unit had made Bobby Curran a cynic years before he should have been, Kay thought. Bobby had probably worked more drug cases than she had, even though she'd been on the streets twice as long. He knew convictions in drug murders were little better than a coin toss. Witnesses were too afraid to talk, or, more often, preferred to take the law into their own hands. The system was clogged and a "speedy trial" wasn't always possible, so, in the end, killers like Dante frequently walked or, at best, took a plea.

Bobby had a point: what was another dead dealer in Baltimore City?

But for Kay, this one was different. Texaco, the dead dealer Bobby was referring to, had a kid brother. And she'd made that kid a promise.

"When exactly did you stop caring, Bobby?" she asked.

"What do you mean?"

She steered north off Edmonson. "I mean, you need to care. If getting someone like Dante isn't important to you, how do you figure you're going to close any murders?"

If Bobby had had a witty rebuttal, he didn't have a chance to voice it.

Kay pointed out the windshield. "Bingo," she said, coming off the gas and easing the Lumina to a crawl.

Two hundred feet down the block she spotted him, shuffling past crumbling stoops and boarded-up doors in his two-hundred-dollar Nikes, and wearing the same Jamaican Rasta Wig hat their witness had described, like he'd just stepped off the boat instead of having been raised six blocks west of these drug corners.

"That ain't Dante." Bobby tipped his disposable cup at him.

"No, Detective Curran, *that* is Quortez Squirl." Adrenaline licked through her. "And my daddy always says if you're aiming to catch the big fish, sometimes you gotta follow the little ones."

Kay checked her rearview: no one behind her. And the occasional southbound car masked the idle of the Lumina's engine.

She reached for the police radio and tossed it into Bobby's lap. "Call it in," she said, unclipping her seatbelt.

But before Bobby had even grabbed the radio, Quortez Squirl turned. In the three seconds it took Dante Toomey's main runner to case the situation, Kay slammed the car into park in the middle of the street and was out the door.

"Hey, Squirl!"

Squirl ran. And so did Kay.

Dodging an oncoming Acura, Kay ignored the horn's blast and the driver's glare from behind the wheel, and headed full tilt down the sidewalk.

At five-foot-eleven, Quortez Squirl covered more ground in those flashy sneakers. Still, Kay gained on him, swallowing up the garbage-littered sidewalk behind him. When Squirl snatched a backward glance, Kay pushed harder.

She thought she heard Bobby in the street behind her. But Kay's eyes locked on Squirl's back, his arms pumping in the oversized hoodie and those dread-locks flapping wildly in the air behind him.

Her heart was beating fast, her senses jacked up. Twenty yards between them. She could hear Squirl's sneakers smacking through the icy puddles.

Nineteen yards. Eighteen. Then Squirl skidded, his laces whirling around his feet. She hoped he'd trip. Instead, he veered left, headlong into the side alley.

By the time she reached the opening, Kay's hand was on the grip of her nine. Behind her Bobby was a half block down, the police radio in one hand, dodging traffic.

She couldn't wait.

Drawing a breath, she ducked around the corner, her eyes taking several precious seconds to adjust to the dark. Searching.

And then Kay spotted the hat. The bright red and

yellow Rasta bobbed at the end of the alley, and there was the clash of chain-link as Squirl scaled the ten-foot fence.

She was running again, negotiating trash cans and flying through greasy pools of refuse. Kay swore, then threw herself at the fence, one eye on Squirl's hat. And when she hit the top, she swung over too fast. She landed hard, slipping on soaked cardboard boxes, and rolled.

She could see him in flashes. The bright hat. The black hoodie. He was heading out to Mount Street. At the mouth of the alley he cut right, bounding into the gray light. When she hit the street, Squirl was zigzagging through traffic, narrowly escaping the grille of a turquoise city sanitation truck.

So close now she could hear his breath, smell his sweat on his slipstream. Kay cleared the corner of the truck in time to see Squirl duck into the next alley. This time she didn't enter as cautiously. And she regretted it the second she rounded the corner.

Squirl was there. Kay saw the flash of gold on his wide black fist and ducked. There was no time to draw her gun. Instead, she took out his leg. With one sharp kick, the thick rubber sole of her duty shoe met the delicate bone and cartilage of his knee. She heard his cry just as she wished she'd aimed higher.

Before he could recover, she spun a kick to his good leg, and he almost went down. But he lunged a second time. And she dodged again, grabbing a fistful of his hoodie and trying to wrestle him to the ground. For one panicked moment, Kay imagined him wriggling out of the oversized shirt and running again.

He swore at her. And then Kay felt his hand. Reaching back. Groping for the butt of her Glock, tugging at the hip holster. She'd lost her gun once. Two years ago. *Never again.*

She brought her elbow back and up in a hard, well-aimed swing. Felt bone and saw a stream of blood fly from Squirl's mouth, spray red against the grime-slicked wall of the alley. When he turned in a flurry of fists, she blocked the blows and felt something hot splash her face. Blood and spit.

" . . . crazy-ass bitch."

"What d'you just call me, Squirl?" She followed the question with a smooth upward arch of her knee and thought she felt a rib crack under the impact as he buckled.

One hand skidded along the sidewalk as he tried to catch himself, and just when Kay thought he was at last going down, Quortez Squirl kicked back. The soft sole of his Nike met her shin. Pain knifed up her leg and she staggered back, catching herself against the alley wall. Then Squirl was crawling, scurrying to get his feet under him, moving toward the street again.

He was almost vertical when Kay nailed him from behind. In a flying leap, she hit him hard, felt the wind rush out of him as they came down together, cold concrete tearing through the knee of her good suit, biting into skin.

"Son of a bitch, Squirl!" She jammed the heel of her hand into the back of his skull, forcing his face into the grimy slush, and brought her knee up between his shoulder blades. "Haven't you learned yet? When you put up a fight, you only go to jail tired."

The cuffs from the back of her belt came out easily and she slid them around his thick, black wrists. Only when they were snug did she dismount him, dragging him to his feet.

"Now, why don't you tell me where your dawg Dante's laying his head these days, hmm?"

She gave him a shove, one hand locked on the cuffs, the other grabbing a fistful of the hoodie.

Quortez Squirl's face glistened with blood and the flesh over his right eye had started to swell. He sucked at his split bottom lip, his chin thrust in the air, his mouth tight as he watched Bobby jog through traffic to join them. The police radio crackled in Bobby's hand.

"Oh shit, Bobby. Sorry about the shirt," Kay said, nodding to the dark stain of coffee down the crisp, white linen.

"Son of a bitch ruined my shirt. See what you did, you dumb-ass? You have any idea how much this shirt cost?"

Kay caught the flash of Squirl's eyes. "You might wanna get out of the way, Bobby."

"What?" But he was too late.

Quortez Squirl's lips pursed, and the runner

hawked a bloody goober, sending it flying against the lapel of Bobby's suit jacket.

"I warned you," Kay said, trying not to laugh as she guided Squirl across the street.

2

JUST OFF A SHIFT of midnights, it seemed like weeks since Detective Danny Finnerty had seen the sun. The gray, mid-April sky pressed down on the grounds of Langley Country High School in Roland Park, and the dusting of snow on the sports fields and tennis courts wasn't melting fast.

The first thing Finn had noticed when he'd arrived a half hour ago was the crows. A turf war had broken out over the narrow strip of woods bordering the west edge of the school grounds. The trees were black with the squabbling, quasi-reptilian birds, and the air filled with their shrieks as they circled and dove like kamikazes, oblivious to the flapping police tape and crime scene below.

Finn warmed his hands in the pockets of his leather car coat and watched the Mobile Crime Lab shoot the scene. What little there was.

"Watch those tracks there," he warned the tech. "To your right. We need those."

Only one trail of prints led from the cul de sac in front of the school to the crime scene at the base of a budding, silver-barked sycamore. The rest of the white expanse was unmarred except for two parallel paths made by the responding officer, Michelle Luttrell, and the witness who'd made the early-morning discovery. And those paths ran west from the back of the witness's home in the opposite direction.

Officer Luttrell had done well in preserving the scene, letting no one within fifty feet of the tree. Finn would have preferred it was a hundred. Still, he'd make sure to have a letter entered into Luttrell's personnel jacket by the end of the week, commending her professionalism on the scene.

She was young and blonde, with a face that looked far too ingenuous for the job. She shivered slightly in her uniform jacket, made bulky from the Kevlar vest she wore underneath, and when she caught Finn's stare she dropped her uneasy, blue-eyed gaze.

"So you think that came from a person?" she asked, gesturing to the tree.

"I don't know. ME's investigator'll be here soon. He should be able to tell us."

She nodded. Pensive. "You need me to do anything else, Detective?" she asked.

Finn glanced back at the cul de sac. Four patrol cars and the Mobile Crime Lab's van lined the narrow drive in front of the columned portico of the private school's main entrance. He shoved a thumb in the direction of the half dozen Northern District uniforms lingering by their vehicles. "Yeah. You can keep those knuckleheads off the snow back there. I don't want my perp's prints messed up. And tell your witness that I need to talk to him."

Luttrell headed across the grounds, carefully retracing her own steps. Finn watched her talk to her fellow officers, gesturing at the tracks in the snow. And when an unmarked pulled in, Luttrell waved it to the side, leaned in to speak with the driver.

Finn recognized Kay as she parked the Lumina. When she rounded the hood of the car, she straightened her jacket over the holster strapped to her waist. She looked tiny next to the uniforms, cradling their coffees in disposable cups. She said something clearly humorous, and one of them let loose a deep belly horselaugh that carried across the grounds. Then Finn heard a "yes, ma'am" and they parted for her.

Finn caught the smile she gave them. Over the past year he'd seen the demons of Kay's past fade, but the memory of them would always be with her. The nightmares had abated, but there were still times, in the dead of night, when he'd hold her sweat-slicked body until she found sleep again.

Some scars even time couldn't erase.

He watched her sure stride as she crossed the field, the rookie Bobby Curran in tow. Only when she neared did Finn notice her slight limp. There was grime on her suit and a small tear in the knee of her slacks.

"What happened to you?" he asked.

"Just brought in Dante Toomey's main runner," Kay said.

"You caught that little squirrel?"

"Let me tell you, Quortez Squirl is *not* so little."

"Well, I hope he ended up looking worse than you. Hey, Hollywood," he said to Curran, nodding at the rookie's stained shirt, "and who'd you arrest this morning? Your coffee cup?"

He was sure Curran shot him a look from behind the Oakley wire-framed sunglasses as he drew the edges of his trench coat together.

"So, what have you got?" Kay asked.

"Might be nothing but a school prank," he said, leading her and Bobby across the field to where the residential yards backed onto the school property. "We have a witness. Says he was letting his cat out. I haven't talked to him yet, but the responding officer says the guy saw someone at this spot. Looked like they dumped something, then headed back to a white panel van and drove off."

"Jesus." Finn heard Curran behind him. "Is that . . . is that someone's heart?"

"Very good, Hollywood. You get an A in anatomy."

Kay squatted several feet from the base of the tree, examining the organ, then lifting her gaze to scan the open fields, the front of the school, and the tracks in the melting snow.

The fist-sized organ glistened dully in the gray light. Smears of blood caked the exterior membrane and stained the snow around it, and where the aorta and arteries had been severed, the edges appeared to be drying.

Kay was silent as she studied the scene. In the past year of partnering with her on more than a dozen cases, Finn had learned how Kay worked. Respected it. That quiet fierceness. The calculation of every angle in a case, like she was playing a game of chess, moving each piece with obsessive deliberation.

Eventually, she pointed to the dozen or so drops of blood in the snow around it. "He must have dumped it from a container or a bag. What time did the witness see this guy?"

"Five. The school lights aren't aimed out this far, so it was pretty dark. Wasn't till daybreak, apparently, that he got curious. I guess he's a birder. Says he used his binoculars, then came to see what it was."

"Look at the snow around it," she said, leaning in closer. "The edge of it. It looks melted."

"Like it was still warm when he put it here," Finn finished for her. "Christ, Kay, what is this? Some kind of cult thing? You ever see anything like this before?"

She shook her head, pointed to the trail of prints heading back to the school. "Are those the perp's?"

"Have to be. The witness walked in from his backyard."

Kay scrutinized the trail. "Ground's pretty sloppy here," she said. "I doubt we'll get any kind of casting."

She came back to the heart.

"Maybe it's from a transplant clinic or something," Curran suggested.

"No," Kay said. "Look at the cuts. Those aren't surgical. This heart was butchered out of someone."

"Well, how do you know it's even human, and not some pig's heart from the school biology lab or something?" Curran asked.

"It's not a pig's heart, detectives."

Officer Luttrell had returned with the witness. "This is Jonathan Durso," she said.

Durso was a small man, with nervous eyes spaced too close together and set too deep in his narrow face. He pushed a pair of glasses farther up his nose and shifted his weight from one foot to the next, his suede-leather deck shoes soaked from snow.

"Dr. Durso," the man corrected Luttrell. "And *that* is not from a pig," he repeated, hugging himself from the cold. "In a porcine heart the left atrial appendage is of comparable size to the right. With this one, the left is appreciably smaller. Also, the shape is wrong. *That,* detectives, is human."